Silver Linings

Silver Linings

Jayne Ann Krentz

WHEELER
PUBLISHING, INC.

★ AN AMERICAN COMPANY ★

Published in Large Print by arrangement with
Pocket Books, a division of Simon & Schuster, Inc.

Wheeler Large Print Book Series.

Set in 16 pt. Plantin.

Library of Congress Cataloging-in-Publication Data

Krentz, Jayne Ann
    Silver linings / Jayne Ann Krentz.
        p.   cm.
    ISBN 1-56895-023-3 : $21.95
    1. Large type books.   I. Title.
    [PS3561.R44S5   1993]
    813'.54—dc20   93-5698

---

*To Claire Zion and baby Rose
and the future . . .*

CHAPTER

One

The only thing she really knew about Paul Cormier was that he was dying.

The blood from the wound in his chest had soaked through his white silk shirt and white linen suit and was running in small rivulets over the white marble tile.

The old man opened his eyes as Mattie Sharpe crouched helplessly beside him, grasping his hand in hers. He peered up at her, as if he were trying to see through a thick fog.

"Christine? Is that you, Christine?" Even in a croaked whisper, his accent was elegant and vaguely European.

"Yes, Paul." Lying was the only thing she could do for him. Mattie held his hand tightly. "It's Christine."

"Missed you, girl. Missed you so much."

"I'm here now."

Cormier's pale blue gaze focused on her for a few seconds. "No," he said. "You're not here. But I'm almost there, aren't I?" He made a sound that might have started out as a chuckle but turned into a ghastly, gurgling cough.

"Yes. You're almost here."

"Be good to see you again."

"Yes." A hot, torpid island breeze wafted through the front hall of the Cormier mansion.

1

The silence from the surrounding jungle was unnatural and oppressive. "It's going to be all right, Paul. Everything will be fine." Lies. More lies.

Cormier squinted up at her, his gaze startlingly lucid for an instant. "Get out of here. Hurry."

"I'll go," Mattie promised.

Cormier's eyes closed again. "Someone will come. An old friend. When he does, tell him . . . tell him." Another terrible gasping sound drained more of the little strength he had left.

"What do you want me to tell him?"

"Reign . . ." Cormier choked on his own blood. "In hell."

Mattie didn't pause to make sense out of what she thought she'd heard him say. Automatically she reassured him. "I'll tell him."

The hand that had been clutching hers slackened its grip. "Christine?"

"I'm here, Paul."

But Cormier did not hear her this time. He was gone.

The horror of her situation washed over Mattie again. She struggled to her feet, feeling light-headed. Without thinking, she glanced at the black and gold watch on her wrist as if she were late to a business appointment.

With a shock she realized she had been in the white mansion overlooking the ocean for less than five minutes. She would have been here two hours earlier if she hadn't gotten lost on a winding island road that had dead-ended in the mountains. At the time the delay had made her tense and anxious. It occurred to Mattie now that if she had arrived on time, she probably would have walked straight into the same gun that had killed Paul Cormier.

The toe of her Italian leather shoe struck something on the floor. It skittered away across the tile.

Mattie jumped at the loud sound in the eerily silent hall. Then she glanced down and saw the gun.

Cormier's, probably, she told herself. He must have tried to fight off the intruder. Dazed, Mattie took a step toward the weapon. Perhaps she should take it with her.

Even as the words formed in her mind she shuddered. The last gun she had handled had been a little plastic model that had come in a box labeled, "Annie Oakley's Sharpshooter Special. For ages five and up." A friend had given it to her on the occasion of her sixth birthday. Mattie had practiced her fast draw for hours, whipping the toy gun out of its pink fringed, imitation leather holster over and over again until her concerned parents had taken it from her and replaced it with a box of watercolors. Mattie had dutifully played with the paints for approximately ten minutes and succeeded in producing a cheerful yellow horse for Annie Oakley to ride. The picture had been cute, but was not deemed good enough to hang on the refrigerator next to her sister Ariel's latest rendition of a bouquet of flowers.

Her training in handguns thus halted at such an early stage, Mattie realized now that she had absolutely no idea of how to use the lethal-looking monster lying at her feet on the white floor.

On the other hand, how complicated could it be? She asked herself as she stooped to pick up

3

the heavy weapon. Every punk on every city street back in the States owned and operated one. It was a sure bet most of them were too illiterate to read the manuals. Besides, it was easy to see which end to point away from herself.

Oh, God. She was getting hysterical. It was a sure sign of losing control. She had to get a grip on herself. She could panic later if necessary.

Mattie took several deep breaths while she fumbled the gun into her elegant black and tan leather shoulder bag. She paused as she noticed the bloodstains on the strap. Cormier's blood. It had come from her hands.

She had to move quickly. A man was dead and among his last words had been the advice to get out of the mansion in a hurry.

She did not doubt that the danger was still hovering. Mattie could sense it as if it were a palpable presence. She took one last look at the body of the silver-haired old man. She had a fleeting vision of white—white linen suit, white buck shoes, white silk shirt, white marble tile, white walls, white furniture. White, endless, pure, unadulterated white. Except for the red blood.

Mattie felt her stomach heave. She could not be sick now. She had to get out of here. She stumbled for the open front door, her heels clattering loudly on the marble. Her only thought was to reach the battered old rental car that she had picked up at the tiny island airport two hours earlier.

She was nearly out the door when she remembered the sword.

Halting, she glanced back into the room of white death. She knew she could not go back.

Valor, the fourteenth-century sword she had been sent to collect, was valuable but not worth the trip back into that room. Nothing was worth going back into that room. Aunt Charlotte would understand.

What was it Aunt Charlotte had told her about the ancient weapon? Something about there being a curse on it. *Death to all who dare claim this blade until it shall be taken up by the avenger and cleansed in the blood of the betrayer.*

The terrible prophecy had apparently been fulfilled in Cormier's case, Mattie thought. Not that she believed in such things. Still, Cormier had claimed the blade and now he was dead. Mattie suddenly had no interest whatsoever in locating the medieval sword and taking it back to Seattle.

She whirled around again and ran through the open door, scrabbling in her purse for the key to the rental car. Perhaps that was why she didn't see the man who stood on the veranda to one side of the open door.

Nor did she notice the booted foot he stuck out in front of her until she tripped over it and went flying. She sprawled on the white planking of the veranda, the wind knocked out of her. Before she could get back enough breath to scream, she felt something cold and metallic against the nape of her neck.

Mattie wondered with an odd, clinical detachment if there would be any small warning sound before the trigger was pulled.

"Hell, it's you, Mattie," said a deep male voice Mattie had not heard in nearly a year. The gun was no longer pressed against her nape but Mattie was still frozen with fear and shock. "You almost got yourself killed. I didn't know who was going to come running out that door. You all right, babe?"

Mattie managed to nod, still fighting for breath. She opened her eyes and realized the wooden planks she was staring down at were less than three inches away. She could not seem to gather her thoughts. It was all too much. *Stress*.

A big hand closed around her shoulder. "Mattie?" The dark, rough-edged voice crackled with impatience.

"I'm okay." A strange relief washed through her at the thought. Then came another chill. "Cormier."

"What about him?"

"He's in there."

"Dead?"

She closed her eyes. "Yes. Oh, God, yes."

"Get up."

"I don't think I can."

"Yes, you damn well can. Move it, Mattie. We can't lie around here chatting." Strong fingers locked around her waist and hauled her to her feet.

"You never did listen to me, did you, Hugh?" Mattie brushed aside the tendrils of tawny brown hair that had come free of the neat coil at the nape of her neck. She looked up into gray eyes that were so light they could have been chips off a glacier. "What are you doing here?"

"That's supposed to be my line. You were due into St. Gabe at nine this morning. What the hell are you doing here on Purgatory?" But he wasn't

6

paying attention to her, not really. He was eyeing the driveway behind her. "Come on."

"I'm not going back into that house."

Predictably enough, he ignored her. "Get inside the hall, Mattie. You're a sitting duck standing in the doorway." Without waiting for a response he yanked her back through the wide opening.

Mattie stumbled after him, keeping her eyes averted from the sight of Cormier's body. She clutched at the strap of her shoulder bag in a vain effort to keep her fingers from trembling.

"Don't move," Hugh said.

"Don't worry, I won't." She hoped she would not be sick all over the marble floor.

He released her and strode quickly over to the body in the white linen suit. He stood looking down for a few seconds, taking in the absoluteness of death in one glance. The expression on his face was difficult to read. It was not shock or surprise or fear or horror—just a remote, implacable sort of fierceness.

Mattie watched him, aware she should be grateful he had appeared at this particular moment in her life. No one else she knew was better qualified to get her out of this sticky situation than Hugh Abbott.

Too bad the mere sight of him enraged her. Too bad that after that humiliating debacle last year she had never wanted to see him again as long as she lived. Too bad that the one man she needed right now was the same one who had devastated her after she had surrendered to him, body and soul.

He had not changed much in the past year, she

realized. Same thick, dark pelt of hair with maybe a bit more silver in it. Same lean, whipcord-tough body that still didn't show any hint of softening, despite his forty years. Same rough-featured, heavily carved face. Same beautiful, incredibly sexy mouth. Same primitive masculine grace.

Same lamentable taste in clothing, too. Mattie noted with a disdaining glance. Scarred boots, unpressed khaki shirt unbuttoned far enough to show a lot of crisp, curling chest hair, a well-worn leather belt and faded jeans that emphasized his flat belly and strong thighs.

Hugh glanced at her. "I'll be right back. I'm just going to get some stuff from the kitchen." He was already moving past the body. He held the gun in his hand so naturally it seemed an extension of his arm.

"*The kitchen*. For God's sake, Hugh. This is no time to grab a cold beer. What if he's still here? The man who shot poor Mr. Cormier?"

"Don't worry. There's no one else here. If there were, you would be as dead as Cormier by now."

Mattie swallowed as he left the room. "No, wait, please don't leave me here with—" Mattie bit off the rest of the frantic plea. She, of all people, ought to know better than to plead with Hugh Abbott to stay. "Damn you," she whispered.

Mattie stood listening to the ring of Hugh's boots on the marble tiles. She heard him move down a hall into another room, and then there was nothing but the awful silence and the hot breeze.

Glancing nervously out the door, she toyed with the keys of the rental car. Nothing said she had to stand around and wait for Hugh. She could drive herself back to the airport. Right now she wanted nothing more than to get on a plane and leave this dreadful island.

But she was feeling very lost and uncertain. Practicing a quick draw with the Annie Oakley special had been one of her few forays into the world of adventure. Her artistically oriented family had emphasized more civilized and sophisticated pursuits.

Hugh Abbott, on the other hand, understood situations involving violence and danger all too well. As chief troubleshooter and free-lance security consultant for Aunt Charlotte's multinational company, Vailcourt Industries, he was on intimate terms with this sort of thing.

Mattie had privately thought of Hugh as her aunt's pet wolf long before she had met him last year. Nothing she had learned about him since had given her any cause to change her mind.

She heard his boot heels on the tile again. Hugh reappeared carrying two large French market-style string bags that bulged with an assortment of unidentifiable items.

"All right. We've spent enough time fooling around here. Let's go." Hugh glided around Cormier's body, not looking down. He saw the keys in Mattie's fingers. "Forget that junker you rented. You're not going anywhere in it."

"What do you mean? Are we going to take your car? Where is it, anyway?"

"A few hundred yards up the road. Hopefully out of sight—but who knows for how long?" Hugh strode toward her. "Here, take one of these.

9

I want to keep a hand free." He thrust one of the string bags into her fingers as he glanced out the door and up at the leaden sky. "It's going to start pouring any minute. That should help."

Mattie ignored the comment about the impending rain. She was too busy trying to juggle the heavy string bag and her purse. "What are these sacks for? We don't need this stuff. I just want to get to the airport."

"The airport is closed."

Mattie stared at him in shock. "Closed? It can't be closed."

"It is. I barely made it in myself. There are armed men on the road, and every plane that didn't get off the island as of forty minutes ago is probably in flames by now. Including mine, goddamn it. Charlotte's going to have to reimburse me for that Cherokee. It was a real sweet little crate."

"Dear heaven. Hugh, what's going on? What is this all about?"

"With your usual fine sense of timing, you walked straight into the middle of what looks like a two-bit military coup here on Purgatory. At the moment I have no way of knowing who's winning. In the meantime the only way off the island is by boat. We're going to try for Cormier's cruiser."

"I don't believe this."

"Believe it. Come on, let's go."

"Go where?" she demanded.

"First to the bathroom." Hugh started down the hall.

"For God's sake, Hugh, I assure you I don't have to use the bathroom. At least, not right at

10

the moment. Hugh, wait. Please stop. I don't understand this."

He turned in the doorway, his eyes cold. "Mattie, I don't want to hear another word out of you. Come here. Now."

Deciding she was too stressed out to think clearly, Mattie trailed after him. She closed her eyes as she stepped around Cormier's body and found herself following Hugh down a white hallway into a luxurious bedroom suite done in silver and white.

"Mr. Cormier certainly didn't like colors very much," Mattie muttered.

"Yeah. He used to say he'd worked in the shadows long enough. When he retired he wanted to live in the sun." Hugh opened a door off the bedroom suite.

"What did he mean by that?"

"Never mind. It doesn't matter now. Here we go." Hugh strode into the bathroom.

Mattie followed uneasily. "Hugh, I really don't understand." She frowned as she watched him step into the huge white tub and push at a section of wall behind the taps. "What in the world—?"

"Cormier built a lot of ways out of this place. He was a born strategist."

"I see. He was expecting trouble, then?"

"Not specifically. Not here on Purgatory." Hugh watched as the wall panel slid aside to reveal a dark corridor. "But like I say, he was always prepared."

"Oh, my goodness." Mattie shivered as she stared into the darkness. The old uneasiness she always felt in confined places stirred in the pit of

11

her stomach. "Uh, Hugh, maybe I should warn you, I'm not very good in—"

"Not now, Mattie." His tone was impatient as he stepped into the black corridor and turned around to reach for her hand.

"Do we have to go this way?" Mattie asked helplessly.

"Stop whining, babe. I don't have time to listen to it."

Thoroughly humiliated now, Mattie found the strength to step into the corridor. Hugh pushed a button and the panel slid shut behind her. She held her breath but discovered she did not have to stand long in the darkness. Hugh switched on a flashlight he'd taken from one of the string bags.

"Thank God you found a flashlight," Mattie said.

"No problem. Cormier kept a couple in every room of the house. I picked this one up in the kitchen, but there's probably one in here, too. Electricity is always a little erratic on an island like this. Come on, babe."

The hallway was narrow but mercifully short. With the assistance of the light and several deep breaths, Mattie was able to control her claustrophobia just as she did in elevators. Hugh was pushing another button and opening an exit in the side of the house before her own personal walls had begun to close in to any great extent.

Mattie stepped outside with a sense of relief and found herself in the middle of a leafy green jungle bower that grew right up to the side of the mansion. She batted at a huge, broad leaf that was directly in front of her. "Well, that wasn't so bad, but I really don't see why we had to leave that way. It seems to me it would have been simpler to walk straight to the car."

Hugh was moving forward into what looked to Mattie like a wall of thick foliage. Once again he ignored her comment. "Stay close, Mattie. I don't want to lose you in the jungle."

"I'm not going into any jungle."

"Yes, you are. You and I are going to do the only smart thing we can do under these circumstances. We're going to stay out of sight until we can get hold of transportation."

"Hugh, this is crazy. I'm not traipsing off into that jungle. In fact, I'm not going anywhere at all until I've had a chance to think."

"You can think later. Right now you're just going to move." He was already vanishing into the greenery.

Aunt Charlotte's pet wolf was apparently accustomed to giving orders and having them followed. He had been known to give orders to Charlotte, herself.

Mattie stood irresolute near the wall of the mansion, the string bag dangling from her fingers. Common sense told her she should be running after Hugh. He was, after all, the expert on this kind of thing. But a sickening combination of disbelief, shock, and an old irrational anger held her frozen for an instant.

Hugh glanced back over his shoulder, eyes narrowing. "Get moving, Mattie. Now."

He did not raise his voice, but the words were a whiplash that broke through Mattie's uncertainty.

13

She hurried forward, fighting with her purse and the string bag.

Two steps past the barrier of broad leaves, Mattie found herself completely enveloped in an eerie green world. Her senses were overwhelmed by the rich, humid scent. The ground beneath her shoes was soft and springy and nearly black in color; a giant compost pile that had been simmering for eons. It sucked at her two-hundred-dollar Italian shoes as if it were a living thing that feasted on fancy leather.

Massive ferns that would have won first place in any garden show back in Seattle hovered in Mattie's path like plump green ghosts. Long, meandering vines studded with exotic orchids billowed around her. It was like swimming beneath the surface of a primeval sea. A couple of fat raindrops landed on her head.

"Hugh, where are we going? We'll get lost in here."

"We're not going far. And we won't get lost. All we have to do is keep the house to our backs and the sound of the ocean to our left. Cormier was a wily old fox. He always made certain he had a bolt hole, and he kept the escape plans simple."

"If he was so clever, why is he dead back there inside that mansion?"

"Even smart old foxes eventually slow down and make mistakes." Hugh pushed past a bank of massive leaves that blocked the way.

The leaves promptly sprang back into position. A mass of beautiful white lilies slapped Mattie right in the face. "Ariel was right," she muttered under her breath at Hugh's disappearing back,

14

"you really aren't much of a gentleman, are you?" She pushed at the lilies, the string bag and her purse banging wildly about her sides.

"Watch out for these leaves," Hugh advised over his shoulder. "They're real springy."

"I noticed." Mattie ducked to avoid the next swinging mass of greenery. She was grateful for the aerobic exercise program she had begun nearly a year ago on her thirty-first birthday. She had taken it up as one of many antidotes to the stress that seemed to press down on her from all directions these days. Without that regular exercise, she never would have had the physical stamina to keep up with Hugh Abbott as they raced through a jungle.

Not that it was ever easy for a woman such as herself to keep up with Hugh under the best of circumstances. As he had once made very clear, she was not his type. Mattie winced at the memory of that old humiliation.

"Not much farther now. How you doing, babe?" Hugh vaulted lightly over a fallen log and reached back to give Mattie a hand.

"I'm still here, aren't I?" Mattie asked between her teeth. The rain was getting heavier. The canopy of green overhead began to drip like a leaky ceiling. Mattie heard something tear as she scrambled over the log. She thought at first it was the seat of her beautifully tailored olive green trousers but realized it was the sleeve of her cream-colored silk shirt instead. It had gotten caught on a vine.

"Damn." Mattie glanced down at the rip and sighed. "Why would Cormier show you his escape route?" she asked, raising her eyes to Hugh's back. "I didn't know you even knew him."

He didn't turn or even slow his pace as he answered. "You'd have found out I knew him if you'd stuck to your original schedule and been on the plane to St. Gabe this morning the way you were supposed to be. Didn't Charlotte's travel department make the reservations for you?"

"They made them. I altered my plans at the last minute when I saw the itinerary. I recognized St. Gabriel Island and realized I was being set up. I decided I didn't need you for a tour guide."

"Even though you were going straight into Purgatory?" he asked dryly. "Come on, now, Mattie. You know what they say. Better the devil you know. Look what happened when you decided to go your own way."

"I suppose you would have realized instantly that there was a military coup going on here?"

"Long before you did, babe. As soon as I contacted the tower, I knew something was wrong. If you'd been with me, we wouldn't have even touched down. I'd have turned and headed for Hades or Brimstone and tried to contact Cormier by phone to see what was happening."

"Hugh, please. I realize that you are ever vigilant and always prepared when it comes to this sort of thing and I'm not. But I really don't need any of your lectures right now."

To Mattie's astonishment, his voice gentled. "I know, babe, I know. I'm still a little shook, myself, that's all."

She stared at his broad-shouldered back, not believing her ears. "You? Shook?"

16

"Hell, yes. I was afraid I was going to walk in and find you dead in that hall along with Cormier."

"Oh."

"Is that all you can say?" The gentleness had already vanished from his rough voice.

"Well, I can see where it would have been a bit awkward explaining things to Aunt Charlotte."

"Christ. There is that, isn't there? She'd have had my head." Hugh came to an abrupt halt. He was looking at a small, fern-choked stream flowing past his boots. "Okay, here we go."

Mattie peered at the twisting ribbon of water. "Now what?"

"We turn left and follow this stream." Hugh glanced back the way they had come. "I think we've got the place to ourselves. Everybody's busy with the revolution. Let's go."

The rain was coming down harder now, battering at the leaves so violently that it created a dull roar. Mattie followed Hugh in silence, her whole attention focused on keeping up with him while she juggled the string bag and her purse.

The black earth was turning to mud. Her shoes were caked with it. Her hair had long since come free of its neat coil and hung in limp tendrils around her shoulders. Her silk shirt was soaked. The rain had cooled things down a little, but not much. The whole jungle seemed to be steaming like a thick, green stew.

Mattie eyes the ground, watching each step she took so that she did not stumble in the tangle of mud and vines. She took a closer look at the vines when she caught her toe on one.

17

"Hugh," she asked wearily, "what about snakes?"

"What about 'em?"

"Do they come out in the rain?"

"Not if they've got any sense."

"Damn it, Hugh."

He chuckled. "Forget about snakes. There aren't any on these islands."

"Are you sure?"

"I'm sure."

"I hope you're right." She dragged the string bag over another fallen log. Something small and green came alive under the hand she had used to brace herself. *"Hugh."*

He glanced back. "Just a little lizard. He's more scared than you are."

"That's a matter of opinion." Mattie forced herself to take several deep breaths as the small creature scuttled quickly out of sight. "Hugh, this really isn't my kind of thing, you know?"

"I know it's a little outside your field of expertise, babe, but you'll get the hang of it. Your problem is you've spent too much of your time with those namby-pamby art collectors whose idea of living dangerously is investing in an unknown artist."

Mattie bristled at this echo of their old argument. "You're quite right, of course."

He didn't seem to notice her sarcastic tone. "Sure, I'm right. You ought to get out of Seattle more often. Go places. Do things. Charlotte says this is your first vacation in two years. When was the last time you did something really exciting?"

Mattie shoved wet hair out of her eyes and set

her back teeth. "About a year ago when I seduced you and asked you to marry me and take me back to St. Gabriel with you. You may recall the occasion. And we both know where that bit of excitement got me."

Hugh was silent for an embarrassing amount of time before he said. "Yeah, well, that wasn't quite what I meant."

"Really?" Mattie smiled grimly to herself and pulled a shoe out of the mud. "I assure you, that was adventurous enough for me. I've been thoroughly enjoying the quiet life ever since. Until now, that is."

"Babe, about last year—"

"I don't want to discuss it."

"Well, we're going to discuss it." Hugh slashed at an orchid-covered vine with his hand. "Damn it, Mattie, I've been trying to talk to you about that for months. If you hadn't been avoiding me, we could have had it all worked out by now."

"There is nothing to work out. You were quite right when you told me I was not your type." She pushed wearily at more vines. "Believe me, I couldn't agree with you more."

"You're just a little upset," he said soothingly.

"You could say that."

"We'll talk about it later." Hugh came to an abrupt halt.

Mattie promptly collided with him.

"Oooph." She staggered backward a step and caught her balance. It was like running into a rock wall, she thought resentfully. No give in the man at all.

"Here we go," Hugh said, apparently oblivious to the collision. He was looking up.

Mattie followed his gaze, aware that the roar of water had grown considerably louder during the past few minutes. She realized why when she peered around Hugh's broad shoulders and saw twin waterfalls cascading out of the old lava cliffs in front of her.

The two torrents plunged fifty feet or more into a fern-shrouded grotto. The pool at the base of the falls was nearly hidden by masses of huge, exotic blooms and the twisted rock formations typical of long-cooled lava.

Mattie frowned. "This is Cormier's escape route?"

"The escape route is behind the falls. There's a network of old lava caves in this mountain. One of the tunnels leads to a cavern that opens in the middle of a sheer rock cliff that faces the sea. The cavern is partially flooded. Cormier always kept a boat in there."

"Caves?" The sense of uneasiness that had been bothering Mattie since they had entered the dense jungle crowded closer. "We have to go through a bunch of caves?"

"Yeah. Don't worry. Nothing tricky. Cormier marked the route so we won't get lost. Ready?"

"I don't think so, Hugh." Her voice was high and thin.

Hugh shot her an impatient glance as he started toward the grotto. "Don't dawdle, babe. I want you off this damned island as soon as possible."

He was right, of course. They could hardly hang around here. There was too much chance of

20

running into the same people Paul Cormier had recently encountered *But oh, God, caves.* Her worst nightmare made real.

Mattie was already damp from the rain and her own perspiration. Now she felt icy sweat trickle down her sides and between her breasts. She took a few deep breaths and chanted the mantra she had learned when she had taken lessons in stress-relieving meditation techniques.

Hugh was already moving along a rocky ledge that vanished into inky darkness behind one of the falls. He balanced easily on the slippery, moss-covered boulders, his movements unconsciously graceful. He looked back once more to make certain Mattie was following, and then he disappeared behind a thundering cascade of water.

Mattie took one more deep breath and prepared to follow. She reminded herself grimly that she had once vowed to follow this man anywhere.

What a fool she had been.

The mist off the falls looked like smoke as she passed through it. If she had not already been soaked by the rain and her own sweat, she would have been drenched by the spray. As it was, she barely noticed the additional moisture.

But her Italian leather shoes had not been designed to undergo this sort of abuse. Mattie clung to her purse and string bag and struggled desperately to balance on the uneven surface. She felt her left foot slide across a slick patch of moss, and everything started to tilt.

"Oh, no. Oh, *no.*" Wide-eyed and helpless to save herself, she started to topple backward into the pool at the base of the falls.

"Watch your step, babe." Hugh's hand shot out of the darkness and clamped around her wrist to steady her. With effortless ease he yanked her to safety behind the falls.

"There you go, babe. No sweat."

"Tell me something, Hugh," she asked acidly. "Were you always this fast on your feet? You move like a cat."

"Hell, no. I used to be a lot faster. I'm forty now, you know. I've slowed down some. Happens to everyone, I guess."

"Amazing." Her voice was drier than ever, but Hugh didn't seem to notice.

He was busy rummaging around in the string bag. "And I'll tell you something else, babe," he added, "No matter how fast you are, there's always someone faster. That's one of the reasons I finally got smart and took that nice cushy job with your aunt."

"I see." His answer surprised her. It also made her curious. She really did not know all that much about Hugh Abbott. "Have you ever actually met someone faster than yourself?"

Hugh was silent for a heartbeat. "Yeah."

"What happened to him?"

"He's dead."

"So he wasn't quite fast enough."

"I guess not."

But their conversation couldn't distract Mattie from the horrible darkness that loomed ahead. *A cave.* She would never be able to handle this, she thought. Never in a million years. This was far worse than any elevator or dark hall or jungle.

This was the real thing, straight out of one of her childhood nightmares.

Mattie's stomach twisted.

She started to tell Hugh she could not go another step when something went crunch under the toe of her expensive, ruined shoe. Automatically Mattie looked down and saw the flattened body of the biggest cockroach she had ever seen in her life.

"That does it," Mattie announced. "You'd better get out of the way, Hugh. I'm going to be very sick."

CHAPTER

Two

"You are not going to be sick." Hugh said with implacable certainty. "Not here, at any rate. Not now. We don't have time for that kind of nonsense. Put down those bags and come here."

Automatically she obeyed, dropping the string bag and her purse to the ground. Her stomach churned. The memory of the blood in the white room mingled with the image of the dead insect at her feet. The gloom of the cavern threatened to swallow her alive.

"Damn it, Mattie, get a hold of yourself."

She felt Hugh's hand close around her arm. She was vaguely aware that he was leading her back toward the entrance of the cavern. But she was totally unprepared for the shock of having her head thrust under one of the waterfalls.

23

"Hugh, for heaven's sake, I'm going to drown!" But the water was refreshingly cool. Her nausea receded. Mattie started to struggle, and Hugh dragged her back into the cavern. She turned to confront him, sputtering. She felt like a drowned rat and knew she probably looked like one.

"Better?" Hugh asked, not unkindly.

"Yes, thank you," she whispered, her tone very formal. She stared straight ahead and realized she could see nothing. "Hugh, I'm not very good in confined spaces."

"Don't worry, babe, you'll do just fine." He went back to rummaging around in his string bag. "Only takes a few minutes to get through these tunnels. Now, where did I put that flashlight?"

"Please do not call me babe."

He acted as if he didn't hear her. "Ah, here we go. I knew I'd stuck it in here somewhere." He pulled the flashlight out of the bag, switched it on, and played it across the cavern walls. "Like I said, no problem. We'll be through here in no time. We just follow Cormier's markings. There's the first of them."

Mattie picked up her burdens and stared bleakly at the small white mark on the damp wall of the cavern. She would never have noticed it if Hugh had not pointed it out. "Couldn't we walk through the jungle to the other side of this mountain and approach Cormier's secret dock from that direction?"

"Nope. That's the beauty of his hiding place. No access from the sea side except by boat, and you'd have to know about the flooded cavern or you'd never notice the opening in the rock face.

24

The only other route in is through these caves, and if someone didn't know the way, he'd get hopelessly lost in minutes."

"I see. How very reassuring," Mattie said weakly.

"I told you Cormier was one sly old fox. Ready?" Hugh was already moving forward with characteristic self-confidence, clearly expecting her to follow without question.

He did everything with that supremely arrogant, blunt, no-nonsense style, Mattie reflected angrily. Literally everything, including making love, as she knew to her cost. She doubted Hugh would have even known how to spell *finesse* or *tact* or *subtlety* if asked to do so. The words were simply not in his vocabulary.

How could she have ever thought herself in love with this man? She wondered in disgust as she trailed after Hugh. She had nothing at all in common with him. He was obviously not even the least bit claustrophobic, for instance. It would have been nice to know he had some small, civilized neurosis, some endearing little weakness, some modern anxiety problem.

She, of course, had plenty of all three.

It took everything she had to follow Hugh through the dark maze of twisting caves. With every step the walls narrowed, trying to close in on her. Just as they used to do in those old, frantic dreams of her childhood, dreams in which there had been no way out.

She'd had enough psychology in college to understand those dreams. They had been manifestations of the anxiety and pressure she had felt during her childhood to find an acceptable niche in a family that considered lack of artistic talent a severe handicap.

The dreams of being caught in an endless tunnel had become less frequent after she had gone off to college. She rarely had them at all these days, but they had left their legacy in the form of her claustrophobia.

Mattie followed Hugh past several dark, gaping mouths that led into other twisting corridors. Her skin crawled as waves of fear moved over her, but Hugh never hesitated, never seemed uncertain. He just kept moving forward like a wolf at home in the shadows. Every so often he paused only to check for a small mark on the cavern wall.

Mattie concentrated on the circle of light cast by the flashlight and tried to picture the view of Elliott Bay she enjoyed from the window of her apartment in Seattle. During meditation training she had learned to summon up such serene pictures in order to quiet her mind.

The walk through the winding lava corridors was the longest walk of her life. Once or twice she felt large, wriggling things go crunch underfoot, and she wanted to be sick again. Every ten steps she nearly gave in to the urge to scream and run blindly back the way she had come. Every eleven steps she took more deep breaths, repeated her mantra, and forced herself to focus on the moving beam of light and the strong back of the man who was leading her through the caves of Purgatory.

She resented Hugh with the deep passion a woman can only feel for a man who has rejected her, but she also knew that she could trust him with her life. If anyone could get her out of here, he could.

"Mattie?"

"What?"

"Still with me, babe?"

"Please don't call me babe."

"We're almost there. Smell the sea?"

With a start Mattie realized she was inhaling brine-scented fresh air. "Yes," she whispered. "I do smell it."

She concentrated on that reassuring rush of fresh air as she followed Hugh around another bend in the corridor. Not long now, she told herself. Hugh would lead her through this. He would get her out of here. He was a bastard, but he was very good at what he did and one of the things he did best was survive. Aunt Charlotte had always said so. But, then, Aunt Charlotte was biased. She had always liked Hugh.

Mattie bit back another scream as the corridor briefly narrowed even further. Her pulse pounded, but the scent of the sea grew stronger. The corridor widened once more, and she inhaled sharply again.

"Here we go. Paul always knew what he was doing." Hugh quickened his own pace.

Mattie remembered Paul Cormier lying on the white marble floor. "Almost always."

"Yeah. Almost always."

"Did you know him well, Hugh?"

"Cormier and I went back a long way."

"I'm sorry."

"So am I." Hugh came to a halt as the passageway abruptly ended in a wide, high-ceilinged cavern.

Relief washed over Mattie as she realized she could see daylight at the far end of the huge cavern. She was safe. Hugh had led her out of the terrible dream.

She dropped her purse and the string bag and hurled herself into his arms.

"Oh, God, Hugh."

"Hey, what's this all about?" Hugh chuckled softly as he let his sack drop to the floor. His arms closed around Mattie with a warm fierceness. "Not that I'm complaining."

"I wasn't sure I could stand it," she whispered into his khaki shirt. She could feel the gun in his belt pressing into her side and smell the masculine scent of his body. There was something very reassuring about both. "Halfway through that awful tunnel I was sure I would go crazy."

"Hell, you're claustrophobic, aren't you?" His hands moved in her wet hair.

"A bit." She kept her face buried against his shoulder. He felt solid and strong and she wanted to cry. She had only been held this close to him once before, but her body remembered the heat and power in him as if it had been yesterday.

"More than a bit. Jesus, I'm sorry, babe. Didn't realize it was going to be that bad for you. You should have said something."

"I did. You said there wasn't any choice."

He groaned, his hand tightening around the nape of her neck. He dropped a kiss into her hair. "There wasn't."

He framed her face with his big palms, lifted

28

her chin, and brought his mouth down roughly on hers.

Hugh's kiss was everything Mattie remembered, disconcertingly intense, just like the man himself.

No subtlety, no finesse, but dear heaven, it felt wonderful. For a moment Mattie surrendered to Hugh's kiss, losing herself in it. But as the lingering terror was pushed aside by this kindling passion, reality crept stealthily back between the cracks.

Mattie tore her mouth free. She was trembling again, but not from the memory of old anxiety dreams this time.

"You okay now, babe?" Hugh massaged her shoulders with strong, reassuring movements. His gray eyes were full of concern.

"Yes. Yes, I'm okay." Mattie was furious with herself for the loss of control. She pulled away from Hugh and turned to gaze around the large cavern as if she had found some extremely interesting modern art sketched on the walls. "What a wretched place."

Hugh released her reluctantly, his narrowed eyes automatically following her gaze. He played the flashlight over the scene. "Well, shit."

"What's wrong?" Mattie glanced around anxiously, following the beam of light.

"The boat's gone."

Mattie very nearly did scream then. She realized just how much she had been counting on the reality of Cormier's escape boat. She fought back the urge with every ounce of willpower at her command.

The beam of light in Hugh's hand told the story. There was a large, natural pool in the middle of the cavern. It was filled with black seawater that lapped against the rocky ledge. At the far end of the pool was a narrow opening that revealed a passageway in the cliff wall that was just large enough for a small boat. A narrow ledge ran along the mouth of the opening like a lip. The rain-spangled sea lay beyond.

"Now what?" She was amazed at the cool tone of her voice. Perhaps she was beyond anxiety now and was well into a state of numbed terror. Except that she was not truly terrified, she realized vaguely. Not with Hugh standing beside her looking so thoroughly annoyed.

Hugh glanced at her, his eyes narrowed consideringly. "We'll figure out something. Don't go hysterical on me now."

"Don't worry, I won't. A good case of hysterics takes energy, and frankly, I'm exhausted. Are you going to tell me we have to turn around and go back out through those awful corridors? Because if so, I think you had better knock me unconscious first. I'm not up to a return trip."

"Relax, babe. This cavern is as good a place to hide as any until we can liberate another boat. There are plenty around. On an island like this nearly everyone has a boat of some kind."

"I don't think I can manage a night in this place," Mattie said honestly.

"It's a big place, Mattie, with fresh air coming in from the sea. When the storm is over we might even get some moonlight in through that opening."

30

Mattie sighed. "I suppose there's no real alternative is there?"

"Nope." He reached out and ruffled her wet hair in a bracingly affectionate fashion. "Come on, babe, cheer up. We'll camp over there near the boat entrance. You'll be able to see out. It will be just like looking at Elliott Bay through your apartment window."

Mattie remembered the night he had stood with her in her apartment and looked out at the bay, and how, when morning had come, she had been standing alone in front of that window. She shuddered. "What about the, uh, sanitary facilities?"

He grinned briefly. "Just walk out along that ledge that borders the entrance. Outside there's a few square yards of jungle growing on a sort of natural veranda on either side of the opening. You can use that."

"What about the tide? Is this cavern going to fill up with more seawater later on?"

"No. This is high tide now. Cormier said the water never gets above that mark on the wall over there. I expect it can get a little exciting in here during a major storm, but other than that, no problem."

"I see. What do you think happened to Cormier's boat?"

"Beats me," Hugh said philosophically.

"Perhaps someone already found this cavern and took the boat. Maybe this isn't such a safe place after all," Mattie said nervously.

"I don't think anyone else knows about this place. But even if someone does, we're staying put."

"Why?"

Hugh was unlacing one of the string bags. "Out in the open jungle we'd be too vulnerable, especially with you clomping around making a lot of racket. No offense."

"None taken," she retorted.

"This cavern, on the other hand, is relatively easy to defend. If someone did come in by boat, we could always retreat into the tunnels if necessary. Any fight in that network of caves behind us would be one-on-one. And we'd have the advantage because we know how to interpret Cormier's wall markings."

"I see." Mattie's stomach clenched at the casual way he talked about a shoot-out in the cavern. She stood still for a moment staring out through the opening in the rocky wall. The fresh air wafting into the big cavern was reassuring. And the cavern itself seemed large enough. It was gloomy, but she did not sense the walls closing in on her the way she had back in the corridors they had just come through.

"Mattie?"

"I won't sleep a wink, of course, but I don't think I'll go bonkers on you," she said.

"Attagirl, babe."

"Do me a favor, Hugh. Try not to be too condescending, okay? I'm really not in the mood for it."

"Sure, babe. How about something to eat? Bet you're starving by now." Hugh pulled a small tin of liver pâté out of one of the string bags and held it aloft for her inspection.

Mattie shuddered. "I gave up meat a couple years ago. It's not very good for you, especially in that form. Pâtés are full of fat and cholesterol and who knows what else."

Hugh eyed the tin with a considering gaze. "Yeah, I'm not real fond of pâté, myself. Give me a good juicy steak any day. But beggars can't be choosers, right?"

"They can be as choosy as they want until they're a lot hungrier than I am right now." Mattie sat down on the nearest rock and cast a withering glance at the liver pâté, the caves that had terrified her, and the man who had humiliated her. She wondered what the instructor in last month's anti-stress class would have advised to do now.

A few hours later Hugh shifted slightly against the rough wall of the cave and watched the wedge of silver moonlight creep slowly toward Mattie's still, silent shape. She was curled up in a semireclining position, her head pillowed on her leather purse. He knew she was not asleep.

Earlier she had managed to eat some of the water crackers he had taken from Cormier's cupboard, but she had not touched any of the other food he had brought along.

Hugh thought about the ashen look on her face when she had emerged from the narrow cavern passages, and his mouth tightened. The lady had guts. He knew what it was like to keep moving ahead when your whole body was bathed in the sweat of fear and your insides felt loose and out of control. He had nothing but respect for anyone else who could manage the trick.

Hugh watched the dark water lapping against rock. He would have given a great deal to know what had happened to the boat that Cormier had always kept at the ready here in this cavern. It was not like his friend to be taken off guard.

Cormier had always been a planner, a careful strategist who had prided himself on being prepared for all contingencies. Now he was dead. And the escape boat was not where it should have been.

There were several logical explanations for the missing boat. It might simply have been sent to a local yard for repairs or a new paint job. Cormier always took care of his equipment.

But there were not many good explanations for how Paul Cormier had allowed himself to be taken unawares by a killer.

On the other hand, Cormier had been an old man, a man who had thought himself safe here in the paradise called Purgatory. The past was behind him now and there had been no reason to fear the future.

Hugh told himself he would worry about what had happened to Cormier later. There was a time and a place for vengeance. He had other things to worry about at the moment.

He watched the moonlight touch Mattie's bare feet. Right now the first priority was to get her safely off the island. Cormier would have been the first to agree with that. The old man had been old-fashioned when it came to dealing with women.

"A man must always protect the ladies, Hugh even when they bare their little claws and assure us they can defend themselves. If we cannot take care of our women, we are not of much use to them, are we? And we would not want to have them conclude we are totally useless. Where would we men be then? A man

34

who is not willing to defend a woman with his life is not much of a man."

Hugh studied Mattie. Her trousered legs were now bathed in pale silver. He recalled the shock on her face a few hours ago when she had emerged from Cormier's mansion. The memory would send a finger of anguish down his spine for years to come. She should not have had to witness that kind of violence. She was a sheltered city creature. She had always been protected from the brutal side of life.

It had been almost a year since Hugh had last seen her. Not that he had not tried. He'd deliberately arranged three separate excuses during the past eight months to report to Charlotte Vailcourt in person at Vailcourt headquarters in Seattle. Charlotte had conspired willingly enough with the pretenses. Acting was easy for her. Before she had abandoned her career to marry George Vailcourt, she had been a critically acclaimed legend of the silver screen.

He and Charlotte had thought their plans to surprise Mattie in Seattle were flawless, but on each occasion Hugh had arrived in town only to find Mattie gone.

The first time she had been off on a buying trip in Santa Fe. The second time she had been visiting an artist's colony in Northern California.

After that Hugh had begun to suspect her absences were not a coincidence.

On the third occasion Hugh had ordered Charlotte not to say a word to anyone about his impending visit. But somehow Mattie had discovered his plans the day before he hit town. She had left that same day to attend a series of gallery showings in New York.

Hugh had been furious and he'd made no secret of it. He had snarled at his boss, told himself no female was worth this kind of aggravation, and taken the next plane back to St. Gabriel.

But a thousand miles out over the Pacific and two whiskeys later, he had forgotten his own advice to forget Mattie Sharpe. He had spent the remainder of the long flight concocting an infallible scheme to force Mattie to meet him on his turf. He'd had it with chasing after her. She would come to him.

Out here on his own territory he would have the advantage. Hell, once her plane touched down on St. Gabriel, she would not even be able to get back off the island without his knowing about it well in advance.

What he'd needed was a reason for her to come out to the islands.

The memory of Paul Cormier's collection of antique weapons had been an inspiration. Hugh had only met one other person who collected such gruesome stuff. That person was Charlotte Vailcourt, who had taken a keen interest in her husband's collection after his death.

Sixty years old, wealthy, shrewd, and delightfully eccentric, the former star turned business wizard had a passion for old implements of violence. She claimed they nicely complemented her executive personality. There were times when Hugh was inclined to agree.

Charlotte had been thrilled with the scheme to strand Mattie on St. Gabriel. Long convinced that

Mattie desperately needed a vacation, she had talked her niece into taking one at a plush resort just a bit beyond the Hawaiian Islands. And as long as she was going that far, Charlotte had said casually, she might as well hop over to Purgatory and pick up a valuable medieval sword from a collector named Paul Cormier.

Nobody had mentioned that the route to Cormier's island was via St. Gabriel.

"Hugh?"

"Yeah?"

"Who is Christine?"

Hugh frowned. "Christine Cormier? Paul's wife. She died a couple years ago. Why?"

"He thought I was her there at the end."

Hugh shut his eyes and rubbed the back of his neck. "Damn. Paul was still alive when you got there?"

"Only for about three or four minutes. No more. He told me there was no point calling for help."

"Christ." Hugh leaned his head back against the wall. He remembered the great red wound in his friend's chest and the blood that had stained the floor and Mattie's clothing. "Was that the first time you've ever had to, uh . . ."

"Watch someone die? No. I was with my grandmother at the end. But that was so different. She was in a hospital and the whole family was there." There was a long pause. "She was a famous ballerina, you know."

"I know."

"I still remember her last words." Mattie said.

"What were they?"

37

" 'Pity the younger girl never showed any signs of talent.' "

Hugh winced. "She was talking about you?"

"Uh-huh. Aunt Charlotte said Grandmother might have been one of the finest prima ballerinas who had ever lived, but that didn't change the fact that she had all the sensitivity of a bull elephant. Even on her deathbed."

Hugh was silent for a moment. He'd seen enough of her multitalented family to guess that Mattie, the only one without any artistic bent, had probably always felt like a second-class citizen. Her decision to forge a career as an art gallery owner had been viewed by the other members of the clan as a final admission that she had not inherited any of the family's brilliant genes. Only Charlotte had understood and sympathized.

"I'm sorry you had to walk in on Cormier like that." Hugh finally said.

"I felt so damned helpless."

Hugh smiled to himself in the darkness. "Paul was probably terribly embarrassed."

"It's hardly a joking matter, for God's sake."

"No, I didn't mean it as a joke." Hugh tried to think of how to explain. "You had to know Paul. He was a gentleman to his fingertips. Took pride in it. He would never have dreamed of inconveniencing a lady. When I saw him a couple of months ago, he gave me a long lecture on how to deal with women. Said my techniques were lousy."

"Did he really? Mr. Cormier was obviously a very perceptive man."

"That's my Mattie. Sounds like you're pulling

out of the shock. What did you say when Paul called you Christine?"

Mattie shrugged as she stared at the moonlight crawling slowly up her rumpled silk shirt. "I did what people always do in a situation like that I held his hand and let him think I was Christine."

Hugh studied her intently. "What makes you think everyone does things like that?"

"I don't know. Instinct, I suppose. There's so little you can do to comfort a dying man." She moved around a little, obviously trying to get more comfortable. "He wasn't hallucinating all the time, though. At one point he warned me to get out of there. Then he said someone would come. Maybe he meant you. And then he made a little joke. It was amazing. Imagine someone being able to joke about his own death."

"What did he say?"

"He said something about intending to reign in hell, I think. You know that famous quote from *Paradise Lost*? 'Better to reign in hell than serve in heaven'?"

"I know it." Hugh smiled to himself with grim satisfaction. "Sounds like Cormier. He probably figured his chances of getting into heaven were slight. But he'll do all right if he goes down instead of up. I'd back him in a contest with the devil any day. Paul may have had the manners of an angel, but I've seen him—" Hugh stopped himself abruptly. No sense bringing up Paul's past. It might lead to questions about his own, and Hugh definitely did not want that.

"Well, he thought he saw Christine again right

at the very end, waiting for him, so maybe he went the other way after all."

"Maybe. He loved her very much." Hugh was silent for a moment, thinking. *I should have been there with you, Paul. After all these years together, I should have been there at the end. I'm sorry, my friend*

"Thanks, Mattie."

"For what?"

"For staying with him for those last few minutes. You probably shouldn't have hung around. You probably should have run like hell. But Paul was a good friend of mine. I'm glad he didn't die alone."

Mattie was silent. "I'm sorry you lost a friend."

"I just wish you hadn't had to go through that," Hugh continued, his voice roughening.

"It was something of a shock," she admitted.

"Why in hell didn't you do as you were told and follow the original flight schedule?" As soon as the words were out of his mouth. Hugh wished he had bitten his tongue.

Mattie sighed. "Please, Hugh. No lectures. Not tonight. I know it will be very difficult for you to resist, but I would very much appreciate it if you would try."

"But, why, Mattie? Was the thought of seeing me again all that terrible? You've been deliberately avoiding me for months. Nearly a whole damned year."

She said nothing.

Hugh eyed her, feeling a deep anger tinged with guilt. He brushed aside the guilt and concentrated on the anger. It was an easier emotion to deal with. "You nearly got yourself killed today because of your stupid determination to avoid me at all costs." He swore under his breath, thinking about what it had felt like to walk up the steps of Cormier's too-silent mansion and see that ominously open door.

There was no response from the still figure on the cavern floor.

"Mattie?" He heard the edge in his own voice and frowned.

She continued to stare silently out into the night.

Hugh swore again, knowing he should not have brought the subject up so soon. But he was not, by nature, a patient man. In fact, Hugh thought he'd exercised more patience with Mattie Sharpe during the past year than he had with every other person in his whole life combined.

The entire, convoluted mess was his own fault, of course, as Cormier had taken pains to point out a few months ago.

"Hell hath no fury like a woman scorned, Hugh. You're old enough to know that. You have only yourself to blame for the situation in which you find yourself. Now you're going to have to work very, very hard to get her back. I rather think the exercise will be good for you."

Hugh, as Cormier had carefully explained, had made the fatal blunder of rejecting Mattie's heart and soul a year ago. But he had compounded his error by taking her body, which she had offered along with the rest.

The lady apparently held a mean grudge. Cormier had warned him that women were inclined to do that.

There had been only one night with Mattie because Hugh had been booked on a plane back to St. Gabe the next morning. His stormy engagement to Mattie's brilliant, dazzling sister, Ariel, had at last ended in a hurricane of tears and recriminations. Ariel never did anything without a lot of melodrama, Hugh had discovered to his disgust. He was only grateful he'd found it out before the wedding. In the end he had wanted nothing more than to escape to his island and lick his wounds.

The last thing he'd intended doing that final night in Seattle was spend it with the quiet, restrained, obviously repressed, business-obsessed Mattie.

Mattie, whom he'd barely noticed while he struggled to deal with the fire and lightning that was Ariel.

Mattie, who had been waiting quietly in the wings all along, knowing that the engagement to Ariel could not last.

Mattie, who had nervously called him that last night in Seattle and asked if he would come to dinner.

To this day Hugh was still not quite certain why he had accepted the invitation. He knew he had not been fit company for anyone, let alone someone as quiet and unassuming and nervous as Mattie. He had been consumed with rage, both at Ariel and at himself. All his fine plans to head back to St. Gabe with a wife in hand had gone up in smoke. Hugh, as Charlotte Vailcourt had frequently noted, was not accustomed to having anyone mess up his plans.

There were a lot of reasons Hugh had not gotten to know Mattie well by the time his engagement to Ariel had ended. For one thing, he simply had not spent much time with her. He had been too busy quarreling with Ariel over her unexpected refusal to move out to St. Gabriel. Ariel had somehow gotten the impression that Hugh had been planning to move to Seattle. The battle, once joined, had taken up every spare minute of Hugh's time.

But another reason why a man tended not to notice Mattie right off was that she was very different from Ariel. Mattie was a quiet, warm rain where Ariel had been a full-blown storm.

Everything about Mattie was more muted and less obvious than her sister.

Ariel's eyes were a fascinating, witchy green. Mattie's almost green gaze was softened with gold into a shade that was closer to hazel. Ariel's hair, cut in a dramatic wedge, was jet black; Mattie's worn in a prim coil, was a warm honey brown.

Both women were slender, but Mattie's figure, which was nearly always encased in a severe, conservative business suit, seemed flat and uninteresting. Ariel, on the other hand, always appeared willowy and dramatic in the one-of-a-kind clothes she favored.

But that last night in Seattle something about Mattie had tugged at Hugh's senses. She had looked like a calm port in which to rest for a while after the storm. He had been lured gently into her web by an oddly old-fashioned womanly charm that was entirely new to him. The home-cooked meal of pasta and vegetables and the quiet conversation had been both soothing and simultaneously arousing. Her anxiousness to please had been balm to Hugh's lacerated ego. Her shy, rather hesitant sexual overtures had made him feel powerful and desired.

He knew she was not his type, but when the time had come he had taken Mattie to bed and lost himself in her warmth. He had been deeply aware of a sense of gratitude toward her.

The next morning Hugh had awakened with a hangover and the gnawing certainty that he had made a really stupid mistake.

The last person he had wanted to get involved with at that point was another Sharpe sister. He'd had it with the women of the clan. In fact, he'd had it with women and city life in general. He just longed to go home and devote himself to his fledgling charter business.

As he had packed his bag and phoned for a cab to the airport to catch his six o'clock flight, Hugh had tried to ease his way out the door by thanking Mattie for her hospitality. That was when she had made her plea, a plea that had echoed in his ears nearly every night since that last one in Seattle.

"Take me with you, Hugh. I love you so much. Please take me with you. I'll follow you anywhere. I'll make you a good wife. I swear it. Please, Hugh."

Hugh had fled after first making a further mess of the matter by trying to explain to Mattie that she was not really his type.

He had not been gone more than a couple of months before he had finally admitted to himself that he had picked the wrong sister the first time around. Trying to rectify his error was proving far more complicated than he would have initially believed possible.

"Had Cormier lived here on Purgatory for a long time?" Mattie asked after a long silence.

"He settled here a few years ago. I think he liked the irony of the name."

"Purgatory? Why is it called that?"

"It's part of the Brimstone Chain. A few of the islands in the group have active volcanos. Guess they made the original settlers think of fire and brimstone. Purgatory's the biggest one in the string. It's been independent since right after World War Two. None of the bigger countries wanted to own it."

"Why not?"

"No commercial or military value. Not even any tourism to speak of."

"Apparently someone's willing to fight for it."

Hugh thought about that. "Yeah. Funny that Paul didn't pick up on that. He usually had an instinct for trouble. He always claimed Purgatory was paradise simply because it wasn't worth fighting over." Paul had long ago grown weary of battle. Just as Hugh had. "Why don't you try to get some sleep, Mattie?"

"I couldn't possibly sleep tonight." There was a shudder in her voice.

Hugh made a decision. He got up, walked over, and sat down right next to her, aware of the tension radiating from her. Deliberately he put an arm around her shoulders. She tried to pull away. He ignored the small, ineffectual movement and gently pushed her head onto his shoulder. Her body was taut and warm alongside his.

45

"Close your eyes, Mattie."

"I told you, I can't." She stiffened. "Hugh, I wish you wouldn't do this."

"Close your eyes and imagine you're dozing off in front of your living room window."

She said nothing more but she did not try to pull away from his grasp. Hugh waited, absently rubbing her shoulder.

Fifteen minutes later he realized she was asleep.

For a long time Hugh sat there enjoying the feel of holding Mattie at long last after all these months. He wondered what Cormier would have advised at this juncture.

"Patience, Hugh. You've already pissed in your chili once, as our dear friend Mr. Taggert is fond of saying. Don't screw up again."

The problem, Hugh thought, was that he'd already been patient for months. He was not sure how much patience he had left. He was forty and he was alone.

And over the past year he had gotten very tired of being alone.

Mattie awoke the next morning to the scent of flowers. Exotic flowers. Rich, lush, vibrant flowers. Their perfume was a heavenly cloud that seemed to envelop her.

She opened her eyes and saw the massive bouquet lying on the floor of the cave directly in front of her face. It was a huge collection of vividly colored blossoms. There were dozens and dozens of flowers—orange, pink, and white lilies, spectacular bird of paradise, red torch ginger, heliconia, and myriad orchids. They were heaped in beautiful disarray. A veritable mountain of gorgeous blooms. Mattie knew that a mass of orchids and other exotics such as this would have cost two or three hundred dollars back in the States.

She smiled and reached out to touch a crimson petal. It was like velvet under her fingertips. Hugh must have gone out very early to collect such a wealth of flora.

Hugh. Of course this tower of flowers was his doing.

Mattie snatched her fingers back quickly and scowled at the huge assortment. It was really quite ludicrous. There were far too many flowers. A single perfect orchid or one golden yellow hibiscus bloom would have been far more tasteful than this colorful, confused heap.

It was no surprise that Hugh was as heavy-handed in presenting flowers as he was in everything else he did. As she had observed before, the man did not have a subtle bone in his body.

That thought brought back unwelcome memories of the one night she had spent in bed with Hugh Abbott. No, *subtle* was not a word that came to mind. What came to mind was the old phrase *slam ham, thank you, ma'am.*

No wonder Ariel had broken off the engagement shortly after returning from Italy with Hugh in town last year. She had explained to Mattie that Hugh had obviously been merely a phase she had been going through. He represented the Elemental period in her evolving artistic style. It was one of her shorter-lived periods.

Mattie sat up stiffly, stretching her limbs

47

cautiously to see how much damage a night on the stone floor had done. She had to bite back a groan. Then she realized that Paul Cormier would not be waking up at all this morning and she sighed.

She got to her feet, aware that she was alone in the cavern. When she glanced at the level of seawater in the small, natural boat basin, she realized the tide must be out.

There was no sign of Hugh. She assumed he was out scouting around or doing whatever men like him did in situations such as this.

When she walked over to the ledge near the cave's entrance and peered out, Mattie could see the small patch of green foliage clinging tenaciously to a rocky overhang that jutted out above the sea.

Above and below the natural veranda there was nothing but sheer cliff. The facilities were definitely primitive, but there was not much choice.

A few minutes later she returned to the cavern and washed her hands in seawater. Then she turned her attention to the contents in the string bags.

Hugh's trip to Cormier's kitchen had been brief, but he had managed to make quite a haul. Mattie found several more small tins of fancy pâtés, marinated oysters, a jar of brine-cured olives, some homemade tapanade, sun-dried tomatoes, bottled spring water, and a wedge of hazelnut torte. There was also a bit of brie and a chunk of Stilton and some day-old French bread. Hugh had even swiped a white linen kitchen towel.

Mattie surveyed the lot and decided the only

thing that vaguely resembled breakfast was the brie. She tore off chunks of the bread and began to spread it with the cheese.

When a boot scraped on the rocky floor behind her, Mattie started nervously and leapt to her feet. She whirled around, clutching the knife she had been using to spread the cheese.

"Hugh." She inhaled deeply. "Don't ever sneak up on me like that again. I'm very jumpy these days."

"Sorry. Didn't know if you'd be awake yet."

He switched off the flashlight he was carrying and sauntered into the main cavern from the tunnel they had used yesterday. He was looking disgustingly refreshed and energetic, Mattie thought in annoyance. An occasional night spent on a gritty stone floor apparently did not bother him in the slightest.

His jeans and khaki shirt were a little stained but basically did not look much different than they had yesterday. Other than a day's growth of beard Hugh appeared none the worse for wear. He looked like Mr. Macho Adventurer, always at home in primitive jungles, barren deserts, or other perilous locales.

Mattie, who had been congratulating herself on surviving the night, suddenly felt weak and puny.

"Want some brie and French bread?" She did not look at him as she held some food for him.

"Thanks. Paul always said living at the edge of the world was no excuse for sacrificing the good things in life."

"So I gathered, Mr. Cormier was obviously a gourmet."

Hugh grinned around a large bite of bread and brie. "Hey, stick with me, babe, and it'll be nothing but the best all the way."

Mattie winced. "Nothing but the best and plenty of it?" She nodded toward the huge pile of flowers.

Hugh looked pleased as he followed her glance. "Nice, huh? I found 'em right outside the front door this morning when I went out to take a . . . Uh, when I went outside."

"For your morning ablutions?" Mattie smiled sweetly.

"Yeah, right. Did you go out?"

"Yes, thank you." She glanced back toward the bright heap. "And thank you for the flowers," she added politely.

Hugh's expectant expression hardened. "Don't fall all over me or anything on account of a few flowers."

"Don't worry, I won't."

"Ouch." He took another bite of cheese and bread. "You're certainly back in fighting form this morning, aren't you?"

"Believe me, the last thing I want to do this morning is fight." She frowned at the tunnel entrance behind him. "What were you doing in there?"

"I left a little before dawn. I was going to bury Cormier."

Mattie bit her lip. "Oh, Hugh. I should have gone with you."

He shook his head. "Wouldn't have done any good. Somebody had already taken him away."

She was startled. "His family, perhaps?"

50

"Cormier had no family. He was alone after his wife died. Whoever took his body cleaned the place out; the sword, the rest of his medieval collection, and everything else that wasn't nailed down."

"Good heavens, I forgot all about the damn sword. Do you think it's possible someone killed him for his collection? Aunt Charlotte said it was extremely valuable."

"Possible. But it's more likely somebody he trusted, maybe a member of his household staff, was overcome with revolutionary fervor," Hugh said.

"You shouldn't have gone back there," Mattie declared. "You might have run into whoever came for Cormier's body."

"I'm not entirely stupid, you know I took a few precautions. The cars are gone, too."

Mattie looked up, startled. "Oh, my God. My suitcase was in that car. All my clothes. And my vitamins."

Hugh cocked a brow. "Your vitamins?"

"I always take vitamins first thing in the morning."

"Why? Don't you eat properly?"

She scowled at him. "My diet is a very healthy one, thank you. But I supplement it with vitamins to counteract the effects of stress and tension."

"I always thought sex was supposed to be good for that."

Mattie looked at him with narrowed eyes. "Well, I don't get a lot of sex, so I have to use other techniques to combat stress."

"Easy, babe." Hugh's eyes gleamed. "I can take

51

care of the shortage of sex in your life for you. Like I said, nothing but the best if you stick with me."

"Oh, shut up. What do you think happened to the cars?"

"Someone must have hot-wired 'em. They got lifted along with just about everything else."

"Looters." Mattie wrinkled her nose in disgust. "Yeah."

Mattie's fingers clenched around the slice of French bread. She looked directly at Hugh. "So what, exactly, are we going to do next, O great, exalted leader?"

"Keep an extremely low profile, as Charlotte would say. We'll stay out of sight today. With any luck the situation, whatever it is, will cool off a little. Tonight I'll go out and see if I can find us a boat."

"We're just going to sit in here all day?" Mattie was alarmed.

"Afraid so. What's the matter? You worried about having to make conversation? Just think of all the stuff we have to talk about. We haven't seen each other in nearly a year."

"We did not have a great deal to say to each other a year ago. I doubt that anything's changed." She began rewrapping the brie. The plastic wrap crackled under her fingers.

"Look, Mattie," Hugh said with exaggerated patience, "you're stuck with me for the next few days. It's not going to kill you to relax and treat me like an old friend of the family or something."

"You're hardly a friend."

"Are you kidding? I'm the best one you've got

at the moment. Who else is going to get you out of Purgatory in one piece?"

"That's blackmail. You want me to be nice and friendly to you because you're doing me a favor? Just how friendly am I supposed to be, Hugh? What will you do if I can't work up any warm feelings for you? Will you get mad and leave me behind when you find a boat?"

He moved so quickly she never had a chance to get out of range. One second he was half-sprawled on an outcropping of stone beside her, the next he had his long, strong fingers wrapped around her wrist in a grip of steel.

"Hugh."

His gray eyes were dangerously cold. "Another crack like that and I'll do something very drastic. Understand?"

"For heaven's sake, Hugh. Let me go." She wriggled her hand in his grasp.

"Damn it, Mattie, I've spent eight months trying to see you again, and you've done nothing but evade me."

"What was I supposed to do? You made it clear you didn't want me." The old rage and hurt welled up out of nowhere. She wanted to lash out at him, hurt him the way he had once hurt her. "As it happens, I spent the past year coming to the conclusion that you were right."

"About what?"

"You told me I was not your type, remember? I agree with you now." Her chin came up proudly. "More important, you're not my type. I should have seen that from the beginning."

53

"How do we know we're not each other's type? We haven't given ourselves a chance."

"I gave you a chance," she reminded him in a scathing voice. "I offered to follow you to the ends of the earth, remember? And you turned me down flat."

"I've told you before, you've got lousy timing. And last year your timing was all wrong."

She was incensed. "Oh, sure. Blame it all on me."

"Why not? I'm tired of having you blame everything on me. And your timing is bad, babe. Look at the way you're starting this stupid fight while we're trapped in this goddamned cave in the middle of an island that's undergoing an armed revolt. Talk about lousy timing."

"You started this, Hugh Abbott."

"Is that so? Then I might as well finish it."

He used the grip on her wrist to yank her into his arms. And then his mouth came down on hers with enough force to swamp her senses.

CHAPTER

Three

Mattie clutched at Hugh's shoulders as he released his grip on her wrist to encircle her with his arms. He pulled her tightly to him and leaned back against the rocky outcropping. She was lying on top of him, her breasts crushed against his chest, her legs tangled with his. Her emotions were in chaos. She wanted to scream. She wanted to swear. She wanted to slap Hugh Abbott as hard as she could.

But most of all she wanted to let herself savor the heat of him and the fierce, hot, masculine passion she had known so briefly all those months ago.

"You feel like you've been waiting in cold storage for me, babe," Hugh muttered. "There hasn't been anyone else this past year, has there?"

"No, damn you, *no*."

"Yeah, Good. I told Charlotte to let me know right away if she saw any man moving in on you. Mattie . . . Mattie, babe, you've been driving me crazy." His mouth shifted heavily on hers and his fingers kneaded her back with hungry impatience. He kissed her throat and then his teeth closed lightly around her earlobe. The small nip was wildly sensual. "Lord, you feel good."

Mattie shut her eyes, inhaling the scent of him. His clothing smelled of sweat but his skin smelled of the sea. The stubble of his beard was like sandpaper against her cheek. She was vibrantly aware of the swift arousal of his body under hers.

"Kiss me, Mattie. Kiss me the way you did yesterday afternoon when you were grateful to me for getting you through those damn caves." He lifted her chin and captured her mouth once more.

Mattie surrendered to the excitement this man seemed able to elicit so easily in her. With a soft little moan of passion she opened her mouth and let him inside.

He accepted the invitation instantly, his tongue plunging hungrily between her lips, his hands sliding down to her breasts. She felt his fingers on the buttons of her silk shirt and then he was inside, unhooking her bra, touching her.

There was a certain rough care in the way he cupped her breasts, as though he was almost in awe of her feminine softness. He touched her the way he would have touched a kitten, his big hands moving a little awkwardly, but cautiously on her. Mattie sighed as his callused thumbs glided over her nipples.

"It's been so long," he breathed. His voice was husky with desire. "Too long. Why the hell did you keep ducking me this past year? We could have had all these months."

His big, warm palms slid down her stomach to the fastening of her trousers. When Mattie heard the metallic hiss of the zipper she finally came to her senses.

The thing you had to keep in mind about Hugh Abbott was that he always moved fast. If a woman was going to say no, she had to say it quickly.

"*No.*" Mattie gasped, levering herself up and back. "No, damn it. What in the world do you think you're doing?" She wriggled farther away from him, sitting back on her heels. "Pay attention, Hugh Abbott. And get this clear. I'm not about to have another one-night stand with you."

"For God's sake, Mattie." He reached for her, his gaze still gleaming and intent with desire.

But Mattie was already scrambling to her feet, her trembling fingers refastening her clothing. "Good grief, I can't believe I let you do this to me. Of all the stupid, asinine . . ."

Hugh swore and gave up the attempt to pull her back into his arms. He collapsed back against the

56

rock and watched her through narrowed, brooding eyes. "You wanted it. You wanted it as much as I did. Don't lie to me, Mattie. Not about that."

"I expect it's the stress," she said with forced calm. "It has odd and unpredictable effects on people."

"Stress? Don't give me that. Do you city people blame everything on stress these days? Even a little old-fashioned lust?"

"I suppose you never suffer from stress?" she muttered, moving several feet away from him. She sat down again, pulled her knees up under her chin, and wrapped her arms around her legs.

"I don't know. I don't think too much about it."

"But lust, on the other hand, is something you do understand, right?"

Hugh started to answer with what looked like an automatic yes and then paused, obviously sensing a trap. "Babe, let's not argue over this," he said with surprising gentleness. "I can see you're kind of on edge. I didn't mean to rush you. If you want to talk a little first, that's all right with me. I mean, I know women like to talk about things: to *communicate*. Paul always said . . . Never mind. It's been a long time since we've seen each other. You probably just feel a little shy, that's all."

"No kidding." Her voice dripped sarcasm.

"Hey, it's okay, babe. We've got all day. We can't go anywhere until tonight. Why don't we just sit here and sort of get comfortable with each other again?"

"Oh, my God." Mattie nearly choked. Hugh

Abbott trying to be modern and sensitive was too much to take. "Ariel was right. You're hopeless."

"Ariel? What the hell has she got to do with this?" Hugh demanded, clearly annoyed.

"You remember my sister, Ariel, don't you, Hugh? You were engaged to her for a couple of months last year. Don't tell me it's slipped your mind. You met her in Italy when she went there to tour the galleries. You two ate pasta, drank cheap red wine, and did kinky things in famous fountains at three in the morning. Then you returned to Seattle with her. The two of you told everyone you were engaged. Does any of that sound vaguely familiar?"

Hugh groaned. "Ariel was a mistake."

"I'm aware of that. I believe I mentioned the fact to you a year ago."

"Yeah, you did."

"She's married again, you know. Her second husband is a man named Flynn Grafton. He's very nice. An artist."

"Charlotte said something about it," Hugh muttered, not showing any great interest in the matter. "Look, Mattie, I don't want to talk about Ariel."

"I do," Mattie said with sudden violence. "I want to know why you fell in love with her and planned to marry her when it was obvious she was all wrong for you. I want to know why you didn't notice me until I threw myself at you, and even then you didn't bother to catch me."

"Forget Ariel. That was a year ago and I've already told you it was a mistake."

"And I was another mistake, wasn't I, Hugh? Do you make mistakes like those a lot?"

"Not often enough to be convenient," he shot back. "Damn it, you aren't the only one who's had a hard year. I haven't been with another woman since you, Mattie."

"You expect me to believe that?"

"Believe what you damn well want to believe. You're really spoiling for a fight, aren't you?" Hugh leaned his head back against the stone and stared out at the sea. "Want to tell my why?"

She bit her lip, horrified to realize how close she was to losing her self-control. It was so unlike her; so alien to her personality. She never made scenes; never screamed at a man; never embarrassed herself with outrageous behavior. A woman like Ariel could get away with that sort of thing. Mattie did not even want to try.

Mattie had been the calm, controlled one in the family for as long as she could remember. The only time she had ever lost her common sense and abandoned herself was a year ago with Hugh Abbott, and she had regretted it ever since. She made it a point not to repeat mistakes.

"Forget it," she said brusquely. "I'm sorry I brought the subject up. I know we're trapped here together until we can get off this island. There's no sense quarreling."

"Why?"

She scowled at him. "I told you why. Because we're stuck in this cave, and we have to work together until we can get out of here."

"I'm not talking about that. Don't worry, I'll get you off the island. I'm talking about why you want to bring up Ariel and the past and fling them both in my face."

At that point Mattie did something she never did. She lost her temper. "Maybe because I want to make certain I don't make a fool of myself a second time!" she shouted.

In the deep silence that followed her words seemed to echo endlessly off the cavern walls. But all Mattie heard was *fool, fool, fool.*

She was appalled. "Oh, God. There. Does that satisfy you, Hugh?" she whispered. "Please. Just let it alone, all right?"

He studied her in silence for a moment. "I can't let it alone, Mattie. I want you."

She shuddered and averted her eyes. "You don't want me."

"Come here and I'll show you." His voice was coaxing now, like velvet.

Mattie rolled her eyes in exasperation. "You wanted Ariel, first, remember? What is it with you? Now that you've gotten over your irritation with her, you're willing to consider another Sharpe sister? If you can't have one of Charlotte Vailcourt's nieces, you'll take the other?"

"Oh, hell."

Mattie hugged her knees more tightly to her chest. "I know Aunt Charlotte wants you in the family. She makes no secret of it. Thinks you have good genes. Says you're a throwback. Says you're not a soft, neurotic wimp like so many modern men."

"Nice to be appreciated for one's finer qualities," Hugh growled.

"She asked you to look up Ariel in Italy because

she figured my sister was her best shot at getting you into her little breeding program. Men have always been attracted to Ariel. They can't help themselves. And you were no different, were you? Aunt Charlotte was thrilled when the two of you came back engaged. But since that didn't work out, she's trying to pair you off with me. I told her you'd turned me down flat last year, but she says it was just bad timing."

"It was. I told you that."

"Well, I've got news for both of you. One chance is all you get, Hugh Abbott, and you've used up yours. I don't care what kind of high-level promotion or how big a cash bonus Aunt Charlotte is offering you to marry me."

The second the words were out of her mouth, Mattie knew she had gone too far. One look at the expression in Hugh's icy eyes told her that. There was an instant of shocking silence and then she prudently leapt to her feet. She did not know where she intended to run, but she knew she had better get going.

She never stood a chance. Moving with the fluid strength that characterized all his actions, Hugh came to his feet and reached for her. A year of aerobic training was no match for that kind of masculine power. Mattie was helpless. Hugh's hands clamped around her upper arms and he held her motionless in front of him.

"You will apologize for that crack," he said, his tone verging on the lethal. "You will tell me you are very, very sorry you said that. You will say you know it's not true. And you will say it now."

Mattie looked pointedly down at his hands on

61

her arms. "Sure, Hugh. I'll say anything you want me to say. You're a lot bigger and stronger than I am and I'm trapped here with you, so you just tell me what you want to hear and I'll say it."

He stared down at her in a kind of awed wonder. "You're really determined to push your luck, aren't you?"

"What luck? I've had nothing but bad luck since I hit Purgatory. Please let me go, Hugh."

"Not until you apologize, by God. We'll stand here like this all day if that's what it takes."

She believed him. "All right, I'm sorry I implied Aunt Charlotte was trying to buy you. There. Satisfied?"

For a few seconds it did not look as if he was satisfied in the least. Then, with a short, explicit oath, Hugh released her abruptly. He jammed his fingers through his hair. "You really know how to get to me, don't you? You know all the right buttons to push."

Mattie stood tensely, watching him. "Hugh, this is crazy. We have got to stop arguing. Who knows how long we're going to be together in this mess?"

He slid her a long glance. "Doesn't it mean a damn thing to you that I've spent the last eight months trying to make up for the stupid mistake I made a year ago?"

She clasped her hands together. "That's just it. You didn't make a mistake last year. You were right to reject my utterly ridiculous offer. We're all wrong for each other, Hugh. I realize that now. What I can't figure out is why you've changed your mind."

"Well, it sure as hell isn't because Charlotte Vailcourt promised to promote me or give me a fat bonus if I marry you," he retorted.

Mattie chewed her lower lip. "I know. I'm sorry. It's just that I was so angry. Dear heaven, I never lose my temper. I don't know what got into me."

Hugh was quiet for a long while. The only sound in the cavern was the hollow echo of water slapping at rock. Then his mouth curved faintly at one corner. "Well, I'll be damned."

Mattie eyed him suspiciously. "What's so funny?"

"Nothing. I was just thinking that maybe it's a good sign you're trying to stick pins in me whenever you get the chance."

She blinked. "A good sign?"

"Yeah. Think about it." His smile broadened into a satisfied grin. "You wouldn't be so prickly about our relationship if you'd really lost interest in me, would you? You wouldn't have gone out of your way to avoid me this past year if you didn't give a damn any longer. You're nervous around me because you're still attracted to me and you're afraid of being hurt again. That's what this jumpy behavior on your part is all about. I'll lay odds on it."

Mattie's brows rose. This was a whole new side to the man. "Since when did you become an authority on interpersonal relationships?"

"You like to think I'm some sort of Neanderthal in the sensitivity department, don't you, Mattie? Why is that? Because it makes you feel superior?"

63

"It isn't just my opinion, you know," she murmured.

"We're talking about Ariel again. I take it? Hell, I already know she thinks I'm something out of the Stone Age. That's why she got interested in me in the first place. She was using me as inspiration for her damned painting. Don't you think I eventually figured that out?"

Mattie flushed and coughed slightly to clear her throat. "I, uh, hadn't realized you were aware of it precisely, no. When the two of you came back from Italy together and announced your engagement, you looked so damned pleased with yourself. Hugh."

He rubbed the back of his neck. "I was pleased. Ariel's a beautiful woman and the timing was perfect. I was getting set to quit doing odd jobs for Charlotte and start working full time at my own business on St. Gabe. I was looking for a wife to take out to the islands with me, and Charlotte set it up for me to meet her niece while I was on assignment in Italy. Said she thought we'd suit."

"I see."

"Hell, there I was looking for a wife and Ariel was just sort of conveniently dropped into my lap. It all seemed to go together into a nice, neat package."

"I know, I know. Let's just forget about it, Hugh."

"I'm willing to forget Ariel," Hugh said. "But not you. I want another chance, Mattie."

"Why? Because you're still looking for a wife, and you think I'll be more amenable to moving out to the edge of the world than Ariel was?"

He frowned. "A year ago you said you'd follow me anywhere."

"That," said Mattie with a bright little smile, "was a year ago. Now, let's stop rehashing the past and start discussing our immediate future. How, exactly, do you plan to find us a boat, and where will we go if we get hold of one?"

Hugh considered her bright smile for a long while. Then he shrugged and smiled back. "Finding the boat is my problem. Don't worry about it. As to where we'll go, that depends on what kind of boat I find and how much fuel I can steal. Don't you worry your pretty little head about such petty details, Miss Mattie."

She folded her arms beneath her breasts and glowered at him. "Wonderful. I'll leave it all up to you."

"You do that. Us Neanderthals have our uses."

Mattie realized he was not going to be forthcoming on the subject of the impending plans for engaging in boat theft. She sighed and looked bleakly around the cavern. Then she glanced down at the bloodstains on her silk shirt and trousers.

"I'd give anything for a hot shower and a change of clothes," she muttered.

"No hot showers, but you're welcome to take a bath. You can use one of those dish towels I found in Cormier's kitchen. Won't take long to dry off in this heat." Hugh strolled over to the opening in the rock wall and pulled the gun from his belt. He idly checked the cartridge.

"You mean take a bath here in the cavern?"

Mattie eyed the saltwater lapping at the edges of the natural basin.

"Why not? I took one this morning. Felt good. You'll be a little sticky afterward because of the salt, but it wears off."

Mattie looked down into the water. "I can't see the bottom."

"So don't go diving for pearls." He thrust the gun back into his belt and pulled a couple of metal packs out of his pocket. "Whoever collected Cormier's body must have picked up that fancy little Beretta he always carried. I found some spare clips but not the pistol. He would have died with that thing in his hand."

Mattie remembered the gun in her purse. "A big ugly pistol? Kind of a yucky blue color?"

Hugh turned his head, one brow cocked. "Ugly is in the eye of the beholder. Paul loved that gun. You saw it?"

Mattie nodded and went over to where her shoulder bag lay. "I picked it up. I didn't know who or what I might run into on the way back to the airport." She picked up the purse, opened it, and removed the heavy blue metal gun. "Here. Is this what you're looking for?"

Hugh came toward her and took the weapon from her fingers. "Well, I'll be damned." He looked genuinely approving. "Nice going, babe. You've just doubled our firepower."

Mattie gritted her teeth. "That does it. I've had it. Never, under any circumstances, call me *babe* again. Understand?"

"You really are touchy today, aren't you, babe?

I imagine all the recent stress has made you a little high strung."

"Damn it, Hugh."

"Going to take that swim?"

"I'm thinking about it." She glanced at the dark water, torn between wanting to wash off yesterday's blood and sweat and a fear of swimming in that bottomless pool. "Where will you go while I do it?"

"Nowhere." He shoved a fresh clip into Cormier's pistol. "I'll just sit right here and watch."

She shot him a disgusted glance. "Then I guess I'll forget the swim."

Hugh grinned. "Hey, I'm just teasing you. I'll turn my back and stare politely out to sea, if that's what you want. But it's not like I haven't already seen you in the buff."

"You were too drunk that night to remember anything you saw."

"Not quite," he assured her, still grinning and totally unrepentant. "If I'd been that drunk I wouldn't have been able to get it up, and I don't recall any problems in that department. And I remember everything I saw. And touched. Believe me, I've thought about it a lot during the past year, and I don't believe I've forgotten a single thing. You were very tight and very wild. A real surprise, I got to tell you. Looking at you dressed for work, no one would have believed it."

"Must you be so crude?"

"It's fun to watch you turn that nice bright shade of pink."

"Well, enjoy it because that's all you're going

to see today. I can stand being hot, dirty, and sweaty another day, if you can."

"Oh, I can stand it. In fact, at the risk of sounding even cruder, there's something real sexy about you the way you are now. I think I like you best when you're not all neat and pressed and ready to sell expensive art to all those suckers you call clients."

"No wonder Ariel got fed up with you."

"Ah, ah, ah. We agreed not to talk about the past, remember? Ariel's not here. It's just you and me, babe."

"Don't call me babe."

"Oh, right. I forgot. Slipped my mind."

"How could it slip your mind?" Mattie raged, skating once more on the ragged edge of her self-control. "I don't think you even have one."

"In that case," he said with grave logic, "I don't see how you can hold me responsible for a few slips of the tongue."

Mattie bit off a muttered oath, vaguely aware that for some odd reason she felt better now than she had since she had walked into Cormier's mansion yesterday. Yelling at Hugh was apparently therapeutic. And she really did want a bath.

"Look, I'll make a deal with you," Mattie said, her hands on her hips.

"Sounds interesting." He was examining the Beretta. "What kind of deal?"

"Promise me you'll go sit by the entrance and keep your back turned while I take a short swim, and I'll give you my word that I won't mention our unfortunate, extremely embarrassing one-night stand last year again. Okay?"

Hugh appeared to turn the terms over in his mind. Then he gave a decisive nod. He never took long to make up his mind about anything. "Deal."

Mattie did not trust the too-innocent expression in his eyes. "Go sit out there on the ledge and watch sea gulls or something." Her fingers went to the buttons of her silk blouse.

"Right. Sea gulls." Hugh obediently ambled toward the cavern entrance and sat down on the rock ledge that lined the opening. He lounged there, one booted foot drawn up, his back to Mattie. "Yell when you're done."

Mattie kept her eye on him as she quickly slipped out of the sadly wrinkled shirt and trousers. When she was down to her bra and panties she hesitated again, making certain Hugh wasn't going to spin around.

She stepped over to the edge of the cavern pool and dipped a toe into the dark water. It felt comfortably cool and inviting. She sat down on the edge and dangled her feet in the seawater. Then she unhooked her prim little bra and slipped it off.

Once into the water she bobbed for a moment, sliding the wet scrap of her modest cotton briefs down over her hips. She lifted them out of the water, squeezed them tightly and placed them on the rocky edge to dry. They would be damp when she put them back on but would no doubt dry quickly against her skin.

She stroked hesitantly toward the far end of the dark pool, letting herself get accustomed to the feel of endless black depths beneath her. It certainly was not as pleasant as swimming in a sunny cove where one could see the white sand below the waves, but it did feel good. The exercise, itself, was soothing, of course. Exercise was very good for stress.

Mattie swam almost to the entrance where Hugh was still sitting with his back to her, turned around, and swam back. It felt so invigorating, she did several more laps.

And then something lightly brushed her leg under the surface.

"Hugh!" Mattie's scream bounced off the cavern ceiling.

Hugh uncoiled from the ledge and was at the edge of the pool nearest her before Mattie, splashing furiously, reached the side. He bent down, holding out his large, strong hands, and Mattie instinctively reached up to grasp his fingers. He lifted her straight up and out of the water in one swift, easy motion. She came out of the sea with a whoosh, naked, wet, and glistening.

"Something . . . something in the water." Shivering, Mattie pushed her dripping hair out of her face and stared wildly at the evil-looking pool. "I felt it. It touched my leg."

"Probably just a bit of seaweed. Or maybe a school of little fish."

"It could have been a shark or something. Damn, I hate swimming in places where you can't see the bottom." Mattie trembled again and hugged herself. Belatedly she realized she was standing stark naked on the rock. Her head came up abruptly and she realized Hugh was staring down at her with open admiration. There was a sexy glint in his eye.

70

"I doubt if it was a shark, babe," he said gently. "Don't get nightmares over it. Up there at the front of the cave the sunlight is bright enough to show the bottom of the pool. I'd have seen something as big as a shark swimming around down there."

"Turn around," she ordered through her teeth.

"Why? The damage is done. Besides, I was going to peek anyway. I was just waiting until you climbed out."

"You," Mattie announced as she stalked quickly over to where she had put the linen dish towel, "are a low-down, sneaky, lying, two-faced, yellow-bellied snake."

"I know," Hugh said sadly. "But I mean well. Most of the time."

"Where did Aunt Charlotte find you, anyway?" Mattie yanked on her trousers and shirt as quickly as possible, aware that he was watching every move with a regretful, hungry look.

"Under a rock."

She frowned at the casual way he said that. She looked back over her shoulder. "What on earth do you mean by that?"

Hugh shrugged. "Where else would you find a low-down, sneaky, lying, two-faced, yellow-bellied snake?"

"Good question." She was not going to apologize. She glared at him as she finally finished dressing. "Thank you for pulling me out of the water so quickly."

He grinned. "That's one of the things I like about you, babe. You always remember your manners, no matter how pissed off you are. And

71

for the record, you look even better naked now than you did a year ago. Stronger in the shoulders and a nice tight, high little ass. Not that it wasn't real cute a year ago, mind you. But it's definitely firmer now. You must be working out or something, huh?"

"Go to hell, Hugh."

He waved a hand to include the entire island of Purgatory. "Haven't you noticed, babe? We're already there. You and me together."

It was still a couple hours before dawn when Hugh materialized in the cavern. Mattie, who had been waiting anxiously for his return from the scouting foray, tried to read his expression in the backglow of the flashlight. He looked cold and savage, she thought uneasily. Back to normal. All the sexy, teasing humor that had lit his eyes earlier the day before was long gone. Hugh Abbott was working now.

Aunt Charlotte had once said that no one worked quite like Hugh Abbott.

"Did you find a boat?" Mattie asked.

"I found one." He crouched beside the string bags, checking to see that they were securely packed. "Good, sturdy, fast-looking cruiser. Full tanks. She'll get us out of here, but we're only going to get one crack at her." He glanced up. "You understand what I'm saying? You do exactly what I tell you and you don't make a sound."

"Yes. I understand." Mattie felt her fingers trembling on the flashlight she was holding. Hugh was telling her this was going to be a dangerous piece of work.

"Right." He stood up and hoisted one of the string bags. He handed her the other one. "First sign of trouble, we drop these. They might come in useful once we're off the island, but we can survive without sun-dried tomatoes and brie if we have to. Ready?"

She glanced at the pistols he was carrying. One was stuck in his belt, the other was in his hand. Aunt Charlotte's pet wolf was ready for the hunt.

"Yes," Mattie said, her pulse thudding in her veins. "I'm ready."

"You going to be okay in the tunnels."

"I think so. If we hurry."

"We'll hurry," he promised her. "Come on, babe. Stick close to me."

Mattie closed her eyes briefly as they stepped back into the tortured passageways. It was not going to be any easier this time than it had been the first time, she realized instantly. She bit her lip and concentrated on Hugh's moving form ahead of her. She struggled desperately not to think about old dreams, old failures, and old fears.

There was only Hugh and right now he was the sole point of focus in her narrow, confined world.

Hugh glanced back once or twice during the endless journey, but he said nothing. Mattie was grateful. It was difficult enough dealing with the feeling of being trapped inside the mountain. She did not think she could have handled sympathy from Hugh on top of it.

She was bathed in sweat by the time they reached the twin waterfalls that marked the entrance to the maze of caves. But she had managed to refrain from screaming, she thought, not without pride.

Hugh edged out from behind the waterfalls and plunged into the jungle.

It seemed to Mattie that they walked for hours through the dense, alien green world, but in reality it probably was not more than forty minutes before they emerged into a wide, sandy, picture-perfect cove.

A shaft of moonlight revealed a handsome, powerful-looking boat bobbing languidly beside an old run-down wooden dock.

Hugh stopped at the edge of the jungle, surveying the cove and its surroundings. He leaned down to whisper into Mattie's ear. "Straight to the boat. Get on board. Lie down on the bottom and stay there. Got it?"

"Got it."

And she did have it. Mattie thought as she obediently started forward out into the open. In fact, she was doing just fine until Hugh whirled around, grabbed her, and yanked her back into the dense undergrowth.

"Shit," he muttered.

The next thing she knew she was being shoved face down into the warm, humid earth.

In that same instant gunfire crackled across the beautiful moonlit cove.

CHAPTER

Four

Silence.

Unnatural, terrifying silence.

Too much silence.

Mattie lay motionless, unable to breathe, her face buried in a pile of decayed vegetation. She was crushed under Hugh's weight as he sprawled on top of her, gun in hand. She could feel the battle-ready tension in him.

"Don't move." His voice was a mere thread of sound in her ear.

Mattie shook her head quickly to indicate she understood. She struggled to breathe. There did not seem to be much point in mentioning the obvious fact that she could not have moved, even if she had wanted to do so. The man weighed a ton.

The ominous silence that hung over the cove continued. It seemed to Mattie it went on for months, weeks, years, eons. She finally began to wonder what would happen next. After the initial terror wore off, the suspense became somewhat boring.

Finally, just when she had begun to think she was going to have a permanent reduction in the size of her already small bustline, she felt Hugh move.

There was no sound, but Mattie discovered the

grip of the Beretta being pushed into her hand. Her finger was guided to a small mechanism.

"Safety. You take it off before you pull the trigger. Got it?" Again. Hugh's voice was a whisper of breath directly in her ear.

Mattie wondered if she should explain about her extremely limited experience with the Annie Oakley Special. She decided this was not the time to tell Hugh she had never fired a real gun in her life. Weakly she nodded her head again, knowing he would sense the movement.

"Stay put. Be right back. And for God's sake, take a good look before you pull that trigger. I don't want to end up like Cormier."

Visions of the horrible red mess in Paul Cormier's chest rose up to temporarily blind Mattie. She clutched the gun and fought a scream of protest.

Then she realized the weight that had been pressing her into the earth was gone. Hugh had risen soundlessly and disappeared into the undergrowth.

Mattie lay where she was and strained to hear some hint of his passage through the greenery. She could hear nothing.

Somehow, the utter lack of noise from Hugh was almost as terrifying as the too-silent cove. It spoke volumes about his unconventional lifestyle. How could she possibly have ever considered marrying the man, she wondered bleakly. Definitely not her type. Absolutely nothing in common.

The answer, of course, was ludicrously simple: She had been certain she was in love with him;

certain that they shared some deep, common bond; certain that she understood him as no other woman would ever understand him; certain that he was lonely and needed her just as she needed him.

The only certainty about the entire situation was that she had been an idiot.

There was a crackling sound off to her right. Mattie instinctively froze like a deer caught on the road in a set of headlights.

The sound came a second time, louder. She thought she could hear heavy breathing.

Not Hugh, then. He would not be making so much noise.

She was slowly turning her head, her fingers clenching the gun, when another shot roared out over the lovely cove. She went totally still once more.

The crackling noises stopped.

Silence.

More cons of silence.

And then the crackling sounds came again. Closer this time.

With a sinking heart Mattie realized that the noises were headed straight for her hiding place. She sat up very carefully and braced her back against the trunk of a vine-covered tree. The vines shifted silently behind her like a nest of writhing snakes. Mattie stifled the impulse to leap away from the tree.

She gripped the Beretta in both hands and pointed it in the general direction of the soft crackling sounds.

From the far side of the cove came a rush of

crashing, breaking, and splintering. A man's startled screech started to climb into the dawn sky but was abruptly choked off.

Mattie did not move. She was fairly sure the scream had not been Hugh's, but that was all she could tell. She kept the gun in her hand pointed into the mass of leaves and vines in front of her.

The crackling sounds escalated abruptly, as if someone who had previously been creeping through the undergrowth was now racing forward toward the sandy beach.

And then the reality of what was happening hit Mattie full force. Someone else was headed for the escape boat.

The thought of another trip back through the caves and another day spent in the cavern while Hugh hunted up a second boat was all the impetus Mattie needed. Her fingers tightened on the Beretta.

A large man burst through the wall of green leaves less than two feet away. He did not look down as he dashed toward the beach.

"You can't have it." Mattie pointed the gun straight up at him. "It's ours."

There was enough dawn light to see the startled expression on the man's unpleasant face. He slammed to an abrupt halt and looked down at where Mattie was sitting with the gun clutched in her hands.

"What the fuck?" The man blinked, first in astonishment and then in growing outrage. "Give me that gun, you little bitch." The voice was a soft hiss.

He stretched out a beefy hand, intending to take the weapon from her as if she were a child.

Mattie fumbled for a second and then found the safety. She slid it off without a word. The soft spick was very loud in the small space between herself and the man.

"Fucking bitch." The huge hand retreated instantly.

"Don't move." Mattie sat very still, holding the gun trained on the man's midsection. "Not one inch."

"That boat ain't yours."

"It is as of now," she told him. It was amazing how quickly the principles of a lifetime could collapse under the pressure of the need to survive, Mattie reflected. Stress, no doubt. She had never stolen anything in her entire life, and now she was planning to participate in grand theft.

"Look, lady, we can do a deal," the man said urgently.

He was interrupted by sounds out on the beach. He turned quickly to look at the boat.

Mattie risked a quick glance and saw Hugh appear from the jungle on the far side of the clearing. He was holding his gun trained on a short, wiry little man.

"Mattie?" Hugh spoke quietly as he neared her hiding place. "It's okay. You can come out now. Hurry, babe. We've got to get moving."

"Uh, Hugh, we have a problem here."

"What the hell?" And then Hugh was close enough to see the still-life scene of woman-seated-on-jungle-floor with-gun-pointed-at-very-large-man.

79

But it was the short, wiry man who burst into a stream of abuse which he promptly hurled at the huge man Mattie was holding at gunpoint.

"Goddamn your sorry ass, Gibbs. I knew you were gonna try for my boat. I damn well knew it." The small man spat viciously into the sand. "You always was a slimy son of a bitch."

"That boat is just as much mine as yours, Rosey," the big man retorted sullenly. "I knew you'd be plannin' to sneak off in it this mornin'. Some pal you turned out to be. All that garbage about how we was gonna get out of here together today. It was all bull. Well, you ain't goin' nowhere without me, you hear me?"

"Gentlemen, please," Hugh said, "restrain yourselves. This is neither the time nor the place for an argument."

"Oh, yeah? Says who?" The small man named Rosey glared up at him. "You ain't any better than Gibbs, here. Worse. You're plannin' to steal my boat, too, ain't ya?"

"Yes, as a matter of fact, I am." Hugh looked at Mattie, who was still sitting on the ground. "Come on, babe. I'll keep an eye on Mutt and Jeff here. Take the bags down to the boat and get in. I'll be right with you."

"Now, see here, mister, you can't just take off and leave us here." Rosey's voice started to rise into a wail. "That boat's ours. We need it to get off this island until things cool down. No tellin' what's happenin' here on Purgatory. It's a goddamned revolution or somethin'. We'll get our throats slit if we hang around."

"Keep your voice down or I'll slit your throats myself and save the revolutionaries the work."

The new and strangely terrifying lack of emotion in Hugh's voice rather than the threat itself had an electrifying effect not only on Mattie but on Gibbs and Rosey. The two men stared open-mouthed at Hugh. It was clear they believed every word.

Hugh flicked an impatient glance at Mattie, who was getting unsteadily to her feet. "I said move, babe."

Very conscious of the heavy weight of the gun in her hand, Mattie edged around the massive Gibbs and started toward the beach. As she passed Hugh she glanced uneasily up at his set face. She thought again about what they were about to do. She started to speak, found she could not, cleared her throat, and tried again.

"Uh, Hugh, this is their boat."

"Jesus, Mattie. Not now, okay? We'll discuss the ethics of the situation later. When we're ten miles out at sea. *Move*."

"I just meant maybe we should take Mr. Gibbs and Mr. Rosey with us. After all, they probably want off this island as badly as we do. And it is their boat."

Rosey and Gibbs turned their heads instantly to stare at her. They looked startled at first, and then a gleam appeared in the short man's eyes.

"I can see that you're a real lady, ma'am. Lord knows why you're hangin' around with this scum," Rosey said, nodding in Hugh's direction. "But I want you to know I sincerely appreciate your thinkin' of us in our moment o' crisis. Poor old Gibbs and me will probably be gutted like a couple of fish by the locals, but I want you to know our last thoughts will be of you. We surely do thank you ma'am."

"Hell," said Hugh. "Mattie, will you do as you're told before the idiots who are running this two-bit coup decide to come down here to take a morning swim and find us all standing around chatting?"

"Like Rosey said, it's real sweet o' you to think of us, ma'am," Gibbs whispered forlornly. "When they're slicin' us up for fish bait or hangin' us in front o' the post office, you can bet your sweet little, uh, backside, we'll sure be thinkin' o' your kindness. Like an angel, you are, ma'am. Just like a pure little angel."

"Move, damn it," Hugh snapped.

Mattie bit her lip. "I don't see why we couldn't take them with us, Hugh. After all, it is their boat and it's quite large. There's plenty of room. If we leave these two men here, they might very well be killed."

"No great loss, I promise you."

"Hugh, please, I'll never be able to sleep at night if we just abandon them to their fates. It's not right."

"Lord love us," Rosey said piously, "you was right, Gibbs. She is a pure little angel. And real good lookin' to boot."

"Hugh, I really think we should . . ."

Hugh groaned. "Mattie, listen to me, it would be downright stupid to take these two with us. They're a couple of professional lowlifes. Trust me on this. We'd have to keep an eye on them every inch of the way. Don't you understand?"

"We could tie them up in the boat or something," she said eagerly, sensing she was making headway.

"No, damn it," Hugh vowed, "I am not going to go against my better judgment just to please a woman who doesn't know what the devil she's dealing with here."

"Please, Hugh. It's just not right. And it's not as if we don't have the room."

Gibbs and Rosey waited with hopeful expressions.

"Shit," said Hugh. "I know I'm going to regret this."

Half an hour later, comfortably ensconced under the canopy of Rosey's swift cruiser. Mattie watched the Pacific dawn explode across the sky. For the first time since she had walked into Cormier's beautiful white mansion, she was able to take a relaxed breath.

Purgatory was no longer in sight. The boat's wake was churning merrily as it made rapid headway toward Brimstone. All seemed right with the world again.

The large man, Gibbs, was sitting across from Mattie, his hands tied behind his back. Rosey was at the wheel. Hugh was sprawled in the seat next to Rosey, his gun still held casually at the ready. He was the only one of the group who did not look cheerful.

"What in the world was happening back there on Purgatory?" Mattie asked to break the ice that had settled over the crew the instant the boat had been untied from the dock.

"Fuckin' idiots, you should pardon my language, ma'am," Gibbs said, pitching his voice over the dull roar of the engines. "Don't have the sense to leave a good thing well enough alone. Ain't that right, Rosey?"

Rosey's small, wiry shoulders lifted in a philosophical shrug. "Right enough. Everyone on Purgatory was happy the way things was. Had ourselves a right nice little government that didn't believe in taxes and committees and paperwork. Kept things simple, ya' know? Didn't interfere in a man's business so long as he kept his nose clean while he was on the island. Worked real well for everyone."

"Fuckin' right," Gibbs volunteered with a sad shake of his massive head. "Worked real well. Can't imagine why some fool would want to mess things up."

"Apparently someone wanted to modernize things," Hugh muttered.

"I guess," Rosey said.

"Had there been an active opposition party on Purgatory?" Mattie asked with a thoughtful frown. "Some group that had been agitating for reforms?"

"Nah. Weren't nothin' to reform," Gibbs told her.

Rosey scowled. "The whole thing just kind o' blew up outa nowhere, ya' know? No warnin' or nothin'. All of a sudden the airport's closed, everyone's told to stay in their homes, and there's armed men in fatigues all over the damned place. No one was ready for that kind of takeover."

"What happened to the president or whoever was in charge on Purgatory?" Mattie inquired.

"Don't rightly know, ma'am," Rosey said. "If he had any sense, which he did, the old pirate, he got hisself off the island right quick like. Either that or he's probably occupyin' the one jail cell we got on Purgatory."

"Or else he's dead," Gibbs said gloomily. "I'll kind o' miss old Findley. Me and him was drinkin' buddies. Man played a mean game o' pool."

"It's incredible," Mattie said, shaking her head.

"It happens." Hugh said, sounding bored.

She shot him a quizzical glance. "What do you mean by that?"

Hugh shrugged. "Just what I said. These things happen. There's always some idiot around who wants to run things."

Gibbs and Rosey nodded in worldly understanding.

"Yep," Gibbs said. "Always some joker around who figures he can line his pockets a little better if he's in charge."

"It usually comes down to money," Hugh explained. "Money and power. They always go together."

"Put the two together and you get politicians," Rosey said in disgust. "There's always a few of 'em, even on a nice peaceful island like Purgatory. Can't trust 'em as far as you can throw 'em. Nothin' but trouble."

There was a profound silence as everyone considered that unalterable fact of life.

"Will you go back to Purgatory?" Mattie asked Rosey.

"Maybe. Maybe not. Depends on what happens."

"Yeah," said Gibbs. "Depends. Had a good setup on Purgatory, but I reckon we can find another patch o' ground, huh, Rosey?"

"Yep. Always a good deal out there somewhere if you got the brains to look for it."

They arrived at Brimstone late in the day. Mattie gazed around with interest as she stepped off the boat. The village looked a lot like other backwater Pacific island communities with its pretty little harbor and a waterfront filled with taverns and small shops. The jungle rose behind the small town, looming over it like a giant green monster that threatened to absorb the small cluster of buildings in one gulp.

Mattie realized she'd had enough of jungles.

"Now what?" she asked, turning to Hugh, who was untying Gibbs. Rosey was securing the boat, his eyes already scanning the waterfront for the nearest tavern.

"Now we say a fond farewell to our two cheerful guides. Then we hunt up a place to spend the night."

"We're going to be stuck here overnight?" Mattie looked askance at the buildings along the waterfront. There was nothing resembling a world-class luxury resort in sight.

"Probably. Brimstone only has one flight out a day. Next one isn't until tomorrow sometime. No charter operation based here. Yet." Hugh finished releasing Gibbs from his bonds and vaulted out onto the dock. "So long, gentlemen. Good luck and thanks for the use of the boat."

"Sure. See ya' around," Rosey said cheerfully. He grinned at Mattie, his eyes crinkling. "Nice to have met you, ma'am, and we sure do thank you for convincing your man to take us off Purgatory with you."

"Fuckin' right," Gibbs said with a toothless smile. "Thanks, ma'am. You all take care now, you hear?"

"Come on, Mattie." Hugh took her arm and propelled her forcefully along the dock.

"Good-bye," Mattie called over her shoulder. "And thanks."

"I'm glad to see the last of those two," Hugh said as he tugged Mattie up the steps to the paved road that fronted the harbor.

"What an odd pair. They seem like the best of friends, yet Gibbs was apparently planning to steal Rosey's boat and Rosey was waiting with a gun to stop him. What on earth do you suppose they'll do now?"

"I don't know and I don't particularly care. But let's get one thing straight, babe. Next time we're in a situation like that, I don't want you trying to call the shots. You do as you're told and you don't stand around arguing with me. Clear?"

"I knew you were just waiting until we were alone to start lecturing me." She lifted her chin. "But I don't have to stand here and let you chew me out. Hugh Abbott. We are now back in civilization. Sort of. I can book my own flight off

Brimstone and be back in Seattle in a day or two. And that's exactly what I'm going to do."

Hugh came to a halt and stood glowering down at her. "What the hell are you talking about? You think that now the excitement's over you can just casually go home?"

"I don't see why not."

"You're supposed to be on vacation, damn it."

"I've got news for you, Hugh. I find life in Seattle far more restful and relaxing than life out here in the islands. Do you know that in all the years I've lived in a city I have never once walked into a house and found a man who had been shot to death? I have never had to crawl through horrid caves or spend a night in a cavern or steal a boat or point a gun at someone?"

Hugh's expression softened in the warm sunlight. "Babe, about that bit with the gun back on Purgatory. You did a fine job of dealing with Gibbs. I was proud of you. I know you haven't had much experience with that sort of thing, but you were terrific. I mean, really terrific. And I also know what it was like for you to have to go through those caves, not once but twice. And I know stealing a boat was kind of a novelty for you."

"Kind of."

"Like I said, I was real proud of you, babe."

"You don't know what that means to me, Hugh." She mocked him with a sugary smile.

"Oh, hell, Mattie. You can't go home now. You've got to give me some time." Hugh stabbed his fingers through his hair. "That's what this whole thing was all about."

Mattie could not bear the expression of chagrin and disappointment in his eyes. She glanced across the street, staring blindly at what appeared to be a small inn. "I'm sorry, Hugh. I really am. But there's no point in trying to pursue this relationship. We both know that."

"No, we both sure as hell do not know that." He clamped a hand around her upper arm and hauled her across the street toward the inn "We'll talk about it later, though. I've got to see about getting us off this island, and you probably want to do some shopping. You've been wearing those same clothes for a couple of days. And you'll probably want to take a bath, I bet."

Momentarily distracted by the mention of clean clothes and a bath, Mattie allowed herself to be led across the narrow street and into the tiny inn lobby. She glanced around with resignation at the nonfunctioning fan overhead, the single worn chair, and the aging copies of *Playboy* on the small wicker table. There was no one behind the desk.

"Is this the best Brimstone has to offer? I've got my bank card I don't mind staking us to something better." Mattie whispered to Hugh.

"Sorry, this is it. Brimstone hasn't exactly been discovered by tourists yet. Don't worry, it's clean. I've stayed here a couple of times myself." Hugh leaned over the counter and hit the bell.

A few minutes later a thin old man with a leathery face stuck his head around the corner. "What you want?"

"A room for the night," Hugh said.

"Two rooms," Mattie hissed.

89

He ignored her, digging into his wallet for several bills. "The best one you've got."

"I know you. Yer name is Monk or Bishop or something, ain't it? You was here once or twice before." The old man eyed the cash and came forward reluctantly. He was working a wad of chewing tobacco with great energy.

"Abbott. Hugh Abbott. The lady wants a room with a bath. Got one?"

"Yep. One. Yer in luck." The old man made the cash disappear from the countertop. He grinned at Mattie. "Take all the baths you want, ma'am. Be stayin' long?"

"Just overnight," Hugh informed him as he reached for the battered-looking register. "We're leaving tomorrow morning on the first flight out of here. Hank Milton still operating out at the strip?"

"No. Hank went back to the States six months ago. Got a new guy comin' in once a day in the afternoons now. Leaves at eight in the mornings. Goes to Honolulu but he'll stop off anywhere in between if you pay him enough. Name's Grover. You better look him up this afternoon if you wanna be on his milk run. That plane o' his is small and usually goes out full."

"What this island needs is more frequent and reliable air charter service," Hugh said as he scrawled something in the register.

"That it do." The old man nodded agreeably. "That it do. We're all startin' to get civilized out here."

Hugh smiled with satisfaction as he picked up the key. "Come on, babe," he said to Mattie,

90

tossing the key into the air and catching it easily. "Let's get you upstairs. You can take your bath while I look up Grover."

Mattie eyed the single key in his hand. "What about a second room for yourself?"

"I'll take care of it later," he assured her as he hustled her up the stairs.

"Hugh, I'm serious about this. I do not intend to share a room with you."

"I hear you." He halted at the landing, glanced at the number on the key, and turned to the left. "I won't say I'm not a little hurt, however. After all, you didn't seem to have a problem sharing a room with me last night, did you? But I won't push it."

"Thank you," she said dryly. Then a twinge of guilt overrode her better judgment. She touched his arm and looked up at him. "Hugh, I'm not trying to be difficult about this. I just feel it would be better for both of us if we don't start something. I really don't think I could stand to go through a second time what I went through the last time you and I got involved."

"This is different, babe." He bent down and kissed the tip of her nose as he stuck the key in the lock.

"You keep saying that, but it's not."

"Take your bath," Hugh said as he pushed open the door. "I'll be back in an hour or so. Besides booking that morning flight, I want to get a shave. We'll have dinner at a little place I know down the street. Great burgers."

Mattie winced. "What about the food in those

91

string bags? There's still some cheese left. Gibbs and Rosey didn't eat all of it on the boat."

"I don't care if I never see another can of pâté or jar of stuffed olives again. What I want right now is some red meat. See you later, babe."

Mattie was too weary to argue anymore about anything. She would deal with it later, she told herself as she stood surveying the hot, horrid little inn room.

The bed looked lumpy. The small rug beside it had once been shocking pink but was now gray with grime. The single bulb in the overhead fixture was probably all of twenty watts.

Hugh had called this a nice, clean place, she remembered. Obviously his idea of decent accommodations was somewhat different from her own. He had not even blinked when he'd opened the door and revealed the sleazy interior of the room.

It made Mattie wonder just what sort of accommodations he was accustomed to. She knew that he brushed up against luxury once in a while simply because he had to in the course of working for Charlotte Vailcourt. Furthermore, he had recognized brie and sun-dried tomatoes when he saw them. But it was equally clear he was totally at home in depressing surroundings such as this.

It occurred to Mattie again that she knew next to nothing about Hugh Abbott's past. In fact, now that she thought about it, neither did Charlotte. Mattie remembered asking her aunt about her pet wolf's background on one occasion and Charlotte had simply shrugged. *"Who knows? Who cares? The man's good at what he does and that's the important thing."*

She put her purse down on the tattered, grimy chenille bedspread. At least no one was pointing a gun at her and there was no blood on the floor. What was more, she could see the ocean from the small window, and the view was spectacular.

Things were definitely looking up.

Downstairs in the narrow lobby Hugh paused to lean over the front desk and bang the little bell.

"What you want now?" the old man asked, not unpleasantly. He was still chewing briskly.

Hugh tugged his wallet out of his jeans pocket and removed a couple of bills. "This is for you."

"For a second room?" The man's brows climbed derisively.

"No. For saying I am booked into another room in the event anyone, including the lady, inquires. Do we understand each other?"

"We understand each other just fine." The clerk pocketed the bills without missing a single chew. "Say, you just come from Purgatory?"

"Yeah."

"What the heck's goin' on over there anyhow?"

"Don't know yet. Some kind of military coup. Heard anything?"

"Nah. Had a few people like yourself passin' through on their way to what you might call more pleasant locales, but no one seems to know what's goin' on back on Purgatory. They just figured they'd best get out while the gettin' was good."

"Smart. I had a friend who didn't make it out."

The clerk sucked on his wad of tobacco for a while. "Sorry to hear that."

"Uh-huh. Do me a favor, will you?"

"What kind of favor?"

"Keep an eye on the lady. If she goes out shopping, make sure no one follows her back up the stairs to her room, okay?"

"Sure. I'll keep an eye on her. But it might be kind of hard tellin' the difference between her visitors and the ones who come to visit the other lady we got stayin' here. The other one, she works out of here, if you know what I mean."

Hugh's mouth went grim. "No one follows my lady upstairs except me, got it?"

"Sure, sure. Whatever you say."

Hugh went out the door and stepped into the hot afternoon sunlight. It struck him that tonight would be the first time he had ever taken Mattie out to a real restaurant meal. He grinned as he started down the street in search of Grover the pilot. It would be a real date. Their first. You couldn't really count that night a year ago at her apartment. At least, Mattie wouldn't want to count it.

Maybe he'd see if he could find a bottle of brandy or rum to take back to the room after dinner, Hugh told himself. Mattie needed to loosen up a bit and relax. She'd been through a hell of a lot lately.

Definitely too much stress.

CHAPTER

Five

"Well, well, well. Hello there. Didn't realize I had competition moving in next door. Welcome aboard, honey. The more the merrier, I always say. The name's Evangeline Dangerfield. What's yours?"

Mattie, who had been standing in the hallway outside her room, struggling with the rusty key in the aging lock, glanced up in surprise. Another woman was lounging in the open doorway of the room next door. Mattie, who would have been the first to admit she had led a somewhat sheltered life until quite recently, had never seen anything quite like her. Not close up, at any rate.

Evangeline Dangerfield appeared to be a few years older than Mattie, although it was difficult to tell precisely how much older because of the thick makeup. Her light brown eyes were heavily outlined in black, and the silver eyeshadow that went all the way up to her brows glittered iridescently. Her full, pouty lips were scarlet, and there was a slash of dark pink beneath her cheekbones. An unbelievably thick mane of improbably blond hair was pulled up high on her head and cascaded down her back in a million curls. The mass was anchored with rhinestone clips that shone in the weak hall light.

The rest of Evangeline Dangerfield was equally exceptional. She was an obviously well-endowed

95

woman who showcased her two main assets in a startling low-cut sarong-style dress. The dress, a flower-splashed creation of red, violet, and yellow, was a size too small for Evangeline's shapely derriere, and the hem was well above the knees. Red heels with three-inch spikes and an assortment of rhinestone jewelry completed the ensemble. Her fingers were tipped with long scarlet nails that obviously required an enormous amount of time and effort.

"How do you do?" Mattie, on her way out to try to find something to replace her much-abused silk blouse and olive slacks, felt rather dowdy. It was a familiar feeling, one she frequently experienced around her sister Ariel. "My name's Mattie. Mattie Sharpe."

"Mattie Sharpe, huh? Nice to meet you, Mattie. Been a while since I talked to another working woman. When did you hit the island?"

"An hour ago. Just got in from Purgatory."

"Oh, yeah. I hear all hell is breaking loose over there. Some kind of revolution or something, huh? Don't blame you for leaving. That kind of thing is hard on business. So how long you here for?"

"Well, I don't know for certain. Hopefully, just a day or so." Mattie looked down at her stained clothing. "I had to leave all my things behind. I was on my way out just now to buy some fresh clothes."

Evangeline was instantly sympathetic as she gave Mattie a swift head-to-toe once-over. "You poor kid. You look like hell. No offense. It must have been real rough over there on Purgatory. I guess you probably need to make a few quick bucks here on Brimstone before you can move on right?"

"Well . . ."

"No problem, honey. There's plenty to go around tonight. Navy ship in the harbor. We'll both have all the trade we can handle and I don't mind sharing."

It dawned on Mattie that she was talking to a professional call girl and that Evangeline assumed that Mattie was in the same business. "That's very generous of you."

"Hey, sisters got to stick together, right?" Evangeline smiled brilliantly. "Look, you aren't going to find any good working clothes in the shops around here. Believe me, I know. Brimstone is the backwater to end all backwaters. I have to make my own things or order them from a catalog. Why don't you borrow some of my clothes for tonight?"

Mattie was fast becoming fascinated. "Do you think they'd fit?"

Evangeline eyed Mattie's slender figure with a critical eye. "You're a little small on top, but we can work around that. I'm pretty handy with a needle. Why don't you come in? We won't be going to work for another few hours. The boys always like to get a few drinks under their belt first, don't they? Plenty of time to run something up for you."

This was rather like falling down the rabbit hole. Mattie wondered what Ariel would say if she knew her prim, conservative sister was being mistaken for a prostitute. Then she wondered what Hugh would say.

And suddenly she could not wait to find out.

"That's very kind of you, Evangeline." Mattie stepped forward. "I can pay you for the clothes."

"Forget it. It's worth it just to have another woman to talk to." Evangeline moved aside to allow Mattie through the door. "That's the thing I miss most out here, you know. Intelligent conversation with another woman. Most of the people I talk to are men, and their conversation tends to be somewhat limited. How about a drink? I make a mean rum punch."

"Thank you." Mattie smiled gratefully as she took in the gaudy room. Everything appeared to have been done in red. Red and gold wallpaper, red velvet curtains, red plush bedspread, red rugs. There were mirrors on the ceiling over the bed and along one wall. "Your room is certainly a lot fancier than mine."

"No thanks to the management of this joint." Evangeline laughed, a rich, throaty sound, as she went over to a small lacquered cabinet and picked up a bottle of rum. "I had to do all the upgrades myself. Took months to get the fabric for the curtains and the spread. This liquor cabinet was a real steal. Got it from a guy who came through on his way to Honolulu with a boatload of stuff he was importing from Singapore."

"It's beautiful. You must have spent a fortune on all this decorating."

Evangeline shrugged. "I figure it's an investment, you know? You got to put some of the profits back into the business if you want to see an increased return. That's my theory."

Mattie nodded, feeling very much on familiar

territory all of a sudden. "That's certainly true, isn't it? During my first couple of years I plowed almost my entire income back into my business. I still have to put a lot into it."

"Ain't it the truth?" Evangeline opened the door of a tiny refrigerator and removed some ice cubes. They clinked as she tossed them into the two drinks she had just finished mixing. "Here you go. Have a seat while I see what I've got in the closet."

Mattie accepted the drink and sat down in a red velvet chair. It was rather like finding oneself in the middle of a play, she thought as she took a cautious swallow of the potent rum-and-fruit-juice mixture. "How long have you been working here on Brimstone?"

"About four years now, I was in Hawaii for a while and it was okay, but I decided to find myself someplace where the competition wasn't so fierce. Here on Brimstone I'm the only working woman on the island." Evangeline opened a closet door and stood, one hand on a gracefully cocked hip, and perused the contents. "Let's see what we've got. Ah, here we go. This should suit you just fine."

Mattie blinked at the tiny little handful of red lace and satin Evangeline was holding out for inspection. "Is that the slip?" she asked weakly.

"Hell, no. It's one of my best outfits. I never wear slips, not unless I get some john who's got a thing for underwear. Takes long enough to get in and out of my clothes as it is. Let's see how this looks on you."

Mattie took a long swallow of her drink before

she rose cautiously to her feet and began unbuttoning her blouse.

Evangeline made more sympathetic noises when she spotted Mattie's prim little bra and briefs. "You poor kid. You didn't get out of that mess on Purgatory with much, did you?"

Mattie was embarrassed by her discreet underwear. She thought of the suitcase full of tasteful traveling clothes she had left in the car on Purgatory. "I had to leave all my good things behind," she explained apologetically.

"Yeah, I can see that. What a shame. Hope things cool down over there so you can go back and collect your stuff. In our line of work a good wardrobe is essential, isn't it?" Evangeline held out the scrap of shiny red satin. "I made this a month ago and it's hardly been worn. Been saving it for a special occasion. Let's get it on and see what needs to be done. You'd better take off that bra. This dress isn't made to be worn with one."

Mattie took another swallow from the glass of rum punch and then did as instructed. No worse than undressing in the ladies' locker room at the health club back home, she told herself. She pulled the red dress down over her head.

There was no problem getting it as far as her waist, but she had to work a bit to get the sarong-style skirt down over her hips. She turned toward the wall of mirrors and stared at herself in amazement.

The dress was not much bigger than a bathing suit. It was cut daringly low in front, and the skirt revealed an incredible length of thigh. There was virtually no back to it at all.

"Not bad," Evangeline said with a critical nod of satisfaction. "A little loose in front, but we knew that would need some work. And I'll have to take it in a bit around the hips but other than that, it's perfect. You look good in red, Mattie. I'll bet you wear a lot of it."

"Actually, I don't," Mattie said honestly. She recalled her closet full of expensive but exceedingly dull clothes. The colors in her wardrobe tended toward gray, beige, and navy blue. "But I may start wearing more of it. I think I like red."

She realized she had never felt quite this way in a dress before. She felt a little wild. Maybe it was just a reaction to all the recent stress she had been under.

"Red definitely does something for you. Kind of brightens you up." Evangeline began pinning the dress, causing the already low neckline to go even lower. "Are those shoes the only ones you've got?"

"I'm afraid so. I left the others behind with my clothes."

"Shame. Shoes are so damn expensive. What size do you wear?"

"Seven and a half."

"No problem," Evangeline said. "So do I. I'll loan you the ones I've got on. They're perfect for that dress. Okay, I've finished pinning. Take it off and I'll make the adjustments."

"This is certainly very nice of you." Mattie said as she slipped the red dress off and handed it over to Evangeline.

"My pleasure. Like I said, it's been a while since I had a nice chat with an intelligent person."

She went over to the closet and wheeled out a small table that held a sewing machine. "How was business on Purgatory before things turned sour?"

"Not bad." Mattie finished dressing in her trousers and silk shirt and sat down again. She picked up her drink. "But I don't think I'll go back."

"Yeah? Where will you head next?" The sewing machine hummed energetically as Evangeline went to work.

"Seattle."

"Been there before?"

"Yes. In fact. I lived there before I, uh, went to Purgatory."

"No kidding? I've always wanted to go to Seattle. Maybe next time I take a vacation I'll go there."

"If you do, be sure and look me up," Mattie said with a rush of good will toward this woman who was going out of her way to be kind. "I'll leave my name and address."

"It's a deal. I make it a practice to take a vacation at least twice a year. A woman needs a break, you know? All work and no play isn't good for you."

"I know. Stress definitely takes a toll."

"That's a fact." Evangeline expertly trimmed the seam of the sarong's skirt. "And we've sure got our share of stress in our line of work, don't we? The business isn't what it used to be, what with these new diseases and all. Which reminds me, you need any rubbers for tonight?"

Mattie choked on a sip of rum and juice. "I didn't bring any with me," she said carefully.

"Figured you might have had to leave those

behind along with your clothes. Check that cabinet over there by the bed. I keep a bunch handy. Help yourself."

Mattie stared at the red wicker cabinet for a moment and then slowly got up and went over to open it. Inside was a large basket filled with little foil packages. She took a handful and dropped them into her purse. "Thank you."

"Can't be too careful these days. Doesn't pay to take chances. By the way, who's your broker?"

"My broker?"

"Yeah, your stockbroker." Evangeline looked up with a quizzical glance and took a pull on her drink. "Or are you into CDs and money market accounts?"

"Oh, I see what you mean." Mattie frowned consideringly as she sat down again. "Yes. I tend to favor certificates of deposit and money market accounts. The stock market is just too volatile for my taste. Not a good place for the small investor anymore."

"I know what you mean. I keep telling myself I should get out, but a part of me likes the thrill, you know? Of course, I don't put everything into the market. Just what I can afford to lose. The rest goes right into T-bills and stuff. I'm no fool. I've seen too many women in this business wind up with nothing after years of hard work. I'm not going to be one of them."

"You're absolutely right. Nobody's going to give us a pension. Self-employed people have to look after themselves."

"Ain't it the truth?" Evangeline nodded as she

went to work on the bodice of the little red dress. "How about another drink?"

"Sounds great. Tell me, Evangeline, what are you going to do when you retire?"

"Funny you should mention that." Evangeline looked down at the red dress she was altering. "I've been thinking about retirement a lot lately. It's time to get out of the business. Like I said, it isn't what it used to be. Don't laugh, but I'd like to open up *a small dress shop* somewhere out here on the islands, you know? Design my own things for tourists. I think I'd be good at it. What do you think?"

Mattie looked at the beautiful workmanship on the red dress. She knew art when she saw it. "I think you'd be terrific at it."

Hugh was smiling with anticipation as he bounded up the inn stairs an hour later. He had a bottle of rum in a paper bag under one arm, and he'd splurged on a new shirt at the little general store on the waterfront. He was ready for the big date with Mattie.

"We're going to party tonight, babe," he announced as he opened the door of the small room. "Got it all planned. A real date. First we'll hit that little place that serves the great burgers, have a couple of drinks and some food, and then I figure later we can come back here and—Holy shit."

Hugh came to a dead halt just inside the door and stared at the exotic creature sitting on the side of the bed.

"Hello, Hugh. As a matter of fact, I am rather hungry." Mattie smiled at him.

"Mattie?" Hugh slowly closed the door behind him without taking his eyes off her. He could not believe what he was seeing.

She was wearing a minuscule red dress that almost revealed her nipples. It clung to her hips like a lover and rode halfway up her thigh. She had her legs crossed, her feet daintily arched in impossibly high, spiky red heels. Her tawny-brown hair danced around her shoulders, soft and loose and inviting. Her green-and-gold eyes were brilliantly outlined and accented with glittering turquoise eyeshadow. Her mouth was a dark red flower. Rhinestones glittered on her fingers and wrists and in the small cleavage revealed by the dress.

"What do you think, Hugh? Is it me?" She grinned at him, her eyes full of an unfamiliar mischief.

"What the hell happened to you?" Dazed, Hugh moved slowly over to a table and set down his packages.

"I met the nicest lady down the hall. A working woman. Just like me. When she realized I had nothing suitable for tonight, she loaned me some of her things." Mattie got up and pirouetted.

Hugh's mouth went dry. His gaze traveled down the length of her spine to where the red dress curved tightly over her hips. "There's no back to that dress."

"I know. Good thing it's warm here on Brimstone, hmmm?"

Hugh took a step closer, eyes narrowing as she

turned back to face him. He had never seen that particular expression in her eyes. "Mattie, have you been drinking?"

"Just a couple of rum punches." She waved her hand in an airy gesture, and the rings on her fingers glittered like diamonds. "Don't worry, I'm in complete control. My friend Evangeline says you can't work drunk. Men tend to take advantage of you if they think you're tipsy. Men are like that, you know. Always trying to take advantage of a woman."

"This Evangeline person. What exactly does she do for a living, or should I ask?"

"I told you. She's a working woman." Mattie laughed up at him. "And she thinks I'm one, too. She took pity on me because I had to flee Purgatory without the tools of my trade." Mattie tossed a handful of little foil packages into the air. They rained down over the bed. "Evangeline is a very nice person, Hugh."

"I don't believe this."

"I know." Mattie giggled. "And neither would anyone else back home in Seattle. I wish I had a camera so you could take a picture of me. Evangeline says I look terrific in red."

"You do," Hugh admitted. "But you need a little more of it."

"Now, Hugh, don't be a prude. Are you ready to go out to dinner?"

"Yeah, but I'm not taking you anywhere dressed like that."

"Then I'll go out by myself."

She was at the door and through it before Hugh realized she meant business. He swung around and went after her. "Now, just one damn minute, Mattie."

"You can't come along if you're going to lecture me," she informed him from the top of the stairs. "I'm sick and tired of your lectures. I intend to have fun tonight."

"Mattie, hold on a second. Damn it, come back here." Hugh started down the hall with long, determined strides.

But Mattie had already scampered down to the lobby and was waving at the clerk as she went past the front door.

Hugh was right behind her.

"Got a navy ship in the harbor," the old desk clerk said as Hugh went past. "You'd better hang on to her or yer not gonna see her till morning."

"Damn," said Hugh.

He caught up with Mattie outside on the street. A beautiful scarlet butterfly flitting through the tropical night, she was already attracting too much attention. A young man in a white Navy uniform leered and let out a loud wolf whistle. Hugh glowered at him and reached for Mattie's arm.

"What the devil do you think you're up to, Mattie?" he demanded as he pinned her to his side.

"Just going out for a bite to eat." She smiled at a man who was tying up a sailboat. The man's mouth fell open and he stopped work to stare. "Isn't this amazing, Hugh? Evangeline is right. Red is definitely my color."

"Babe, the way that dress is cut, it wouldn't matter what color it was." He realized she was enjoying herself. "Look, I don't want to rain on your parade, but it's not exactly safe for you to be running around in that outfit."

She looked up at him with innocently widened eyes. "Why ever not, Hugh? After all, I've got you along to protect me, don't I?"

He exhaled on a low groan. Then he decided two could play at that game. "Who's going to protect you from me, babe?"

"No problem. You've seen me in less and you weren't exactly overwhelmed, were you?"

"If you misjudge other men as badly as you misjudge me, you're going to be in a lot of trouble."

"Nonsense." She patted his arm with condescending affection. "We both know you'll behave yourself. What would Aunt Charlotte say if I told her you'd gotten out of line?"

He tightened his grip on her arm. "You ought to know better than to wave a threat at me, babe," he warned softly. "I only answer to Charlotte when it comes to business. She doesn't have anything to do with the rest of my life."

"Tough talk." Mattie gave a gurgle of husky laughter. "But I don't believe a word of it. What would you do if you didn't get all those nice, lucrative assignments to clean up little messes around the world for Vailcourt?"

"I'd spend more time on my own business." Hugh abruptly decided against dragging her back to the room. A sexy, teasing Mattie was a wonderful thing. He had never seen her in quite this mood, and he realized he did not really want to squelch it. She was having too much fun and— if he played his cards right—so could he.

He steered her toward the open-air tavern at the end of the street. There was no absolutely safe place to take her tonight. Brimstone was full of sailors, and even at their best, the local taverns and bars tended to be rough. He would just have to make certain everyone realized she was private property.

"And just what is this mysterious business of yours, Hugh? It's got something to do with airplanes, doesn't it?" Mattie clung to his arm, practically draped over it as she gazed up at him with wide, inquiring eyes.

"I told you, I'm building up a charter business on St. Gabe." He eased her through the tavern's entrance and was immediately aware of the sensation Mattie caused. Catcalls and whistles echoed from one end of the long bar to the other. Hugh wondered if he was going to get through the evening without a fight. "This is really stupid," he muttered as he aimed Mattie toward a booth near the railing.

"It's fun." Mattie slid across the vinyl seat, exposing another three inches of thigh. "I feel good tonight. I think it's a new me. I'll have a rum punch, please."

"You'll have dinner," Hugh informed her.

"What a grouch. Very well. Dinner first. And then a rum punch."

"We'll drink it back in the room." Hugh decided, giving the man at the end of the bar his coldest glance. The man, who had been staring intently at Mattie, heaved an obvious sigh of regret and turned back to his drink.

"A beer for me," Hugh told the middle-aged

waitress. "And a cola for the lady. Then a couple of hamburgers. Big ones. Make mine a double."

Mattie smiled past his shoulder up at the waitress. "I'd like to make a couple of changes in my order, please. I'll have fruit juice instead of cola. And put some rum in it, will you, please? And instead of a hamburger, I'll have a salad. And, um, let's see, what else have you got that doesn't have meat in it?"

"No meat? You want fish instead?" the woman asked.

"No pieces of dead animal of any kind," Mattie stipulated. "I don't eat dead meat. And neither should he," she added, patting Hugh's arm. "One of these days I'll cure him of the habit."

The waitress looked bemused. She glanced at Hugh for guidance. When he simply shrugged in resignation, she looked at Mattie again. "We've got French fries. You want some of those?"

"All right," Mattie agreed. She turned back to Hugh as the waitress disappeared. "So tell me more about this charter business," she said in a deliberately provocative tone. "I want to hear every little detail about it. I'm just fascinated by that sort of thing. I'll bet you're a big honcho in the air charter business out here in the islands, aren't you?"

"This lady who put you in that dress give you lessons in how to talk to a client or something?"

"How can you say that?" Mattie looked hurt. "I'm serious, Hugh. I want to know everything. I've just realized there is a great deal I don't know about you."

The beer arrived. Hugh hadn't really wanted

one, but he knew the bottle would be useful if things turned rowdy before dinner was over. He looked speculatively down at Mattie. "Are you trying to flirt with me?"

"What if I am?" She hunched her shoulders and the neckline of the red dress dipped so low for a second or two that it revealed the dusky curve surrounding one nipple.

Hugh realized he was staring. Already half aroused, he could feel himself getting very hard, very fast. He took a quick swallow of beer. "I'm not complaining. I just want to be sure you know what you're doing."

"I'm just trying to learn a little more about you, Hugh Abbott. Do you realize I know almost nothing of your past?"

With great effort he managed to lift his gaze back to her eyes. "You're not missing much. Sit up straight, will you?" She really was flirting with him. *Damn*. He just wished they didn't have an audience. Every man in the room must be aware of the look she was giving him. He was torn between his own roaring desire and a need to protect his newfound treasure from the lustful gazes of other males.

"What did you do before you went to work for my aunt?"

"This and that. Odd jobs. Mattie, you'd better sit a little straighter. I mean it. That dress is about to fall off."

"Evangeline designed it to look that way. She's very talented when it comes to dress design. I think she may have missed her calling."

"Yeah. Maybe." Hugh moved slightly, trying

to ease the tightness of his jeans. "What did you say her name was?"

"Evangeline Dangerfield."

"Hell of a name. Wonder where she picked that up."

"She says it's not her original name. It's sort of a *nom de mattress*, I believe. She suggested I think of something a little more interesting than Mattie Sharpe, myself. What do you think?"

Hugh's mouth curved briefly. "I think Mattie Sharpe is just fine."

She frowned slightly. "But do you think it's sexy enough? Does it have romantic allure? Does it promise passion and excitement and fulfillment?"

"Yeah," said Hugh. "It does."

"Advertising and image are so important, you know."

"I'll keep that in mind as I build up Abbott Charters."

Mattie leaned closer, her eyes smoky. "Tell me more about Abbott Charters."

And then, to his own astonishment. Hugh found himself doing just that. He could not resist. She was hanging on every word as if nothing in the world were more important than his hopes and plans and dreams for the future.

Nobody had ever listened to him with such intensity, he realized vaguely at one point. He rambled on about his goal for getting some contracts with the United States government and some with local businesses. He talked about the difficulties of getting aircraft serviced out here in the islands. He explained how St. Gabe was starting to become more popular with tourists and how he planned to encourage them to use Abbott Charters. He talked about organizing scuba diving tours at nearby islands. On and on he talked.

Mattie was obviously enthralled. She prompted him with questions now and again, but mostly Hugh just talked.

And talked.

The food arrived and Hugh kept talking as he ate. He described his plans to become the most reliable charter operator in that section of the Pacific. He detailed his goal to provide a first-class professional operation that would supply everything from fishing boats for tourists to freight service for business.

"I'm thinking about a franchise operation eventually," he said. "For example, the guy who's going to take us off the island in the morning is running a shoestring operation with one plane. If he bought an Abbott Charter franchise he'd instantly look bigger and more successful than he is. He'd get more business, and I'd have another base of operations."

Hugh discovered he was still talking about his schemes and ambitions half an hour later when they left the tavern and started back down the street. He was a little surprised to have gotten through the meal without having to bash a few heads, but he wasn't complaining. Obviously everyone had figured out right away that Mattie was not available, he thought proudly. Probably had something to do with the way she was focusing so completely on him.

"I'll pour you a drink now." Hugh said

magnanimously when they reached the privacy of Mattie's room. "Sit down."

Sitting down meant sitting on the bed. There were no chairs in the room. Mattie obediently kicked off her red heels, leaned her delightfully bare back against the old wicker headboard, and stretched her legs out in front of her. "When will you tell Aunt Charlotte you won't be accepting any more free-lance jobs for Vailcourt?"

"The way things are going, I'll be in a position to do that in another six months or a year," Hugh said as he poured a shot of rum into two glasses. "It's going to be good out here, Mattie. You'll see. Abbott Charters is going to work. A year from now I'm going to start work on a house. I've already picked out a chunk of property that overlooks the prettiest little cove you've ever seen."

Footsteps sounded outside in the hall. They went past the door and stopped at the next room. Evangeline Dangerfield's door opened. There was a murmur of voices and then silence. Hugh sat down beside Mattie on the bed and went on talking about his dream house. Mattie sipped at her rum.

A short time later the unmistakable squeak of bedsprings could be heard through the thin walls. Hugh ignored the sound as he described the veranda he was going to build around his spectacular dream house. Mattie took another sip of rum.

A man's guttural shout of sexual release rumbled through the walls. Mattie bit her lip as her eyes met Hugh's and then slid away. She giggled.

Hugh pretended to ignore the second set of footsteps in the hall while he explained that his beautiful dream house would be open to the island breezes on three sides.

When the third set of footsteps went past the door on the way to Evangeline's room, Mattie wriggled a little on the bed. "Hard way to make a living," she observed, yawning.

"Yeah." Hugh was finally beginning to have a problem concentrating on what he was talking about. The rhythmic squeak of bedsprings and the noisy sounds of masculine climax kept interfering with his train of thought. Mattie's yawn had done interesting things to the top of the little red dress.

"I guess I'd better stick to running an art gallery," she said, easing herself down onto the pillows. She put her glass on the table beside the bed. "I don't think I'd have the energy for Evangeline's kind of work. Do you know, Hugh, I am absolutely exhausted all of a sudden."

"You've been through a lot today," he started to say sympathetically. Then he realized her eyes were closing. "Hey, Mattie?"

"Good night, Hugh. Be sure and turn off the light and lock the door when you leave." With a soft little murmur, she went to sleep.

Hugh sat watching her for a long time while he finished his drink. He hadn't gotten around to telling her about the bedroom in his dream home, he realized. It was going to be a big room with a big bed and a view of the sea. He was sure she was going to like it.

The bedsprings next door began to squeak again.

Hugh put down his glass, stood up, and slowly undressed down to his briefs. Then he pulled

115

down the bedspread and eased Mattie under the sheet. He thought about undressing her but finally decided the red slip of a dress was a perfect nightie.

He went over to his shopping bag and found his revolver. Then he turned out the light and slid under the sheet beside Mattie. He put the revolver under the pillow.

Hugh folded his arms behind his head and listened to the endless parade of footsteps in the hall. He began to wonder if he was going to stay in this painfully aroused condition all night long.

When one particular set of footsteps stopped outside Mattie's door instead of going on to Evangeline Dangerfield's room, Hugh was still awake.

He sighed and quietly reached under the pillow for the gun.

CHAPTER

Six

Hugh felt Mattie move beside him as the door opened. She turned in her sleep, her leg sliding along his, her hand settling on his bare chest. He could feel his body's instantaneous response all the way down to his toes. The lady always did have lousy timing. One of these days he hoped she would get it right.

He forced himself to keep his eyes on the widening crack of light in the doorway. First things first.

A familiar figure was revealed briefly in the weak light that entered the room from the hall. The figure crept stealthily into the room, easing the door shut behind him.

Hugh pulled the hammer back on the revolver. The soft, deadly click was as loud as a cannon in the small room. The figure near the door froze, obviously recognizing that particular sound at once. A man of the world.

Mattie's hand shifted slightly on Hugh's chest at that moment, her fingertip grazing his flat nipple. Hugh stifled a groan and watched his quarry.

"I knew I was going to regret taking you off Purgatory, Rosey," Hugh kept his voice to the level of the softest of whispers, but he knew Rosey heard him.

"What the hell . . . ?" Rosey's muttered exclamation was nearly as soft as Hugh's words had been.

Mattie murmured in her sleep and her fingers began to slip gently through Hugh's chest hair to his belly, which went taut at the caress. He held himself as still as Rosey.

"Wake her up and I'll be real pissed, Rosey."

"I thought you was sleepin' down the hall. Desk clerk said so." Rosey sounded peevish, but he obediently kept his voice low.

"You thought wrong."

Mattie's foot came into contact with Hugh's leg. He could feel her toes nibbling at him like tiny little fish. The delicate, unconscious caress sent a ripple of electricity through him.

"Look, no hard feelings or anything, okay? It

was all a mistake, see." Rosey started to edge backward to the door.

"A big mistake. What were you after?"

"Just a few bucks. I know she's got a wad in that fancy purse of hers. You can always tell by the purse and the shoes, y'know? Real leather. High-quality stuff."

Hugh relaxed slightly, aware of the ring of truth in Rosey's whining voice. His initial annoyance had been generated by the certainty that Rosey must have seen Mattie in the red sarong earlier this evening and had come to her room with something more reprehensible in mind than simple motel theft. "You're lucky I'm feeling in a good mood tonight, Rosey. I'm not going to blow your head off. At least not right at the moment."

"You wouldn't do it anyway," Rosey declared with rash insight. "*She* wouldn't like it. Just like she didn't approve of you threatenin' to cut me and Gibbs' throats on Purgatory. Like she wouldn't let you leave us behind."

"She might not approve, but she couldn't stop me. Get me mad enough, Rosey, and I won't give a damn what she thinks. Keep that in mind and we'll get along just fine."

Mattie sighed softly and her hand moved lower, her fingers sliding inside the opening of Hugh's briefs and tangling lightly in the thick, curling hair there. A distinct bulge appeared in the sheet that covered his thighs. Hugh stifled another groan and through monumental willpower managed to keep most of his attention on Rosey.

The wiry little man had sidled back to the door and was starting to open it.

118

"Hold it," Hugh ordered quietly just as Mattie's thumb gently trailed across the base of his heavy erection. He realized his manhood had come free of the briefs. His muscles were all violently taut, and the hand that held the gun trembled faintly.

With great care, Hugh uncocked the revolver. No sense accidentally spraying Rosey's few brains against the wall in a moment of uncontrollable passion. "I want to talk to you for a second, Rosey."

"Look, I told you, it was all a mistake. I wasn't gonna hurt her. Just needed a few bucks. Me and Gibbs didn't have much with us when you stole our boat, y'know. We're kinda short."

"Something tells me it wasn't the first time you've had to leave town in a hurry. Rosey, before you go, I want to make certain we have an understanding. First, come anywhere near Miss Sharpe again and I'll be very, very annoyed. Clear?"

"Yeah, yeah. Clear. Now, don't get up or nothin'. I'll see myself out."

"One more thing."

"Sheesh. Don't you ever stop givin' orders?"

"Not until I get what I want."

Rosey hovered near the door. "What the hell do you want?"

"A name. A friend of mine died on Purgatory."

"Yeah? Who?" Rosey sounded vaguely interested now.

"Paul Cormier."

There was a small pause. "I knew Cormier. He was okay, him and his white shoes and all. Made me a couple of loans when I needed 'em bad to

119

pay off some folks. Bought the farm, huh? I'm sorry to hear that."

"Somebody shot him and left him to die. If you ever hear a name, Rosey. I want it. I want it very badly."

"I don't know who killed him." Rosey said hastily.

"There's money in it, Rosey. A lot of money. Come up with a name and the money's all yours. Contact me or a guy named Silk Taggert over on St. Gabe. Got that?"

"Yeah, sure. I got it. I'm leavin' now, if that's okay with you. Got things to do, people to see, places to go. Say good-bye to the little lady for me."

"I'll do that." Hugh sucked in another deep breath as Mattie's fingers slipped between his thighs. "And lock the door behind you."

"Anything you say." The wedge of pale light from the hall widened briefly once more as Rosey hurried out of the room, and then there was darkness again. Hugh waited until he heard the lock click.

Mattie's leg slid over his thigh and she stirred gently, nestling closer.

Hugh shoved the revolver under the bed where it would be within easy reach. Then he reached beneath the sheet and found Mattie's hand. It was resting alongside his upthrust shaft, her fingertips just touching the full globes underneath.

"Oh, Christ."

He thought he would lose it all right then and there.

Holding his breath, Hugh pushed his briefs

120

down over his hips and fumbled free of them. Every inch of the way he feared he would wake Mattie and bring his own dream to an abrupt end. But she just wiggled a bit and snuggled closer.

When he had stripped off the underwear, Hugh carefully folded Mattie's fingers around himself. He moved experimentally, lifting his hips slightly. Her hand tightened briefly.

"Damn." Hugh squeezed his eyes shut and inhaled deeply.

For a moment or two Hugh seriously considered torturing himself to death in that position until morning. But he did not think he had the stamina for it. He was already too close to exploding.

Mattie stirred again and her lips brushed against his shoulder. He looked down and in the pale light from the window he saw that one soft, sweetly rounded breast had escaped the bodice of the red dress.

Fascinated, Hugh touched Mattie's nipple with his thumb and felt it grow as hard as a berry. The soft fingers clinging delicately to his manhood tightened again for an excruciating instant.

Hugh caught hold of the top of the red sarong and eased it down so that Mattie's other breast came free. For a long moment he simply lay there feasting on the beautiful sight spread out in front of him.

Then, deciding to push his luck, he moved one hand down to her thigh and slid his palm up under the short red skirt of the sarong.

Mattie released him and rolled onto her back, her eyes still closed. Her legs shifted restlessly.

Hugh edged his fingers higher under the red

satin. The warmth and softness of the inside of her thigh almost sent him over the edge. When her legs parted slightly of their own accord, he stifled another muffled groan.

His questing fingers found the scrap of cotton that shielded the moist, feminine flower he sought. For a moment or two he contented himself with stroking her through the fabric, but when he felt the cotton grow damp he knew he was not going to be able to stop there.

Mattie moved again, arching her hips slightly against his touch. She mumbled something in her sleep, something that sounded like an impatient demand. Hugh slid his fingers inside the leg opening of the cotton panties.

Mattie inhaled quickly and her lashes fluttered. Through sensually narrowed lids, her eyes met his in the shadows. Hugh did not dare move. He realized he was holding his breath.

Then, without a word, she reached up for him, twining her arms around his neck and pulling him down to her. Her eyes closed again.

She wanted him. Hugh thought he would go out of his mind then. He groped roughly at the satin skirt, shoving it quickly up over Mattie's hips to her small waist. Then he yanked the cotton panties downward.

She was ready for him, moist and welcoming. Hugh came down on top of her, probing hungrily. He buried his lips against her warm throat and simultaneously thrust deeply.

Mattie cried out, her whole body stiffening.

"Oh, babe. *Oh, babe, Mattie.*" Hugh's voice was hoarse with his desire. She was tight and hot and wet, just as he had remembered. Months of shattering dreams had finally crystallized into a glittering reality. *She wanted him.* He pounded into her, a year's pent-up need fueling his passion.

He heard the soft little gasps, felt her arching herself beneath him, and he reached down to find the little nub hidden in the thick, soft curls at the apex of her thighs. When he touched it, she went off like a rocket. She convulsed beneath him. She went wild. She clawed at his back. She clung to him as if he were the only man left on earth.

He hastily covered her mouth, drinking in the gentle, feminine sounds of release. And then he was going up in flames himself, his entire body uncoiling like a powerfully compressed spring that had been under tension far too long. The sensations ripped through him, seeming to last forever.

When it was over at last, Hugh was covered in sweat as if he had just completed a long-distance run. He raised his head to look down at the woman in his arms and realized she had gone back to sleep.

Hugh exhaled heavily. He really did not feel like talking now anyway. He felt too good, too replete, too content. Why mess up the perfection of the moment with a lot of idle chitchat? Slowly, reluctantly, he eased himself out of Mattie's clinging warmth. Then he rolled onto his back and gathered her against him.

"Babe, we're going to be damn good together," he whispered. "Just like you told me a year ago. Damn good." For a long time he lay looking up at the ceiling of the shabby little room and listened to the sounds of footsteps in the hall.

It occurred to him that this waterfront fleabag of an inn was probably not at all the sort of place Mattie usually chose to stay in when she traveled.

Mattie's first thought when she awoke the next morning was that the mattress must have been ever lumpier than it had looked yesterday. She felt stiff for some reason.

And a little sticky between her thighs.

And uncomfortable. The red sarong was bunched awkwardly around her waist.

Then she opened her eyes and the all-too-vivid dream she'd had during the night flooded back.

It had not been a dream, of course.

Mattie groaned, turned onto her stomach, and buried her face in the pillow.

Idiot. Fool. Dolt. Dunderhead. Half-wit. Dunce.

She was trying to think of other suitable terms of endearment for herself when she heard boot heels in the hall and a cheerful masculine whistle. A few seconds later the door of the room opened.

"Hey, babe, you awake yet? Time to rise and shine. Got a plane to catch. I brought you some coffee and a roll. The roll is a little stale, but it's edible."

"Oh, my God," Mattie said into the pillow. Hugh's voice held the unmistakable tone of a man who is very certain he's in control of his woman and his world.

"Up and at 'em, babe." Hugh put something down on the dresser and stepped over to the bed to give Mattie an affectionate swat on her rear. "Believe me, I know how you feel. Nothing I'd like better than to crawl back into that bed with

124

you, but we've got to get moving. Plenty of time for fooling around later."

Mattie turned her head on the pillow and opened her eyes with a strong sense of foreboding. Hugh was grinning down at her, gray eyes gleaming with sexy satisfaction. He looked his usual vital self dressed in his jeans, boots, and khaki shirt. His hair was still damp from a recent shower. She looked past him, gauging the distance to the tiny bath.

It was worth a shot.

"Excuse me," Mattie said very politely as she slowly sat up, tugging the sheet around herself. "I'm not at my best in the mornings."

"Have some coffee. Got it next door at a little hole in the wall joint. Stuff tastes like a cross between burned tires and battery acid. It'll wake you up." Hugh thrust the cup of steaming brew into Mattie's fingers.

Clutching the sheet, Mattie looked down at the thick, black liquid. It looked and smelled stronger than the espresso all her friends drank back in Seattle. "I prefer herbal tea in the mornings."

"You look like you need something powerful to get you going this morning, babe. Drink up."

She did not have the fortitude to argue. She sipped obediently. The dark coffee sent a severe jolt through her entire system. "Yes, that certainly will wake me up."

"Told you so. Off you go to the showers, babe."

Exerting heroic effort, Mattie stood. She headed straight for the bathroom, the sheet trailing behind her like the train of a somewhat tattered and stained wedding gown.

125

She would be home soon, she told herself over and over again. In a day or two she would be back in comfortable, familiar surroundings where she did not have to worry about waking up in sleazy waterfront inns with strange men.

Damn. How could she have been such a fool?

Mattie shut the bathroom door quite forcefully and turned to gaze at her reflection in the cracked mirror over the sink. She looked like a walking disaster, she decided critically. Her hair was a wild, tousled mess, there were shadows in the hollows of her cheeks and under her wide, dazed eyes. She wondered if this was how Evangeline looked after a hard night.

Slowly Mattie let the sheet slide to the floor. The red sarong dress that had seemed so sexy and daring last night looked cheap and tacky this morning as it bunched around her waist. Mattie stepped out of it, turned, and entered the small tin-walled shower. She stood under the weak rush of cool water for a very long time, trying to think of how to handle the situation she had created for herself.

One thing was for certain. Hugh was going to be impossible to deal with now. Mattie strongly suspected that as far as he was concerned, last night had settled everything. Hugh was a very linear thinker, a straightforward, insensitive sort of man when it came to most things. She knew that he would assume his "relationship" with Mattie was back on track after last night.

The bathroom door opened. "Here you go, babe. Your fancy shirt and trousers. They're looking a little beat up, but don't worry, we'll get you some new things on St. Gabe."

The door closed once more. Mattie decided that one of the hardest things to deal with this morning was Hugh's cheeriness. It was intolerable.

Her spirits began to revive as she finished showering and got dressed. The brilliant sunlight pouring in through the window and the sight of the turquoise sea did wonders to help dispel the sense of doom that had been hanging over her when she first awakened.

She could handle Hugh Abbott.

She *must* handle Hugh Abbott.

She would be cool and casual and ever so sophisticated and blasé about the whole thing.

She would not give him so much as an inkling of how much the entire event had upset her.

"When do we leave?" Mattie forced herself to ask calmly as she emerged from the bathroom.

Hugh looked at her, his eyes warm and possessive. "In about twenty minutes. We'll be on St. Gabe by noon."

"Great. I can't wait to get out of here." Mattie's gaze flickered around the dingy little room. She knew she would never forget it as long as she lived.

Hugh followed her glance. "Not exactly the honeymoon suite at the Ritz, is it?"

"Not exactly."

"Things on St. Gabe aren't a whole lot fancier, but I've got plans, babe. You'll see. I just need a little time."

"Right. Time cures all, doesn't it?" Mattie picked up her purse and slung it over her shoulder.

"I want to say good-bye to Evangeline before we leave."

"Doubt if she's up yet. A woman in her line of work tends to sleep days."

Mattie smiled coolly. "You're an authority?"

Hugh's brows rose in silent warning. "Now, don't go implying anything, babe. I told you. I've been keeping myself pure and chaste for you. And after last night I've got to admit it was worth the wait."

Mattie felt herself turning pink under the intent gleam in his eyes. She busied herself removing a business card from her purse and scrawling a note on the back. "I'll just leave this under her door."

"Tell her thanks from me for the red dress," Hugh murmured as Mattie picked up the scrap of red satin and the red heels and stepped past him.

She ignored him as she went down the hall to Evangeline's room and knelt to push the business card and the red dress under the door.

"What the hell . . . ?" Evangeline sounded sleepy and disgruntled as she abruptly opened the room door. "Oh, it's you, honey. Have a good night?"

Mattie got quickly to her feet. She blinked at Evangeline's attire, a see-through black nylon peignoir trimmed in fluffy fake fur at the hem and neckline. She had taken time to put on a pair of fake-fur-trimmed matching black high heels.

"I was just leaving," Mattie said. "I wanted to say good-bye. And to remind you that if you ever get to Seattle to be sure and look me up. My number is on that card."

"You bet." Evangeline smiled through a yawn and gave Mattie a quick hug. "Good luck, honey."

Then she glanced past Mattie. "You leavin' the island with him?"

Mattie glanced over her shoulder and saw Hugh leaning negligently against the upstairs railing, arms folded across his chest. "Uh, yes. We're flying out in a few minutes."

"Watch out for the kind that like to do favors for you." Evangeline warned. "Sooner or later they get the idea that they own you."

"I'll remember. Good-bye, Evangeline. Take care of yourself."

"Bye, honey. Hey. Keep the dress, why don't you? It looks terrific on you, and I don't feel like letting it out again."

Mattie looked at the red dress thinking she never wanted to see it again. "Oh, I couldn't possibly—"

"No, no, I mean it. A present, you know? One working woman to another. Like I said, we got to stick together."

"Thank you." Mattie knew there was no polite way to turn down the gift. She stuffed the red sarong into her shoulder bag and smiled weakly. "Well, good-bye."

"See ya." Evangeline yawned sleepily and closed the door.

Mattie turned to find Hugh still watching silently from the railing. She stood there looking at him, unable to think of anything clever to say.

"Ready?" He came away from the railing.
"Yes."

The small chartered plane landed on St. Gabriel's single runway five minutes before the rain squall hit. By the time the pilot had taxied up to the main terminal, a building that was not much more than a large shack of corrugated aluminum, the rain was coming down in buckets.

Mattie was surprised to find herself invigorated by the wild downpour. She actually laughed as she jumped down onto the tarmac and raced toward the metal shack.

"Don't worry, it'll be over in a few minutes," Hugh assured her as he grabbed her wrist and tugged her into the shelter of the terminal building.

Mattie shook the rain from her hair and listened to the roar on the roof as she glanced around curiously. Several figures were lounging around inside the terminal. They greeted Hugh with easy familiarity, their eyes going straight to Mattie.

"Hey, Abbott. What's that you brought back with you? A little souvenir?" one of the men asked.

"Meet my *fiancée*. Mattie Sharpe."

Mattie winced. This was going to be more awkward than she had thought. Things were even more settled in Hugh's mind than she'd feared.

"Pleased to meet ya, Mattie."

" 'Good luck to ya, ma'am. Abbott here could use a woman around to polish up his manners."

"When's the wedding?"

Hugh was grinning as he led Mattie through the small terminal. "Don't worry, boys. You'll all be invited to the party."

Mattie found herself back outside and being stuffed into a Jeep. The rain was already moving on, leaving a steaming green landscape in its wake.

In spite of her forebodings, a new sense of excitement gripped her. This was Hugh's island; his home. This was the place she had been willing to move to sight unseen a year ago. She could not help wondering what her life would have been like if Hugh had taken her up on her offer to follow him out here.

"You're going to love it here, Mattie," Hugh announced as he slid behind the wheel.

Mattie said nothing.

"First thing we'll do this afternoon is get you some clothes. That red thing is cute as hell, but you can't wear it all the time, can you?"

"Probably not."

"We'll stop in town before I take you on out to the house. You can do some shopping while I check in at the office."

The road into the tiny town of St. Gabriel followed the cliffs above the sea. Thick jungle vegetation hugged it on one side, and down below on the other side Mattie could see pristine white beaches and foaming breakers. There was a gray Navy ship and a big, sleek white cruise ship anchored just off shore.

"Navy puts in here regularly. Has for years. But now we're starting to get a little more tourist trade," Hugh explained above the noise of the wind rushing past the open Jeep windows. "Cruise ship comes in once a week. One of the big hotel chains is talking about putting in a first-class resort. Lot of divers are starting to come here. St. Gabe is on the way, babe. You and me are going to be part of it."

Hugh drove the twisting, narrow road with the

casually efficient competence that characterized everything he did. Mattie found her gaze straying to his strong hands as they curved around the wheel. Memories of those hands on her body during the night flooded her mind.

Hugh's lovemaking could hardly have been described as artful, but there was a raw power and an elemental passion in it that had been as overwhelming this time as it had been the first time, a year ago. Mattie shivered as she recalled her own uncontrollable response. Last night, when she had awakened to find him looming over her, nothing in the world had mattered except having him become a part of her.

Fool. Idiot.

The small town hugging the waterfront of a beautiful, natural harbor looked faded and worn. It was obvious no one went out of the way yet to attract the trickle of tourists Hugh claimed were starting to come to St. Gabriel.

"We're still not used to tourists here yet," Hugh explained as he parked the Jeep in front of a building that had *Abbott Charters* painted on the front. "But one of these days St. Gabe is going to start waking up to the fact that we're all going to get rich. When it does you'll see some civic action downtown. Come on, babe, I'll introduce you to a couple of the guys who work for me."

Curious in spite of her mixed emotions regarding Hugh, Mattie followed him into the interior of Abbott Charters. It was a warehouse-style building with a small office in one corner. On the walls there were a couple of pinup calendars featuring overly endowed females in clothes that resembled Mattie's red sarong.

"Mattie, this is Ray and Derek. They fly for me," Hugh announced as two men, one young, one middle-aged, took their feet down off a desk and stood up.

Mattie smiled and shook hands. The two men had the look of bush pilots the world over: a sort of easy machismo and an aura of bravura. They gave Mattie the once-over with raffish eyes, but they seemed to acknowledge that Hugh's presence beside her made her private property.

"You get that government shipment over to St. Julian?" Hugh asked as he stopped beside a battered metal desk and picked up a sheaf of papers.

"Took it over yesterday, boss," Ray, the younger of the two pilots, said laconically. "What have you been up to? Heard there was some trouble on Purgatory. Get caught in it?"

"Mattie did. I found her in time, but Cormier's dead."

"Damn. Who got him?"

"Don't know yet," Hugh said, tossing aside the papers. "But sooner or later I'll find out."

Mattie heard the cold certainty in Hugh's voice, and she turned to glance at him in surprise. She had not realized he intended to try to track down Cormier's killer. "Hugh? What do you mean, you're going to find out? How can you do that?"

"Never mind, babe." He smiled at her and turned to the older pilot. "You finish the inspection on that Cessna?"

"Yeah, boss. No major problems."

"Check out that fuel line on the Beech?"

"It's fixed."

"Keep an eye out for corrosion?"

"Sure, boss. Like always." Derek winked at Mattie and added conspiratorially. "The man's a damn tyrant when it comes to maintenance."

"You want to get caught out over the water with corroded equipment, that's your privilege," Hugh said. "But do it in someone else's plane. Not one of mine. I can always find more pilots but good, reliable aircraft are hard to come by."

Ray grinned widely at Mattie. "Don't worry, his bark is worse than his bite. Most of the time, that is."

Mattie smiled back. "I'll keep that in mind."

Hugh looked at her. "I'll bet you're ready to do some shopping, aren't you, babe? There's a couple of stores farther down the street. Why don't you go have a look while I finish checking up on things here? I'll be along in a few minutes."

"Fine." Mildly irritated at being sent off as though she were a child who was too young to hear an adult conversation, Mattie turned on her heel and strode toward the door.

"I think she's mad, boss," Derek observed.

"She's been under a lot of stress lately," Hugh explained.

Two doors down from Abbott Charters Mattie saw a window display that included jeans and short-sleeved shirts. She went inside and made her selections quickly. There was not much choice.

When she reemerged a few minutes later she walked across the street to take a closer look at the wide variety of boats bobbing in the harbor. There

134

were several sailboats, a few fishing boats, and one large cruiser that had *Abbott Charters* printed neatly on the bow. Apparently, Hugh was in the boat as well as air charter business. An astute businessman covering all the bases.

She strolled along the waterfront for a short distance, taking in the picturesque setting with a weird sense of déjà vu. *This would have been her home if she had come here a year ago.* Somehow it all looked exactly as it should, as it had in her dreams and fantasies.

She leaned over the concrete balustrade and found herself staring into the uncovered stern section of one of the boats. For a second she could not believe her eyes.

She was looking straight down at a half-finished painting. It was sitting on an easel that had been set up in the aging boat amid a welter of brushes, paints, coiled ropes, and fishing gear.

The painting was incomplete, but it was stunning.

The artist had obviously taken the lazy, sun-drenched scene of the main street of St. Gabriel as his starting point. But the painting had gone far beyond a mere reproduction of the quay, bars, and faded storefronts that lined the waterfront. This was no tranquil scene of a picture-postcard island paradise. It was a primitive, incredibly sensual image of savage beauty.

In the half-finished painting the jungle behind the town throbbed with both unseen menace and a sense of life in its rawest form. The beautiful waters of the harbor threatened the tiny outpost of civilization yet somehow held promise for the future.

The painting was at once a universal statement on the human condition and a compelling landscape scene. It was a work of art on several levels, totally accessible to a wide variety of viewers.

And Mattie knew immediately that she could sell it for a small fortune back in Seattle. Perhaps for a very large fortune if she shrouded the painter in enough mystery.

All of her instincts as a businesswoman snapped to full, quivering attention. Like a hound on the scent, she hurried down the dock steps and peered through the windows of the boat's cabin. She had to locate the artist, and she hoped like hell he was not already represented by another dealer.

She leaned down to call into the cabin. "Anybody home?"

There was no response.

She waited impatiently for a moment or so. When there was still no sign of life, she glanced at the name painted on the hull of the old boat and tried again.

"Excuse me. Is anyone home on board the *Griffin*?"

"Don't go holdin' yer breath waitin' for an answer from ol' Silk, lady. He's already up at the Hellfire. Won't be back till Bernard rolls him out the door sometime after midnight."

Mattie glanced down the dock and saw a grizzled old man crouched over a coil of rope. His skin looked like leather and his eyes had a permanent, sun-induced squint. He was wearing a pair of old pants that hung precariously on his scrawny frame and a cap that looked as if it might once have been decorated with a military insignia.

"Hello," Mattie said politely. "I'm looking for whoever painted that picture."

"That'd be Silk, all right. He's always fiddlin' around with those paints o' his. 'Cept when he's busy workin' or drinkin', o' course."

"Of course. And I take it he is now drinking?"

"Yup. Take a look at the time. Dang near four o'clock. Silk always heads for the Hellfire at three sharp on Wednesdays. Real regular in his habits. Silk is."

"Thank you for the information," said Mattie, turning. "I'll try the Hellfire. Is it up there on the waterfront?"

"Yup. But I don't reckon you want to be goin' in there, ma'am." The old man eyed her skeptically. "Silk can get a might difficult to manage once he's had a few. Specially when it comes to females. Silk likes females and he don't get a shot at very many around here. Just an occasional tourist." The man spit a wad of chewing tobacco into the harbor. "None of us gets much shot at females. Not many females get this far. They usually stop in Hawaii. Worse 'n livin' in a dang monastery."

"Really? If that's the way you feel, then why do you choose to live way out here?"

"Used to it, I reckon. What you want with Silk?"

"I just want to do a little business with Mr. Silk."

"Yeah? Funny. Wouldn't have pegged you right off for the type. Kinda thin for that sort o' work, ain't ya? But if that's your aim, I'd get the money up front if'n I was you. Silk don't like payin' for it after the fact, if you know what I mean."

"I'll keep your advice in mind," Mattie said as she started toward the steps that led up to the street.

The novelty of being mistaken for a professional prostitute had begun to wear thin, she reflected. Definitely time to go home.

Just as soon as she had acquired some paintings from this Silk person.

She did not want to have to label her Pacific trip a complete disaster, which, until now, was what it definitely had been.

CHAPTER

Seven

The Hellfire bar was another classic island dive. Mattie decided she was in a position to judge now, after having spent most of yesterday evening in one. This tavern was open to the breezes, just as the one last night had been. It had a sluggish ceiling fan and a long, long backbar filled with the basics: beer, whiskey, rum, vodka, and gin. There was no white wine as far as Mattie could see.

The crowd was light and appeared to consist entirely of men who looked as if they had spent their lives working around docks and fishing boats. In one corner sat a handful of sailors who were presumably off the Navy ship that Mattie had seen at anchor in the harbor.

In another corner near the rail that separated the interior of the Hellfire from the street sat a mountain of a man. He had an overgrown beard and a shock of hair that had obviously been bright red at one time. He was dressed in a flower print shirt that hung unbuttoned to the waist and revealed a great expanse of massive, tanned chest. He also had on a pair of shorts and a pair of thongs. There was a glass of what looked like whiskey on the rattan table in front of him.

The splotches of paint on the shorts were all the clue Mattie needed. Smiling her best gallery-owner smile, she started across the room, deliberately ignoring the wolf whistles and moist sucking sounds that came from the group of sailors.

"Mr. Silk? I'm Mattie Sharpe from Seattle. I just saw the painting you're working on down on the *Griffin*, and I think it's absolutely wonderful. I'd like to talk to you about representation."

The big man turned his head very slowly to stare at her with slightly bloodshot blue eyes. His leonine face went well with the rest of him, Mattie decided. He was truly huge all over, but everything about him appeared to be very, very solid.

The blue eyes lit up as they settled on her. She continued to smile back, feeling quite hopeful. She had never met an artist who was not more than anxious to sell his work.

"Well, well, well." The voice fit the man, a deep, booming, Southern drawl. "Who the hell did you say you were?"

"Mattie Sharpe. I own a gallery back in Seattle

139

called Sharpe Reaction, and if the painting I saw on board your boat is a sample of the body of your work, I would love to represent you."

The man's grin was slow and magnificent and revealed two gold teeth. "The body of my work, eh? Sit down. Mattie Sharpe, and let me buy you a drink. We can have us a real nice discussion on the subject of my body."

Mattie sat down. "Thank you. Is Silk the name you prefer or would you rather I use your first name?"

"Honeypot, you can call me anything your little heart desires. But if you can't think of something better, Silk'll do just fine." Silk turned and called out to the bartender. "Bernard, my lad, bring the lady whatever she wants."

"What's she want, Silk?" the bartender called back.

Silk turned to Mattie. "What'll it be, Mattie Sharpe?"

"Iced tea would be nice."

"Hey, Bernard, you got any iced tea for the lady?"

"I think I got some tea and I know I got ice. I guess I can put the two together. Take me a few minutes, though."

Silk nodded in ponderous satisfaction. "No rush, Bernard. No rush at all. Me and the lady are going to just sit right here and get to know each other. Ain't that right, Mattie Sharpe?"

It occurred to Mattie that the man called Silk might be a little farther gone than he had originally appeared. "About your painting, Silk."

"Forget my painting. We can talk about that

later. Much later. Tell me about yourself, Mattie Sharpe. Tell me what you like to eat, what your favorite color is, and how you like for a man to ball you. Tell me all the little details. I always aim to please."

Mattie stared at him, uncertain whether she had heard him correctly. Surely he had not actually said what she thought he had said. "My gallery is quite successful, Silk," she began earnestly. "I feel certain your work would do very well there. It has the timeless appeal of landscape art and the immediate impact of a powerful, passionate statement."

Silk's grin got bigger. "That's me, Mattie Sharpe. I ain't nothin' if not passionate."

"All good artists are passionate about their work. Look, I'm only going to be here on St. Gabriel for a very short time. But if we can work out a suitable contract, I would like to take some of your paintings back with me."

Silk put one elbow on the table and rested his broad chin on his hand. "Do you like it slow and easy or hard and fast?" he asked. "I can go either way, but they don't call me Silk for nothin'. I'm at my best when I'm going slow and easy. Maybe with you on top, huh? You're kind of a little thing, and I wouldn't want to accidentally squash you. Yeah, I think slow and easy would be best."

Mattie groaned and reluctantly got to her feet. "I think we had better have this conversation at some other time, Silk."

"Nonsense. We're doing just fine, Mattie Sharpe. Sit down and keep talking." Silk's big hand snaked out with an astonishingly quick, flashing movement, locking around her wrist. There was enormous strength in his fingers.

Mattie gasped as she was jerked back down onto her seat. She stared at the huge paw wrapped around her wrist. Artists were notoriously difficult at times, but this was getting out of hand.

"Let go of me," Mattie said very firmly.

"Now, now, don't be in such a rush, honeypot. Bernard'll be here with your iced tea in a minute or two, and you can drink it while we talk. Then we'll just wander down to the *Griffin* and fuck each other's brains out. How does that sound?"

"I said, let go of me."

"Now, honeypot, don't go getting impatient. I told you, slow and easy. All in good time." Silk leered happily at her. "I'll be at my best after another couple of drinks. Smooth as Silk, like they say."

"I have no intention of seeing you at your best." Mattie snatched up his half-finished whiskey with her free hand and hurled the contents straight in Silk's face. The big man yelped and his grip slackened slightly on her wrist. She yanked her hand free and stepped quickly back out of reach.

"Hey, man, what do you think you're doing?" one of the sailors bellowed, getting to his feet. "Let the lady alone."

"Yeah, let the little gal alone!" yelled another man at the same table. "She'd much rather have some civilized company, I'll bet. Wouldn't ya, lady?" The second sailor stood up also, staggering slightly as he found his balance.

The rest of the men at the table quickly got to their feet, exhibiting varying degrees of stability.

Instantly chair legs scraped on the scarred wooden floor of the Hellfire as everyone else in the room scrambled to his feet. Enthusiastic shouts rose to a clamor.

Silk lost interest in Mattie at once. His whole face glowed with a beatific expression as he rose majestically. "Well, now, lads, looks like we have us a slight difference of opinion here. What say we settle the matter like the gentlemen we all are?"

"Any time, Silk. We'll back you against these sweet little Navy pussies any time. You just say the word."

Silk glanced over his shoulder at Mattie. "Don't go nowhere now, Mattie Sharpe. I'll be through here in just a minute or two, and we can carry on right where we left off."

With a roar, Silk launched himself toward the group of sailors. The regular patrons of the Hellfire followed suit.

Mattie was stunned by the speed with which the brawl erupted. With one hand instinctively going to her throat, she sidestepped to avoid a flying chair. Then she backed hurriedly toward the door.

A man who had apparently abandoned shaving and deodorant upon moving to St. Gabriel made a grab for her arm. "What d'ya say we just kind o' slide on outa here, sweetheart? Nobody's gonna miss us."

Mattie rammed her elbow into the man's ribs and extricated herself from his grasp when he bent double. She fumbled with the catch of her shoulder bag.

"Can you hear me, Silk?" she called out above the din.

143

"I can hear you just fine, Mattie Sharpe. Be right with you." Silk smashed a beefy fist into a hapless face and turned to show Mattie a wide grin.

Mattie plucked one of her business cards out of her purse and waved it in the air. "I'm going to leave my card here on the bar. I'll look you up tomorrow morning when you're, uh, recovered. I really feel we can do business together, and I— Oh!"

Mattie's voice rose on a yelp of alarm as her business card was snapped out of her fingers. A familiar male hand closed around her arm with a force that was just short of bruising.

"Damn," said Hugh. "I should have known. Can't leave you alone for a minute, can I?"

"*Hugh,*" Mattie breathed a sigh of relief. "Thank heavens it's you. I don't mind telling you, I was getting a little nervous. Artists are usually somewhat eccentric, but I've never had anything like this happen before when I've approached one."

Hugh wrapped a hand around the nape of her neck and hauled her toward the door "I suppose you started this?"

Mattie was outraged. "Me? What a nasty thing to say. I had nothing to do with this stupid brawl. I was just trying to conduct a little business."

"Uh-huh."

"Yep. She started it all right, Abbott," Bernard the bartender announced. "Walked right in and sat right down at Silk's table. Silk being Silk, you know what happened next. And we both know Miles is going to expect someone to pay for it."

"Send the bill to Silk," Hugh suggested.

"Can't do that. He'll try to pay for it with another painting. We already got enough of his pictures stashed away in the back room. Don't need another one."

"All right, all right. Bill me for whatever you can't get out of the Navy."

"You got it." The bartender went back to polishing glasses as the bar fight raged across the floor of the Hellfire.

"Now, hold on just one hot minute," Mattie said.

"You shouldn't pay for any of the damage being done in here. It's not your fault, Hugh."

"We all know whose fault it is." Hugh yanked her toward the door. "But don't worry. I intend to get reimbursed. I'll just take it out of your soft little hide."

"Don't you dare talk like that," Mattie retorted indignantly. "I am a totally innocent victim."

Before Hugh could respond to that statement, a familiar voice boomed out across the sounds of thudding fists and flying chairs.

"Now, just a dadblamed minute, Abbott. What d'ya think you're doing? You can't go running off with that little gal. I already got dibs on her. You just leave her be. I'll be through here right quick."

Hugh halted and turned around to confront Silk, who had emerged from the center of the brawl to reclaim his departing victim.

"Sorry, Silk. A slight misunderstanding here. Mattie belongs to me. Brought her with me from Purgatory."

Silk's eyes widened in outrage as he glared at Mattie. "The hell you say."

"Afraid so. Now, if you'll excuse us, we're out of here."

"Now, see here, this just ain't fair, Abbott."

"I know, Silk, but that's the way it goes. Finders keepers."

Mattie was incensed. "Will you two kindly stop discussing me as if I were a side of beef?" A glass whizzed past her head and she ducked instinctively. A split second later it shattered against the wall behind her.

Silk's massive hand closed around Mattie's free wrist. "Don't you worry none, Mattie Sharpe. I'll be glad to teach Abbott here some manners. He gets kinda uppity at times."

"Oh, my God," Mattie said.

"Let her go, Silk. You've got business to attend to." Hugh sidestepped a chair as it went skidding past his booted foot.

"But the whole point of this here business is so me and Mattie Sharpe can go screw . . . umph."

Silk lost his balance and toppled to the floor like a felled oak as Hugh did something very fast and very efficient with his foot and one hand.

"I said, let her go, Silk." Hugh spoke with surprising gentleness. "You know I always mean what I say."

Silk propped himself up on his elbows and eyed Mattie through slitted eyes. "You said you brought her with you from Purgatory?"

"Yeah. I'm going to marry her as soon as I can get things arranged."

Silk looked up at him in open astonishment.

146

"No fooling? Hey, can I come to the party? I haven't been to a real live wedding party in years."

Mattie sighed.

"Sure." Hugh said easily. "You can come to the party."

Silk staggered to his feet, dusted himself off, and gave Mattie a huge grin. "Don't you worry none, Mattie Sharpe. I'll make sure it's a real wingding of a party. It'll be a party to remember, that's for sure. We'll invite the whole damn island."

He turned and waded back into the fray.

"Let's just hope he doesn't do any damage to his hands," Mattie said as Hugh hauled her out the door and into the street.

"Damn it to hell." Hugh shoved her into the passenger seat of the Jeep and got in beside her. "Is that all you can think about?"

"Talent is where you find it I'd hate to see his artistic career ruined because his hands got injured in a barroom brawl."

"Silk hasn't got an artistic career. He works for me when he works at all, and the rest of the time he just sits around in his boat painting or else he sits in the Hellfire drinking." Hugh sent the Jeep roaring out of town. "Once in a while he gets real lucky when some stray lady tourist wanders in and decides he's picturesque."

"I see."

Hugh slid her a dangerous sidelong glance. "Can't really blame the guy for thinking he'd gotten lucky this afternoon, can I? The way you behaved, it's no wonder."

147

"For heaven's sake. You make it sound like I went in there to pick him up," Mattie said tightly.

"Well, didn't you?"

"No, I did not. I went in there to do business with the man."

"What the hell did you think you were doing wandering into a waterfront bar all by yourself and sitting down at the table of a complete stranger?" Hugh snapped. "Where's your common sense, Mattie?"

"Stop acting as if what happened back there was all my fault."

"It was your fault. I told you that."

"Hugh, I don't want to hear another word about it, understand? I've told you before, I don't like listening to your little lectures. And while we're on the subject, there's something else I'd better mention. I'd rather you stopped telling everyone we're going to get married."

"Why? It's the truth."

"It is not the truth. We have no plans for marriage. You're only going to embarrass yourself if you go around telling everyone you're about to become a groom."

He took his attention off the narrow road just long enough to shoot her a searing look. "What the hell do you mean, we're not getting married? We got that all settled last night, damn it."

"We did not settle anything last night!" Mattie yelled back. "All we did last night was have sex together. If you will recall, we did that once before and it didn't end in marriage."

"Christ, woman are you going to throw that in my face again?"

"Yes, I am. You deserve it." She braced herself on the window frame of the Jeep as Hugh slammed the vehicle to a halt. "Why are we stopping?"

"Because we're in the middle of an argument and I want to give it my full attention." Hugh swung around in the seat to confront her, one arm draped over the wheel, the other lying along the back of the seat. "Mattie, what's gotten into you? You knew I figured everything was okay between us this morning."

"I knew you were probably making some assumptions, but who am I to try to set you straight? You never listen to me."

"Give me a chance. Talk to me. Tell me why you won't marry me," he said roughly.

"Try it the other way, Hugh. Why should I marry you?"

"Because you love me."

"Is that right?" She faced him with fury and passion now. "How do you know that for certain?"

"I've always known it." He looked exasperated and helpless in the way only a man can when caught in the middle of a dreaded *relationship* discussion. "Since that night we spent together a year ago. Before that, if you want to know the truth. I wasn't completely blind to the way you acted around me. You were always sort of anxious and uneasy."

"Stress."

"Don't give me the stress excuses. If I wasn't sure how you felt about me back then, I got a damn good idea during the past eight months when you deliberately avoided me every chance you got. You were afraid to see me because you knew the effect I'd have on you."

"Bull."

"And if there was any doubt left, you cleared it up last night. You wanted me, Mattie. Admit it, damn it. You wanted me."

"I don't know what came over me last night. I went a little crazy. It was the stress. It must have been."

"It was not the goddamned stress. You wanted me. You can't hide a thing like that."

"Wanting is not necessarily loving. You're old enough to know that."

"It is with you."

"You don't know that, damn you!" she shouted.

"Mattie, babe, you're getting upset."

"Of course I'm upset. You're trying to tear my world apart again. I won't let you do it a second time, Hugh. It took me long enough to put myself back together last time. Do you hear me? I won't let you do it to me."

"Babe, listen to me. I've told you I'm sorry. I didn't know what the hell I was doing last time. I made a mistake. I've been regretting it ever since. But this time around things are going to be different."

"Are they?" she asked, almost viciously.

"Damn right."

"Prove it."

That stopped him for an instant. He looked blank. "What do you mean, prove it? How am I supposed to do that?"

"Are you sure you really want to marry me?"

He began to look wary now. "Hell, yes. Why else would I be going through this kind of nonsense?"

"Because you've got your one-track brain set on getting yourself a wife. Because I'm convenient. Because I once volunteered to move out here to the edge of the world, so you figure I won't give you a hard time about it the way my sister did. Because you think you can handle me."

Hugh rammed his fingers through his hair. "You're trying to make it sound like a business deal or something."

"I think it is, in a way. You want a wife and I appear to be available. You don't have a lot of opportunity for finding suitable wives out here on this backwater island, do you? Some man down at the docks said living on St. Gabriel was rather like living in a monastery."

"Now, Mattie, babe—"

"It's pretty clear why you fixated on me after Ariel opted out of the engagement. I'm a known quantity and I must have looked like I'd be a great deal easier to manage than Ariel. After all, I don't make scenes. I don't quarrel in public. I'm not melodramatic."

"Come on, babe, you're being ridiculous."

"No," Mattie said tightly. "I don't think I am. I'm being realistic. What you don't seem to realize is that I'm not the same woman I was a year ago. I made some decisions that morning after I humiliated myself."

"What decisions?"

"I told myself that never again would I settle for playing second fiddle to my sister. I had enough of that while I was growing up. Enough of watching her get the dates while I prayed the phone would ring just once for me. Enough of having her cast-off boyfriends come to me for sympathy and comfort. Enough of watching her win all the prizes and get all the applause."

"For crying out loud, Mattie."

But Mattie was too wound up to stop this time. "It was humiliating always being second best. It was miserable having people chalk up her tantrums to a budding artistic temperament while I always got a lecture on self-control. I hated being sent to counselor after counselor to find out if I was an underachiever or if I was just a hopeless case."

"Spare me a dissertation on your early child-hood traumas, okay? I'll tell you something, babe, you don't know what real trauma is," Hugh said through clenched teeth. "You with your fancy private schools and your art lessons and your rich aunt Charlotte."

"Is that right?" she raged back.

"Damn right. You know what trauma *is*? It's having your old man run off when you're six years old and you're glad to see him go because it means the beatings will stop. It's having your mother give you up to foster care because she can't figure out how to deal with you and her own miserable, screwed-up life at the same time. It's having people tell you you're bound to wind up in jail sooner or later because you come from bad stock."

Mattie stared at him, aghast. Then her eyes narrowed. "Oh, no you don't, Hugh Abbott. You're not going to pull that old trick on me."

"What old trick?" he roared.

"You're not going to belittle my feelings by making me feel sorry for you. All my life my feelings have been less important than anyone else's. Everyone else got to be temperamental, but not me. I was expected to be *nice*."

"Oh, yeah? Well, I've got news for you. You're not being very *nice* at the moment, babe. You're yelling louder than a damned fishwife."

"You know something? It feels good. Right now I have a right to feel used, damn it. You are trying to use me. You're accustomed to giving orders, accustomed to having things go the way you want them to go. Ariel gave you a setback last year, but that didn't stop you, did it? You've regrouped and decided to attack a weaker target this year. Well, I won't stand in for her. Not this time. Do you hear me?"

"Mattie, that is not the way it is" Hugh clearly had himself under control again.

"Isn't it? You're picking me this time because you think I'll be so damn grateful to marry you I'll get down on my knees and thank you. Well, that's not how it's going to be."

"Babe," Hugh said soothingly, "take it easy."

"I will not take it easy. We're going to settle this here and now. If you really want me, you can damn well prove it."

"I'm going to marry you. What the hell more do you want?"

"I'll tell you what I want." She was feeling goaded now—dangerous, reckless, and up against a wall. "You can stop expecting me to give up my career and my friends and everything else back in

Seattle to move out here to the edge of the world to make a home for you."

"But, babe—"

"*Stop calling me babe*! If you really want me, Hugh Abbott, then you can give up your business and your lifestyle and your friends and move to Seattle."

Hugh's mouth fell open as he stared at her in stunned amazement.

Mattie realized with a sense of shocking satisfaction that it was the first time she had ever seen Hugh Abbott caught completely by surprise. She sat back in her seat, folding her arms protectively under her breasts, and studied him through cool, narrowed eyes.

"Are you nuts, Mattie? Me leave St. Gabe? With everything I've got going here?"

"Yes, that does put a different slant on the subject, doesn't it?" she noted sweetly. "Rather like asking me to leave Seattle."

Hugh closed his mouth. His big hand tightened ferociously around the steering wheel. "Is this some kind of game, Mattie? Because I don't like games."

"It's no game. I told you, I'm tired of being second best. Just once, *just once*, mind you, I want to know I'm first. I want to be wanted for myself, not as a fill-in for Ariel. Just once I want to finish in front. And if I can't be first. I don't want to even enter the damned race this time."

Hugh was silent for a long time, his hooded eyes never leaving her set face. "I don't believe this," he finally said.

"Believe it, Hugh."

"You want me to give up Abbott Charters? Forget the house I was going to build for us? Live in a damned city and go to gallery openings and drink espresso?"

She smiled grimly. "It is a lot to ask, isn't it? Just as much as you're asking of me."

"But I've got a business to run."

"So do I."

"How the hell am I supposed to get Abbott Charters on its feet from Seattle?"

"How the hell am I supposed to run Sharpe Reaction from St. Gabriel?"

"It's not the same thing," Hugh shot back. "Damn it, Mattie, when you move out here, I'll take care of you."

"If you come to Seattle, I'll take care of you. I make enough to support both of us."

"I'm not going to let you make me into some goddamned kept man," he said through gritted teeth.

"Well, I don't want to be a kept woman."

"Babe, be reasonable. You were willing enough to move out here a year ago. You begged me to take you with me when I left Seattle."

"That," said Mattie, beginning to feel like a broken record, "was last year."

"Shit." Hugh sat back in his seat and wrenched the key in the Jeep's ignition. The engine started with a roar.

Mattie closed her eyes tightly, but she could not stop the tears from trickling down her cheeks. Angrily she brushed at them with the back of her hand.

"Mattie? Are you crying?"

"No. I won't let you make me cry a second time, Hugh. I will never let you make me cry again."

There was silence from the other side of the Jeep. And then Hugh said quietly. "All right. We'll try it."

She blinked away more moisture. "Try what?"

"I'll try proving to you that you're first. I'll go back to Seattle with you. I can go on working for Charlotte,so you won't be supporting me. We'll see how it goes."

Mattie jerked her head around to stare at his hard profile. "You don't mean that."

He shrugged. "I never say things I don't mean."

"You can't come with me to Seattle. You'd hate living there."

"I've lived a lot of places that were a lot worse."

"Hugh, this is crazy."

"Yeah. I agree. But I can't think of any other way to prove I want you more than I wanted Ariel. And that's what this is really all about, isn't it? Proof? You'll get your proof, Mattie."

She heard the grim determination in his rough-edged voice and she shuddered. "I don't believe you'll really pack up and come back to Seattle with me."

"You sure don't trust me very much, do you, babe?"

"Frankly, no. You're hatching some kind of scheme. I can tell."

"I'm going back to Seattle with you. Let's leave it at that, okay?"

"No," Mattie said defiantly. "I won't leave it at that. While we're on the subject, I think I should tell you that there will be no repeat of last night's little incident."

"I agree. I don't want you wearing that little red job out in public, anyway."

"I'm not talking about the dress," she yelled, "I'm talking about us! Sleeping together. Sex. You and me in a bed. No more of it. At least not until I figure out what you're up to."

"Shit," Hugh said.

"I am beginning to realize you have an extremely limited vocabulary, Hugh Abbott."

"It's the stress. When I get under a lot of stress, I always say *shit*."

CHAPTER

Eight

"Are you out of your tiny little mind?" Silk Taggert shoved a bottle of beer into Hugh's hand. "Go to Seattle? And stay there for who knows how long? After you're just getting the business going here? Why in hell would you want to do that? It's damn stupid, Abbott. You're a lot of things, but stupid you normally ain't."

"It's a relationship thing, Silk. Hard to explain." Hugh took a long pull on the beer and leaned back against the bulkhead. He was sitting in the stern of the *Griffin* waiting for Mattie to finish picking up the ingredients for dinner from one of the local shops down the street. "Hell, I don't know if I understand it myself."

"You tried this relationship stuff once before,

remember? It didn't work out then. What makes you think it'll work this time?"

"Mattie's different."

"Don't sound like it. Sounds just like the other one. Leads you on and gets a proposal out of you and then refuses to move out here and set up housekeeping." Silk sat down in front of the easel and picked up a brush.

"I made a mistake last year." Hugh said. "I'm paying for it."

"How long you going to go on paying?" Silk dabbled the brush in water and then in blue paint.

"Don't know." Hugh took another swallow of beer and thought gloomy thoughts. "Until I can convince her of something, I guess."

"What's she want to be convinced of?" Silk studied the blank white canvas and then put in a wash of blue that came close to the color of the afternoon sky over St. Gabriel.

"That she's more important to me than her sister was, I guess."

"Well, shoot." Silk studied the blue wash with slitted eyes. "You could spend a lifetime trying to convince a woman she's the most important thing in your life. Women are never satisfied."

"Mattie will be. Eventually. She just needs a little time to get used to the idea that I mean what I say."

"What are you gonna do with the charter business while you're busy convincing Mattie she's Number One?"

"That, my good man, is where you come in."

"Oh, no, you don't. I ain't running it for you. I don't mind making a few flights when you're short of pilots, or doing some maintenance for you, but I don't want to play boss. You know I can't stand paperwork."

"I need you, Silk. You're the only one I can trust to handle Abbott Charters while I'm in Seattle."

"Forget it."

"It'll only be for a few weeks or so at the most." Hugh leaned forward, resting his elbows on his thighs and cradling the beer bottle between his palms. "I just need some time in Seattle."

"She know you're only planning to spend a few weeks convincing her?"

Hugh scowled. "No, and if you open your big mouth, I will personally close it for you."

"You're gonna keep working for Vailcourt, aren't you?"

"Might as well. The money's good. Work's easy. Charlotte Vailcourt thinks handling Vailcourt security is hard and dangerous, but she doesn't know the meaning of the words *hard* and *dangerous*. Don't see why I should be the one to set her straight. Not as long as she's willing to pay me a fortune to consult."

"Yeah, you got it cushy working for Vailcourt, all right." Silk added a lemon tinge to the blue sky. "You ever tell this Mattie Sharpe what you used to do for a living?"

"Hell, no." Hugh gave his friend a cold stare.

"Don't worry. I'll keep my mouth shut," Silk said quietly. He deepened the yellow. "But you don't know women. If they think there's some mystery in your past, they won't stop digging until they uncover it."

"I can handle Mattie."

Silk snorted. "Sure. That's why you're leaving everything behind here on St. Gabe and traipsing off with her to Seattle. Who's handling who, boss?"

"Look, let's just forget this whole subject, all right?"

Silk heaved a massive shrug. "Whatever you say, boss. But take it from me, you're wasting your time. Things ain't what they used to be in the old days when a good woman would follow a man to the other side of the world and stick with him come hell or high water. Nowadays we got this new liberated female who wants her own career and a fancy condo and what you call a sophisticated lifestyle. What's more, she wants to marry a man who works for a corporation, drinks white wine, and drives a BMW."

"So now you're an expert on the modern woman?"

"A wise man learns by observation." Silk informed him loftily. "I watched you screw up last year. I ain't looking forward to watching you shoot yourself in the foot again. It's embarrassing."

"Mattie's different," Hugh insisted stubbornly. "Once she's sure of me, she'll stop fussing about where she lives."

"Sure."

"Hey, you want to come over to dinner tonight?"

Silk's bushy brows climbed. "You making another batch of that godawful chili?"

"No. Mattie's going to be doing the cooking." Hugh could not help feeling smug. It was curiously pleasant to be able to extend an invitation for a home-cooked dinner to a friend. He liked the idea of entertaining in his own home. Just like a real married man. "She's a great cook. I told her to pick up some nice thick steaks and stuff for a salad. Maybe dessert. What do you say?"

Silk considered that. "Sounds good, I haven't had a real home-cooked meal since that little blond tourist lady made me scrambled eggs when she stayed overnight on the *Griffin*."

"That was damn near a year ago."

"Yeah. I'm drooling already. Don't mind telling you. But I doubt if Miss Mattie Sharpe will want me coming to dinner. I didn't exactly get off on my best foot with her yesterday."

"I explained all that," Hugh said.

Silk put a dark blue wash in over the area that would be the sea. "Well, if you're sure she won't poison me, I'd be mighty pleased to join you."

"Good. Six o'clock." Hugh glanced up and saw Mattie approaching along the quay. She was wearing the new jeans she had bought yesterday and a flower-splashed top. She had complained that the jeans were too tight and that the bright, short-sleeved camp shirt was rather garish, but he thought she looked terrific. Which only went to show how low-class his tastes were, Hugh supposed. He got to his feet. "One more thing," he said to Silk, "Don't stop off at the Hellfire first."

Silk contrived to look offended. "I got manners when I need 'em, Abbott. Don't worry, I won't embarrass you by showing up three sheets to the wind. You hear anything yet from Purgatory?"

161

"No. It might take a little time. But the word is out. Bound to hear something sooner or later." Hugh vaulted onto the dock. "We'll get whoever did it."

"I get first crack at the bastard who blew Cormier away when we do find him," Silk muttered.

"You're going to have to get in line. I'm first. Whoever it was came too close to getting Mattie, too, remember?"

Silk frowned thoughtfully at Mattie, who was making her way down the harbor steps, two large sacks of groceries in her arms. "You know, I still say she's going to lead you around like a bull with a ring through its nose and then dump you, but I got to admit she's got some sass and spirit. Handled me real good yesterday when I got out of line. Threw a glass of whiskey right in my face. Saw her punch out another guy who tried to grab her on the way out of the bar."

Hugh grinned with expansive pride as he recalled Mattie holding a gun on Gibbs. "Yeah, She's definitely my kind of woman. Now all I've got to do is convince her of that."

"I think it's going to be a little tougher than that, boss. What you got to do is convince her you're her kind of man. Again."

As far as Hugh was concerned, dinner was a roaring success. This was part of what a real home was all about, he decided in deep satisfaction. This was the way it was supposed to be, a man and a woman creating a warm and happy little world where friends were welcome. It had never been this way for Hugh in the past, but he was determined that it would be in the future.

He admitted to himself he'd had a few qualms when Mattie had calmly announced she had not bought the steaks as instructed but was going to make a fancy pasta dish instead.

Hugh had not been at all certain of how Silk would react to trendy health food. But after the first bite, he knew he need not have worried. After one curious glance, Silk had immediately begun putting away the pasta by the truckload.

Taggert had appeared a bit anxious when Hugh opened the door of the small, wooden framed beach cottage earlier. But once Mattie broke the ice by asking questions about his paintings, he'd mellowed instantly.

"So you and my old buddy Hugh, here, are going to tie the knot, huh?" Silk reached for a third helping of salad and bread.

"Right," said Hugh.

"We're thinking about it," Mattie demurred.

Hugh scowled at her, but she appeared oblivious. He reached for another bottle of beer, started to drink straight from the bottle, and then remembered his manners and poured it into a glass.

"More pasta, Silk?" Mattie smiled and held out the bowl.

"You bet." Silk reached for the bowl. "This is the fanciest spaghetti I've ever had, although I got to admit I've come across some pretty interesting noodle things in places like Malaysia and Indonesia. I remember one dish of rice noodles and peanuts and hot peppers that—"

Hugh kicked his friend under the table. Silk

gave him a reproachful glance. The problem with Silk was that he usually meant well, but he did not always know when to keep his mouth shut. As far as Hugh was concerned, the less said about Indonesia and other exotic locales from their shared pasts, the better.

"I think I know the dish you're talking about," Mattie was saying. "It uses lemon grass and coconut milk, doesn't it?"

"Uh, yeah," Silk said, eyeing Hugh with a side-long glance. "Something like that."

"I've made it myself, once or twice. Tell me, how many paintings do you have completed and ready for purchase?" she asked.

Silk shrugged. "Who knows? Probably a couple dozen or so. I can get some back from Miles at the Hellfire if you want 'em. You really serious about taking 'em back to Seattle?"

"Deadly serious," Mattie said.

"Dang. What makes you think you can sell 'em there? I can't hardly give 'em away around here."

"Probably because the general level of artistic taste here on St. Gabriel is pathetically low," Mattie said dryly. "Most of the art I've come across so far has been the sort one finds on the girlie calendars hanging in the offices of Abbott Charters."

"Now, hold on," Hugh interrupted. "I didn't hang those up. Ray and Derek did that."

Mattie gave him a skeptical look and turned back to Silk. "Don't worry, Silk. I can sell your work. Guaranteed."

"What makes you think folks back in Seattle will think my work is worth a lot of money?"

164

"They'll think it is worth a great deal of money because I will tell them it is worth a great deal of money," Mattie explained very gently.

Silk's eyes widened appreciatively. Then he gave a great shout of laughter. "I like your style. Mattie Sharpe. Something tells me you and me were born to do business together."

Hugh was about to comment on the unlikely friendship budding before his eyes when the phone rang. He got up reluctantly to answer it. The only calls he ever got were business calls, and he really didn't want to take one right now. The only problem was, he could hardly afford to ignore one.

"Abbott Charters," he said automatically, his eyes on Mattie and Silk, who were engaged in an animated discussion on the subject of art gallery contracts.

"Abbott? That you?" The voice was low, rasping, and familiar.

Hugh was suddenly paying full attention to his caller. "This is Abbott."

"It's me, Rosey. Remember me?"

"Yeah, Rosey, I remember you."

"Remember what you said? About being willing to pay big bucks for some info?"

"The offer's still open."

"Good." There was gloating satisfaction in Rosey's rasping voice. "I'm here and I got what you want. I think. But it'll cost you, pal. This is dangerous stuff."

"You're here? On St. Gabe?"

"Yeah. Got in this afternoon. I been lyin' low, waiting to see if I was followed. But it looks like

I'm in the clear. I've done some checkin' around. Know that old, abandoned warehouse just north of town? Right near the beach?"

"I know it. Lily Cove." Hugh realized that the conversation at the table had ceased. He looked across the small room and saw that Mattie and Silk were both watching him intently.

"Meet me there in half an hour."

"All right."

"And Abbott?"

"Yeah, Rosey?"

"Bring cash. A thousand big ones."

"Christ, Rosey, I'm buying information, not a bridge."

"This information is worth it. If you don't want it, I can sell it somewheres else."

"Come on, Rosey. We both know you're bluffing. Who else would want this kind of information?"

"I don't know yet, but I got a feeling there's more than one guy who'd pay for what I've got."

"But you're in a hurry, right, Rosey? You need the money tonight. You can't afford to sit around and wait for another buyer."

"Goddamn it, Abbott." Rosey said, his voice taking on the characteristic whine, "if you want the name you're after, be at that warehouse in half an hour. With the thousand."

"Five hundred and that's it, Rosey."

"Sheesh. Okay, okay. Like you say, I can't hang around. Five hundred."

The receiver on the other end was slammed down in Hugh's ear. He gently replaced the phone and looked at Silk and Mattie.

"That was Rosey?" Mattie asked.

"Yeah." He met Silk's steady blue gaze. "He's got a name. Wants five hundred in cash for it."

Silk shook his head. "Poor guy's got delusions of grandeur."

"What name?" Mattie demanded, starting to look anxious.

"The name of the guy who shot Paul Cormier. Or so he says. Who knows with a rodent like our friend Rosey." Hugh walked over to the tiny kitchen and opened a chipped metal cabinet. He found his revolver behind the sack of pinto beans he kept for making chili.

"You're going to see Rosey? Tonight? Hugh, what is this all about?" Mattie got to her feet clutching the spoon she had been using to serve the pasta "Why are you taking your gun?"

"Yes, I'm going to talk to Rosey, and I'm taking the gun because when one is dealing with the Roseys of this world, one feels more secure when one is armed." He shoved the revolver into his belt and went over to the table. He felt ridiculously pleased by her unnecessary concern. "Now, don't worry. I won't be gone long."

"I don't like this," Mattie stated emphatically. "I don't like it at all."

"I'll be back before you know it." He bent his head and kissed the tip of her nose. "Silk will stay here with you until I get back. Won't you, Silk?" He met the big man's knowing eyes.

"Sure," Silk said. "If that's what you want."

Hugh nodded. "That's what I want."

Silk shrugged. "You're the boss. You going to give him the five hundred?"

"Probably. If the information is good."

"Where you going to get that kind of money at this time of night?"

"I'll stop off at the office on the way. There should be a couple of grand in the safe. Derek and Ray got paid in cash for delivering those medical supplies to St. Julian."

Mattie followed as Hugh went toward the door. "You will be careful, won't you?"

"I'll be careful."

"How will you know if Rosey is telling you the truth? Maybe he'll just give you a name, take your money, and run."

"He wouldn't get far," Hugh said. "And I think he's just barely smart enough to know that." He kissed her again and firmly closed the door in her anxious face. He went out to where the Jeep was parked in the drive.

It was starting to rain again. Another squall was about to sweep over the island. The palms rustled in the breeze and the night scents of the jungle were strong.

He was going to miss St. Gabriel for however long he had to stay in Seattle, Hugh thought as he started the Jeep and drove toward the main road. It was odd how the island had become home during the past couple of years. It was the first real home he could remember. He couldn't wait to start building his dream house overlooking the sea. He just knew Mattie was going to love it.

But first he had to survive Seattle.

He drove into town, past the loud taverns and bars, and parked in front of Abbott Charters. He let himself in the front door and walked through the darkened interior to the small office, where he kept a big old-fashioned safe. He switched on the light.

There was nearly five thousand in the safe. Hugh reminded himself to get it to the bank in the morning, and then he counted out five hundred in large bills, folded it up, and stuffed it into his pocket. He'd put it down on the books as petty cash.

On the way out of the office Hugh automatically glanced around with a proud, possessive eye. Abbott Charters was starting to thrive. Another year or two and he would be ready for serious expansion. He considered the business his first and only real accomplishment in life other than keeping himself alive. It was the one positive thing he had ever created from scratch. It was his dream, his future, his hope for a different sort of life than the one he had been living for the past forty years.

He wondered if that was how Mattie felt about her art gallery. The thought was unsettling and he pushed it aside. Mattie would be okay out here. He would see to that.

On the way out the door Hugh ripped the nearest girlie calendar down from the wall and tossed it into the trash can.

Ten minutes later Hugh pulled the Jeep off the road and parked it a discreet distance from the abandoned warehouse on Lily Cove. He walked silently through the jungle to the edge of the clearing, where the sagging structure crouched like a dinosaur carcass in the pale moonlight.

Trust Rosey to pick a suitably picturesque spot for the deal. Hugh frowned as he scanned the clearing for signs of life. Something like this was better handled in the loud, noisy, well-populated environment of the Hellfire. But Rosey obviously preferred scuttling around in the shadows. Once a rat, always a rat.

There was one vehicle parked near the precariously tilted loading dock, a small, rusty compact Rosey had probably picked up at the airport.

The gaping dark opening above the loading dock was the obvious way into the building. Hugh considered it briefly and then decided to enter the warehouse through a side door that hung on its hinges.

There was no sound from the black interior. Outside the rain was starting to fall more heavily. It swept into the building through the wide-open loading dock entrance.

Hugh eased the revolver out of his belt and edged through the doorway and into the shadows. Knowing how swiftly aging wood rotted in this climate, he slid one booted foot along the floor.

The toe of his boot found thin air. Hugh yanked his leg back and glanced down. He could see almost nothing in the shadows but he knew his suspicions were correct. The floorboards had rotted away in sections. He would have to move carefully or risk breaking a leg.

"Rosey?"

There was no response. Hugh kept his shoulder in contact with one wall as he worked his way silently around the building to the loading dock entrance. The rain was thrumming on the roof now, hiding any small sounds that he or anyone else might make.

Something was wrong and Hugh knew it. If all had been well, Rosey would have made his presence known by now and demanded his money.

The figure lying in the rain on the loading dock looked like a heap of old clothing at first. Hugh crouched in the shadows, gun in hand, and stared at the too-still bundle. He swore silently.

Rosey, you damned fool. Why didn't you meet me in town? Why play games?

He waited another minute or two, but his senses told him the warehouse was empty except for himself and Rosey. Hugh straightened and went reluctantly over to the rain-soaked body.

Very gently he reached down and turned the bundle over. In the weak light Hugh could see the dark, wet stain that soaked the front of Rosey's shirt. Hugh checked for a pulse.

Rosey groaned softly.

Startled, Hugh hunkered down beside him. "Rosey?"

"That you, Abbott?" Rosey's eyes fluttered.

"Yeah, Rosey, it's me."

"Son of a bitch got me. Thought I was being so careful. Tell Gibbs, will ya, if you see him. He'll wonder."

"I will, Rosey, who did this?"

"Rain . . ." There was a curious, wondering tone in Rosey's voice before the single word ended in a choking, bloody gargle.

"I know it's raining, Rosey, I'll get you out of it. Who was it, man?"

But Rosey was gone.

Hugh got slowly to his feet and looked down at the little man who had died in the pouring rain.

Two deaths in less than a week. *Damn*, Hugh thought in disgust. Life had been going so well lately, too. And now this.

Just like old times.

Mattie poured another cup of green tea for Silk and watched as he polished off the last of the sweet potato pie she had made for dessert. He had eaten nearly the entire pan.

"So how long have you lived here on St. Gabriel?" Mattie asked.

"Couple of years," Silk said around a mouthful of pie.

"About as long as Hugh, then?"

"Right. Me and him moved out here together."

"Really? Where were you before you arrived here?"

"Here and there." Silk grinned. "No fixed address, I guess you'd say. Hugh was doing odd jobs for Vailcourt, and I just sort of drifted around with him, helping out sometimes."

"Fascinating. Did my aunt know you were on the payroll?"

"Nah. Hugh figured why bother her with the details. She's an executive type. Folks like that only care about the bottom line. He just put me down under petty expenses when he sent his bills into Vailcourt Accounting."

"I see." Mattie hid a smile. "I take it you've known Hugh for a long time?"

"Sure. We been working together for years."

"Where did you meet him?"

Silk scowled, looking thoughtful. "As best as I can remember, I think it was a bar somewhere along the coast of Mexico. I forget the name of the town. Neither of us stayed there long. Had a little trouble."

"You were working in the area?"

"Abbot and I was flying charter for a guy who was running a little operation there Pretty cushy job but it didn't last long."

Mattie propped her elbows on the table and rested her chin on her folded hands. "You said that job did not last long. What did the two of you do after that?"

Silk grinned. "You plying me with sweet potato pie and tea in order to get me to talk?"

"Just idle curiosity," Mattie explained airily as she got up to clear the table.

"Yeah, well better exercise your idle curiosity on the boss. He'll nail my hide to the wall if I get too chatty."

"Why?" Mattie inquired innocently.

"He doesn't like to talk too much about the past."

"Any particular reason?"

Silk leaned back in his chair, replete. "He pretty much likes to forget his past for the most part. Not the sort who looks back, you know? Abbott's got his eye on the future these days."

"Was Paul Cormier a big part of Hugh's past?"

Silk's engaging grin belied the shrewd intelligence in his big blue eyes. "Cormier? You could say he was an old friend. Hugh's real loyal to old friends. Probably because he hasn't got too many of 'em."

"Anyone else besides you now?"

173

"Well," said Silk very smoothly, "I reckon there's you, too."

Mattie shot him a quick glance as she filled the cracked sink with hot water. "Hugh and I have not really known each other very long," she murmured. "This is the first time I've seen him in nearly a year."

"I know. He told me you'd been ducking him. He didn't like that." Silk shook his head. "Never seen a female who could make Abbott run around in circles the way he's been doing these past few months. And now you're dragging him all the way off to Seattle. He's gonna hate Seattle."

"Yes," said Mattie. "I know. Don't worry, Silk. He won't be there long."

Silk's eyes narrowed abruptly. "What the hell's that supposed to mean?"

"Just that I'm certain Hugh will soon get tired of Seattle and bored with me when he realizes I have no intention of moving here to St. Gabriel. He'll give up on his big plans to marry me, and he'll be back here before you know it." She smiled bleakly. "After all, he's got a business to run."

Silk looked baffled. "You mean you're taking him back with you even though you know he won't be staying long?"

"I'm not taking him back with me. He's insisting on accompanying me on the return trip."

"Yeah, but that's so's he can convince you that he likes you better than your nitwit sister. He told me all about it."

The sound of the Jeep in the drive halted Mattie's reply. Relief poured through her. "He's back."

"Sure. What did you think he was going to do? Spend the rest of the night drinking at the Hellfire or something? Hugh ain't the type."

"No, I was afraid he was walking into trouble. That Rosey he went to see is not a very nice little man." Mattie quickly dried her hands on the ragged towel and went toward the door.

It opened and Hugh strode into the small hall, shaking the rain from his hair.

"Hugh, I've been so worried. Thank heavens you're all right." Mattie raced forward and threw herself into his arms.

"Well, well, well," Silk said from the other side of the room. He surveyed the couple with a beatific smile. "Ain't that a picture. Maybe this little trip to Seattle is going to turn out all right after all. I left you a slice of pie, boss."

"Thanks." Hugh said over the top of Mattie's head. His eyes met Silk's.

"Trouble?" Silk asked.

"Yeah."

"Mattie had a hunch there would be." Silk said with a sigh.

"I still can't believe that Rosey's dead," Mattie said two hours later as she paced the floor of Hugh's small beach house. "Whoever killed him could have killed you, too. I knew that meeting was going to be dangerous. I just had a feeling."

"Well, it wasn't. Not for me, at any rate." Hugh opened the refrigerator and reached inside for a beer. "Just for Rosey."

"So now you and Silk are back to square one as far as finding Cormier's murderer goes." Mattie rubbed her palms up and down her bare arms. Silk had left an hour ago after Hugh had gone through all the details of his late-night meeting at the warehouse. The big man had not seemed particularly shocked by Rosey's death. It was almost as if he was accustomed to that kind of news.

"We'll find him."

"How are you going to do that in Seattle?" Mattie asked.

"Silk will be in touch if anything turns up. Seattle's not the end of the world."

"Aren't there police or federal agencies who should be handling this kind of thing?"

"Not on Purgatory. They're in the middle of a coup over there, remember?" Hugh went across the room and opened a cupboard.

Mattie watched him pull out a well-worn khaki green duffel bag that looked as though it had been hauled around the world several times. She sank down onto a wicker chair and watched as Hugh carried numerous changes of underwear and shirts out of the bedroom and dumped them into the duffel bag.

"Why the rush? Why do we have to leave tomorrow?" she asked. The sense of urgency had been hovering in the air ever since Hugh had walked back in the door.

"No sense hanging around here. Silk's going to look after Abbott Charters for me. We might as well head to Seattle."

"There's more to it than that, isn't there? You're more worried about this second murder than you want to admit. You're afraid there might be some danger here for me, aren't you? Hugh, if finding Cormier's killer is so important to you, why don't you stay here on St. Gabriel and I'll go home by myself?"

"Sure. And start ducking me again every time I try to call or see you? Not a chance, babe. I'm not letting you out of my sight this time. You want proof I'm serious about marrying you. You're going to get it."

"Damn it, Hugh, I know you're serious about marrying me. That's not the point. It's the *reason* you want to marry me that I don't trust."

He stopped packing the duffel bag and stood, feet braced, hands on hips, and regarded her with grim intent. "Now, you listen and listen good, babe. I want to marry you for all the normal reasons. I want a wife and a home, a real home. I want to have someone to talk to in the evenings, someone to warm my bed, someone to eat with, someone who gives a damn if I come home late. What's not to trust about that?"

She stared at him, her hands twisting together in her lap. "There are a lot of women who would be glad to do all that for you."

"I don't want a lot of women. I want you." He took two long strides over to where she was sitting and lifted her to her feet. "And I do not want to hear another word about my staying here on St. Gabe while you flit back to Seattle. Understood?"

Mattie looked up at him sadly. "I don't think it's going to work, Hugh."

"Leave it to me, babe. I always get the job done."

CHAPTER

Nine

Three days later Mattie picked up a canapé from a passing tray and surveyed the throng of well-dressed people milling around a prestigious Seattle gallery.

Plastic champagne glasses were everywhere. They were in people's hands, overflowing the wastebaskets, and standing around on every available empty surface. There were also a lot of little paper napkins, bits and pieces of canapés, and discarded programs. Most of the people in the room seemed more interested in being seen themselves than in looking at the art that hung on the walls.

Not that the art on the walls was not good. It was. The gallery was showing some of the best avant-garde stuff ever done on the West Coast. The show was, after all, a retrospective display of the works of Ariel Sharpe.

The canvases had been grouped according to the artist's four clearly recognized periods, her Early Dark period, her Exploratory period, her short-lived Elemental period, and the latest, which had been dubbed her Early Mature period.

Mattie caught a few of the snippets of conversation going on around her. *"The emotion is incredible, right from the first . . . such brilliant use of color, even in the Early Dark period, when she was using only black and brown . . . a sense of cataclysmic inevitability . . . a surprisingly shocking use of line, but she was getting divorced from Blackwell at the time, and that kind of thing always has an impact with her. She's so emotional . . . a bit rough and crude, Art Brut, if you will, but it is from her Elemental period, after all . . . ."*

Mattie had no trouble recognizing the talent in her sister's work. The strong sense of line and color added an emotional sophistication and a visually compelling quality to the abstract designs which took them far beyond the ordinary and into the realm of the brilliant.

And the expensive.

Mattie nibbled her canapé and unconsciously began tapping the toe of her black leather pump. She glanced at the black and gold watch on her wrist.

Hugh was due a half hour ago. He had promised to show up at the opening right after his meeting with Charlotte Vailcourt. The meeting had been scheduled for four o'clock and it was now nearly six.

She knew he had not been looking forward to tonight's event, but Mattie had insisted he attend. Going to openings was part of her world, and if he was determined to fit into that world, he could darn well make an effort to learn something about it.

Mattie glanced impatiently at her watch again. She was beginning to suspect that Hugh was deliberately stringing out the meeting with her aunt in order to avoid the gallery show. She was wondering if she should phone Charlotte's office

179

when a voice hailed her from halfway across the crowded room.

"Mattie, you're back from paradise. I thought you'd be gone another week or so. It was supposed to be a vacation, wasn't it?"

Mattie turned her head to smile at the tall, blond Viking god making his way toward her through the throng. "Hello, Flynn, I got back early. Paradise is not all it's cracked up to be. Things didn't go according to schedule, but I guess that's what happens when you take the budget tour package."

"Well, glad you're back safe and sound. And glad you could make it here tonight." Flynn Grafton was a striking man by any standards. His mane of pale hair was pulled back in a ponytail at the base of his neck, a dramatic contrast to his all-black attire, which consisted of black multipleated pants, a black shirt with wide, flowing sleeves, and black boots polished to a high gloss. The only ornament was a silver Egyptian ankh he wore around his throat.

"Looks like another successful show for Ariel." Mattie observed.

Flynn nodded proudly. "It turned out well, didn't it? Elizabeth Kenyon always does a great job. Good crowd. The usual number of moochers who always float from one opening to another for the free munchies, naturally, but what the heck. They add color."

Mattie chuckled. "I thought I saw Shock Value Frederickson and a couple of her friends nibbling her way through the hors d'oeuvres."

"Starving artists, one and all. But there are

some genuine buyers here. It's going well. Ariel will be pleased."

"Speaking of Ariel, where is she? I've been here over half an hour, and I haven't seen her yet."

Flynn's noble brow contracted in a brief frown of concern. "I don't know. She was due fifteen minutes ago. She was planning on making her usual entrance after everyone had arrived. I called home, but there was no answer."

"She must have gotten held up in traffic."

"Probably." Flynn's expression of concern relaxed slightly. "She's been sort of tense lately. To tell you the truth, I'm a little worried about her."

"Ariel's high strung, Flynn. You know that."

He shook his head and munched a canapé. "This is different."

"Any idea why she's more tense than usual?"

"Sure. I've been pointing out that her biological clock is ticking. She's three years older than you, Mattie. Thirty-five. If we're going to have a kid, we'd better get moving. The whole notion has her panicked."

Mattie gave him a startled look. "I can imagine. I thought Ariel had decided not to have children years ago. I distinctly remember her telling me that the day she married you. Said it would interfere with her art."

Flynn smiled complacently. "She's just scared because of her track record in love and marriage. After all, she's already been divorced once and lord only knows how many engagements got broken along the way."

"Ariel? Scared? That's a crock. Believe me,

181

Flynn, my sister has more pure, unadulterated self-confidence than anyone else I know except possibly a certain party she was once engaged to last year."

"You may be her sister, Mattie. But you don't really understand her the way I do. Never mind. I'm glad she's running late and I'm glad you're here. Gives us a chance to talk. I've been thinking it over, and I want to do some stuff for your gallery. Were you serious about taking a look at some of my work?"

"Any time, Flynn. But you know as well as I do the kind of thing I hang. I'm very commercially oriented. That means I can't use your experimental work."

"I know, I know. But I've got a series in mind that would be perfect for Sharpe Reaction clients."

"Ariel will have a fit," Mattie warned gently. "She'll probably try to strangle us both. You know what she thinks about the kind of stuff I sell."

Flynn smiled wryly. "Yeah. Commercial schlock. Don't worry about Ariel. I'll handle her. This is between you and me."

"If you say so. Flynn, you know I'll be glad to look at anything you bring me. You really have a great talent. Ariel's quite right about that. You're just undiscovered, that's all. Unlike her."

"I'll tell you something, Mattie. Undiscovered talent is about as useful as feathers on a hog. Look, why don't I bring some canvases by in a few days?" He broke off and glanced toward the door. "Ah, there she is. About time she got here. Who's that with her?"

Mattie turned her head to follow his glance. Her stomach clenched with a sick feeling that could only be jealousy. She fought to control it. "That," she told Flynn, "is Hugh Abbott. Ariel was once engaged to him."

"Oh, yeah. The guy from her Elemental period, right?"

"Right."

"That was really a dead-end direction for her," Flynn said, dismissing Hugh with ease.

"Yes, I thought the same thing at the time." Mattie watched her sister descend like a queen on the gathering.

Ariel was especially striking tonight. But, then, her sister always looked dramatic. Her lustrous black hair, translucent white skin, and exotic green eyes lent themselves quite naturally to drama of all kinds.

Ariel applied the same intuitive sense of design to her clothes as she did to her art. She had favored black for years, ever since her Early Dark period. It still suited her, although her painting had become much more colorful. Tonight she was riveting in a totally black strapless gown and black high-heeled sandals.

Her jewelry consisted of only a pair of jet earrings that dangled to her shoulders. Her sleek black hair was parted in the middle and worn in a shining wedge that gave her finely chiseled features the air of an Egyptian princess.

The only touches of color on Ariel were her scarlet mouth and her startling green eyes.

Mattie thought wistfully of the little red satin sarong she had brought back with her from the islands. It would have made quite a splash here tonight. But, of course, it would have been totally inappropriate, she told herself firmly. The conservative gray business suit and pastel silk blouse she had on was what she always wore to this sort of function. Only the artist was supposed to look exotic or outrageous.

She saw Hugh scanning the room with an impatient glance. He was wearing the one jacket he owned, a rather battered-looking navy blue blazer over a white shirt and his usual pair of jeans. He also had on his boots. There was no tie.

His eyes met hers, and she smiled wryly. He started toward her, leaving Ariel amid a circle of admirers.

"How well do you know this guy?" Flynn asked, helping himself to another canapé.

"Why do you ask?"

"Because he looks annoyed."

"That's his usual expression." Mattie locked her smile in place as Hugh came to a halt in front of her and glanced pointedly at Flynn.

"Hello, Hugh," Mattie said. "I don't believe you've met Flynn Grafton. A wonderful artist. He married Ariel about six months ago."

Hugh nodded brusquely and shook the hand Flynn offered. "Congratulations," he said crisply.

"Thanks. I hear you're the guy from Ariel's Elemental period."

Hugh's expression got darker. "That's not exactly how I think of it."

"Hey, don't be embarrassed. I can see why you wouldn't want to be associated with that particular time frame in her work. I mean, we all know it was a useless digression when taken in the total context of her art, but the stuff she did during that period is very collectible. People are paying a fortune for it simply because it was such an odd detour, professionally speaking."

"Is that right?" Hugh muttered.

"Personally, I've always kind of liked some of the stuff from that period. There's a certain rough-edged, primitive quality to it. Rather like early Ashton or Clyde Harding."

Hugh's mouth was a humorless line. "Look, do you mind if I talk to Mattie for a few minutes? In private?"

"No, no, take your time," Flynn said. "I'll see how Ariel's doing. Talk to you later, Mattie."

"Fine." Mattie took a sip of her champagne and watched Flynn saunter away through the crowd.

"All right, spit it out." Hugh grabbed a plastic glass from a passing tray.

"Spit what out?" Mattie asked politely.

"You want to know why I'm late and why I arrived with Ariel." Hugh swallowed most of the contents of the glass in one gulp.

"I do?"

"The answers are that, A, the meeting with Charlotte ran late and, B, Ariel was just getting out of a cab in front of this joint when I arrived. I couldn't avoid walking in with her."

"I see."

"Good." Apparently considering the subject closed, Hugh glowered down at her. "Now, what's with you and Grafton?"

Mattie glanced up in astonishment. "What on earth are you talking about?"

"He was looking at you the way a dog looks at a bone. Real intense."

Mattie shrugged. "He's an artist. Artists are always intense in one way or another. He wants me to look at some of his work. I said I would. That's all there was to it. What did you and Charlotte decide?"

Hugh frowned, looking as if he wanted to pursue the topic of Flynn Grafton. But he reluctantly altered course. "Everything's swell, just like I told you. She's happy to keep me on the payroll and says I can work here at the home office for as long as I want. Won't have to travel."

"What are you going to do here at headquarters?"

"She wants a new security plan worked up that can be implemented at all the Vailcourt offices around the world. I told her no problem."

"And how long will you be happy doing that, Hugh? I see you as a field man, not an office type."

"The experience will be good for me," he told her. "The more I learn about the business end of running a corporation, the better."

"Because you plan to go back to St. Gabriel to run Abbott Charters eventually, don't you? Admit it. You see this Seattle jaunt as just a short hiatus you have to tolerate until I come to my senses and see the light, right?"

"Forget Abbott Charters and forget St. Gabe. I don't feel like arguing right now. Who's this heading our way?"

Mattie looked across the room and heaved a small sigh. "It never rains but it pours."

"What's that mean?"

"Just that there's quite a crowd of Ariel's exes here tonight. That's Ariel's first husband, Emery Blackwell. From her Early Dark and Exploratory periods. They were married five years."

"He looks drunk as a skunk."

"He probably is." Mattie bit her lip in concern.

Emery hid his problem fairly well. He was in his late fifties, but he had the craggy, slightly dissipated good looks that suited authors whose status had once been near-mythical in high-level literary circles. He was aging well, in spite of his increasing fondness for the bottle. It was true his jaw was getting a bit thick and there was evidence of a certain softness around his midsection, but he paid attention to his clothes, and they, in turn, hid a multitude of sins. His shock of silver-gray hair was as stunning as ever, and his pale eyes brimmed with intelligence, even when they were slightly bloodshot.

Mattie had always liked Emery, and he had always treated her with an avuncular affection.

"He's been under a lot of stress in the past few years." Mattie confided softly to Hugh as Emery approached. "His career has been in the doldrums for ages, although he still gets tapped for lectures and readings occasionally."

"More stress, huh? Is that the cause of everybody's problems back here in the States these days?"

"A large portion of them, yes." Mattie smiled at Emery as he came to a halt in front of her and inclined his head with regal grace.

"Mattie, my love, you look positively splendid, as always. How would you like to join me on

Whidbey for a few days? I could use a muse. Bring something comfortable to change into, dear. We'll drink cognac and talk about poetry."

"You know I never really got the hang of poetry, Emery. And you look pretty splendid yourself, tonight." Mattie went on tiptoe to give him a small peck on the cheek. "But, then, you always do."

"It's called style, my dear. Some of us have it—" Emery broke off to give Hugh an amused head-to-toe glance. "And some of us don't. Pray introduce me to your rustic friend, Mattie. He is a friend, I assume, and not a hired thug?"

"Hugh Abbott," Hugh announced coldly. "I'm going to marry Mattie."

"Good lord, Mattie." Emery turned back to her with an expression of stagy astonishment. "I told you that you should have invited me to go along when you went on vacation. Send you out to the wilds of the Pacific alone and look what happens. You come back with a really tacky souvenir."

"I may be tacky, but Mattie thinks I'm cute." Hugh shoved an entire canapé between his teeth and bit down hard.

"Mattie's tastes have always been a little plebeian, to say the least. That's why she's been so successful with her gallery. And it may explain her problem with men."

Mattie scowled at both males. "That's enough out of both of you. If you want to squabble, go outside in the alley."

"Much too physical. I wouldn't lower myself to that sort of activity, my dear," Emery demurred.

"I would." Hugh stuck another entire round of cheese-and-pimiento-decorated cracker into his mouth and chewed vigorously, showing his teeth. "Any time, Blackwell."

"Dear, dear. Where ever did you find him, Mattie?"

"I didn't. Aunt Charlotte did. He works for her."

"That explains it, of course." Emery smiled benignly at Hugh. "Charlotte Vailcourt is a noted eccentric."

"Pay's good, too," Hugh said.

Mattie lifted her eyes toward heaven in a silent plea that was answered almost immediately when a handsome, rather hard-eyed woman in her late forties joined the small group. She was an imposing female built along statuesque lines, who favored southwestern turquoise and silver jewelry.

"Hello, everyone," Elizabeth Kenyon said cheerfully. "I do hope you're enjoying yourselves." Her hazel eyes were bright with the glow of success.

Elizabeth Kenyon's gallery was one of the most important on the West Coast, and everyone knew it. She catered to wealthy collectors whose only goal was to be considered at the vanguard of the contemporary art movement.

Elizabeth, herself, was important both socially and in the art world. She could make or break an artist, and she had done both frequently. She had a reputation for being able to cow clients into buying anything she told them was collectible, and she had broken the creative spirits of artists whose works she deemed retrograde.

Mattie admired Elizabeth Kenyon enormously. Although Mattie, herself, had a different taste in art and knew she was much too soft-hearted for her own good when it came to dealing with artists and clients, she respected Elizabeth's success. Someday. Mattie sincerely hoped, Sharpe Reaction would be in the same league as Elizabeth Kenyon's gallery.

"Good evening, Elizabeth," Emery said with another gracious inclination of his head. "Fantastic bash, as always."

"Thank you, Emery. You know how thrilled I am that you were able to attend. Your presence is always an asset at this sort of thing." She turned to Mattie. "Who is your friend, Matilda, my dear?"

"Hugh Abbott," Mattie said.

"Mattie's fiancé," Hugh drawled, sliding Mattie a mildly disgusted glance as he completed the introduction. The warning gleam in his eyes made it clear he was getting tired of having to explain his status in Mattie's life.

"Abbott. Abbott. Abbott. Now, where have I . . . ? Oh, yes," Elizabeth's eyes brightened. "Weren't you the one from Ariel's Elemental period?"

"Excuse me," Emery Blackwell said, drawing himself up and reaching for another glass of champagne. "I believe this is where I came in. I think I shall go mingle. See you later, Mattie. Elizabeth." He ignored Hugh, who, in turn, ignored him.

"Later, Emery," Mattie said, raising her glass in a small farewell.

Elizabeth frowned at Emery's retreating back. "I'm afraid dear Emery has not only become rather passé, but he doesn't handle his liquor as

190

well these days as he used to. I rather wish he had not bothered to attend tonight. But I suppose he couldn't resist. In spite of the divorce, he still feels a sort of paternal interest in Ariel's success."

"Well, he was a major influence on her early work," Mattie said, feeling obliged to defend Emery. "And he introduced her to all the right people back at the beginning. That certainly didn't hurt."

"Nonsense. She already knew most of the right people through her own family connections." Elizabeth smiled at Hugh. "How long will you be staying in Seattle, Hugh?"

Hugh caught Mattie's eye. "As long as it takes."

"I see." Elizabeth looked momentarily blank at the oblique answer. Then she nodded to both of them and moved off through the crowd.

"Matilda, dear, how are you?" said a new voice at Mattie's elbow. "I just spoke to your sister a few minutes ago. She tells me your parents couldn't be here tonight."

"Hello, Mrs. Eberly. Good to see you again. Ariel's right. Mom and Dad are both busy. Mom's teaching in an artists-in-residence program at a private college back East this spring, and Dad went with her. He wants to finish his book on the Modern-Postmodern continuum and thought this would be a good opportunity to do it. Do you know Hugh Abbott?"

The elderly woman turned to Hugh. "Abbott. No, I don't believe I do." Her bright eyes widened. "Unless, of course, you're the one from Ariel's—"

"Don't say it." Hugh advised with a wry smile.

"If I hear about Ariel's Elemental period one more time tonight, I think I'm going to be sick all over a tray of canapes."

"Well, it wasn't one of her best periods, was it?" Mrs. Eberly said, patting his hand consolingly. "But that's not to say you should feel personally responsible for it, my boy. After all, some good did come out of it."

"Yeah. She broke off the engagement. I've been feeling grateful for months."

"That wasn't quite what I meant," Mrs. Eberly murmured. "What is this rumor I hear about you and Matilda, here, being engaged?"

"It's a fact," Hugh said roughly. "Not a rumor."

"Where did you hear that, Mrs. Eberly?" Mattie asked.

"Gossip, my dear. You know how it is. I pride myself on being something of a sponge when it comes to gossip. I soak it up wherever I go. Can't imagine you married to someone who wears boots and jeans but, then, they always say opposites attract."

"Mattie and I actually have quite a bit in common," Hugh said.

Mattie smiled brilliantly up at him. "Such as?"

"You want a list?" he asked with soft menace.

"That would be fascinating." Mattie deliberately turned back to Mrs. Eberly, who was watching the scene with a fascinated gleam in her shrewd brown eyes. "By the way, Mrs. Eberly, I've got another one of Lingart's red pieces in the gallery, if you're interested."

"Thank you, Matilda. Hold on to it for me, will

192

you? I do believe he's starting to move into his yellow period. There won't be too many more reds, I'm afraid. And I do so want to corner the market."

"It's yours." Mattie promised. "But if you think the Lingart painting is good, just wait until you see what I brought back with me from the islands."

"You mean besides this fine specimen of machismo?" Mrs. Eberly gave Hugh a smiling glance.

"Much more collectible, I assure you," Mattie said. "The artist's name is Taggert. Silk Taggert. I'm planning an opening for his work a week from Friday."

"Count on me, dear. I love everything you've ever sold me." She swept the art that was hanging around Elizabeth Kenyon's gallery with a single raking glance. "I realize this sort of thing is very avant-garde and quite the in thing. Quite formidable in its own way. But the sad truth is, I really don't want it hanging in my home, if you know what I mean. I don't *enjoy* looking at it. When I buy something for my own home, I want to just love looking at it every time I walk into the room."

"You're in good company, Mrs. Eberly. The Medicis and the Borgias and a few other notable art collectors from the past had the same idea about art collecting."

Hugh frowned and started to make a comment, but at that particular moment the crowd parted to reveal Ariel sweeping down on them. Her exotic emerald eyes were on her sister.

"Mattie, I can't believe this thing about you and

Hugh." Ariel gave her sister a delicate hug of greeting while she narrowed her eyes at Hugh. "What in the world do you think you're doing?"

"Well, I—"

"Never mind," Ariel said briskly, stepping back, "we'll discuss it later. This isn't the time or the place. I understand you've been talking to Flynn. I want to discuss that little matter with you, also. I'll drop by the gallery tomorrow sometime."

"Fine," Mattie said quietly.

A group of moneyed-looking people moved up to commandeer Ariel's attention. She turned to them at once and moved off toward one of the paintings from her Exploratory period.

Elizabeth Kenyon materialized beside Mattie again. "Mattie, dear, would you do me an enormous favor?" she whispered.

"What's that?"

"Get Blackwell into a cab or something. He's becoming a bit obnoxious. I don't want him upsetting any of the clients. I swear, I'll be forever in your debt if you'll get him out of here for me."

Mattie groaned, glancing across the crowded room to where Emery Blackwell was in serious danger of dumping the contents of his glass into the cleavage of a Wagnerian lady of middling years. "All right, Liz. But, remember, you owe me."

"Thank you, dear." She smiled as she turned away, her hard eyes straying once more toward Hugh. "You always did have a way of picking up the bits and pieces Ariel leaves behind in her wake, didn't you, Mattie?"

Mattie gritted her teeth and went toward

Emery. She was vaguely aware that Hugh was following her through the throng.

"There you are, Emery," she said when she reached his side. "I've been looking for you." Mattie deftly removed the glass from his hand. "There's someone just dying to meet you." She flashed the large woman a placating smile. "Will you excuse us? Emery is always in such demand."

"Of course," the woman said, looking vaguely disappointed.

"Mattie, my love, you arrived just in the nick of time," Emery murmured as she led him away. "I do believe I was about to make a descent down an extremely treacherous precipice without benefit of proper climbing apparatus. Haven't seen a woman built along those lines in a good ten or fifteen years." Emery cast a last, wistful glance at the massive bosom he was forsaking. "They just don't make them like that anymore."

"Oh, I don't know about that," Hugh said easily. "I've got some calendars back in my office that have pictures of females built like that."

"You would," Emery agreed.

Mattie sighed. "Emery, you're getting drunk and you always get obnoxious when you drink."

"Kind of you to notice. I do try. Where are we going?"

"You're going home in a cab," Mattie said as she steered him toward the door.

"I've got a better idea. Why don't we go get a bite to eat? Just you and me, of course. Leave the Elemental creature behind."

Hugh crowded close as he followed the pair

out the door. "Forget it, Blackwell. Mattie and I already have plans."

"Pity," Emery said.

"Hey, Mattie." Flynn called, hurrying toward the three, who were halfway through the door. "Leaving already?"

"Afraid so," Mattie said.

"Don't think it hasn't been fun," Hugh growled.

"Look, I'll get those canvases to you as soon as possible, Mattie." Flynn followed them all out onto the sidewalk and stood waiting with them until a cruising cab pulled into the passenger loading zone.

"That'll be great, Flynn. But, like I said, Ariel is not going to approve."

"Don't worry about it." Flynn opened the cab door and ushered Blackwell inside.

Mattie slid in beside Emery.

"Where the hell are you going?" Hugh demanded as he watched Mattie get into the cab.

"Home. I think I've had enough champagne and soggy canapés tonight. Want to come along? We're on Emery's way."

Hugh glared at her in frustration and then got into the backseat of the cab beside her.

"You three have a nice evening, Flynn said casually, bending down to say good-bye.

"Shit," said Hugh.

"My sentiments exactly," Emery Blackwell intoned as the cab pulled away from the curb.

"You shouldn't have been there tonight, Emery," Mattie admonished. "You promised me you would stay up at your place on Whidbey

Island until you got the second book of the Byron St. Cyr series completed."

"Now, don't scold, Mattie, my love. I deserve a break. I swear on my honor as an aging scholar who has sold his soul to the devil of commercial fiction, I will head straight back to Whidbey tomorrow. I just couldn't resist attending that opening tonight." He looked across Mattie at Hugh, who was filling up a large chunk of the cab. "What about you, Abbott?"

"What about me?"

"Don't you feel a certain perverse pleasure in seeing your influence in Ariel's work? A little claim to artistic immortality, eh?"

"Bull."

"Succinctly put. A man of few words. Well, as for myself, all I can say is, I'll take my moments of fame when and where I can. All glory is fleeting. Do you know I actually had to explain to a couple of people in that gallery just who I was, Mattie? A humbling experience."

"Don't worry, there will be a whole new level of fame waiting for you when you emerge as the mysterious author of the best-selling Byron St. Cyr series," Mattie said gently. "Stop feeling sorry for yourself and start looking forward to the day you get to sign autographs at the mall."

"Dear Lord," Emery moaned. "What a fate. Autographs at the mall. I have truly made a devil's bargain, Mattie Sharpe. And it's all your doing."

"Your first book will be out in the stores in a couple of weeks, Emery, and you're going to feel much different when you see it selling like hotcakes. Trust me."

"My future is in your hands, Mattie, love."

Ten minutes later the cab pulled up in front of the restored early-nineteenth-century building in Pioneer Square that housed Mattie's large loft apartment. Mattie and Hugh climbed out, and after a bit of quiet nudging, Hugh reluctantly paid the fare, including enough to cover the cost of getting Emery Blackwell to his Capitol Hill residence.

The cab departed with Emery sitting regally in the backseat. Mattie dug out her keys and opened the security door of her building.

"What an evening," Hugh muttered as he punched the elevator call in the hallway.

"A little different from the Hellfire on a Saturday night, isn't it?" Mattie observed.

"Give me the Hellfire anytime."

"You'd better get used to evenings like this one, Hugh," Mattie told him sweetly. "I go to several openings a month and hold a lot myself during the year for my own artists. I'm sure you'll want to accompany me to each and every one. After all, you intend to be a part of my life here in Seattle, don't you?"

"For as long as it takes," Hugh said grimly.

CHAPTER

Ten

That night it occurred to Hugh for the first time that things were not going to go as smoothly or as easily as he had anticipated.

He sprawled on Mattie's black leather couch amid a tangle of sheets, his hands folded behind his head. It was nearly two in the morning, but the view through the high, curving windows that lined Mattie's huge studio was neon-bright. The glow of city lights at night always irritated Hugh. He preferred the velvet, flower-scented darkness of an island night. If he closed his eyes he could conjure up a mental image of pale moonlight falling like cream on the sea.

Seeing Mattie in her world tonight had been more of a shock than it should have been. After all, he knew what she did for a living; knew her sister and something about the family. Why had it been surprising to see Mattie looking so at home amid that crowd at the gallery? he wondered.

A part of him knew the answer. He had not wanted to admit that she was a part of that world. For the past several months he had been remembering the night of passion followed by her soft plea to take her with him back to the islands. *Take me with you, Hugh. I love you so much. Please take me with you.* And for the past week he'd had her out there on his territory, where he made the rules and where he felt comfortable.

When he had arrived here in Seattle with her three days ago and moved into her glossy apartment, he had been confident of his ability to convince her to move to St. Gabriel within a matter of days. He had been so certain that all he needed was a little time to overcome the feminine pique she felt because of his past engagement to Ariel.

Now things were looking a lot more complicated

than they had appeared from St. Gabe. A new sense of uncertainty was gnawing at his insides.

And after two nights he was already damn tired of sleeping on the couch.

Hugh tossed aside the covers of his makeshift bed and got to his feet. He crossed the red and gray carpet that designated what he thought of as the living room area of the huge studio and padded over the gleaming wooden floors to the windows. He stood there for a long while watching a late-night ferry crossing Elliott Bay.

Still restless, he wandered over to the kitchen area and rummaged around in the shadows until he found the sack of oat bran muffins Mattie had bought for breakfast. He pulled one out and took a bite. He didn't think he was ever going to become a big fan of oat bran, but he'd eaten worse things in his life. Paul Cormier's sun-dried tomatoes, for instance.

That recollection brought back a lot of other memories, some of them unpleasant. But most of all it brought back the image of the gaping red hole in Cormier's chest.

Hugh had never had a lot of friends. Cormier had been one of the few. Truth was, for a while there, Cormier had been more than a friend. He'd been almost a father in some ways back in the early years, when Hugh had still been searching for himself and a way to test his own young manhood. From Paul he had learned a lot of the important things, like how to have pride in himself, how to live by a code of honor. And how to survive.

Hugh was suddenly, acutely aware of his deep

loneliness. The sensation came more and more frequently of late. The only time it was ever really banished was when he was making love to Mattie.

A soft sound from above made him turn and look up at the open loft-style bedroom that jutted out over the living area. The loft had a shiny red metal railing around it. Mattie's bed was lost in the shadows behind the railing.

Mattie was the one who could banish the loneliness.

Hugh came to a decision. He put down the half-finished oat bran muffin and walked over to the narrow spiral staircase. Silently he climbed up the wrought-iron steps to Mattie's bedroom aerie.

Tonight at the gallery he had experienced genuine uneasiness as he had watched Flynn Grafton and Emery Blackwell hover around Mattie as if they had a prior claim on her.

This was not a sure thing he had going with Mattie, after all. He could lose her, Hugh thought, and he knew of only one way to reassert his own claim on her. He needed some reassurance. He had to know she still wanted him physically, even if she was trying to talk herself out of wanting him as a husband.

He had to know that on some level, at least, she was still his, the way she had been since their first night together all those months ago.

Mattie was still wide awake when she sensed Hugh's presence near the bed. She had been unable to sleep since she had climbed the stairs to her little fortress in the sky two hours ago.

Some part of her had known this would happen,

if not tonight, then tomorrow night or the next. Soon. The inevitable could not be postponed for long. The attraction between herself and Hugh ran too deep, and the fear that she might still be in love with him was too strong to ignore. She turned slowly to see him standing beside the bed, wearing only his briefs.

"Hugh?"

"Tell me you want me, Mattie. At least give me that much."

"I want you. You know that. That isn't the point."

"It is tonight." He leaned down, lifted the covers, and crawled in beside her. "If you don't want me to touch you, I won't. But I can't take any more nights alone down there on your couch." He reached out and caressed the curve of her shoulder. "I've spent too damn many nights alone, babe."

Mattie searched his face for a long moment and then, with a small sigh of surrender, she raised herself up on her elbow and kissed his sensual mouth. Her lips grazed fleetingly across his. Her fingers glided over his hard chest like butterflies.

"*Mattie.*" Hugh's groan of relief came from deep within him. He half lifted himself and pushed her eagerly back onto the pillows. Then he came down on top of her like a ton of bricks.

Mattie lay crushed beneath Hugh's weight, her mouth open to him. She was aware of his big hands moving hungrily on her, sliding down over her breasts to her stomach and lower. He wedged his leg between her thighs, prying them apart, and then his hand was on her in an intimate caress.

Mattie gasped, feeling herself growing warm and moist almost instantly. His tongue filled her mouth. She arched her hips, straining against him, and her head tilted back over his arm.

"That's it, babe. God, yes. So hot. So wet. So good." He settled himself quickly between her legs and reached down to wrap her thighs around his hips. "Squeeze me tight, babe. Take me inside and hold me."

Mattie felt the heat and excitement flood her senses. She wanted to tell him to slow down, but she could not find the words. It was all so hard and fast and overwhelming with Hugh. Making love with him was as primitive an experience as swimming in the sea or running through a jungle. There seemed to be no slow, delicate, civilized way to do it.

She could feel his manhood prodding at her now, feel his fingers parting the soft petals, guiding himself into her.

"Tight," he said in husky wonder as he flexed his hips to drive himself deep inside. "Babe, you feel so damn good."

And then he was in all the way, filling her, stretching her, setting off five-alarm fires at each of her nerve endings. His mouth covered hers again, and his possession of it was as deep and damp and complete as his possession of the slick, tight, sensitive sheath between her legs.

Mattie closed her eyes and let go of whatever strings still bound her to earth. She put her arms around Hugh and clung to him with all her strength.

It was a wild, glorious run through the night

with a giant wolf. She was free at last and with her true mate. There was nothing soft or gentle about the trip, but when it all ended in a shower of tiny, delicious convulsions that rippled through her, Mattie was exultant.

She turned her face into the pillow and took long, deep breaths.

"Mattie?"

"Yes?"

"From now on I sleep up here with you. Do we agree on that much, at least?"

"Yes."

"You see?" Hugh chuckled in the darkness as he rolled onto his back. "We do have a lot in common."

"Sex isn't everything, Hugh."

"No, but it's a start," He sounded lazy and satisfied. "A damn good start. And it isn't all we've got going for us," he added around a huge yawn. "I told you that earlier tonight."

"So just what do we have in common?" She was curious in spite of herself. Mattie propped herself up on her elbows and looked down at him. "Go on, Hugh. Name one thing."

The intensity in his silver-gray eyes was clear even in the shadows. "Don't you understand? We're both misfits, babe. Changelings. Round pegs in square holes for most of our lives."

Mattie blinked, startled. Then she frowned. "That's not true."

"It's true. I think you recognized it first. That's probably why you begged me to take you with me a year ago. You understood it instinctively then, but after I left you behind you were too angry to

204

give me a second chance. Now you're making up excuses, telling yourself I only want you because I didn't get Ariel. You're bent on trying to convince me our lifestyles are too different to allow us to get together."

"Our lifestyles *are* too different. There's no compromise possible for us, Hugh. And you did want Ariel at first. You can't deny it. You still wanted her even after you made love to me that first time."

"No."

"Yes, it's true, damn it. You said I wasn't your type, remember? Thank you very much for the roll in the hay, but I've got a plane to the islands to catch."

"You're running scared, Mattie," he said gently. "Why don't you admit it? I know it took everything you had to make your big offer a year ago, and I was a fool for turning it down. But you've got plenty of guts, babe. I know that for sure now after watching you handle yourself out in the islands. Why not give our relationship another chance? A real chance?"

She sucked in her breath on a fierce exclamation. "I don't have to make my offer again, remember? You've already made yours. You chose to follow me to Seattle. You're here now, so I don't have to go back there, do I?"

They were silent for a long time while they gazed at each other through the shadows. It was a contest of wills. Mattie could feel Hugh's determination beating at her, looking for weak spots. She held herself very still, the way a rabbit did when confronted by a wolf.

And then the wolf grinned. "Relax, babe. It's going to work out. You'll see. You just need a little time to learn to trust me. Now, go to sleep. We've both got to go to work tomorrow."

"Hugh," Mattie said on a wave of genuine anxiety, "do you like working at Vailcourt headquarters?"

"I've worked in worse places."

"You don't like it. You hate it, don't you? You're not an urban person. Hugh. We both know that."

"Don't worry about it. Like I said. I've worked in worse places."

"But, Hugh—"

"Hush, babe. Go to sleep." He pulled her against his side, cradling her close to his hard, lean strength, and put one muscled leg over her slender calf.

Mattie sensed him slipping into sleep within minutes. But she lay awake for a long time.

Mattie lounged back in her chair behind the tiny desk in her office and studied the bizarre-looking creature in front of her.

Shock Value Frederickson, as she was calling herself this month, was about twenty-five years old. She was thin to the point of being scrawny and had a lot of chartreuse hair that stood out in a stiff, gelled halo around her head. She was wearing a couple of dozen clanking metal bracelets on each arm and four rings in each ear. She also had a ring in her nose, a delicate steel one. Her light hazel eyes were outlined in black and gold, and her clothes were a hodgepodge of Salvation Army rejects held together by a heavy metal belt.

"So what do you think, Mattie?" Shock Value indicated her latest metal sculpture, which was sitting on the floor beside her chair. "Will you handle it for me?"

Mattie sighed. "You're obviously still in your End-of-the-World period, Shock. It's interesting, but we both know it's not going to appeal to my clients. Maybe Christine Ferguson's gallery can handle it."

Shock Value squirmed uneasily in her chair. Metal jangled on her wrists and ears. "She didn't want it, either. Neither did anyone else I tried. Mattie, I'm in kind of a bad spot at the moment. I spent my last ten bucks on supplies, and I haven't sold anything in months."

"I thought you were getting by with that restaurant job I lined up for you."

"I was. And it was really great of you to get me that job, Mattie, but they just didn't understand me there." Shock Value leaned forward earnestly. "You know what? They actually canned me just because I came in late a few times. Can you believe it? I told them I'd been working all night in my studio and time had sort of gotten away from me, but the manager wouldn't listen."

"I see."

"Mattie, please. I'm working on some really strong stuff. I just need a little time and a little cash to carry me for a few weeks until I can finish it."

"More stuff like *Dead Hole*?" Mattie nodded toward the piece on the floor.

Shock Value shook her chartreuse-fringed head impatiently. "No, no, that's all gone. I've worked through that period. I mean, it was useful and everything because it got me focused, you know? But now I'm working toward the important stuff. But I need to be able to *work*."

"You should have spent your last ten bucks on food instead of supplies, Shock. You're getting too thin."

"I don't care about food. I've got to be able to buy my materials. You know how expensive metal-working supplies are."

"The whole point of getting you that job in the restaurant was so you wouldn't starve yourself for your art. That place allows the employees one free meal a day."

"I know. But I usually missed it."

Mattie groaned. "Have you looked into food stamps? Welfare?"

"Mattie, the government wants you to prove you're looking for work. I can't do that. I'm already working. My art is my work. I swear I'll go back to being a waitress just as soon as I finish the piece I'm designing now. I just need a few more weeks of freedom. I've got to get some cash. Fast. If you can't sell *Dead Hole*, could you at least make me a small loan?"

Mattie surveyed the piece Shock Value had brought with her. *Dead Hole* was one of several creations the young artist had done lately using wire, rusted iron, and used Styrofoam cups.

There was no doubt but that Shock Value's work was uniquely robust and filled with energy. Mattie had seen the possibilities in it right from

208

the start. But the art was not quite ready to be born. Mattie knew that no matter how energetic it was, *Dead Hole* was never going to sell in her gallery. It had a power all its own, but it was the power generated by ugliness.

Still, one of these days Shock Value Frederickson was going to be brilliant and in the meantime the woman had to eat.

"Will a hundred hold you for a while?" Mattie finally asked.

Shock Value nodded quickly. "Anything. You can keep *Dead Hole* as collateral."

Mattie reached for her purse in the bottom drawer of her desk and took out the five twenties she had just picked up at the bank. "Here you go. You can take *Dead Hole* with you, but I want you to swear on your life that you'll let me have first crack at whatever it is you're working on now. Deal?"

"You got it." Shock Value beamed in relief as she scooped up her metal sculpture and plucked the twenties from Mattie's fingers. "You won't regret this, Mattie, I promise. Thanks."

Shock Value whirled and headed for the door of the small office with her usual frenzied energy. She nearly collided with Ariel, who was just about to enter.

"'Scuse me," Shock Value mumbled, rushing past with *Dead Hole* clutched in her hands.

Ariel looked at Mattie. "How much did you give her?"

"A hundred."

"You'll never see it again." Ariel walked in and

sat down in the chair Shock Value had just vacated.

Mattie put her purse back in the drawer. "I don't know about that. Shock's going to be very good one of these days. Maybe even commercial once she gets control of her talent. Her work has an edgy, vibrant quality that might translate very well into the sort of thing I can sell here at Sharpe Reaction."

"You mean if she makes her work *pretty* enough to appeal to your middlebrow businessmen, shop-keepers, and computer-nerd clients?"

Mattie grimaced. "I know you don't have a high opinion of the sort of people who buy the work in my gallery, Ariel, but I could do without another lecture on the subject. Face it, I'm one of those hopeless cases who really does believe there's such a thing as good art for the masses. Like Mrs. Eberly says, why hang something in your living room that nauseates you whenever you look at it?"

Ariel's smile was bitter. "Yes, we both know your own tastes, don't we? But that's not really what I want to talk about."

"What do you want to talk about?"

"Tell me, sister dear, do you like playing Earth Mother to my Castrating Bitch role? Personally, I'm getting a little tired of it. I'd appreciate it if you'd leave my men alone."

"Oh, hell," Mattie said. "It's going to be one of those unpleasant big sister versus little sister chats, isn't it? You know how I hate those. You always win." Mattie leaned precariously back in her chair and checked to see that there was water

210

in the small hot pot sitting on the floor behind her. When she saw it was full, she switched it on.

"Mattie, this has gone too far."

"You want some herbal tea and some oat bran muffins? I have a couple left over from breakfast."

"For God's sake, Mattie, no, I do not want an oat bran muffin. How can you think about health food at a time like this? But that's you right to the core. I can't stand it. I have never been able to stand it. No one in the family can stand it. The rest of us vent our emotions in a normal, healthy way, but not you, you always try to change the subject."

"You know I'm not very good at confrontations," Mattie reminded her humbly. She eyed the oat bran muffin and decided she wasn't hungry. "They make me tense."

It was true. When it came to arguing with anyone in her temperamental, high-spirited, high-strung clan, she was always at a disadvantage for the simple reason that she was the only one in her family who truly dreaded scenes. They made her physically sick. Everyone else thrived on them. What's more they were very good at them. On the rare occasion Mattie had tried to stage a major scene, she had always felt outclassed, outgunned, and outacted.

Except when she had staged one with Hugh, she realized. She had actually lost her temper with Hugh more than once, and she had not felt nauseated at all.

"Maybe you don't handle scenes well because you're such a wimp, Mattie. If you'd just fight back once in a while, you wouldn't get so tense."

211

Mattie sighed. "I don't have the personality for the kind of dramatics you and Mom and Dad and everyone else in the family enjoy so much. That kind of thing just puts me under a lot of stress. You know I try to avoid stress these days."

"You don't know what stress is," Ariel shot back. "I'll tell you what real stress is. Last night was real stress for me."

"Last night?" Mattie glanced up in surprise. "What was so stressful about last night? The retrospective of your work was a great success."

"Oh, sure. You think it was my work everyone was talking about after you left? Well, it wasn't. The main topic of conversation was that cozy little scene of you and Flynn and Emery and Hugh all huddled together out on the sidewalk talking like the great friends you obviously are. And then you, my dear sister, had the gall to get into a cab with my ex-husband and my ex-fiancé and drive off into the night. How do you think that made me feel?"

"I didn't think anyone noticed," Mattie said weakly.

"Bullshit. You like doing things like that, don't you? You like making me look like the Wicked Witch while you play Snow White." Ariel sprang to her feet and took a turn around the room.

"That's not how it is, Ariel." Mattie watched her sister warily. Ariel was working herself up into one of her full-scale storms. She was capable of generating real thunder and lightning when she got going.

"Don't tell me how it is. I know how it is. It's always been like that. Everyone thinks I'm some

212

sort of Amazon goddess in a cast-iron bra who gets her kicks from destroying men. But it's not true." She spun around and glared at Mattie. "The divorce from Emery was not my fault, you know."

"I know, Ariel."

"No, you don't know, damn you. How could you know? You've never been married. Why should you bother? You're having too much fun comforting the men who get bruised and battered by me, aren't you?"

"Now, hold on, Ariel . . ."

"Too much fun letting everyone think you're the only one with any real sensitivity; too much fun compensating for your lack of artistic talent by demonstrating the depths of your womanly empathy and understanding. You've already hooked Emery and Hugh, but you're not satisfied. Now you've finally got your claws into Flynn, too."

"That's not true." Mattie sat stunned in her chair. It had never occurred to her that Ariel might actually be jealous of Flynn. Ariel always seemed so self-assured when it came to men, as assured as she was about her talent.

"It is true. You want to add Flynn to your collection of scalps, don't you? You want to prove you can make him turn to you for a comforting bosom to cry on just like the others do. Do you know what Emery once said about you? He said you were such a sweet, old-fashioned sort of woman. Very gentle on a man's ego. The kind who was born to be waiting faithfully back at the castle when the warrior came home from battle."

Mattie put her head in her hands. "God, that

does sound awful, doesn't it? Especially when everyone knows that in real life men are bored to tears by that kind of woman."

"I won't let you do it, Mattie."

"Do what?" Mattie looked up again.

"You can have Emery and you can have Hugh, if you really want them, although Lord knows why you would. *But you cannot have Flynn.*"

"I don't want Flynn, damn it." Mattie shot to her feet as the stress of the moment finally galvanized her into action. "I didn't want Emery, either. We've never been anything more than friends and that's the gospel truth. The only one I ever wanted was Hugh, and he wasn't particularly interested when I offered myself on a silver platter last year. So stop making it sound like I'm some kind of Jezebel who specializes in your cast-off men. I don't want your leftovers, Ariel, I never did."

Ariel was staring at her. "What do you mean, you offered yourself to Hugh on a silver platter last year?"

"Oh, damn, why did I let you drag me into this stupid argument. Forget it. Forget everything." The rare and unfamiliar passion of rage died as quickly as it had arisen. Mattie sank back wearily into her chair, surprised to discover that although she felt drained, she didn't feel sick to her stomach. She was getting better at anger. Maybe it was from all the practice she was getting with Hugh.

"Tell me what you mean about that silver-platter crack," Ariel insisted, planting her hands on Mattie's desk.

"There's nothing to tell. I made a fool of myself last year after you dumped Hugh. That's all. Believe me, I learned my lesson." The water was boiling in the hot pot. Mattie reached down to flick the switch and noticed her fingers were trembling. *Stress*, she thought. She was shaking from the stress. She must be sure to get to her lunch-hour aerobics class today. The exercise would help deal with the anxiety.

"How did you make a fool of yourself? What happened between the two of you? Were you seeing him while I was engaged to him?" Ariel yelled in fury.

"No, of course not. Your men never notice me until after you've finished with them. You ought to know that. They're all much too dazzled by you."

"What happened? How did you make a fool of yourself?"

"Let it go, will you, Ariel?"

"No, I will not let it go. I want to know. Tell me what happened."

Mattie exhaled heavily. "This is so embarrassing. The night before Hugh was scheduled to fly back to St. Gabriel, I called him. Told him he could spend the night at my apartment. Made some idiotic excuse about my place being cheaper than an airport hotel, which is where he was planning to stay."

"Oh, Mattie."

"I know. It sounded just as lame then as it does now. But he showed up on my doorstep around dinnertime. He was not in a good mood. He was angry and restless, like a caged wolf. He'd already

215

had a couple of drinks. I made the mistake of giving him a couple more along with dinner."

"My God. You were playing with fire."

"Umm, yes. It was a new experience for me," Mattie admitted dryly. "I'm sure you can imagine the outcome of the evening. Hugh downed a good deal of very expensive after-dinner brandy and then he more or less fell into bed with me. I confess I gave him a small shove."

"What did you think you were going to accomplish?" Ariel demanded tightly. "Were you trying to prove you could seduce him?"

"No. Not exactly." Mattie fiddled with a pen on her desk. "I wanted him to take me with him when he left town on the flight to St. Gabriel the next morning."

Ariel stared at her sister in amazement. "You wanted to run off to the islands with him? You? I can't believe it."

"What can I say? I went a little crazy. Believe me, it won't happen again."

"But he claims he's engaged to you. He's staying with you at your apartment."

"He's the one talking about marriage. I'm thinking of our present arrangement as an affair." Mattie smiled bleakly. "Don't worry, Ariel, it won't last. One of these days Hugh will get on another flight back to St. Gabriel."

"Poor Hugh."

Mattie scowled. "Poor Hugh?"

But Ariel had already made one of her lightning-swift mood swings. "And poor Emery. You know, lately, I've begun to wonder why I always seem to attract losers. It's awkward, you know, because people think I'm the one who ruined them, but the truth is that they carry the seeds of their own destruction within them. I'm like a catalyst or something that speeds up the process."

"For Pete's sake, Ariel."

"I'm not responsible for Emery and Hugh ruining their lives."

"Of course you aren't. And their lives aren't exactly ruined. They've both got plenty of big plans for the future, I promise you."

But Ariel was off on a new dramatic tangent. "Last night I felt so guilty when I saw you with the three of them out there on the sidewalk."

"There's absolutely no need for you to feel guilty." Mattie was used to this role, too. She had spent years soothing Ariel and everyone else in the household.

"Maybe it is my fault, somehow. Maybe I do something to destroy them."

"Ariel, stop it. That's not true and you know it." Mattie was getting alarmed now. Ariel's emotions could be unpredictable. "For heaven's sake, don't start wallowing in a lot of unearned guilt. It's not your style and it will take days for you to get back out of it so that you can paint."

"It doesn't matter. I haven't painted in weeks. I'm too frightened by what's happening between me and Flynn."

"Afraid of what?"

"That I'll do to him whatever I did to Emery and Hugh." With a sob, Ariel fled to the door.

CHAPTER

Eleven

Mattie got off the elevator on the twenty-sixth floor of the downtown highrise and walked along a wide, carpeted hallway. She took several deep breaths to force back the familiar tension and realized she had a death grip on the paper bag she was holding as well as on her purse strap. It had been a long ride up and the elevator had been very crowded.

Memories of the caves of Purgatory had started to nibble around the edges of her thoughts by the twelfth floor, when five more large specimens of corporate humanity had gotten on board. Real anxiety had set in by the twentieth, when the doors had stuck shut for a moment. She had literally leaped off the elevator when it had finally arrived at the twenty-sixth floor.

She always had some problem in elevators, but this last experience had been especially difficult. The fact was, she was having more trouble than usual handling the normal stresses in her life these days. Perhaps that was because she was experiencing more than the usual amount, she reminded herself grimly. Living with Hugh Abbott under the same roof was not exactly conducive to serenity. It was like having a large beast underfoot, one who was just waiting for the day when he would go back to the wild. Dragging her with him, of course. She knew that was always in the back of his mind, no matter how often he reassured her that he was willing to stay in Seattle indefinitely.

Indefinitely, hah. She knew Hugh Abbott better than that. The man was extremely low on patience.

Perhaps she should start doubling up on her vitamin B and niacin tablets in the mornings, Mattie thought. They were good for stress.

There were several excellent paintings hanging on the walls of the twenty-sixth floor of the Vailcourt building. It was one of the three management floors. Mattie had chosen the art for the offices at her aunt's request, and she was pleased to see that it still looked as good now as it had the day the pictures were hung. Some art did not wear well, even though it looked terrific when it first went up. It was a fact of life in the business. Only the truly good stuff looked terrific five, ten, or a hundred years later.

Mattie halted at the open door of one of the offices and glanced inside. Two people were seated at two large desks, a young man and a woman of about fifty. There was a desktop computer on each desk. Around the room was an array of state-of-the-art office equipment: Fax machines, exotic telephones, laser printers, and assorted computer peripherals. There was also a lot of paper stacked up on various surfaces. Modern machines seemed to generate more paper than the old ones.

The attractive, well-groomed young man at the first desk looked up and saw Mattie standing in the doorway.

"May I help you?" he inquired in plumy accents.

"I just dropped by to see Hugh, that is, uh, Mr. Abbott, if he's in," Mattie said, moving slowly into the office. She felt oddly ill at ease and realized it was because it was very difficult to imagine Hugh working in such sophisticated surroundings. It just wasn't *him*, somehow.

"Mr. Abbott is very busy," the young man said smoothly. "Did you have an appointment?"

"No, no, that's all right," Mattie said quickly. "If he's busy, don't bother him. I happened to be in the building, and I thought I'd say hello while I was here."

"I'll be glad to give him your name and see if he can find time for you," the young man offered.

"Mattie Sharpe. But, really, it's okay. Don't worry about it. I'll just run along. Here, you can give him this, if you will." She held out the paper bag she was holding in one hand. "He forgot it this morning. On purpose. I suspect."

"Miss Sharpe." The name obviously clicked immediately. The young man, who had been reaching out to take the paper bag, dropped his hand and smiled. "One moment please." The secretary pressed the intercom button on his desk and started to speak into it.

At that moment the door of the inner office was yanked open, and Hugh stuck his head out. "Gary or Jenny, one of you bring me that report on the Rome office, will you? And make it quick, I haven't got all day."

"I've got it right here, Mr. Abbott," the woman said calmly, reaching for a thick folder on her desk.

"Great. Thanks." Hugh held out his hand as the secretary got to her feet.

"Excuse me, Mr. Abbott," Gary said. "You have a visitor."

"Not now, Gary, I'm busy." Hugh started to flip through the folder. "I told you I don't have time to see anyone until this afternoon." He looked up and spotted Mattie standing near the secretary's desk. "Hey, it's you, babe. Didn't see you there."

"Probably because my suit is the same color as the carpeting," Mattie grumbled, glancing down at her beigy-brown attire.

"Well, I'll admit you do stand out better in red," Hugh said with a grin. "Come on in." His easy smile changed abruptly to a scowl as he examined her more closely. "What happened to you, anyway? You look like hell."

"Thank you. The suit isn't that bad, is it?"

"Forget the damned suit. You're white as a sheet." Hugh closed the door behind her and waved her to a chair near the floor-to-ceiling windows. "You look the way you did when we went through those caves on Purgatory."

"The elevator was a bit crowded," Mattie explained as she sat down. She gazed around at the plush surroundings, taking in the polished wooden desk, the thick carpeting, and the designer chairs. "Nice office. Not a girlie calendar in sight."

"Don't worry. I've ordered a few to put up around the room to make myself feel more at home. What are you doing here?"

"A royal summons. My aunt phoned me up this

221

morning and said she wanted to see me. Said she could fit me in around ten o'clock."

"This is Thursday. She always has a massage at ten o'clock downstairs in the health club on Thursdays." Hugh sprawled in the big, elegant executive chair and put his booted feet up on the gleaming surface of the desk.

"Right. She's invited me to join her. She says we can talk while we're getting massaged."

"What are you two going to talk about?" Hugh asked with narrowed eyes.

"You, probably. That's what most people seem to want to discuss with me lately. I just stopped off here to give you this." Mattie opened her brown paper bag and drew out a container of thick, brightly colored juice. "You ran off and left it behind this morning."

Hugh looked shocked. "My bug juice? After all that special effort you went to this morning to mix it up for me in the blender? I accidentally left it in the refrigerator? I can't believe I'd do a thing like that. I'm getting forgetful lately, aren't I?"

"Stress, no doubt."

Hugh chuckled. "So what is it this morning?"

"A combination of lime, papaya, banana, and wheat grass with some bran added for texture. I told you when I was making it this morning that it's great for supplying you with plenty of midday energy. Lots of vitamins and special enzymes."

"Gary makes a pretty good cup of coffee," Hugh said, looking hopeful. "Lots of energy in coffee."

"But no real nutrition," Mattie said with an admonishing frown.

"Right. No real nutrition. Okay, stick the bug juice in that little refrigerator over there, and I'll drink it later. When are you supposed to meet Charlotte?"

"I should go on up there now," Mattie said, opening the section of bookshelving that was humming softly on the other side of the room. "This is impressive, Hugh. Your own refrigerator. All the comforts of home."

"Not quite," he drawled. "I could use a couch."

"Why would you want a couch?" she asked as she straightened, and then her eyes met his faintly mocking, very sexy gaze. She blushed. "Oh. You have a one-track mind, Hugh Abbott."

"I'd just like to be better prepared for visits from you," Hugh said as he took his feet down off the desk. He cast a thoughtful glance at the polished wooden surface. "Of course, there is the desk, isn't there?"

"Forget it," she said firmly, memories of the night flooding her veins with heat. "I'm due upstairs. Got to run."

"Some other time, maybe. Come on. I'll escort you up to Charlotte's palace."

"That's not necessary. I know you're busy."

"Not that busy."

He took hold of her arm and guided her out through the office and into the hall. There was a crowd of people waiting to board the elevator that had just opened.

"Excuse me, folks," Hugh said in a cool commanding tone as he tugged Mattie past the small group and into the empty elevator.

223

"Emergency security check. Next elevator will be along in a minute."

The doors closed on a row of startled expressions, leaving Mattie and Hugh alone in the elevator. Hugh punched the button for the presidential floor.

"What was that all about?" Mattie demanded.

"Figured you'd had enough of crowded elevators today." Hugh folded his arms and propped his shoulder against the wall. He smiled.

"So you kicked everyone off this one just so I wouldn't have to ride in a packed elevator?" Mattie began to giggle. "Honestly, Hugh."

"What's so funny?"

"Watching you throw your weight around. You're very good at it, you know. It must come naturally."

"You don't get what you want in this world unless you go after it." He reached for her, pulling her close and kissing her fiercely just as the elevator doors opened. "I learned that a long time ago, babe."

"This feels incredible, Aunt Charlotte. Absolutely incredible," Mattie was lying facedown on the massage table while a white-jacketed woman with amazingly strong hands worked on her bare back. She was being kneaded, punched and pounded, and it felt wonderful. "You say you do this once a week?"

"At least," Charlotte Vailcourt said from the next table. "Sometimes more frequently if I'm under an unusual amount of stress."

Another woman in white was working earnestly

on Charlotte. Mattie opened her eyes and glanced over at her aunt. Charlotte Vailcourt had always been a beautiful woman. She was nearly sixty now, but she still managed to draw every eye whenever she walked into a room. It was not just a case of physical beauty, although she had plenty of that left thanks to a fine bone structure and a great deal of money; it was also a matter of grace and style.

Charlotte Vailcourt was loaded with grace and style. Those qualities had been the hallmark of her career as an actress, and they had carried her safely through the deep, dangerous waters of the international business world after she had taken control of Vailcourt Industries upon the death of her husband. It was Charlotte who had expanded the firm into the international realm of operations. The business had thrived under her leadership.

"I'm going to have to try this on a routine basis myself," Mattie said languidly as she felt tension dissolve throughout her body. "So relaxing."

"I had a hunch you'd enjoy it. You've been under an unusually high level of stress yourself, lately. Hugh gave me a full report on what you went through on Purgatory. I was absolutely shocked. Poor Mr. Cormier."

"I have to tell you, it certainly made me wonder if there wasn't some truth to the old legend surrounding that sword, Aunt Charlotte."

"You mean that bit about 'Death to all who dare claim the blade until it's been taken up by the avenger and cleansed in the blood of the betrayer'? Typical medieval nonsense. All first-class ancient swords like *Valor* have legends and curses attached to them. Part of what makes them interesting. No,

I'm afraid Mr. Cormier's problem was a combination of the usual, bad luck and bad timing."

"It was bad, all right," Mattie agreed with a small shiver of memory.

"You needn't have stumbled into the middle of it, you know. Why on earth didn't you stop at St. Gabriel, the way you were supposed to? You could have avoided that nasty little scene on Purgatory altogether. Hugh would never have walked into that sort of thing with you. He has an instinct for trouble."

"You know why I changed my reservations."

Charlotte sighed. "So much for my attempt at playing matchmaker. Still, on the whole, I didn't do too badly, did I? Hugh tells me you're engaged."

"Don't look so satisfied, Aunt Charlotte. I don't think I'd go quite so far as to call our present arrangement an engagement."

"That's what Hugh's calling it, so that's what I'll call it."

"I see. You two took a vote and I've been outvoted, is that it?"

"Now, don't go getting tense again, Mattie. You'll undo all the good work these nice women are accomplishing. When do you think you'll move out to St. Gabriel?"

Mattie stiffened and her masseuse responded by digging her thumbs into a pressure point. "Ouch. I'm not moving out to St. Gabriel. Didn't Hugh explain that part? He's decided to move to Seattle."

"Not permanently."

Mattie smiled grimly. "Then you'll have to ask him when he's leaving."

"Mattie, you know you can't keep him here long. Hugh Abbott will never be happy in the city. He's like a wild animal. He'll never become completely civilized, no matter how much sushi and white wine he consumes. All his hopes and dreams are waiting for him back on his island."

"I know. I'm waiting for him to admit that and go back to St. Gabriel."

"He won't go back without you."

"Then he'll wait until hell freezes over."

"You're tensing up again, ma'am," the masseuse said, sounding annoyed.

"Sorry," Mattie mumbled.

"The thing is," Charlotte said gently, "you're part of his hopes and dreams now. He won't leave you behind."

"He did once before."

"Are you going to hold that against him for the rest of his life?"

Mattie thought about it. "Maybe. At least until I can be sure I'm not a stand-in for Ariel."

"I don't believe it. That's not like you, Mattie. Hugh made a mistake a year ago, but that's because he was mad as hell and didn't know his own mind. For heaven's sake, dear, he's a man. Men aren't very good at analyzing themselves, you know."

"I know. But I'm tired of analyzing him, too. I thought I had him figured out a year ago. I thought I understood him and that once he was free from Ariel's spell he'd see the light. But he didn't, Aunt Charlotte."

"It only took him a couple of months to come to his senses. Be reasonable, Mattie." Charlotte sighed. "He was really thrown for a loss when Ariel broke off the engagement. He needed time to get his act together again. Poor Hugh, he thought he'd wrapped everything up in a nice, neat package for himself. All his plans were in order, and he's very accustomed to making things work out according to his own plans, you know. Even if he has to sort of hammer them into place."

"You can say that again."

"I blame myself, in part. I should never have arranged for Hugh and Ariel to meet."

"Why did you?" Mattie asked tightly. "You've made no secret that you'd like him in the family, but why choose Ariel for him the first time around? Why didn't you toss me into his lap?"

"Oh, dear. I had a feeling you might be harboring some resentment on that score."

"Forget it, Aunt Charlotte. I'm used to Ariel getting picked first, I've always been her understudy."

"Really, dear, must you sink back into that old self-pity routine? I thought you'd outgrown that years ago."

Mattie winced as the masseuse crushed her shoulders. "Sorry. Old habits are hard to break."

"Well, it's not as if you don't have cause in this instance, I suppose. In this case I did consciously choose Ariel for Hugh. And I admit it was a big mistake. All I can say is that at first glance they somehow seemed very suited to each other. They're both very vibrant, colorful, dramatic people. I thought they would strike sparks off each other."

"They did. More than sparks. Explosions."

"But they didn't set any long-term fires, Mattie. You and Hugh did."

"It's another mismatch, Aunt Charlotte. Trust me."

"Well, one way or another, you'd better be prepared for real fireworks if you insist on tying Hugh to Seattle. Because he can't stay here indefinitely, and he won't leave without you."

"Is that right?" Mattie retorted, feeling pressured again. "What about me? Why should I pull up stakes and move to his godforsaken little island? What about my career? What about my sushi and white wine? I'm happy here, Aunt Charlotte. Finally. After all these years I'm actually happy."

"Are you, dear?" Charlotte asked softly.

"I think I'm getting tense again," Mattie declared.

"Just relax, dear."

"Aunt Charlotte?"

"Yes, dear?"

"What do you know about Hugh's past?"

"His past? Well, he's worked for Vailcourt on a freelance consulting basis for nearly four years."

"I mean, before he went to work for you."

"I'm afraid I can't tell you much."

"Because it's confidential? Personnel policies don't permit telling me?"

Charlotte smiled. "It's not so much a matter of personnel policy as it is the plain and simple fact

229

that I don't know exactly what Hugh was doing before he came to work for me."

Mattie frowned. "I find it hard to believe you'd hire someone you knew absolutely nothing about, Aunt Charlotte."

"Something about his style rather appealed to me," Charlotte said thoughtfully. "He just walked into my office one day without an appointment and told me I needed him. Said one of the South American field offices of Vailcourt Mining was in jeopardy because a group of rebels was about to destroy it in order to make a political statement. Hugh told me that for ten thousand dollars he would deal with the situation."

"And he did."

"Oh, yes, dear. He certainly did. The rest, as they say, is history."

Hugh sprawled in his executive chair, heels stacked on the desk, and eyed the magnificent view of Elliott Bay through the office windows. When he got back to St. Gabriel, he'd have to see about ordering up a chair like the one he was presently occupying. But he already knew he had a better view back in the islands. There was something about having to look at the expanse of the bay through solid glass windows that could not be opened that bothered him.

But, then, there were a lot of things about city life that irritated him. The sooner he got Mattie out of here, the better.

"Where the hell have you been, Silk?" Hugh said when Taggert eventually rumbled inquiringly into the phone. He could hear the sounds of the

Hellfire evening crowd in the background. "I've been trying to reach you for two days."

"I was off island," Silk said, sounding stone-cold sober. "Took a little trip to Hades to see if I could pick up any leads."

"Any luck?"

"Word is that things have settled down on Purgatory. The revolution or whatever you want to call it is over, and it's business as usual over there, apparently."

"Who's in charge?"

"Good question, boss. A lot of the old crowd, believe it or not, including Findley, the pool-shooting president. The official word is that the coup failed and things are back to normal. But the rumor is there's a new man in charge behind the scenes and that the important government officials now answer to him."

"In other words, the coup worked but the new strongman has enough sense to stay out of the spotlight."

"Sounds like it. And whoever it is, he's also smart enough to use money, not guns, to buy the loyalty of the local officials."

"Money always did talk over on Purgatory," Hugh observed. "That's one of the things Cormier liked about it."

"As Cormier pointed out, money talks everywhere. It's just a bit more obvious on a small island like Purgatory. Don't forget, in the old days, that island was a pirate stronghold. It hasn't changed all that much."

"Yeah. Interesting." Hugh was silent for a moment, running possibilities through his head.

"You ever find Gibbs? The guy who was Rosey's partner?"

"Nope. No trace. Looks like he's skipped."

"Probably for good reason. Must have found out what happened to his friend. Sounds like the next step is to try to track down some of Cormier's former house staff. See if we can get one of them to talk. Find out if they saw anything the day Cormier was killed."

"My guess is that they're all going to be suffering from amnesia. Assuming we can even find one or two of 'em."

"If we can find one, we can make him talk. Keep working on it, Silk. I'm going to try something from this end."

"Like what?"

"Ever heard of computers? Information networks? Worldwide data bases?"

"Where the hell are you going to get hold of a computer with enough information to help us find out something about Cormier's killer?"

"I'm sitting on top of one of the most sophisticated computer networks in the world, Silk. Call me when you get a handle on something."

"Right."

"By the way," Hugh said, "Mattie's scheduled your opening for tomorrow evening. There's going to be champagne and all kinds of free eats. They do that kind of thing up big around here."

"Damn. Wish I could be there. Sounds like my kind of party." There was a pause on the other end of the line. "She really think my stuff is going to sell?"

Hugh was amazed at the degree of uncertainty

in Silk's voice. It wasn't like the big man to be uncertain of anything. "She says you're going to make her rich."

"Damn," Silk said again in tones of great wonder. "When I think of how I had to ram those canvases down Miles's throat in order to cover my tab here at the Hellfire, I could just spit. He'll have to beg for 'em now, by God."

"Revenge is sweet."

"Ain't it just?"

Hugh hung up the phone and took his boots down off the desk. He got to his feet, went over to the small refrigerator, and removed the bottle of juice Mattie had brought with her that morning.

The two secretaries that had been assigned to Hugh looked up inquiringly as he strode through the outer office on the way to the elevators.

"See ya," said Hugh.

"What shall we say concerning your estimated time of return to the office, Mr. Abbot?" Gary asked just as Hugh reached the door.

"Tell 'em I'll be back in a while." Hugh went out into the corridor and punched the elevator call button. Secretaries who tried to set schedules and run a man's life were a nuisance. He knew the two he had were among the best in the business, but they annoyed him as often as not.

Hugh was doing his best to learn how to manage a staff, however, because he figured that sooner or later he would be hiring office help for Abbott Charters. He sure as hell did not want to keep doing all the filing himself, and he could not trust Derek or Ray or Silk to do it. Their idea of file management was to toss everything that wasn't edible or spendable into the nearest wastebasket.

"What in the world have you got in that bottle?" Charlotte Vailcourt asked when Hugh sauntered through her office door a few minutes later.

"Bug juice. Mattie made it." Hugh set the bottle on Charlotte's vast slate desk. "Want some?"

"Another one of her high-energy, antistress concoctions, I presume?" Charlotte eyed the juice warily.

"Yeah, I haven't tried this particular formula yet, but if it's like the others I've tasted, we'll be lucky to survive." Hugh went over to the black lacquer wet bar across the room and found a couple of glasses in the cupboard.

"Why do you keep drinking her 'bug juice,' as you call it, if you can't stand the stuff, Why not just toss it into the nearest flowerpot?"

Hugh shrugged as he came back across the room and poured two small glasses full of the juice. "It's not that bad. I've had worse things to drink." He swallowed the entire contents of his glass in one long gulp and grimaced. "But I can't recall just when."

Charlotte grinned as she sipped tentatively at hers. "I suppose the fact that she goes to so much trouble to elevate your health consciousness is a sign of how much she cares about you."

"That's what I tell myself when I'm eating pasta and veggies instead of a nice bloody steak." Hugh sank down into a black leather and chrome chair.

His gaze went briefly to the large glass cabinet that held several of Charlotte's most interesting specimens of old armor. The lighted case displayed a row of swords with unusual hilts, some gilded, some studded with semiprecious stones, and an arrangement of daggers of various sizes.

"Is that rapier new?" Hugh asked idly. "I don't remember seeing it in there last time."

"Yes. It arrived yesterday. Seventeenth century. Rather nice, don't you think?"

"If you like that kind of thing." Hugh brought his gaze back to his boss. "Charlotte, I need a favor."

"I thought you might. You don't normally come up here just to visit. What sort of favor?"

"I want to borrow some of your computer people. I need a little research done."

"On what?"

"On what might have happened on Purgatory."

"According to the one short article I saw in the newspaper the other day, the coup was crushed almost immediately."

"That's the official version, but a friend of mine says there's a rumor that someone else is in charge now. Someone working behind the scenes. I figured if I could do a little fishing in some of your data banks, I might be able to come up with a name."

"My data banks or someone else's?" Charlotte asked with arched brows. "Never mind. I don't think I want to know the answer to that. Go ahead and talk to Johnson down in Systems. He can use our computers to talk to just about any major data bank in the world. Just don't give me too many details, all right? And tell Johnson I don't want any tracks left that could lead back to Vailcourt."

Hugh grinned. "Appreciate it."

"Consider it a wedding present."

"I'll do that." Hugh stood up. "You want the rest of that bug juice?"

"No, thank you. I'm afraid you're going to have to finish it all by yourself."

"I was afraid of that." Hugh reached for the bottle and headed for the door.

"By the way, Hugh," Charlotte said behind him.

"Yeah?" He turned, one hand on the doorknob.

"How is Vailcourt's master security plan coming along?"

"Be finished with it in another couple of weeks or so at the outside."

"And then what?"

"Then, with any luck, I'll be on my way to St. Gabe with Mattie."

"I'm afraid you've still got some convincing to do in that department."

"It'll work out."

Charlotte absently tapped a gold pen on the desk. "I hope so. I honestly think she would be happy with you if she lets herself."

"Damn right," Hugh said forcefully. "I'll make her happy, Charlotte, I swear it."

"None of us can actually make someone else happy, not really. We each have to find our own happiness within ourselves. We have to work at it. It takes courage."

"She's got guts." Hugh said. "She'll be all right. She just needs a little time to get used to the idea of being with me on a permanent basis."

"I hope you're willing to give her the time,

Hugh," Charlotte said with a meaningful look. "I hope you won't try to push her too fast. You do tend to operate rather quickly, you know."

"Well, I can't hang around here forever. I've got a business to run and a house to build. And I'm not getting any younger."

"You really think she's just going to toss it all away for you, don't you? Her business, her lifestyle, her friends. Isn't that somewhat arrogant on your part, Hugh?"

He scowled. "I'll take care of her."

"She doesn't need to be taken care of. She's perfectly capable of taking care of herself. Lord knows, she's had to do it for years. No one in the family knew how to take care of her. She wasn't like the rest of them. Her needs were different. Her talents were different. No one knew quite what to do with her when they found out she wasn't going to fall into the same mold as the rest of them."

"You seem to understand her."

Charlotte smiled. "Probably because I left the artistic world many years ago and went into the business world. When I found myself at the reins of Vailcourt, I learned a great deal about an area of life I had previously ignored. The experience has taught me to recognize and respect people such as you and Mattie. You're both entrepreneurs at heart. You both are inclined to take risks."

"You think Mattie is a risk taker?"

"Certainly, although she doesn't think of herself that way. She takes risks frequently. She took a major one when she started Sharpe Reaction. Ariel and the rest of the family had a fit because she went for the commercial market. They didn't support her at all and believe me, in the beginning it would have helped a great deal if she had been allowed to hang some of her mother's work or a few of Ariel's paintings."

"They didn't want her to succeed."

"No, not because they didn't love her. They simply didn't approve of what she was doing. The Sharpe clan is very elitist when it comes to art."

"Except for you."

Charlotte smiled. "As I said, running Vailcourt has broadened my horizons. But my point about Mattie is that she is quite capable of taking risks. Heaven knows she does it every time she discovers a previously unknown artist and features his work in her gallery. Her reputation rides on the quality of the artists she hangs, you know. She can't afford to make many mistakes. And like any good businesswoman she makes it a practice to learn from her mistakes."

Hugh got the point. He felt himself turning a dull red. "She didn't make a mistake with me. It was just a case of bad timing. Sooner or later she'll get that through her head."

Charlotte considered that. "I suppose it's a good sign that she's starting to get very curious about your past. We talked about it while we had our massage this morning, you know. She had a lot of questions."

"Shit." Hugh felt his insides tighten. "My past has nothing to do with my present or my future. I've told Mattie that. She doesn't need to know anything more than she already does."

"Women, especially women who have learned

from experience to be prudent when it comes to men, sometimes take a slightly different view."

"Shit," Hugh said again as he went through the door and slammed it behind himself.

"Enjoy you bug juice," Charlotte called after him.

"What do you think about putting the lagoon series on the right-hand wall and the paintings of the town itself on the left-hand wall?" Mattie stood in the center of her gallery, studying the blank white walls. She'd been puzzling over Silk Taggert's work all afternoon. She had deliberately waited until after closing time to hang the paintings in order to create an air of expectation and curiosity in the local art community. She wanted to surprise everyone. She had all the placements carefully planned out and all she had to do was hang the work in its prepared locations. But time was getting short and she was in a hurry.

It was proving difficult to concentrate on the design of the display, however, because her sister was pacing furiously up and down the room. Ariel's fluttering black skirts and voluminous black silk top made her look like an exotic black butterfly as she flitted from one end of the gallery to the other.

Mattie automatically glanced down at the tailored little navy blue suit, white blouse, gold chain necklace, and black pumps she, herself, was wearing and felt like a moth rather than a butterfly. She wished the suit were red instead of navy blue. Thoughts of the daring little red sarong that she had brought back with her from the islands danced in her head. It was neatly tucked away in the darkest corner of her closet.

"Will you stop blathering on and on about those paintings? I'm trying to talk to you about something important," Ariel waved her hands in a graceful gesture of total frustration, whirled, and strode back the other way.

"These paintings are important. Right now they're more important than anything you've got to say to me, Ariel. You know I've got an opening scheduled for tonight." Mattie bent over the stack of pictures leaning against the wall. She had just finished uncrating them and was anxious to see how they would look on the walls of her gallery.

"Another opening for another one of your boring artists who paints pretty little pictures for people who like *nice* art?"

Mattie was incensed on Silk's behalf. "There is nothing boring about Silk Taggert or his pictures." She picked two at random out of the stack and put them up on the wall. "Take a look at these, Ariel. Take a good look, damn it, and tell me they're boring."

Ariel heaved a dramatic sigh and swept the pictures with a single cursory glance. One was an oddly disturbing harbor scene, the other a painting of the jungle that caught both a sense of primitive menace and the feeling of abundant life.

"Island landscapes? Give me a break, Mattie.

That's the sort of thing hotel chains hang in the rooms. You can buy them by the dozen anywhere. They all look alike. I'm sure *your* clients will love them, of course. They're only one step beyond putting posters on their walls, anyway. This stuff will probably look like great art to them."

"Ariel, you are elitist and self-centered and you've got a really bad case of tunnel vision when it comes to art. What is it with you? You think the only good art is the kind that does nothing more than express the artist's personal neurosis? I've got news for you, you and your kind wouldn't have survived in business for more than five minutes during the Renaissance."

Ariel, not surprisingly, looked taken aback at the unexpected attack. It was axiomatic in the Sharpe family that Mattie did not disagree on matters of artistic taste with the other members of her clan. It was understood she did not have a proper grasp of the subject.

"For heaven's sake, Mattie, there's no need to get all worked up about it. Besides, I want to talk to you about something else entirely."

But Mattie was all worked up. It felt good to be arguing with Ariel. Odd how she found herself doing it more and more frequently of late. Ever since she had come back from the islands, in fact.

"You know something?" Mattie snapped. "Back in the good old days people understood what art was supposed to do. It was supposed to appeal to them. It was supposed to speak to them, not just to the artist. It was supposed to mean something important, something universal. It was supposed to be beautiful. And it was supposed to represent certain ideals and values and hopes and dreams."

"Really, Mattie, I think this has gone far enough."

"Back then people knew good art when they saw it, and that's what they bought. Artists created work to please the customer, and you can't deny that some of the greatest art in the world was produced under those conditions. Nowadays you elitist insiders in the art world are trying to tell the customer what he's supposed to like, and you've managed to cow a lot of them into buying what you tell them is good art. But my customers are different. They're buying what they really want to buy, stuff they enjoy hanging in their homes."

"Mattie, this is crazy. I don't want to discuss the art establishment with you."

"Take a close look at Silk Taggert's paintings and tell me they're bad art!" Mattie yelled.

"Mattie, for heaven's sake, keep your voice down," Ariel hissed.

"Why should I? It feels good to yell at you. I think I'm releasing a great deal of stress this way. Years of it, in fact. Look at Silk's pictures, damn it."

"All right, all right, I'm looking at them. Get a grip on yourself, will you? It's not like you to be so . . . so emotional." Ariel turned to study the paintings. She peered at them for two or three long minutes. Her eyes narrowed thoughtfully.

"Well?" Mattie challenged. "Are you going to call them boring?"

"No," Ariel admitted reluctantly. "They're not boring. This guy has talent, I'll grant you that."

"A lot of talent."

"Okay, okay. A lot of talent. Too bad he's wasting it on pretty seascapes and landscapes."

"The fact that he's using familiar subjects is what makes his work so accessible. Can't you understand that? It makes the pictures work on several different levels. The appeal ranges from the physically attractive to the mentally stimulating. People, real people, like art that does all that. And I'll tell you something else, Ariel. This is just the sort of appeal Flynn would have if he tried doing more realistic art."

Ariel whirled on her, raw fury in her eyes. "Don't you dare try to seduce Flynn into doing this kind of thing for you. Do you hear me? Don't you dare."

Mattie groaned, her anger evaporating. "Forget it. Look, Ariel, I've really got a lot of work to do here before the show. If you don't mind, I'd like to get to it."

Ariel hesitated. "Here, I'll give you a hand I think you're right about grouping the pictures by subject. I'll handle the jungle scenes."

Mattie stared at her in astonishment. "Thank you."

"Don't look so amazed. I'm not a bitch goddess all the time, you know I told you I want to talk to you, and this looks like the only way I'm going to be able to do it."

"I was afraid there was an ulterior motive." Mattie centered a painting of the harbor and stepped back to eye it. "Let's get on with it. What do you want to lecture me about?"

"I want to know what you think you're doing

getting engaged to Hugh Abbott." Ariel hung a jungle scene. "How did it happen, Mattie?"

"It's a bit difficult to explain. I'm not quite certain how it happened, myself. And I'm not sure I'm engaged. That's Hugh's interpretation of the situation, not mine. I haven't made up my mind yet."

"Oh, Mattie, be honest. The man's living with you. He's telling everyone he's going to marry you. Did you have to go this far just to prove you can have what I once had?"

"I didn't do it to prove anything."

"Yes, you did. You've always envied me. My talent, my success, my men, my looks. Everything."

"That's not true. Oh, sure, maybe when we were kids. But that was a long time ago. People grow up, Ariel."

"Is that right? Then how come the one man you finally decide to get serious about is one of my exes? An ex-fiancé, in this case. Don't you think that's too much of a coincidence? Why choose that particular male? Tell me, Mattie. Go on and admit the truth."

"I didn't choose him. At least, not this time around. He chose me." Mattie stalked back into her office to look for some tools.

Ariel followed, sweeping through the doorway behind her. "He chose you? What's that supposed to mean?"

"Ask Hugh. He's the one who insisted on getting engaged. I've been deliberately avoiding him for a year. He set things up for us to meet out on Purgatory, not me. Whatever happens doesn't concern you."

"Doesn't concern me? He's my ex-fiancé, damn it."

"So what?" Mattie snapped. "You threw him back, remember? You didn't want him."

"And neither should you. Mattie, listen to me. I'm saying this for your own good. He's all wrong for you. Trust me. I know him. If you must have one of my men, take Emery. At least he's genuinely fond of you."

"Thanks a lot."

"Okay, so he's much too old for you and his career is on the skids, but he knows your world and the people in it. You can talk to him about things like art and wine and books. He'll respect your career. He won't try to drag you off to some godforsaken island and expect you to sit around under a palm tree and shell coconuts."

"I'm not interested in marrying Emery, thank you very much. And I don't plan to sit around twiddling my thumbs under any palm trees."

"What else can you do out there in the middle of nowhere? Or do you have some illusion about changing Hugh? If so, you're in for a rude awakening. I should know. I thought I could civilize him, too. But I was wrong. And if he wouldn't change to please me, what makes you think he'll change to suit you?"

Mattie sorted through a toolbox until she found a screwdriver. Clutching it tightly she turned back to face her sister. "Excuse me, Ariel. I still have a lot of paintings to hang."

Ariel's face softened. "Oh, Mattie, I'm sorry if

I hurt your feelings. I'm doing this for your own good, I swear it. I am speaking to you now as your older sister. For a while I was sure I could convince Hugh to see reason and move back to the States. But I soon found out the truth. He won't leave that damned island of his for any woman."

"Get out of my way, Ariel. I've got work to do."

"Mattie, you don't want to marry him. The man is a throwback. He belongs in the Middle Ages or something. His attitude toward women and marriage is several hundred years out of date. Oh, I know the macho approach in bed is kind of interesting at first, but you'll get tired of it, believe me."

Mattie felt herself turning a fiery shade of red. "You may be my sister, Ariel, but I don't have to discuss my love life with you."

"Why not?" Ariel snapped, exasperated. "Just think of the sisterly confidences we can share now that we've both slept with the same man. Let's be blunt about this. I know for a fact he's not that good."

"Shut up, Ariel." The anger was rising once more.

"It's true. Mattie, I'm warning you, that slam-bam-thank-you-ma'am approach gets old real fast."

"*I said, shut up Ariel.* I don't want to hear another word."

"Hugh is not the man for you. He wasn't the man for me. As far as I can tell, he's not the right man for any modern woman. He's an outdated, inconsiderate, insensitive clod. Mattie, Listen to me. We're talking about your whole future here."

"All right. You want me to say it? That I'm scared? That I'm not real sure what I'm doing? Okay, I'm scared. I'll admit it. I don't know what—"

The small, crackling sound of a paper bag being opened drew Mattie's startled attention to the doorway behind her sister. Hugh lounged there, one shoulder propped against the frame. He was fiddling with a sack from the Thai take-out restaurant around the corner. He looked up from a perusal of the contents of the bag as a sudden silence fell on the office.

"Hey, don't let me interrupt," he said calmly, withdrawing a small carton from the sack. "I just stopped by with some dinner for Mattie. Figured she needed something to fortify her energies before the big opening."

"My God," Ariel breathed. "Look at you. So damned cool. So disgustingly sure of yourself. How could you be such a complete and utter bastard. Hugh Abbott? How could you?"

"Well," Hugh began, looking thoughtful, "it's not easy, I can tell you that."

"Oh, shut up." Ariel brushed past him, black silks streaming behind her.

A moment later the outer door opened and closed with a reverberating slam.

Silence descended again on the small office.

Hugh eyed the viselike grip Mattie had on the screwdriver. "Tell you what. If you put that down slowly and carefully on the desk, I'll serve dinner."

Mattie realized she was trembling. She dropped the screwdriver onto the desk, went around to the back, and sank abruptly into her chair. Her knees felt weak.

In numb silence she watched Hugh lay out a meal that featured noodles and vegetables in a spicy peanut sauce.

"Eat up," Hugh said as he spread a napkin across her lap and pushed a paper plate full of noodles in front of her. "When we're finished I'll help you hang the rest of Silk's pictures."

"Thank you." Mattie stared blindly down at the noodles.

"Think nothing of it. Even us outdated, inconsiderate, insensitive clods have our uses."

Mattie continued to stare at the noodles.

Hugh started to eat his. He munched in silence for a full minute, and then he arched a single, inquiring brow. "Slam-bam-thank-you-ma'am?"

Mattie blinked and at last picked up her chopsticks. "It's not that bad."

"Thank you," Hugh said with great humility. "I do try, you know. And I'm willing to study hard and learn. I'm a fast learner."

And suddenly Mattie couldn't help herself. She thought of his intense, highly erotic, incredibly sexy brand of lovemaking, and she started to giggle. The giggle mushroomed into laughter, and a moment later she was convulsed with it. Hugh watched in quiet amusement, looking obliquely satisfied.

It was only later that she realized that the laughter had been as effective at reducing her stress level as venting her anger had been earlier.

And it was Hugh who had somehow given her the gift of both kinds of freedom.

The Silk Taggert show was a huge success. Hugh spent most of it leaning negligently against one wall, a glass of champagne in his hand, and wishing his friend could see what was happening. Silk would have gotten a kick out of all these sophisticated, trendy people going crazy over his work. Hugh made a note to try to remember as many of the comments he had overheard this evening as possible.

"... *It leaves me with the strangest sense of longing ... I can't wait to get that lagoon scene on my wall ... Such spectacular colors, real colors ... What a change from all the gray and brown and black you see so much of in Seattle galleries these days ... So bold and vibrant ... A nice change. I get so tired of subtlety ... That jungle feels alive ... Dangerous but beautiful ... Captures the power of nature ...*"

Mattie was everywhere, looking very business-like in a proper little suit, her hair neatly coiled at the nape of her neck. She was mingling with the crowd, chatting with potential buyers, and turning a blind eye to the serious inroads a few apparently starving artists were making at the buffet table. She had told Hugh earlier she considered the free food eaten by artistic moochers at these events as a contribution to the arts.

"This stuff isn't bad," a young woman with chartreuse hair and a lot of metal hanging from her clothing announced to Hugh.

He looked at her. "You mean the art?"

"Nah. The food. The art's good, but the food

is really terrific, isn't it? Mattie always puts on a first-class feast. She's not stingy like some of the gallery owners." The young woman squinted up at Hugh. "Who are you? The artist?"

"No. A friend of his. He couldn't be here."

"Too bad. It must be nice to watch people going nuts over your work. I'd give anything to have them go apeshit like this over my stuff."

"What sort of stuff do you do?"

"Metal sculpture. The name's Shock Value. Shock Value Frederickson. But I'm thinking of changing it. It doesn't go with my new direction, you know?"

"Yeah?"

"My work is getting more refined." Shock Value explained patiently. "Things are just flowing for me now, thanks to Mattie, and the flow is changing everything."

"Mattie? How the hell is she involved?"

"She's sort of like one of those old-fashioned patrons, you know? She's keeping me in groceries while I work on my latest project. One of these days I'll pay her back."

"Uh-huh. How much has she loaned you?"

"I don't remember exactly." Shock Value said carelessly. "Wow, there's a friend of mine. Haven't seen him since he broke his ankle doing some performance art in the park last month. Nice talking to you, whatever your name is. See you around."

A long time later Hugh watched Mattie carefully lock the door of Sharpe Reaction. She looked quietly elated.

"Went well, huh?" Hugh took her arm to walk down the sidewalk to her apartment.

"Very well. I sold everything I had. I hope Silk will be pleased."

"Yeah. He'll be as excited as a little kid at Christmas. He's never had any real success before. Not in anything. I can't wait to tell him." Hugh was silent for a while, thinking. "You're really good at that kind of thing, aren't you?"

"What kind of thing?"

"Handling that crowd of potential buyers tonight. Showing Silk's work. Running your gallery. The whole bit."

"It's what I do for a living," she said quietly.

"Yeah."

"What's wrong, Hugh?"

"Nothing."

"Are you sure?"

"Watching you this evening just made me think about some things, that's all," he muttered, wishing he'd never opened his mouth.

"Like what?"

"Never mind." But the truth was, he was definitely beginning to worry. Mattie was very much at home in this world. She was successful in it. She had friends here. She was a part of the art community.

Tonight he had seen just how well she moved in this environment, and the realization haunted him. Until now he had been telling himself that she would adapt easily enough to St. Gabe when the time came, but now he was beginning to wonder if the time would ever come.

He had been so blithely certain that once he had

convinced Mattie she was not just a stand-in for Ariel that she would give up everything to move to St. Gabriel.

Now he was beginning to wonder if that would be the case. Viewed objectively, what did he really have to offer her compared to the life she had created for herself here in Seattle?

Only himself.

Silk was right. These weren't the good old days when a man could expect a woman to pull up stakes and follow him anywhere. Maybe Charlotte had a point when she called him arrogant.

"Hugh? Is something wrong?" Mattie was looking up at him with worried eyes as they came to a halt in front of the door of her apartment building.

"Nothing's wrong. Forget it, Mattie." He opened the security door, walked Mattie down the hall, and punched the elevator button in silence. Mattie continued to throw small, anxious glances in his direction, but he ignored them. He was thinking.

In fact, Hugh was concentrating so hard on the host of new worries that had arisen to confront him this evening that he almost failed to notice that the bolt on the front door of Mattie's apartment was not in position.

He, himself, had locked it earlier. He never made that kind of mistake.

Someone had opened the door tonight and failed to set the dead bolt again. Whoever it was might still be inside.

Hugh stepped back and clamped a hand over Mattie's startled mouth to prevent her from saying anything. She went very still, her eyes widening in silent question.

"Someone inside," he breathed into her ear. He took his hand away from her lips when she nodded her understanding of the situation.

Mattie mouthed a single word. "Police."

He shook his head and pulled her quietly along the corridor to the door that opened onto a utility room. He opened it, reached inside, and found the switch that operated the hall lights. When he flipped it, the hall outside Mattie's apartment was immediately plunged into darkness except for the pale glow of the emergency sign at the end of the corridor.

"Hugh?" Mattie's faint whisper was now laced with anxiety.

"Wait right here."

"What are you going to do? There might be a burglar inside. You're not supposed to confront them. You're supposed to go use a neighbor's phone and call the police."

"Give me two minutes. If I haven't got the situation under control, go ahead and call the cops."

"I'd rather you didn't—"

"Hush, babe. I'll be right back."

It was the thought that it might not be a simple thief at all that was making him do this the hard way. After all the excitement on Purgatory followed by the death of Rosey and the disappearance of Gibbs, a man had to wonder if there might, just possibly, be something besides an everyday, garden-variety burglary in process inside the apartment.

253

And if there was, Hugh wanted some answers. The opportunity was simply too good to miss.

His eyes were adjusted to the shadows now. Hugh pushed the door open and went in fast and low. He was counting on the darkness behind him to give him the cover he needed.

A picture of the layout of the big studio firmly etched in his mind, he dived behind the leather sofa and flattened himself. He glanced up at the bedroom loft first. There was no one up there. He could tell that much from the glow coming in through the high windows.

The entire room was shrouded in darkness. Whoever had invaded it earlier had turned off the light that Hugh had deliberately left on in the kitchen alcove.

Hugh was processing that piece of information when he heard someone shift on the sofa cushions. Leather squeaked softly.

Hugh rolled to his feet, vaulted over the back of the sofa, and slammed into the body on the cushions.

A man yelped in startled surprise as the wind was knocked out of him. Gasping, the intruder thrashed about like a fish on a line. His wild gyrations succeeded in causing both Hugh and his victim to slide off the sofa and onto the carpet with a dull thud.

Hugh pinned the man to the floor and then wrinkled his nose as the unmistakable odor of brandy fumes assailed his nostrils.

Whoever he was, the guy had been into Mattie's small supply of liquor.

"Hey," the intruder managed in strangled tones. "Take it easy, damn it. Let go, will you?"

The lights went on. "I've called the police," Mattie said forcefully from the open doorway. "They'll be here any minute. Hugh, are you all right?"

Hugh looked down at the man he had trapped beneath him. "Shit. You'd better cancel that call to the cops."

"Well, actually, I didn't call them," Mattie explained, moving into the room. "I haven't had a chance. I just said that in case whoever was in here got any ideas of shooting his way out. I thought he might think twice if he knew the police were on their way." She stopped abruptly, her eyes widening in shock. "Good grief. What are you doing, Hugh? That's not a burglar."

"Hi, Mattie." Flynn Grafton looked up at her from his prone position on the floor. His blond hair was spread out in a pale fan around his head and his gaze looked distinctly red and watery. "Sorry about this."

CHAPTER

Thirteen

"Good grief, it's Flynn." Mattie hurried forward, deep concern in her eyes. "For heaven's sake, let him up, Hugh. Did you hurt him? Flynn, are you okay?"

"He's fine." Hugh got to his feet, annoyed with

255

the speed with which Mattie's concern had shifted from him to Ariel's husband.

"I think I'm okay." Flynn shook his head slightly as if to clear it. He sat up slowly and blinked in the light as Mattie crouched beside him. "Christ, You landed on me like a tank, Abbott. Who did you think I was? Jack the Ripper?"

"It was a possibility. What the hell are you doing here, Grafton? How did you get inside?"

"Ariel has a key. I borrowed it." Flynn's words were slightly blurred.

"Why?" Hugh demanded roughly.

Mattie scowled at him. "Stop badgering Flynn. Can't you see he's still trying to recover from your assault? I hope there's no serious damage. That sort of trauma can cause all kinds of stress-related injuries from back problems to headaches. You definitely overreacted, Hugh."

"I overreacted?" Hugh stared at her in disbelief. "The guy sneaks into your apartment, drinks your booze, and sacks out on your couch waiting for you to come home, leaves all the earmarks of a burglary in progress and you call it an overreaction when I jump him?"

"Thank heavens you weren't carrying your gun. This is exactly how accidental shootings occur."

Hugh looked up toward the ceiling for inspiration and patience. "Give me a break. I've never accidentally shot anyone in my life. That kind of thing I tend to do on purpose."

"Calm down, Hugh," Mattie said, her voice soothing. "I realize you're still a little wired from the adrenaline, but there's no need to get short-tempered."

"Wired? Short-tempered? You haven't seen anything yet, babe."

She smiled brightly. "Why don't you make us all a nice pot of herbal tea? I have some chamomile in the kitchen. That will settle everyone's nerves."

"My nerves are just fine, thanks. I'm not real happy, but my nerves are in great shape."

"Well, perhaps Flynn would like some herbal tea," Mattie said, glancing down at the artist who was struggling to his knees.

"No," Flynn whispered, holding up a pleading hand and looking seasick. "No herbal tea. To tell you the truth, I'm feeling a little rocky at the moment. Don't want to puke all over your nice rug."

"Don't even think of getting sick in here," Hugh warned.

Mattie frowned. "Don't sound so menacing, Hugh. You're just going to make him more tense."

"This may come as a serious shock to you, Mattie, but I really don't give a damn about Grafton's stress level." He turned to Flynn, who was pulling himself up onto the couch. "Stop playing the wounded innocent and tell me what you're doing here before I really get stressed out to the max and take you over to that window, open it, and drop you onto the street."

"*Hugh.*" Mattie sent him a reproachful glance.

Hugh ignored it, his eyes on Flynn. "Let's have the explanation, Grafton."

Flynn made it to the couch and sank wearily down onto the cushions. He put his head in his hands. "I came to ask Mattie if I could spend the night."

"The hell you did. That settles it. I am going to drop you out the window. But first I'm going to do a neo-impressionistic job on that pretty face of yours." Hugh started forward.

"No, Hugh, stop. Stop this at once." Mattie threw herself into his path, holding up an imperious palm. "This isn't Purgatory or St. Gabriel, damn it. You're back in civilization now, and you will behave in a civilized fashion, do you hear me?"

"Out of my way, Mattie."

"No, I will not get out of your way. This is my home and I run things here. Now, you are not going to beat up Flynn. Is that clear? I'm sure he didn't mean what you thought he meant when he said he wanted to spend the night."

"He meant to spend the night with you. You heard him. He said so himself," Hugh snarled. "Get out of my way, Mattie."

"He just wanted to sleep on my couch, didn't you, Flynn?" Mattie turned to her uninvited guest for confirmation.

Flynn raised his head, looking baffled by the commotion. "Sure. Just wanted to sleep on the couch. Ariel and I had an argument. Came over here to see if you'd put me up, Mattie. What's the problem?"

"I don't believe this." Hugh pinned Mattie with his coldest gaze. "Does he spend the night on your couch regularly?"

"Of course not." Mattie looked anxiously at Flynn. "This is the first time he's ever asked to stay here. I take it the argument was pretty bad, Flynn?"

"Bad enough." Flynn collapsed back against the cushions, closing his eyes wearily. "I keep telling myself she's entering her Early Mature period, but I'm not so sure anymore. I know she's temperamental by nature, but lately it's been downright crazy. Her moods are all over the place."

Mattie patted him gently on the shoulder. "What did you fight about?"

"Same old thing. My painting. But this time she really went bonkers."

"Why?"

"Because I told her my mind was made up. I've got some stuff ready to show you, Mattie. I want you to tell me if you think you can sell it to your crowd of upwardly mobile Borgias and Medicis."

Mattie sank down onto the couch beside Flynn. "No wonder Ariel blew up. She's been fighting you every step of the way on this project."

"Yeah. But I've made up my mind to do it, Mattie. I can't live on her money any longer. Besides, truth is, I'm damned tired of doing art for art's sake. Hell, maybe I just want to prove my old man wrong after all these years. Maybe I want to show him that I can make a living at my art. I don't know. All I know is that I want to try putting some stuff into your gallery."

"I understand," Mattie said, still patting his shoulder.

"Look, I'm sure this is all very touching." Hugh interrupted sarcastically. "And believe me, I'm well aware of how temperamental Ariel can be. But that's no excuse for you to come here looking for a place to bed down for the night, Grafton. Nobody is spending the night in Mattie's apartment except me. Clear?"

"Now, Hugh," Mattie said, her tone soothing once more, "there's no need to run around beating your chest and defending your territory. Look at the time. It's much too late for Flynn to find somewhere else to stay. There's absolutely no reason he can't spend the night here on my couch."

"He's history," Hugh stated. "Get out of here, Grafton. Now."

Flynn nodded, his eyes bleak. "I'll call a cab."

"There's no need for that, Flynn," Mattie said firmly. She shot Hugh a defiant glance and turned back to Flynn. "Where would you go at this hour, Flynn? A hotel? It would cost a fortune, and you don't have any money, remember?"

"I've got Ariel's credit cards."

"Great idea." Hugh muttered. "Use one of your wife's credit cards to pay for a fancy suite in some big downtown hotel while you hide out from her. There's a certain poetic justice in that."

"No, I guess that wouldn't be right, would it?" Flynn straightened, looking very noble and stoic. "I'll think of something. Mattie. Don't worry about me. I'll find somewhere to spend the night. It's too late to get into any of the missions, but I can always find a doorway or something."

Mattie was aghast. "But, Flynn, you can't possibly sleep on the streets. I won't allow it."

Hugh eyed the pathetic little scene while he dug his wallet out of his jeans. "Tell you what. I'll make this even easier. I'll stake you to a night in a hotel. Grafton. It's worth it just to get you out of here."

Mattie sprang up from the couch and came toward Hugh with a determination in her gaze that made him immediately uneasy.

"Will you stop behaving like a jealous Tarzan? There is no reason Flynn can't stay here. It's past midnight. I am not sending him out at this hour."

"Then let him go home and sleep in his own bed."

"This is my apartment, he is my brother-in-law, and I say he can sleep here."

Hugh sensed defeat in the making, but he braced himself, planted his fists on his hips, and tried his most intimidating glare. "I say he goes."

"You don't have any right to make demands around here."

"Is that a fact? In case it has escaped your notice, we happen to be engaged. That gives me a few goddamned rights."

She eyed him for an icy moment and then switched tactics with dazzling speed. "Hugh, I don't want to quarrel over this. Flynn's had too much to drink, he's very depressed and under a lot of stress, and he has no money of his own. It won't hurt you to let him sleep on the couch just this once. Please?"

"Damn it, Mattie." It was not fair that a woman's pleas could break through a man's defenses so easily, Hugh told himself as he started to weaken.

A gentle snore interrupted the low-voiced argument. Hugh glanced toward the couch and saw

261

that the man he was trying to evict had gone back to sleep. Hugh knew a strategically indefensible position when he saw one. Sometimes the only good option was a carefully orchestrated retreat.

And revenge, of course. There definitely remained the pleasures to be had in exacting vengeance.

Half an hour later Hugh stretched out beside Mattie in the loft bed and pulled her into his arms. He had waited patiently while she had found a blanket to throw over Grafton, brushed her teeth, taken her evening ration of vitamins, and changed into her prim little flannel nightgown.

"Hugh, I want to thank you for backing down on this little matter of letting Flynn sleep on my couch." Mattie whispered earnestly as she snuggled close, "I know you were annoyed to find him here, and I realize that under the circumstances you had every right to react as you did. It won't happen again, I promise."

"You're right. It won't happen again." He kissed her throat, inhaling the sweet, feminine scent of her body. He was already hard with sexual anticipation, he realized. He let his hand glide down her arm.

"Hugh?"

"Yeah, babe?" He slowly pushed her proper little nightgown up over her knees and then edged it higher.

"Hugh, we can't. Not tonight." She batted ineffectually at his roving hands. "Flynn might wake up and hear us. It would be horribly embarrassing."

"Then you'll just have to try real hard to be very, very quiet, won't you?" He gently pried apart her tightly closed thighs. She was so soft, he thought. Her skin was like velvet. He smiled to himself when he felt the first small, delicious shiver go through her. He loved it when she trembled like that.

"Stop it," Mattie hissed. "You're doing this to get even with me, aren't you?"

"No way, babe. I'm doing this on account of I'm such a sweet, sensitive guy who happens to be hornier than hell." He tugged the nightgown off impatiently and tossed it over the loft railing.

Mattie gasped in horror as the gown fluttered downward. "For heaven's sake, Hugh. What will Flynn think when he sees that nightgown down there in the morning?"

"He'll think what he's supposed to think. That I'm staking out my territory."

"Well, I suppose I should be grateful you don't do it in the usual manner of wolves and other wild animals," she retorted tartly. "Really, Hugh, there's no need to be quite so primitive about all this. *Oh.*" She clapped a hand over her own mouth as she realized she had moaned aloud.

"Hush, babe, or he'll hear you. Think of the embarrassment." Hugh slid down between her legs, moving lower and lower along the delightfully curving length of her until he could taste her essence.

"Ummph, no, I said no, *oh.*" Mattie held the pillow over her face. She used one hand to hold it in place and clenched her other first quite painfully in Hugh's hair.

He used his thumbs to part her carefully, and then he used his tongue.

"*Mmmmph,*" Mattie yanked the pillow away from her face. "Oh, my God, Hugh." She slapped the pillow back in place. "*Mmmmph.* No, Oh. Hugh."

Hugh waited until she was arching frantically, her muffled moans threatening to turn into the now-familiar cries of delight that he had gotten addicted to hearing during the past several days.

When he decided Mattie was too far gone to remember to use the pillow to muffle her breathless little moans, he moved heavily back up along her soft body, spread her thighs more widely apart, and thrust himself slowly, deeply, into her wet heat.

When he yanked the pillow away from her face, she looked up at him with huge, luminous eyes. He saw her teeth were clamped on her lower lip in an effort to keep from crying out.

"Slam-bam-thank-you-ma'am?" Hugh murmured on a soft, husky laugh.

"Like I said, it's not so bad."

He grinned and covered her mouth with his own. A moment later he swallowed her soft shriek of ecstasy as she contracted tightly beneath him.

Then he quickly released her lips and buried his own face in the pillow to stifle his groan as he poured himself into her.

His own muffled shout of triumphant release made the bed vibrate.

The angry shrill of the telephone brought Mattie out of a sound sleep with a start. She flailed around in the rumpled bed until she managed to silence the offending instrument by the simple expedient of lifting the receiver in the general direction of her ear.

She regretted the action immediately. A tearful Ariel was screaming more loudly than the phone had been ringing.

"He's there with you, Mattie, isn't he? I know he is. He went to you just like all the others did. Put him on the line right now. I want to tell Flynn Grafton to his face that he will never be able to crawl back into my bed. I don't care how hard he begs."

"Good morning to you, too, Ariel. Nice of you to call." Mattie opened her eyes and gazed at the ceiling. She was alone in the bed. Down below she heard the low rumble of men's voices and the clink of a pot. The aroma of strongly brewed coffee wafted upward.

"I hope you're satisfied, Mattie." Ariel sniffed. "After all these years I hope you're finally satisfied. You've done it, haven't you? You've gotten your sneaky little claws into the only man I ever really wanted."

"Ariel, contrary to popular opinion around here, Flynn and I are not having an affair."

There was a click followed by the hollow sound on the telephone line that indicated someone had picked up the downstairs receiver.

"Oh, God, an affair," Ariel whispered, apparently unaware of the other presence on the line. "An *affair* I knew it. I was praying that it was just a one-night stand." Something done in the heat of the moment like that stupid fling you had with

Hugh last year. Something you might have at least had the decency to regret the way you regretted that. But, no. No, you're bragging about it, aren't you?"

"Ariel, you're not listening. I just told you, I am not sleeping with your husband. I have never slept with your husband. I have no desire to sleep with your husband. And he has no desire to sleep with me. He loves you."

"He went to you last night. He didn't come back home. He went straight to you. Did you comfort him, Mattie, the way you did the others? Offer him herbal tea and sympathy? Tell him you understood all the stress he was under? Damn you."

"For Christ's sake, give it a break, Ariel," Hugh ordered brusquely. "Grafton's here, all right. He slept on the couch. I should know. I'm the one who spent the night in Mattie's bed. I would have noticed a third party in the sheets, believe me, I'm fussy that way."

"Hugh? You're there, too?" Ariel's sobs halted with dramatic swiftness.

"I'm here, all right."

"You were there all night?"

"Where the hell else would I be? I'm engaged to Mattie, remember?"

"Thank God," Ariel said, switching instantly from pathetic victim to vengeful shrew. "Put Flynn on the line at once."

"My pleasure," Hugh said.

There was a brief, fumbling sound and then Flynn's voice spoke very coolly into the phone. "Ariel?"

"Flynn, how could you do this to me? I was so frightened when I woke up this morning and realized you'd never come home. Do you have any idea of what I've been through? Do you know what it was like having to call my own sister to find you? How dare you do such a thing?"

"You're the one who told me to get out and stay out, remember?" Flynn sounded vaguely preoccupied. He also sounded as if he were munching on something.

Mattie dropped the receiver back into the cradle, got out of bed, and reached for her robe. She went to the edge of the loft and looked down over the waist-high red metal railing.

The first thing she noticed was her modest nightgown. It had been tossed rather negligently, Mattie thought, over the back of the chair Hugh was occupying.

Hugh himself looked arrogantly at ease, quite the master in his own home, as he sprawled in the chair. He had a mug of coffee in his hand, and there was a plate of bran muffins on the low table in front of the couch. He had not bothered to put on anything except a pair of jeans, Mattie realized. His bare feet were propped on the coffee table, and his bare shoulders gleamed in the morning sunlight.

Flynn, rumpled from a night in his clothes, was eating one of the bran muffins as he listened to Ariel's tirade.

"I hear you, Ariel," he said calmly. "Ease up, honey. You've made your point."

Flynn took another bite of muffin and wrinkled his nose while he listened to Ariel's response.

"What was I supposed to do after you locked the door? Stand out in the hall and beg?" he finally asked.

More munching while Flynn listened.

"No," he finally said during a pause. "Nothing's changed. I know you don't like it, but I've done a lot of thinking about this and my mind is made up. I'm going to ask Mattie to hang my more commercial stuff and that's final." Flynn finished the muffin and picked up his mug of coffee. "Ariel, I may be the greatest undiscovered artist who ever lived, but I'm also your husband. With any luck, one of these days I'll be a father. I've got some pride, okay? I want to carry my own weight in this family. Maybe I'd better talk to you later when you're feeling calmer."

Flynn hung up the phone quite gently and sat hunched over his coffee. "The lady is very unhappy," he said to Hugh.

"I got that feeling," Hugh replied. "Wish I could help you out with a few tips on handling her, but the truth is, I never did understand Ariel. She and I were like oil and water. Or gasoline on a fire. Whatever."

"Yeah, I know. It's not that I can't deal with her usual moods. I understand those. They're part of what makes her a great artist. She's very sensitive and she needs to be handled delicately. But last night I just lost it, you know? Told her I was tired of feeling like a kept man. Tired of feeling like I'm standing in her shadow, making no contribution to the relationship. We really got into it. Sorry I turned up here. That was a mistake."

"I guess one time isn't going to be a problem," Hugh allowed magnanimously.

"It won't happen again," Flynn promised.

"Right." Hugh sounded satisfied.

"It's just that this was the first place I thought of when I found myself locked out. The thing is, Mattie always seems so quiet and calm and levelheaded. So sensible and unemotional. Sort of soothing."

"She has her moments," Hugh said dryly. "But she sure is a hell of a lot different than Ariel, I'll give you that. I could never get a handle on Ariel during our engagement. She was either moping around in some tragic state of depression or else she was exploding. It was a real roller-coaster ride, and it didn't help matters any that I had no patience for any of it after a couple of weeks."

Flynn nodded wisely. "Like I said, Ariel needs to be handled delicately."

"I'm not the kid-glove type."

"No. I can see why you two never made it. I take it you don't seem to have the same problem dealing with Mattie?"

"No sweat," Hugh assured him. "Sure, sometimes she gets a little feisty. You've got to watch out for that streak of pride she has. But I understand pride. I can deal with it. Given a little time I can always find a way to settle Mattie down when she occasionally gets a little temperamental."

Mattie looked around for something convenient to drop over the loft railing. She considered the tall, heavy black vase but discarded it as overkill. She picked up the glass of water she kept beside the bed instead.

"The thing about women like Mattie." Hugh was saying down below, "is that you've got to make them understand . . ."

"For the record, Hugh Abbott," Mattie called as she leaned out over the railing and tipped the full glass of water, "no lady worth her salt likes to hear first thing in the morning that she is so dreadfully dull a man can handle her with 'no sweat.' But, then, I've always said you have a lousy way with compliments. No finesse at all."

Hugh yelped very nicely and scrambled up out of the chair with amazing speed as the water splashed down over his head and bare shoulders.

Flynn looked on, amused.

"Like I said," Hugh muttered, using a napkin to wipe water off his shoulder, "she has her moments."

"I can see that." Flynn picked up another bran muffin and eyed it critically. "You really like these things?"

"You get used to them," Hugh said. "It's the herbal tea and the bug juice that are a little hard to swallow."

Mattie sat in her office chair later that morning, her hands folded on the desk, and watched her sister storm back and forth across the room. Ariel had been alternating between tears of rage and tears of self-pity for the past fifteen minutes. It was getting hard to tell the difference. But in either mood she managed to look her usual exotic self in flowing black trousers and a black blouse with billowing sleeves.

Mattie was again painfully aware of the bland,

businesslike look of her coffee-colored suit and beige blouse. Maybe it was the string of pearls that really elevated the outfit to the level of total forgettableness, she decided critically. Or perhaps it was the low-heeled pumps. She really was going to have to go shopping one of these days. The desire for a red business suit was becoming irresistible.

And maybe, if she got very adventurous, she would invest in a pair of three-inch red spike heels, just like the ones Evangeline Dangerfield had loaned her for that wild night on Brimstone.

"I'm sorry I blew up at you on the phone this morning," Ariel said, sniffing delicately into a tissue. "I can't believe I did that. Lately, it's almost like after all these years our roles have been reversed or something. For the first time. I've actually been jealous of you. It's so ludicrous."

"Simply ludicrous."

"It's irrational."

"Right. Totally irrational."

"Especially when I know there is absolutely no real reason for it," Ariel concluded.

"True," Mattie agreed.

Ariel swung around and looked at her with eyes that brimmed with sincerity. "I want you to know that I really do realize there is no basis for my irrational jealousy, Mattie. I don't understand it, but I just don't seem to be completely sane on the subject of Flynn. I've never felt this way before about any man."

"Maybe that's because you've never been afraid of losing any of your previous men. After all, none of the others have been terribly important to you."

Ariel nodded. "I guess that must be it. I really do love Flynn. What I feel for him is so different than what I felt for any of the others. He's the only one who's ever understood me. Well, that's not entirely true. Emery understood me, but it was sort of the way a mentor understands his protégée, you know? Toward the end of our relationship, he just could not handle my success at all."

"Did you understand him? What he was going through as he saw himself slipping slowly into obscurity?"

"It was hardly my fault he couldn't write anymore." Ariel retorted.

"I know, I know. Forget I said that."

Ariel nodded willingly enough. "Hugh, of course, never did understand me. Not at all. He was really just a sort of wild fling for me. I don't know how on earth I managed to get myself engaged to him."

"Probably the same way I did," Mattie observed. "By fiat. Hugh has a way of taking command."

"Yes, I know. It's very annoying, isn't it? However do you tolerate it, Mattie?"

"Sometimes I don't," Mattie said, thinking with a sense of pride of how she had won the battle over Flynn's sleeping arrangements last night. And she *had* won it, by God. She had actually made Hugh Abbott back down. Even better, she had dumped cold water on him this morning. She was definitely showing signs of genuine spirit, Mattie decided.

"Well, you're certainly welcome to him,

although I still think you're making a big mistake."

"Thank you," Mattie murmured.

"Damn. I've gone and offended you again, haven't I? And the truth is, I came here to apologize, Mattie. I made an absolute fool out of myself this morning on the phone, and I want to tell you how sorry I am for screaming at you."

Mattie felt her brows climb. Apologies for an outburst from Ariel or any other member of the family were rarer than hen's teeth. In the Sharpe clan temperamental explosions were considered normal. Nobody except Mattie ever got upset over one.

"Don't worry about it, Ariel," she said gently. "It was perfectly understandable. I'd have made the same kind of fool out of myself if I'd quarreled with Hugh and then discovered he'd spent the night at your place."

"Thank you, Mattie. That's very generous of you."

"All right, you've apologized and I've told you to forget it. You knew I would. So what do you really want from me this morning, Ariel?"

Ariel sniffed into the tissue again. "You think you know me so well, don't you?"

"Well, I have known you all my life." Mattie reminded her, smiling.

"You've really had to put up with a lot from me over the years, haven't you?"

"It wasn't that bad." Mattie said, feeling a little wary now.

"Sometimes when we were growing up I'd feel guilty about it, even though I knew I had no reason to feel that way, of course. I mean, it wasn't my fault I inherited talent and you didn't, was it?"

"Of course not."

"I used to wish you'd find something you could really excel at so I wouldn't have to feel so damned sorry for you. You worked so hard trying to prove yourself at so many things, and they were all disasters. Remember the year you determined to become a ballerina like Grandmother?"

"Don't remind me. I limped around for weeks from all that work at the barre."

Ariel smiled. "And then there was the time you were so sure you could become a great artist like Mother. You used to sit up until three in the morning practicing your drawing. You never could do a proper nude, could you?"

"Never got much past fruit," Mattie admitted. "And then there was that year in college when I was certain I was going to write, just like Dad. You don't have to remind me of that, either, Ariel, what's the point of all this?"

Ariel heaved a dramatic sigh. "It's hard to put into words. It's just that, maybe because you tried so many things and failed before you started this gallery, you learned something the rest of us never had to learn."

Mattie studied her, remembering all the depressing years of failure. "Just what is it you think I learned?"

"I don't know." Ariel waved the hand with the damp tissue in it. "How to cope with normal life or something. How to take risks, maybe. How to try and fail and then be able to accept the failure and go on to something else. None of the rest of us ever had to do that, you see. We always knew we had talent. It might have made us a bit neurotic at times; we might have had to struggle to master it or sell it, but we always knew deep down we had it. You've never had that kind of inner certainty."

"Well, I definitely floundered around for years getting my act together. I'll admit that much."

Ariel blew into the tissue. "But all that floundering made you more adaptable or something. More understanding of other people. More accepting of their little foibles and weaknesses. More approachable."

"So I'm an easy touch. What do you want from me now?"

Ariel raised her head, her eyes tragic. "I want some advice, damn it."

"Advice? You're asking me for advice?"

"Please, Mattie. Don't make me grovel. Help me, I don't know where else to turn. You seem to understand men so much better than I do. They feel comfortable around you. I've never worried about making a man feel comfortable. I've never needed to worry about it. But now I want you to give me some pointers on handling Flynn. I don't want to lose him. Mattie, I'm scared. And I'm pregnant."

CHAPTER

Fourteen

"You're pregnant?" For a long moment Mattie could think of nothing else to say. "Does Flynn know?" she finally asked.

Ariel shook her head. "No I've only just realized it myself. I haven't told him yet."

Mattie considered the matter. "Is there a problem here? Do you want a baby?"

"Yes, but Mattie, I'm scared. I told you, I'm not like you. I can't take things in my stride the way you do. I don't cope well. I stopped taking precautions because Flynn kept talking about having children and how my biological clock was running out. But now that the inevitable has happened, I don't know what to do next. I'm starting to do stupid things like fight with Flynn and accuse you of sleeping with him. I can't paint. I feel like I'm floundering. It's just awful."

"When are you going to tell Flynn?"

"Don't you understand? I'm scared to tell him. I'm scared to death that when he finds out he's going to be a father, he'll be more determined than ever to get into the commercial mainstream with his painting. I don't want him giving up his art for me, Mattie I can't let him make that kind of sacrifice."

"Because you know deep down inside that if the situation were reversed, you wouldn't do it for him?" Mattie suggested quietly.

Ariel froze, an expression of shock on her face. "Oh, Lord, you're right of course. You're absolutely right."

Mattie examined her fingernails for a long moment. They were blunt, neatly curved nails with no polish on them. "You want advice? I'll give it to you for what it's worth. From what I know about Flynn. I would say that underneath that trendy facade, he's really a decent, old-fashioned guy who needs to feel he's doing the right thing as a man. So let him do it. Tell him about the baby. Encourage him to go ahead with his more commercial style of painting. Let him know you respect him as a man, not just as an artist, and that you need him. Let him feel he's holding up his end of the marriage."

"I'm afraid he'll be seduced by success," Ariel whispered.

"What's wrong with that? What's wrong with finding out he can do stuff that will sell like hotcakes? I think it's what he really wants, Ariel, so stop trying to force him into a different mold."

"But, Mattie—"

"These days a lot of artists are beginning to be a lot more personally ambitious again. They want success in their lifetimes, not posthumously. It hasn't been fashionable to be artistically ambitious for the past hundred years or so, but things are changing. Very soon it's going to be just like the old days, the way it was before somebody got the notion that the only good art was art nobody understood."

A sound in the doorway made Mattie glance up. Shock Value Frederickson stood there, her hair tinted silver and black. She was holding a large metal object in her arms that was very nearly as large as she was.

Mattie smiled slowly. "Speaking of great art. Lord love us, Shock Value, what have you got there?"

Shock Value glanced diffidently at Ariel. "Am I interrupting anything? Suzanne out front said you weren't busy in here."

Mattie was already out of her chair, circling the desk for a better look at the metal sculpture Shock Value was holding. "You can interrupt me anytime as long as you've got something like this in your hot little hands. This is fantastic, Shock. Absolutely fantastic."

Shock Value grinned, looking enormously relieved. "I'm calling it *On the Brink*. You really like it?"

"I love it. I always knew you had talent, Shock, but this is unbelievable. Take a look at this, Ariel." Mattie took the soaring, powerfully worked metal from the artist's hands and placed it on the floor in front of her desk.

Ariel studied the piece thoughtfully. "You're right, Mattie. It's really something. Very strong stuff. You're going to display it here in Sharpe Reaction?"

"You bet I am, so that Shock gets the public exposure. But it's not for sale. As of this moment this piece is mine, all mine. Let's make a deal, Shock."

Shock Value smiled. "Mattie, you can have it for free. I owe you. A lot, I think. I don't even remember how much."

"You don't owe me this much." Mattie assured her. "If you won't put a price tag on it. I will sit down while I write up a bill of sale."

Shock Value took a seat. "I'm really sort of relieved that it's okay. I wasn't sure what I was doing. You know, I think it would be a good idea for me to get away from the city for a while. Too many distractions, you know? I think I need a change of environment. I need to go somewhere and refresh myself while I work out this new direction in my style."

Mattie glanced up from the paperwork. "You really think so?"

Shock Value nodded quickly. "I turned a corner when I started working on *Brink*. I could feel it I need to focus this new energy. I don't want to work in isolation, but I really think I have to get away from the city. Someplace quiet and sort of inspirational, if you know what I mean."

"Someplace where they don't sell colored hair gel and metal-studded leather pants?" Ariel asked with a little smile.

"I guess," Shock Value admitted. "But a nice place."

"Some place like a tropical island perhaps?" Mattie said slowly.

"Man, that'd be perfect," Shock Value said with a grin.

"You've got to come with me, Mattie. I simply don't have the guts to do this alone. Lord knows, I'm no Hemingway." Emery Blackwell slumped dejectedly in the chair in Mattie's office. "You got

279

me into this, and you simply cannot abandon me now in my hour of need."

"Of course I'll come with you," Mattie assured him. "I can't wait to see it. Just give me a minute to finish off this paperwork. I'm right in the middle of something. Would you like a cup of herbal tea or something to calm your nerves?"

"A shot of whiskey, maybe, not tea."

The door of Mattie's office opened, and Hugh took one step into the room before he spotted Emery. He scowled. "Why is it I can't go anywhere these days without tripping over you or Grafton, Blackwell? The two of you are getting to be damned nuisances."

Emery looked up with lofty disdain. "If my presence offends you, Abbott, feel free to take yourself off elsewhere. You're not needed around here at the moment, as it happens. Mattie and I have an appointment in a few minutes."

"The hell you do." But Hugh's voice contained more resignation than heat.

He sauntered over to the desk, tipped Mattie's face up, and kissed her ruthlessly. It was a kiss of possession, rather than passion. The kind of kiss a man uses when he's drawing lines and issuing challenges in front of another man. The woman's response was not particularly important. It was the impact on the other male that counted.

Mattie smiled frostily. "You've made your point."

"Dear me," Emery murmured. "However, do you tolerate all that dreadful machismo, Mattie? Ariel could only put up with it for a few weeks."

"Most of the time it can be ignored," Mattie explained cheerfully.

Hugh growled with mock menace. He lounged against Mattie's desk and folded his arms across his chest. "All right, let's have it. What are you two up to this afternoon?"

"We are proposing to walk all of two blocks down the street to the bookstore," Emery informed him. "I do hope that doesn't offend your hopelessly antiquated sense of male territoriality."

"Heck, no," Hugh said. "I'll go with you, sport that I am."

"Shouldn't you be working?" Emery suggested pointedly.

"Took the afternoon off. I get to do that, you know. I have this really important, fancy, executive-level job that lets me do that."

"How odd," Emery murmured.

Mattie leaned back in her chair. "There's no need to go with us. Hugh, Emery and I will only be gone a few minutes."

"No sweat, babe. I've got nothing better planned. And I wouldn't mind hitting a good bookstore."

"Oh, do you read?" Emery asked.

"Without even moving my lips on my good days," Hugh assured him.

"Congratulations. Quite an accomplishment for a man of your rather peculiar abilities."

"Gentlemen." Mattie interrupted forcefully, "I would appreciate it if you would do your sniping outside of this office and away from me. If you cannot be civil to each other, please leave. Otherwise, you will both shut up while I finish

281

this paperwork and then we will all go together to the bookstore."

"Sure," said Hugh. "By the way, just why are we making this trek as one big, happy family, anyway?"

"We are going to look at the first book in Emery's new mystery series. It arrived in the shop yesterday, and they got it out on the shelves this morning."

"How do you know?"

"I called." Emery said coldly. "Anonymously of course."

Hugh grinned. "Of course. I'll bet you've been calling anonymously for the past couple of weeks, right?"

Emery sighed. "Really, Mattie. What do you see in him?"

"It's kind of hard to explain sometimes," Mattie admitted.

"Don't start," Hugh warned.

"She tells me you're claiming this is a more or less permanent move to Seattle," Emery murmured, crossing his legs and adjusting the crease in his trousers. "Personally, I think you're lying through your teeth."

"Is that right?"

Mattie looked up uneasily as she heard Hugh's voice go cold.

"Yes," Emery said, "that's right. You're just playing games, aren't you, Abbott? I'll wager you're just biding your time, secretly planning to sweep Mattie off to that godforsaken little hellhole of an island you call home."

"What if I am?" Hugh drawled. "Would you have any objections?"

"As a matter of fact, I would. Mattie's a civilized woman and deserves civilized surroundings. She will make her own decisions, naturally, but let me make something perfectly clear, Abbott."

"And what would that be?" Hugh asked, voice dropping another ten degrees below zero.

"Mattie is a friend of mine. If it should come to my attention that you are not treating her well or if you fail to make her happy, you will hear from me. Is that understood?"

"What'll it be, Blackwell? Pistols at dawn?"

Mattie got to her feet, outraged. "Stop it, both of you. Stop it at once, do you hear me?"

Emery rose majestically. "Just watch your step, Abbott. You may be a few years younger than I, but that only means I've had that much longer to get meaner and craftier." He turned to Mattie. "Are you ready to go, my dear?"

"Well, I'm not sure." Mattie eyed both men consideringly. "This is a totally new experience for me, you realize. I've never had two men fighting over me. I'm having so much fun listening to the two of you snarl and growl and snap that I hate to see the entertainment end."

"Don't worry," Hugh said as he took her arm and started toward the door. "It's not likely to stop just because we're out in public."

"Actually," Mattie said, "that's what I'm afraid of. I do have a reputation in this neighborhood, you know. I'm the quiet Sharpe. I don't take part in public scenes."

Emery smiled grandly, "I assure you, Mattie.

283

I, for one, will not embarrass you. I cannot speak for your hellhound here, however, I leave it to you to control him."

"Relax, babe," Hugh said. "I promise not to rip Emery's head off his shoulders while we're inside the bookstore."

"I suppose I'll have to be satisfied with that much. Let's go." Mattie led the way out the door and through the gallery. She waved casually to her assistant as the trio went past the front desk. "We'll be back in a few minutes, Suzanne."

"Sure thing, boss," Suzanne answered with a wave.

St. Cyr's Axiom was sitting face out on the new-books shelf in the mystery section of the large bookstore. Right where it was supposed to be. It even had a neatly lettered sign under it advising browsers that this was a work by a local author.

Mattie took one look at the evocative cover with its subtle, sexy, menacing appeal and hugged Emery.

"It's gorgeous!" she exclaimed. She released Emery and stood back to admire the book from all angles. "Absolutely beautiful. It's going to sell like crazy."

"Why should it? Nobody's ever heard of the author." Emery examined his pseudonym on the book and shook his head. "Just one more new mystery in an already overcrowded genre."

"The cover will sell it," Mattie assured him. "And once the average browser reads the first page, he'll be hooked. Here, I'll show you. We'll run a little experiment." She plucked a copy of

St. Cyr's Axiom from the stack and handed it to Hugh.

"What am I supposed to do with this?" Hugh demanded, examining the cover.

"You get to volunteer as our average bookstore browser for this on-the-spot consumer test. Read the first page."

"Without moving your lips," Emery added.

Hugh looked at Mattie. "Do I have to do this?"

"Yes, you do. Get busy."

With a great show of reluctance. Hugh opened the book and scanned the first paragraph of *St. Cyr's Axiom*. Then he went on to the second and third paragraphs.

Mattie grinned as he started to turn the page. "That's far enough. It proves my point." She snatched the book out of Hugh's hand. "See what I mean, Emery? If even Hugh couldn't resist turning the page, nobody will be able to resist."

Emery turned a most unusual shade of red "I am deeply flattered, Abbott."

"No big deal," Hugh muttered. "I was just going to finish the sentence, that's all."

"Buy a copy of your own if you want to finish it." Mattie put the book back on the stack. "Well, I've got to get back to work. Emery, your new career is launched. Congratulations."

"St. Cyr is never going to win any Pulitzers," Emery said.

"Who cares? It's going to sell, and that's even better than winning prizes."

Emery finally permitted himself a small, rueful smile. "How can you be so damn sure of yourself when it comes to second-guessing the market-place, Mattie, my love?"

"It's a knack," Mattie told him. "Hugh, stop trying to sneak a peek at the second page of Emery's book. Buy it and be done with it. I'll bet Emery will autograph it for you if you ask him nicely, won't you, Emery?"

"Certainly," Emery said.

Hugh took the copy of *St. Cyr's Axiom* over to the counter, "Forget the autograph."

Emery sighed. "Mattie, love, it does worry me so to see you engaged to a man of such astonishingly limited social polish. You really do deserve better, my dear."

"I know, but at my age a woman can't afford to be too picky," Mattie said with a daring grin. It occurred to her that teasing Hugh could be rather amusing at times.

Hugh ignored them both as he paid for the book.

The trio returned to Sharpe Reaction in thoughtful silence. At the door of the gallery Emery came to a halt and looked down at Mattie with deep affection.

"Mattie, my love, I owe you more than I can say, and I am only just beginning to realize it. Do you know, I must confess it really was something of a thrill to see all those copies of *St. Cyr's Axiom* stacked up in that bookstore. Much better distribution than I ever get with any of my important literary stuff."

"Just wait until the paperback edition comes out and you see it sitting on a rack at a supermarket checkout stand right next to the tabloids and flashlight batteries," she advised with a chuckle. "Then you'll know you've really arrived."

Emery laughed and kissed her forehead, "Who would have guessed? Life takes odd turns now and again, doesn't it?"

"It certainly does."

"Well, I suppose that's what keeps it interesting." He arched a laconic brow at Hugh, who was watching the little scene with an irritated expression. "I wish you the best of luck with your odd turn, Mattie. But watch him closely. I wouldn't trust him any farther than I could throw him, if I were you. He has plans to carry you off, my dear. Mark my words."

There was a short, charged silence between Mattie and Hugh as they watched Emery walk away down the sidewalk.

"Do you?" Mattie finally asked quietly.

"Do I what?" Hugh's narrowed gaze was still on Emery's back.

"Have plans to carry me off, or are you really going to settle down here permanently in Seattle?"

"You still don't trust me, do you, babe?"

"Hugh, I'd trust you with my life. In fact, I have on a couple of recent occasions."

"But not with your heart?"

"I'm thinking about it."

"You do that, babe," he said as he pulled her close and kissed her full on the mouth. "You think about it real hard. Because one way or another this is going to work."

Hugh removed a massive pile of computer print-outs from the one visitor's chair in Johnson's office and sat down. The intense young man in horn-rimmed glasses, running shoes, polyester slacks, and an unpressed white shirt looked up warily.

"I told you I'd call if I got anything. Mr. Abbott."

"I happened to be going by your office, so I thought I'd just drop in and check on the progress." Hugh lied. The Vailcourt computer facilities were located several floors below management and were definitely not on his way to anywhere. "You told me yesterday you'd verified that there's a new presence on the political scene on Purgatory. I wanted to see if you'd come up with a name or some background yet."

Johnson sighed, took off his glasses and rubbed the bridge of his nose. "Nothing yet, I told you I'd call. Scout's honor, Mr. Abbott. I know this is important to you."

"Real important."

"I get the picture. Look, all I can tell you at this time is that the situation has changed slightly on Purgatory, but no one really knows how yet. Nor does anyone seem to care. I've given you everything I've been able to dig out of two or three fairly good intelligence data bases. There just isn't much available. Mostly because the situation on that dipshit little island is not of great interest to anyone."

"Except me."

"Yes. You." Johnson picked up a pen and tapped it impatiently on the desk. "I'll call when I get something."

"Any time. Night or day." Hugh got to his feet.

"Right. Night or day," Johnson agreed wearily.

Hugh paused at the door. "You actually went into two or three government data bases? *Intelligence* data bases? Just like that?"

"Just like that. It's my job, Mr. Abbott."

Hugh nodded, impressed. "You know, I could have used you in the old days. You and that computer of yours would have been worth your weight in gold."

"Really? What sort of work did you do in the old days?"

"Nothing very important. Call me. Soon."

Johnson called at five-thirty that afternoon, just as Hugh was getting ready to walk out the door of his office. The two secretaries had already left, so Hugh reached for the phone himself when it rang.

"Mr. Abbott? This is Johnson down in Systems. I think I may have a little more information for you. Some of it's just coming in now, and there may be more later. It's not much, but it could be something."

"I'll be right down." Hugh hung up and dialed Mattie's gallery. She answered on the third ring. "It's me, babe. Listen, I'm going to be a little late getting home. There's some info on Purgatory coming in on one of the computers downstairs."

"All right. How late will you be?" she asked sounding distracted. He heard voices in the background and realized she was probably with clients.

"Don't know. Be there when I get there."

"Be careful on the way home," she said automatically. "It'll be dark. First Avenue can be rough in the evenings."

Hugh allowed himself to wallow briefly in the luxury of having someone worry about him.

"Sure, babe, I'll be careful. See you later." He tossed the phone back into its cradle and headed for the elevators.

Mattie could feel the walls closing in.

"Knees up high and *kick*. And *kick*. And *kick*."

The heavy throb of rock music combined with the thundering herd of aerobic dancers to make the wooden gym floor shudder. Mattie kicked out as hard as she could, skipped, turned, and joined the herd as it pounded to the far end of the room.

Her grandmother the ballerina would be turning over in her grave. Mattie sent up a silent apology as she always did during aerobics class and then kicked out even more wildly, skipped, turned, and thundered back down to the other end of the room. Technique and grace were not big factors in this kind of thing. Grandmother had always been a fanatic about technique and grace. Mattie could still hear her lecturing the little girl at the barre during that period when Mattie had determined to follow in grandmother's footsteps.

What a mistake that had been. Another wrong direction.

Electric guitars screaming in her ears, Mattie whipped around in a frenzied movement. She had her heart rate up good and high now. The sweat was dampening the thin, supple fabric of her leotard.

The decision to go to the after-work aerobics class at her health club had been an impulse that had struck right after Hugh had announced he would be late getting back to the apartment. Mattie had missed her regular noon-hour class, and she always did some form of aerobics three or four days a week. She could practically feel the stress levels sink after thirty or forty minutes of strenuous dancing.

"Grapevine!" the instructor yelled out over the pounding music. "And kick . . . two, three, four, and grapevine, two . . . three . . . four . . ."

Mattie kicked vigorously, aware that she had a great deal of stress to work off. The tension was building daily. The sense of pressure had been mounting. She could feel it, a palpable field of energy pressing on her as surely as claustrophobia.

She knew that sooner or later she was going to have to make a decision. Emery and Ariel and Aunt Charlotte were all probably right about Hugh. He wasn't planning to stay in Seattle permanently. He was playing a waiting game, and he was not a patient man.

One of these days he would come home from work and announce that he had given her enough time to get used to the idea of trusting him. He would tell her he was leaving for St. Gabriel on the six o'clock plane the next morning.

And she would have to make her decision.

The walls were definitely closing in on her.

"And up and out and up and out and up . . ."

She was not ready to take the risk a second time. She would not be a stand-in for Ariel.

"Reach and pull. Reach and pull. Move it, people. Reach and pull . . ."

Hugh had claimed he would stay here in Seattle as long as necessary. But Mattie knew better. She could feel him getting restless. The last three mornings she had awakened to find him already awake beside her, gazing out at the dawn. She had known instinctively that he was thinking about his island and Abbott Charters and his dream home.

"Slide and skip, two . . . three . . . four. Slide and skip, two . . . three . . . four . . ."

Aunt Charlotte was right. Hugh was not meant to live in the city. He had started to build a dream for himself out in the islands, and now, half-finished, it called to him. Mattie tried to tell herself that her dreams were right here in Seattle, but a part of her denied it.

". . . And two, three, four, and slide, turn, kick . . . and two, three . . ."

A part of her knew that her dreams were forever linked to Hugh's.

So she would have to make a decision.

Mattie wondered how much time she had left. The walls were definitely closing in.

Half an hour later, showered and changed back into the well-tailored pin-striped suit she had worn to the office that day. Mattie left the health club and started the five-block walk to her apartment. It was dark and a light rain was beginning to fall. Hugh was going to get wet on the way home tonight. He never remembered to take an umbrella with him to the office.

Mattie had just unfurled the umbrella she always carried with her in her briefcase when she heard the footsteps behind her.

Footsteps on a city street were hardly unusual, but there was something about the pace of these particular footsteps that sent a flicker of anxiety down her spine. A woman who lived alone in the city soon developed a certain degree of street savvy. There were footsteps and there were *footsteps*.

The sidewalk was uncrowded at this hour. The rain and the cold had driven most people indoors. The few people who were still out were hurrying toward the shelter of bus stops, restaurants, or parking garages. She listened for a change in the pace of the person walking behind her.

But the footsteps behind Mattie did not quicken or slow. They beat a steady tempo that matched her own brisk stride.

She was getting paranoid, Mattie told herself. There was no cause for alarm. If worse came to worse, she could always run out into the middle of the street and scream bloody murder.

Unless whoever was following her jumped her suddenly and dragged her into a dark alley.

She clung more tightly to her purse and brief-case and hugged the outer edge of the sidewalk. She remembered reading somewhere that it was safer to walk near the curb.

The sense of being followed was sending chills down her spine now. At the corner Mattie swung around abruptly and looked back in the direction she had just come.

Two men were on the sidewalk behind her. One had his keys out and was heading toward a car parked at the curb. The other was staring into a shop window. He was wearing a cap and had the collar of a khaki-green trenchcoat pulled up high around his neck. But Mattie caught a glimpse of his face and realized he was a young man, probably in his early twenties. He didn't look like a street thug; he looked more like a soldier, especially in that military-style trenchcoat.

She *was* getting paranoid. Maybe she'd lived a little too long in the city. Mattie crossed the street and hurried down the next block. Midway she whirled around and saw that the man who had been looking into the window was still behind her. An aura of menace hung in the air.

Mattie gave up trying to fight the anxiety. She was probably going to regret this, but there was only one appealing option available. She turned and stepped into the first warmly lit doorway she saw.

And found herself in a sleazy, smoke-filled tavern. Music blared from tinny loudspeakers. The smell of alcohol fumes, burning tobacco, and old cooking grease were thick in the air. A couple of men at the bar swiveled around on their stools and eyed her with lecherous interest.

Mattie ignored them as she clutched her purse more tightly than ever. A waitress paused and looked her up and down.

"Help you?" the woman asked without much real interest.

"I'd like to use the pay phone, please."

"Back near the rest rooms."

Mattie kept her gaze averted from the crowd at the bar as she walked the gauntlet of staring eyes toward the phone.

It seemed ridiculous to call a cab for a two-block ride. The driver would probably be furious at the cheap fare. She would try the apartment first.

Hugh answered the phone on the first ring.

"Where the hell are you, Mattie? It sounds like a bar, for God's sake."

"Smells like one, too." She wrinkled her nose at the unpleasant odors emanating from the bathrooms. "I'm only two blocks away from the apartment, Hugh. Look, I hate to ask this, but could you come get me? There's someone outside on the sidewalk. I think he might have been following me."

"Which bar?" Hugh's voice now had that familiar cold edge.

Mattie gave him the address.

"Stay put near the front door. Don't move until I get there. Understand?"

"I understand," Mattie hung up and made the endless trip back past the crowd seated at the bar. She could handle anything this lot might try, she told herself. After all, she had survived a barroom brawl on St. Gabriel. The thought gave her confidence.

Nevertheless, when Hugh came through the front door five minutes later looking lethal, she didn't hesitate for an instant.

She went straight into his arms.

CHAPTER

Fifteen

"What the hell did you think you were doing walking home alone in the middle of the night?" Hugh raged as he stood towering over Mattie.

"It wasn't the middle of the night, Hugh. It was

only seven o'clock." Seated with her legs curled under her on the couch. Mattie sipped a reviving cup of herbal tea. "I knew I shouldn't have called you. I knew you'd only start yelling."

"I've got a right to yell. You had no business out there at this hour."

"I've never had trouble coming back from the after-work class before."

"It only takes once. Damn it, a city is not a safe place for a woman alone."

"I can tell you right now, you'll never get me to move out into the burbs. It's a jungle out there."

"This isn't a joke, Mattie." Hugh leaned over her menacingly and flattened his hands on the back of the couch on either side of where she was sitting. "City streets are dangerous and you can't deny it. You're the one who warned *me* to be careful on the way home tonight, remember?"

It was hard to argue that one. "Well, yes. But that's because you're not used to Seattle. You haven't lived here long enough to develop street smarts. You kind of have to get the hang of living downtown."

"Is that right? And you've got the hang of it. I suppose?"

"Oh, yes," she said easily. "The sort of thing that happened tonight really isn't typical. I handled it, didn't I?"

"Hell. This is a really stupid argument. I'm right and you're wrong and that's all there is to it. You'd be a lot safer living out in the islands than you are here in Seattle. I can guarantee it."

"May I remind you that I encountered more

violence out in your neck of the woods than I have ever encountered in my whole life?"

Hugh ran his fingers through his hair. "That was an unusual situation."

"So was tonight."

"Damn it, Mattie . . ."

"The thing is," Mattie said slowly, "I'm not used to having someone chew me out like this just because I had a little trouble on the way home."

"Get used to it. And while you're at it, get used to not coming home alone at night, period," Hugh advised forcefully.

"I'm not sure I like it."

"Not sure you like what? Having me tell you that you can't come home alone at night? Let me tell you, you ain't seen nothin' yet, babe. There are going to be all kinds of rules after we get married."

"I've been doing just fine without any of your rules for thirty-two years, Hugh. Damn. I should never have called you. It wasn't any big deal."

He glared at her. "No big deal? You get followed by some creep who might have intended anything from grabbing your purse to slitting your throat or rape? You don't call that a big deal?"

"I probably overreacted. Maybe no one was following me. Maybe that man on the street behind me was innocently walking home, too."

"Hah. You say that now because you're all safe and sound and cozy and warm again. But that's not what you were saying twenty minutes ago when I found you in that damn bar. And while we're on the subject, why the hell did you have to pick that joint? It was a real dive. Every jerk in there was leering at you."

"It was the first place I saw when I decided to get off the street. Hugh, are you going to keep yelling like this or can we get something to eat? I'm hungry."

"I've got a right to be concerned here, Mattie."

"I know. But as I said, I'm just not used to it," she explained softly.

He eyed her for a long, thoughtful moment. "No, I guess you're not, are you? You're too accustomed to taking care of yourself."

She tried a tentative smile. "Just like you."

"Yeah. Sort of. Come on, let's eat. I'll finish chewing you out later."

Mattie started to get up off the couch. "I've got some buckwheat noodles and vegetables I can fix."

"Forget it. After all the excitement, I need something more substantial." Hugh was already reaching for the phone. "I'm going to order in a pizza."

Mattie was horrified. "A *pizza*."

"I've had a hard day, Mattie. I need real nourishment. I'll tell you something. This business of being able to order up a pizza in the middle of the night and have it delivered is about the only really good thing about the city living I've discovered yet. While we're waiting for it to get here, we'll have a drink. I think we both need one."

Forty-five minutes later Mattie had to admit the aroma of a fresh pizza was far more captivating than it ought to have been. She decided to forget about a well-balanced meal that evening and decided to enjoy herself. She deserved a break.

"So how did it go with the guy in the computer lab at Vailcourt?" she asked around a dripping bite.

"He didn't have a whole lot. Just a possible name to pin on whoever it is that seems to be running things behind the scenes on Purgatory."

"What name?"

"McCormick. John McCormick. It doesn't mean anything. He seems to have come out of nowhere. There's no paper on him, no background, no history at all. Which means the name's an alias. Johnson is going to try to check deeper, but he says he probably won't find much. I called Silk and told him what I had. The name may mean more out there by now."

Mattie nodded. "Any sign of Gibbs yet?"

"No. He definitely lit out for safer country. I'd sure as hell like to know what spooked him and who killed Rosey."

"This McCormick person?"

"Looks like it, but why? Apparently, he's safely in power there on Purgatory. Why should he care if a couple of bit players learned his name? Hell, the name is showing up in the computers now. He can't hope to keep it a secret."

"But you said it doesn't mean anything," Mattie said slowly. "Maybe Gibbs and Rosey found out it does mean something. Maybe they found out who he really is, and McCormick didn't like it."

"Or maybe they saw something they shouldn't have seen," Hugh said thoughtfully. "A couple of bozos like those two could easily have stumbled into the wrong place at the wrong time."

"Or Rosey's death might have nothing at all to do with this McCormick person," Mattie pointed out. "It might all be a remarkable coincidence."

Hugh gave her a wry look. "Yeah. Remarkable."

"Coincidences do happen, you know."

"Not where I come from."

Mattie studied the three acrylic paintings Flynn had propped up in front of her desk. Ariel was hovering near the door in an uncharacteristically reticent fashion.

The silence in the small room was laced with the peculiar tension that always exists at such moments between artist and dealer.

Mattie smiled slowly. "I love them," she said, enthralled. "I absolutely love them."

"You sure?" Flynn asked, breathless with relief.

Mattie felt the delicious thrill of discovery. The paintings were vivid, evocative images that tapped Flynn's undeniably powerful inner vision. But they were not the dark, grotesque, unidentifiable scenes that had formerly characterized his work.

These pictures were filled with color and light and energy. Mattie knew they would sell in a red-hot minute.

"They're perfect," she told him, unable to look away from one particular painting, a shimmering image of a woman standing at a window that looked out on a jarringly primitive landscape.

"Absolutely wonderful. I'll hang all three immediately. Deal?"

Flynn's eyes lit with elation "Deal." He watched her go around behind her desk to pull out a blank contract.

"They're really good, aren't they, Mattie?" Ariel moved forward, radiating a more familiar self-confidence now that judgment had been passed. "I don't know why I gave Flynn such a hard time about trying something for you. It was stupid of me to worry that he might be prostituting his talent. How can you prostitute talent anyway? It's either there or it isn't."

"That's been my guiding philosophy since the day I set up Sharpe Reaction," Mattie admitted.

"And Flynn is loaded with talent, isn't he?"

"Yup. Loaded. And now he's found a way to make that talent accessible to other people. People who have enough money to pay for it."

Out of the corner of her eye Mattie saw Flynn turning red under the unstinting praise. He deserved it, she thought. It was more amusing to witness Ariel's dramatic about-face. There was nothing quite like the fervor of the newly converted.

"What does it matter if Flynn caters to mainstream tastes for a while?" Ariel demanded passionately. "All the great artists of the past did it. Just think, Raphael, Michelangelo, Rubens, all of them. They all had to please their patrons. Art has always had to walk the fine line between pursuing individual vision and making that vision compelling to the public."

Mattie slanted Flynn an amused glance as she

301

opened a drawer and pulled out the paperwork she needed. "I agree. But, then, I sell commercial schlock for a living, so I'm somewhat biased."

"Don't say that, Mattie," Ariel instructed fiercely. "It's hardly as if you're pushing pictures of matadors painted on black velvet, you know. You're developing the next of great artists such as Flynn and thereby expanding their consciousness of art in general."

"My God." Mattie murmured. "My sister has turned into a raving supporter of art for the masses. I don't know if I can handle the shock."

"You're teasing me," Ariel complained.

"I know. Sorry."

"It's all right. I deserve it."

Mattie looked at a smiling Flynn. "She's really appalling when she's in her noble repentant role, isn't she?"

"Appalling, all right. Fortunately, that's one of her least favorite acts." Flynn grinned at his wife.

Ariel stuck her tongue out at both of them and then chuckled happily. "I told Flynn about the baby, Mattie."

"And that settled the matter of what I'm going to paint for a while," Flynn stated firmly. "Pretty exciting, isn't it? Imagine me being a daddy. I went out and bought a set of watercolors and brushes for the kid this morning."

"You're going to be a terrific father," Mattie told him. For the first time she allowed herself to wonder just what sort of father Hugh would be. Probably an overprotective one, she decided. But definitely a committed one. A man like Hugh took his responsibilities very seriously.

She remembered what he had once said about his own childhood in the heat of an argument. She knew instinctively that he was the kind of man who did not repeat the past, but rather learned from it and thereby changed the future.

Men like Hugh were very rare in the modern world. Perhaps they always had been.

The walls threatened to close in again. Mattie took a grip on herself and several deep breaths. She had some time. She did not have to make any decisions right now at this very moment.

The office door opened and Hugh sauntered in carrying an open bottle of Mattie's favorite mineral water.

"This place is sure crowded a lot lately," he announced. "Every time I come in here I trip over a past, present, or future member of the family."

"Speaking of family," Ariel said coolly, "on behalf of Flynn and myself, I'm warning you that you'd damn well better take good care of Mattie. I don't know what she sees in you, but as long as she sees something she wants, you'd better behave. Make her cry a second time, Abbott, and you'll regret it."

Hugh glowered at Mattie. "Promise me you won't cry under any circumstances," he ordered. "I can't stand the idea of having to explain myself to these two and Emery Blackwell and Charlotte Vailcourt and your parents and God knows who else happens to think you need protection for me."

Mattie grinned wickedly, feeling suddenly lighthearted. "Looks like you'll have to watch your step, won't you, Abbott?"

"The stress is definitely beginning to take its

toll on my good nature." He drank the remainder of the mineral water in one gulp and made a face. "Christ, this stuff is awful."

"Why drink it?" Flynn asked curiously.

"Mattie thinks it's better for me than soda pop."

"What you need is a good cup of espresso." Flynn said. "Come on, I'll buy you one. I'm celebrating."

He had been joking back in Mattie's office, Hugh told himself later as he stood watching her choose fresh broccoli at a stall in the Pike Place Market. But the truth was, he was getting a bit stressed out.

Maybe *stressed out* was not quite the right phrase. Maybe what he was feeling was a little old-fashioned guilt.

Hugh did not like guilt. For most of his life it had been an alien emotion. Usually he was sure enough of himself and of his own personal code of honor that he did not experience guilt. Regrets, yes, but not guilt.

He knew his present uneasiness had not been caused by the rash of folks, such as Emery Blackwell and Ariel, who had felt compelled to warn him to treat Mattie well. Hugh already knew he was going to treat her well. Hell, he would protect her with his life, if necessary, and he would see to it she never went without. When it came to the basics, he was sure he would make a good husband for her in the old-fashioned sense.

The problem was that while parts of Mattie were delightfully old-fashioned, there were other parts of her that were very modern. Very sophisticated. Very New Woman.

Hugh wondered again, as he did more and more frequently these days, if his long-range goal of dragging Mattie away to the islands was really the right thing to do. She looked so at home here in Seattle, he thought as he watched her move from the broccoli to the piles of red, orange, yellow, and purple peppers.

Damn it, she was happy here. He could hardly deny it. She was also financially established here. And independent. She had friends, family, a career, and a lifestyle. She mingled with artists, writers, and businesspeople, all of whom accorded her a lot of professional respect.

Compared to all that, Hugh knew he did not have a lot to offer out on St. Gabriel. Silk was right. The days of dragging intelligent, accomplished women off to the frontiers were over.

It had all been a lot easier in the old days. Hell, it would have been a lot easier last year if he'd had the sense to take Mattie up on her offer the first time around.

"Wait until you taste these peppers sautéed in a little olive oil and with some olives and capers," Mattie said in a confidential tone as she paid the produce dealer. "Fantastic. It'll be great served with focaccia or this great potato and cabbage soup I make."

"Mattie?" Hugh took the sack of broccoli and peppers from her as they started toward another stall.

"*Hmmm?*" Her attention was clearly on dinner.

He did not know what to ask or how to ask it.

He had been so sure of himself until now. So sure she would come with him when the time arrived. He smiled crookedly. "I should have taken you out to the islands with me last year."

"Who knows?" she said quietly. "Maybe things turned out for the best after all."

"No," he stated categorically. "They did not. We wasted one goddamned entire year."

She did not respond to that.

Mattie sensed that something had changed in Hugh's attitude toward her. She could not put her finger on it, but it made her uneasy. She wondered if his limited patience was finally at an end. He was probably getting ready to give her an ultimatum, she thought as she watched him pour her a glass of wine.

"How's the job going?" she asked as she sliced the multihued peppers in lacy circles.

"It's okay." Hugh sat on a stool at the counter hunched over his glass of wine and watched her prepare dinner.

"You don't sound exactly fired up with enthusiasm."

"Like I said. It's okay."

"How much longer will it take you to get a security plan worked up for Aunt Charlotte?" She was fishing for an answer to the question of how much time she had left, Mattie realized. But she was afraid to ask Hugh directly.

Hugh turned the glass of wine between his palms. "It depends."

"On what?"

"Lots of things. You want me to do anything?"

Mattie sighed. She wasn't going to get any answers tonight. "You can rinse the broccoli."

"Sure."

The phone rang just as Hugh dumped the broccoli into a colander, and Mattie went across the room to answer it. The sultry voice on the other end of the line took her by surprise.

"Evangeline? Is that you? I can't believe it. Where are you?"

"Right where I was when you left Brimstone. Look, Mattie, this isn't exactly what you'd call a social call."

"Is something wrong?" Mattie glanced over at the kitchen and saw that Hugh was watching her curiously from the sink.

"No, not exactly. At least I don't think so. But I'm not real sure. Does the name Rainbird mean anything to you?"

"No." Mattie frowned. "Nothing at all. Why?"

"'Cause I had a trick last night who was stoned out of his gourd, and he kept talking about this guy named Rainbird. Said he was looking for someone who had slipped off Purgatory during the coup. A man. Said it was worth a lot of money to find him. I remembered that man you had with you."

Mattie's eyes widened in shock. "Good grief."

"You sure the name doesn't ring any bells?"

"No. But I'll ask Hugh."

"He's still around, then?"

"Well, yes, as a matter of fact. I still see a lot of him."

"I was afraid of that. Look. I know it's none of my business, but isn't that kind of risky, honey?

I mean, you know how it is. Get close to a John, and the first thing you know, he wants a cut of the profits. Then he starts telling you that you need him for protection. Then he starts giving orders. Next thing you know, you've got a lousy pimp."

"I'll keep that in mind," Mattie promised.

"You do that. Besides, if this jerk Rainbird is after him, you don't want to be standing nearby. Innocent bystanders have a way of getting hurt, if you know what I mean. What do you want with a man, anyway?"

"Well . . ."

"Face it, honey. Men aren't any good for women like us. We're too independent by nature. Look, I've got to run. I can hear someone coming down the hall. Probably a customer. You take care of yourself now, you hear? And watch out for this guy named Rainbird."

"I will. Oh, and Evangeline?"

"Yeah, honey?"

"Thanks for calling. It was good to talk to you again." Mattie slowly replaced the phone and looked thoughtfully at Hugh.

"Evangeline Dangerfield? What the hell did she want?"

"For one thing, she was rather alarmed that I'm still seeing you. She says men aren't any good for a working woman such as myself."

Hugh swore. "This is why a man has to keep tabs on his woman's friends. You start hanging out with females like Evangeline, and you pick up idiotic notions. That the only reason she was calling?"

"No. Hugh, does the name Rainbird mean anything to you?"

"*Shit.*" Hugh dropped the pan of broccoli into the sink as if it had suddenly become red hot. "Rainbird? Did you say *Rainbird*?"

"I think that was the name." Mattie was alarmed by Hugh's reaction.

Hugh came around the edge of the counter. He was across the room in a matter of seconds, reaching for her. His eyes had gone the color of cold crystal.

Mattie instinctively tried to take a step backward, but she was too late. He seized her and held her still in front of him.

"Where did you get that name?" Hugh demanded.

"Evangeline." Mattie swallowed.

"Jesus Christ."

"She said one of her customers had gotten drunk and talked about a man named Rainbird looking for someone who had slipped off Purgatory during the coup. Do you think it was Rosey? Or Gibbs?"

Hugh ignored that question. "Why did Evangeline call you?"

"Because she knew I had just come off Purgatory with you, and she wondered if you were the person this Rainbird was after. But that's impossible, isn't it? Hugh, what is this all about? Why are you acting like this?"

"Rainbird. So that's what Rosey was trying to say."

"Hugh?"

"I asked him who had attacked him." His

mouth was a grim line. "He opened his eyes for a second, looked up, and said *Rain*. I thought he was talking about the rain that night. But he was trying to say *Rainbird*. He never finished the word."

Mattie took a deep breath, remembering Paul Cormier's last words. "Reign in hell."

Hugh stared down at her. "*Rainbird* in hell. Paul was trying to leave a message for me that Rainbird was there on Purgatory. *Shit*."

"Who is he?" The repressed violence in Hugh was making Mattie tense. She could feel his fingers clenching into the flesh of her upper arms. "What do you know about him?"

"He's supposed to be dead, for one thing." Hugh looked at the phone. "Damn, I should have talked to Dangerfield myself. Where was she calling from? Her room in that inn?"

"Yes. She said a customer was on his way down the hall."

"The customer can damn well keep his pants zipped for a while longer." Hugh dug out his wallet and fished through some bits and pieces of paper. "Here it is."

"What?"

"The receipt for our room. The phone number is on it." He was already punching out the number.

Mattie could feel Hugh's tension radiating from him in cold waves. It was a battle-ready sort of tension, a terrifyingly masculine thing that assaulted her on all fronts. She waited in silence while Hugh put through the call. A moment later he had the inn clerk on the line.

"She can't be gone." Hugh said into the receiver. "She just called us from there. She's with a customer and not answering the phone, that's all. Go upstairs and get her. *Do it now.*"

Mattie shivered a little at the savage tone in Hugh's voice. She looked around, thinking that the temperature in the apartment seemed to have dropped several degrees in the past few minutes. Hugh spoke again after a couple of minutes. "Goddamn it." He tossed down the phone.

"She's gone?"

He nodded brusquely. "Left right after she called you. Walked out the front door. With a suitcase."

"Alone? Or with whoever was coming down the hall to her room? Hugh, do you think she's in any danger?"

"I don't know." Hugh was already punching out numbers on the phone.

"Who are you calling now?"

"Silk."

There was another tense pause before Hugh gave up in frustration and dropped the receiver back into the cradle. "Shit," he said again. "Goddamn it to hell. Rainbird. After all these years."

Mattie sat down on the edge of the couch, her arms crossed under her breasts. "Don't you think you'd better tell me what this is all about?"

He looked at her as if surprised to see her still there. She could tell he was a million miles away in his mind. "No."

She stared at him, nonplussed. "No? Hugh,

311

you can't just say no like that. You have to tell me what's going on here. I'm involved in this, too."

"No, you're not involved and you're not going to get involved. Silk and I will take care of Rainbird, and then it will all be over. For good this time."

"You can't shut me out like this."

"I'm not shutting you out. This has nothing to do with you."

"The hell it doesn't," Mattie said, gritting her teeth.

"Let it be, Mattie. I'll deal with it."

Something snapped inside Mattie. She jumped up in front of Hugh, clenching her small fists at her sides. "Now, you listen to me, Hugh Abbott. I've had about enough of taking orders from you, and I've had enough of your refusal to talk about your past. You've got some nerve, you know that? You won't tell me anything about yourself, but you expect me to give up everything and move out to that stupid island with you."

"Now, babe, I never said that."

"You didn't have to say it," she stormed. "It's been perfectly obvious from the beginning. Why do you think I've been so tense lately? I knew that sooner or later you'd pin me down and force me to make a decision. But how can I do that when you won't even tell me who you really are or where you've been most of your life? It's obvious your past has come back to haunt you. That means it affects our future. I demand to know the truth."

"My past does not affect you," he said, spacing each word out carefully, as if by stating the concept forcefully enough he could make it reality.

"Everything that affects you affects me." Mattie was near tears. "Don't you understand? I love you, Hugh. *I love you*. I have to know what's going on here."

He stared down at her for a long while. Then, without a word, he opened his arms and she stepped into them. He buried his lips in her hair and held her so tight Mattie thought her ribs might crack.

"Babe," he muttered, his voice husky. "I never wanted you to know. I didn't want you to find out about any of it. Not ever."

CHAPTER

Sixteen

"Once upon a time," Hugh said slowly. "I worked for Jack Rainbird." Hugh let his arms fall away from Mattie, and he moved over to the window to stare out through the rain-streaked glass. "It was not one of my more rewarding enterprises."

"What did you do for him?" Mattie's voice was soft and laced with deep concern.

Hugh wondered how long it would be before the concern turned to disgust. "A lot of things."

"Hugh, this is no time to be evasive. I have to know what's going on here."

He exhaled heavily. "Yeah, I guess you've got a right. Okay, here's how it went down. When I got out of the Army, I got a job with a fly-by-night air charter outfit that operated down in South America. The guy who ran it would take any

313

cargo, fly in any weather, and not ask any questions. The pay wasn't bad. And I learned almost everything I know about running a charter service from the wild man who ran that one. That's where I met Silk, by the way."

"He was working for the same outfit?"

Hugh nodded. "Silk and I became a team. What one of us couldn't handle in the air or on the ground, the other usually could. Sometimes getting the plane back into the sky after making a delivery was a real challenge."

"Because the planes were not properly maintained?" Mattie asked.

He studied the reflection of her frowning face in the window. "No, the planes were kept in great shape. That was one of the boss's two rules. The planes got properly serviced even if everyone in the operation went hungry for a while."

"Then what was the problem?"

"The problem," Hugh said quietly, "was that sometimes the clients did not want witnesses who might have snooped around the cargo. Sometimes the clients had enemies who did not want the cargo transported in the first place."

"I see. It was dangerous."

Hugh shrugged. "Sometimes. On the whole it wasn't bad work. Silk and I, we sort of liked it. There was hardly any paperwork, no dress code, and like I said, the boss only had two rules. I told you the first one: take care of the planes."

"And the second?"

"Don't come back without one of the planes. Planes are expensive, you see. A lot more expensive than pilots."

"That sounds a little cold-blooded."

"Just good business."

"Planes are more expensive than pilots. I heard you say something like that to Ray and Derek." Mattie smiled faintly. "But you didn't really mean it. You were just emphasizing the importance of maintenance."

Hugh's brows climbed at her naive faith in his basic good nature. "Well, my boss meant it. Every word. At any rate, things went fairly well for me and Silk for quite a while. We made a little money, did a lot of flying, and got the planes back in one piece. And then one day we broke the rules."

"What happened?"

"We were flying a cargo into a very remote location in South America. It was supposed to be supplies for some fancy scientific research team, but Silk and I knew it was probably something else."

"Like what?"

"Like guns. But, as usual, we didn't ask any questions. We just tried to do the job and get out. But this time we almost didn't make it. The plane got shot up. I got it back in the air but not for long, and we went down in some bad country."

"My God," Mattie whispered.

Hugh smiled in spite of his mood. "Hey, don't look so horrified. Obviously we made it out."

"Obviously. But you lost the plane."

"And our jobs. Silk and I were not in the best of shape when we finally walked out of that damned jungle. The jungles in South America are different from the ones out on the islands. They're a lot more dangerous. A lot can go wrong. And it seemed like just about everything that could go wrong did go wrong, from Silk picking up a fever to us meeting up with some folks who wanted to use us for target practice. But the worst thing that went wrong was that we had no cash left by the time we paid Silk's medical bills."

"But you got another job?"

"Yeah. Working for Jack Rainbird."

Mattie chewed on her lower lip. Her expression as reflected in the window was very determined looking. "Doing what?" she finally asked.

"Rainbird was the head of a group of professional mercenaries," Hugh said bluntly. "He sold his team's services all over the world."

Her eyes widened in the glass. "You became a mercenary? A hired gun?"

"Yeah." Hugh braced himself against the shock and disbelief in her voice. He had expected both, but they still came as quick jabs in the gut. Perhaps that was because there were times when he had the same reaction to his own past.

A hired gun. A man who signed on to fight somebody else's war, carry out somebody else's vendetta. For cold, hard cash, up front.

People from Mattie's world, where the big battles were all verbal ones fought over weighty questions of artistic merit, could only be expected to recoil in horror from such a truth. In Mattie's world a man could be forgiven for showing up for a date with paint stains on his hands but not old blood.

In Mattie's world a man did not make a living at warfare.

In Mattie's world a man was expected to have a civilized past.

In Mattie's world there would be no place for a man like the one Hugh had once been.

Hugh was aware of the old, familiar chill in his gut. He could hear it reflected in his voice. The cold sensation was automatic after all these years. It was a way of protecting himself when things were about to turn very bad. He could hardly feel anything at all when he went real cold like this.

Hugh kept his gaze fixed on Mattie's reflection, waiting impatiently now for the look in her eyes to change to one of shock and disgust; waiting for her to turn away from him.

He was waiting, as usual, for things to turn very, very, bad, the way they had so often over the course of his life.

"Obviously not your sort of work," she said thoughtfully, her brows drawing together in a considering fashion. "It wouldn't really suit you at all."

"Not my sort of work?" Hugh stared at her, openmouthed and momentarily speechless. "Uh . . . well . . ." There was no point telling her he'd been damn good at that kind of work, he decided. He was not especially proud of that fact. And she was right, the job hadn't suited him at all, even if he had been competent at it.

"Silk was also part of this team run by Jack Rainbird?" Mattie asked.

"Yeah. And Paul Cormier. Silk and I were in charge of logistics. We were responsible for figuring out how to get the team in and back out again once a job was done." Hugh spoke slowly, his mind still on Mattie's unexpected reaction to his grand confession. "Rainbird dealt with the client, took the money, and gave us our shares. It was run sort of like a corporation in that respect."

"Who were the clients?"

Hugh shrugged. "CIA as often as not. Or some front operation they were backing."

"A nasty lot."

"The work is steady. They pay well. And on time," Hugh told her, his voice harsh.

"Well, of course. They could hardly expect people to continue taking risks doing their disgusting little jobs all over the world for them if they didn't pay well and on time, could they?" Mattie asked practically. "What happened in the end? Why do you hate Rainbird so much?"

"He betrayed the team."

"Betrayed you?" For the first Mattie really did look shocked. "How did he do that?"

Hugh shrugged. "He took the client's money, as usual, but he also took money from the opposition. The opposition was paying better, I guess. Or maybe they had something more valuable to offer. Who knows? Maybe Rainbird just wanted out of the business and thought he'd take the opportunity to cash out big. But the net result was that he set all of us up on that last aid. The opposition knew when, where, and how we were going to be coming in, and they were waiting."

"Oh, my God, Hugh."

"Silk, Paul, and I and a couple of other guys made it out alive. But we lost most of the team."

"And Rainbird?"

"He vanished. Word was he'd been killed by

318

the opposition after he'd pulled his little trick. That was a logical possibility. Silk and I and the others assumed it was probably true. After all, the guys who'd paid him off to betray the operation knew better than anyone else they couldn't trust him."

"I suppose that's true."

"The only thing a mercenary has to sell is his sword and his guarantee of loyalty. Both belong to the client for the duration of the contract. Once he gets a reputation for changing employers in midstream, business has a way of declining."

"Yes. I can understand that," Mattie said weakly. She sank down onto the couch. "So you all thought he was dead."

"He knew he had better be dead as far as we were concerned," Hugh said.

"I see. Because he knew that those of you who had survived his betrayal would hunt him down?"

Hugh's hand, which was braced against one of the window frames, bunched into a hard fist. "Yeah He knew it."

Mattie looked up. "You said Paul Cormier was also part of this . . . team of professional merce-naries?"

Hugh nodded. "Cormier was the strategist for the team. He'd been in the business a long, long time. Long before Rainbird was on the scene. Paul worked with me and Silk to set up the Rainbird operations. Like I said, he was one of the few who got out of that last operation alive. Hell, one of the reasons we did get out was because of Cormier. He believed in contingency planning. He told me later Rainbird wasn't the first team boss he'd worked for who had turned sour."

"It's beginning to look like Cormier wasn't killed by some marauding rebel or houseboy who went crazy on Purgatory, isn't it?" Mattie noted quietly.

"It's a lot more likely Rainbird was behind the coup in the first place. He would have gotten to Cormier right at the start because Cormier would have recognized him."

"And Cormier would have come looking for you and Silk and the others so that you could all go after Rainbird."

"That's about the size of it. Looks like the Colonel decided to come back from the dead, and Cormier was in the way."

"Now what happens, Hugh?"

"Now Silk and I have to take care of some old business."

"I was afraid you were going to say that." Her hands twisted together in her lap. "I don't suppose it would do any good for me to ask you not to try to hunt him down?"

"No."

"I'm so afraid," she whispered. "There's only you and Silk. Rainbird apparently runs a whole island now."

"He won't have more than a few people around him. Five or six at the most. I know him. I know how he thinks. He never trusted anyone completely. Always said it was smart to keep the leader's inner circle down to a small number. The more people around, the more of a chance of betrayal. He ought to know."

"But how can he maintain control of the island with so few people?"

"There were probably more at the beginning until he'd established himself. But now, according to Silk's information and the stuff Johnson pulled out of the computer, the guy behind the scenes on Purgatory is keeping a low profile. That means he's cut some deals with the people in charge."

"You mean Rainbird's using money, not raw firepower, to run the show?" Mattie asked shrewdly. "Makes sense."

"Yeah. He's bought himself the perfect safe harbor out in the middle of nowhere. He can do just about anything he wants there, launder money, run drugs, organize mercenary teams, *anything*. And no one could touch him."

"Why did he pick Purgatory?"

Hugh shrugged. "Things are a little loose politically out in the Pacific, but even so, there aren't that many islands you can just take over without some larger power noticing or getting annoyed. Purgatory was one of the few that nobody gives a damn about. No military bases, no tourism, nothing."

"Damn. I don't like the idea of you and Silk taking him on yourselves. There must be some other way to stop Rainbird. Can't you tell the government or something? Let them handle it?"

"They have no interest in Rainbird or in Purgatory. Besides, as far as the government is concerned, there is no Rainbird. Just some joker named Jack McCormick, remember? A small-time strongman who may or may not be pulling the strings in a two-bit island government. Unless he gives them a problem somehow, he'll be ignored."

Mattie's eyes narrowed. "Besides, as far as you're concerned, this is personal, isn't it?"

"It's personal, all right."

"What is this Rainbird really like, Hugh?"

"Remember I once told you that no matter how fast a man was, there was always someone around who was faster?"

"I remember. You told me that on Purgatory."

"Well, Rainbird is the guy who is always faster."

Mattie's eyes widened. "What do you mean?"

Hugh shrugged. "Just what I said. He's damn good at what he does, Mattie. Fast, utterly ruthless, and smart. But most of all, fast. I've never seen reflexes like Jack Rainbird's. A natural fighting machine. Good with everything, his hands, a gun, a knife, a rock, you name it. He literally moved like greased lightning. Just like they used to say about those old western gunslingers. Jesus, could he move. You never knew he was behind you until you looked down and realized your throat was bleeding."

Mattie hugged herself, her eyes huge with horror. "How old is he?"

"My age. Maybe a year older."

"You said you'd slowed down a little. Maybe he has, too."

"Maybe." But Rainbird had always been faster, Hugh reminded himself. So even if he'd slowed down some, he was still going to be slick. Very, very slick.

322

"Is that all you know about him? That he had unusually swift reflexes and fighting abilities?"

"No, I know a few other things," Hugh admitted.

"Such as?"

"Women were drawn to him like moths to a flame. All kinds of women, young and old, rich and poor, single and married. One, a very beautiful, very rich wife of an American diplomat in Brazil, told me once that women knew he was dangerous, but that that was part of the thrill. She said there was something hypnotic about him. Something to do with his eyes, she said."

"The man sounds like a vampire." Mattie said with disgust.

"All I know is that he had something. Rainbird was never without a woman when he wanted one. And he got any woman he wanted. Cormier always claimed that a man who could have any woman never learned how to love one woman properly. But I never noticed Rainbird complaining."

"Of course not. He wouldn't even know he was missing something. A man like Rainbird is essentially incomplete emotionally and pretty much of a coward at heart."

Hugh blinked in astonishment. "A coward? Rainbird? You don't even know him."

"No, but I've met men who go from woman to woman and never seem to be able to bond permanently with one. Every woman has met a man like that at some time in her life. They can be very amusing because they've usually developed a lot of surface charm, but a smart woman doesn't do anything more than entertain herself for a while

323

with one. Men like that are useless in the long run. Bad genetic material, as Aunt Charlotte would probably point out."

"The hell you say." Hugh was fascinated.

"It's true. It's hard to explain. It's just that, once you scratch the surface on a man like that, there's nothing underneath." Mattie's shoulders rose and fell in a small shrug. "They're empty shells. Something important is missing. When a woman says a man is literally no good, that's the kind of man she's talking about. He's no good to her in terms of bonding and survival because he has no guts or staying power. He can't be trusted to make a commitment and keep it. Like I said, he's simply no good."

"Do all women look at men in those terms?" Hugh asked, stunned.

"Smart ones do."

He stared at her, his mouth abruptly gone dry. He was afraid to ask the obvious question, but he could not resist. "Mattie, is that how you look at me? Is that why you didn't want to give me a second chance? Is that why you wouldn't move to St. Gabe? You think there's nothing under my surface?"

She shook her head, then went to him in a soft little rush and wrapped her arms around his waist. "Oh, no, Hugh. You aren't anything like that. You're as solid as a rock."

He grinned faintly in relief. "And just as dense?"

"Maybe. At times." She lifted her face, smiling at him with misty green-gold eyes. "But I suppose you've found me a little dense lately, too, haven't you?"

"Nothing I can't work around." His voice felt thick in his throat as he cradled her head in his hands. "Babe, I've got to go back out to the islands."

"I knew you were going to say that. I know I can't talk you out of it. But I want you to take me with you," she begged. "I can't stand the thought of waiting here, not knowing what you're doing or what kind of trouble you'll be facing. Let me come with you."

He was startled. "Hell, I can't do that, babe."

"At least let me come with you as far as St. Gabriel. I could wait there until you and Silk take care of this Rainbird person. Please, Hugh. You can't leave me behind. Not this time."

"Not this time? Mattie, what are you saying? This isn't like the last time. There's no connection at all. It simply isn't safe. Christ, babe, I can't take you with me."

Her eyes filled with tears. "That's what you said the last time."

"*It's not the same thing.* Mattie, don't cry. For God's sake, don't cry, okay?"

"I want to go with you," she said. "Please, Hugh. Take me with you. I'll be safe on St. Gabriel."

"No, damn it." He was beginning to get angry now. This was crazy. "No way. I don't want you anywhere near this. You're going to stay right here, safe and sound."

"You can't make me stay here this time."

"The hell I can't," he shot back. He clamped

his hands around her shoulders and gave her a small shake. Then he looked down into her tear-filled eyes. "Listen to me, babe. You're going to stay here and that's all there is to it. That's an order."

"You're very good at giving orders, aren't you?" She sniffed and stepped back quickly away from him, dashing toward the little spiral staircase that led up to her sleeping loft.

Hugh watched her run up the metal steps and throw herself down onto the bed. Then she was out of his line of sight. But he could hear her sobbing into the pillow.

Not for the first time in his life, he felt like a real jerk. He went into the kitchen, tossed his unfinished wine down the sink, and poured himself a glass of whiskey.

Mattie was still sniffling up in the loft when he sat down near the phone and started thumbing through the yellow pages. Ten minutes later he had his flight booked to St. Gabriel. Another early morning departure.

Just like last time.

Hugh was sitting in the same chair, still working on the same glass of whiskey a half hour later when he heard muffled noises from the loft. He glanced up but still couldn't see Mattie. He went back to staring out the rain-lashed window and wished Rainbird were already in hell.

Mattie had been able to accept his past, Hugh realized. He was still dazed by that miraculous fact. But she seemed unable to forgive him for abandoning her a second time, even though it was for her own protection. He wished he could make her understand his own need to keep her safe.

She was not accustomed to being taken care of, he reminded himself. That was the crux of the problem. He had tried to tell her this wasn't like last time. He wanted to explain that for his own sanity he had to know she was thousands of miles away from Rainbird.

"Hugh?"

He heard the soft footsteps behind him, but he was reluctant to turn around and face her. He had handled a lot of things in his life, but he did not want to deal with the accusation he knew he would see in her eyes. "Yeah, babe?"

"When does your plane leave?" Mattie moved up behind him.

"Six."

"I should have known."

"Mattie, I'm sorry," he said roughly. "But this is the way it has to be."

There was a small silence. "You'll take care of yourself?"

"Word of honor."

"You'll come back to Seattle?"

"God, yes, babe. Count on it." He did turn around then, and the first thing he saw was that she was smiling slightly.

The second thing he saw was that she had changed into the little red sarong she had worn that night on Hades.

"Jesus, babe."

"I didn't want you to forget me," she whispered as her arms slid around his neck.

"Never. No matter what happens." He reached

up and tumbled her down into his lap, kissing her with a hunger that he knew could only be temporarily assuaged, a hunger that would be with him all of his life. "I'll be back."

Mattie refused to cry the next morning when she drove him to the airport. She kept a determined smile pasted to her face the whole time, even when she waved good-bye at the gate.

She did not allow the tears to fall until the jet had backed slowly away from the loading ramp and was headed for the runway. Then she went into the nearest ladies' room and sobbed for a long while.

When the tears were finally finished, she bathed her face in cold water and went back out to the parking lot to find her car.

He would be back, she told herself. He would not do something really stupid like get himself hurt. He had survived this long. No one could take care of himself as well as Hugh. He was a survivor.

But so, apparently, was this mysterious Rainbird.

Mattie parked the car back in the garage beneath her building and changed into a neat little gray checked business suit. Then she coiled her hair into its familiar bundle at the nape of her neck and left for the gallery. The only way she would stay reasonably sane until Hugh returned was to keep herself so busy she would have no time to think.

She phoned Charlotte later in the day and told her what had happened. Her aunt commiserated with her but seemed convinced Hugh would be fine.

"He's taken care of himself for quite a while. I'm sure he'll handle this little problem in no time," Charlotte said. Then she hesitated. "So he finally told you about his mysterious past, did he?"

"I gather he lived a little rough," Mattie said carefully.

"Well, we guessed that much."

"He was a professional mercenary for a while, Aunt Charlotte."

"Yes, I wondered if that might not be the case. It accounts for many of his skills and a lot of his inside knowledge of certain matters, doesn't it? How did you take the news, Mattie? He worried excessively about that, you know."

"I told him it was obviously not a suitable line of work for him."

Charlotte laughed at that. "Did you really? How odd."

"Why do you say that?"

"Oh, no particular reason. Just that I would have imagined he'd have been rather good at that sort of thing."

"I don't care what he did in the past or how well he did it," Mattie said fiercely. "He's built a different life for himself now."

"He's going after this Colonel Rainbird," Aunt Charlotte pointed out gently.

"Old business," Mattie said quietly. She knew then she had accepted the inevitable. Hugh had to be free to live his new life, and he was the only one who could close the door on the past. "It has to be cleaned up. And it's not exactly something that can be turned over to the police. Aunt Charlotte, although I wish to God it were."

"It sounds as though you've come to terms with things. But it doesn't surprise me that you've got the inner fortitude to deal with this. You're a strong woman. Always have been. And Lord knows. Hugh needs a woman who is strong enough to handle his past as well as his present and future."

"Hugh may have lived a harsh life, but there is one thing I know for certain."

"And that is?" Charlotte prompted.

"He would never have lived a dishonorable life."

"Umm, yes, I'm inclined to agree with you. Now, why don't you have some of your famous bug juice, Mattie dear? Take a few antistress vitamins, go do your aerobics workout, and try not to worry about Hugh too much. He'll be back for you."

"That's what he said."

"The problem, of course," said Aunt Charlotte, "is what are you going to do when he does come back?"

She hung up the phone before Mattie could think of a response.

The next morning on the way to work Mattie spotted the figure huddled in the gallery doorway from halfway down the block. She sighed inwardly. It was not all that unusual to find a street person had spent the night sleeping in the minimal shelter provided by the shop entrance. Sad, but, unfortunately, not unusual.

She would wake him up and send him on his way with enough money for a cup of coffee.

She was fishing in her purse for a dollar when she realized it was no stranger who was crouched against the gallery window. The figure was wearing an outrageously fake fur coat and a pair of three-inch spike heels. She had a mass of unlikely blond curls boiling around her heavily made-up face.

"Evangeline!" Mattie shouted, breaking into a run. "What on earth are you doing here?"

"Hi, honey. Sorry about this. Got in this morning and came straight here. You said to look you up if I ever got to Seattle, and this was the address on that card you left me. When the cab let me off here, I thought there'd been a mistake." She glanced quizzically at the paintings in the window. "This gallery really belong to you?"

"All mine." Mattie thrust the key into the lock and opened the door. "Come on inside and warm up."

"Jeez. This is really something. It's an art gallery, isn't it?" Evangeline eyed the contents of the shop with astonishment as Mattie turned on the lights. "You're not really in the business, at all, are you?"

"You mean, your particular business? No. But I am in business. How about a cup of tea?"

"Yeah, anything. I've had nothing but lousy airline food for the past twenty-four hours." Evangeline followed her into the office and watched her plug in the little hot pot. "Got a bathroom?"

"Over there." Mattie nodded toward the small door.

"Thanks. Be right out."

When she returned, Evangeline had taken off the fake fur. She was wearing a skin-tight island-style sheath. She looked like an exotic flower that had been freshly plucked in the jungle and plunked down in Mattie's mundane little office.

"I suppose you wonder what the hell I'm doing here," she said, sniffing suspiciously at the herbal tea.

"The question did cross my mind. You're more than welcome, though. It's good to see you again. You look great. I love that dress."

"Just a little something I whipped up a couple of weeks ago. I had to leave a lot of really nice stuff behind, damn it."

"I take it you left Hades in a hurry? Hugh tried to call you back after you phoned the other night, and the desk clerk said you'd already left with a suitcase. I was worried. What happened, Evangeline?"

"Remember I told you some trick was coming down the hall to my room and I had to get off the phone?"

"Yes?"

"Well, it wasn't a john. It was some guy named Gibbs. He wanted to talk to me about a friend of his. Someone named Rosey."

"Rosey's dead. He was killed over on Purgatory."

"That right? Well, his friend Gibbs was afraid of that. Wanted to know if I knew what the hell was going on. Mentioned this Rainbird guy again and said he sounded like trouble. He told me about the way your friend Abbott had stolen his boat to get off Purgatory and how Abbott had offered money for information on whoever might have shot a man named Cormier. When the name Rainbird came up again, I got real nervous. It occurred to me that I might already know a little too much. I've always trusted my instincts, you know?"

"So you decided to leave Brimstone?"

"Not just Brimstone. I decided to put a lot of distance between me and this Rainbird character until things cooled down. It occurred to me I needed a little vacation and it wouldn't hurt to come back to the States to check up on my investments. Brokers and accountants can get a little sloppy if you don't breathe down their necks once in a while, you know?"

"That's true," Mattie agreed. "I make it a point to check in with mine in person a couple of times a year."

"Right. So I figure I'll kill a couple of birds with one stone. Take care of business back here and wait for things to settle down out there."

"That may have been a very smart move. I don't know for certain what's going on, but there's real trouble brewing. Hugh left yesterday morning."

"Yeah? What's he going to do?"

"I wish I knew," Mattie said sadly. "Look, if you don't mind sleeping on a big couch, you're welcome to stay with me for a while until you decide what you want to do."

Evangeline looked startled at first and than

strangely grateful. "That's real nice of you, honey. Sure you don't mind?"

"Not in the least. I think I'll rather enjoy having company."

Evangeline grinned. "I'll take you out to dinner. My treat."

"Sounds great. We can talk business investments."

They made a decidedly odd-looking pair that evening as they walked into the lounge of one of Seattle's best restaurants and sat down for a drink. Every eye in the place turned at least briefly toward Mattie's companion. And then, having assessed Evangeline and come to certain conclusions, those same eyes turned with great curiosity to Mattie.

Evangeline looked extremely dashing in another of her own creations, a flower-splashed, low-necked dress with long sleeves and a hem that ended mid-thigh. Mattie felt quite staid in the demure, heather-toned, high-necked dress that Evangeline had decided was the only wearable garment in Mattie's closet aside from the red sarong. Mattie had declined to wear the sarong out in downtown Seattle on the grounds that it was too cold. This wasn't the islands, after all.

"This is great, you know?" Evangeline glanced around at the ferns, polished wood, and dapper customers. "Usually when I'm in a bar, I'm working. Nice to be able to come in and just sit down and relax."

"I'm glad you're enjoying it. Evangeline, I'd like to ask a favor."

"Sure, honey."

"Would you go shopping with me tomorrow? I could use some advice."

Evangeline laughed and heads turned again. "You bet. Can't think of anything I'd rather do than go shopping." She leaned forward. "And confidentially, honey, you could use some help."

"I know."

"I didn't want to say too much, but the truth is, I was a little shocked by what you've got in that closet of yours. All the wrong colors. And you need a style that makes the most of your figure. You're a little thin, but that's okay. The right styles will make you look sleek. Those business suits just sort of cover you up, if you know what I mean."

"I had a feeling they weren't quite me." Mattie smiled. "At least, not any longer."

"So you and this Abbott are together full-time, huh?" Evangeline sipped her wine. "For real?"

Mattie nodded. "He says so."

"Is he planning on moving here to Seattle or are you going out there?"

"That's one of the things we're still working on," Mattie admitted.

"I'll bet you end up out there." Evangeline said thoughtfully. "I don't know Abbott very well. Just saw him with you that morning. But my guess is that he ain't the city type."

"No, I don't think he is."

"And men aren't very adaptable. Ever notice? They tend to get real set in their ways. Much more so than women."

"I expect that's one of the reasons why women

have usually had to do the adapting," Mattie agreed with a sigh. "It's not fair, is it?"

"Nope. But that's life, I guess. So what will you do if you go out to St. Gabe with him? Lie around and get a tan?"

"Tanning is no longer considered a healthy leisure-time activity," Mattie said.

"I heard that. Sort of like sex. I'm thinking of going out of the business real soon."

"You're going to open that little dress boutique you talked about? Design your own clothes for tourists?"

Evangeline nodded. "I think I've got enough in certificates of deposit, T-bills, and stocks to do it now. First thing I've got to do is find a good location, though Hawaii is too crowded. Commercial rents are sky high. I need a place that's just about to get discovered, you know? Some place where the tourists are just starting to head. Brimstone ain't it."

"Hugh says St. Gabe is on the way to being discovered," Mattie said almost to herself. "The tourists are starting to show up regularly."

"Yeah? Hey, maybe you and me could both go into business there. Wouldn't that be a kick?"

"I can't sew." Then Mattie smiled slowly. "But I can sell paintings. And if I can sell art, I can probably sell anything. Tourists always buy souvenirs, don't they?"

"You're serious, aren't you?"

"I've got to figure something out. And fast. The walls are starting to close in on me."

"I know the feeling. Been closing in on me for years. This Rainbird thing was the last straw."

Mattie was never quite certain what woke her that night. She had been sleeping fitfully anyway, so perhaps it was simply the change in the pattern of shadows on the ceiling when the door to the huge studio was stealthily opened.

Whatever it was, she knew that something was very wrong. For a few seconds she lay absolutely still, wishing desperately that Hugh were there beside her. Then she heard the tiny squeak that signaled the door being closed.

Mattie took several deep breaths fighting to overcome the panic that gripped her. She could not just lie here like this while someone burglarized the apartment. Evangeline was asleep on the couch. Whoever had come into the studio would see her.

Mattie pushed back the covers and silently got out of the bed. She tiptoed to the railing and looked down.

There, silhouetted in the light coming in through the high windows, was the figure of a man. The faint neon glow glinted off the gun in his hand as he aimed it at Evangeline.

Without skipping a beat, Mattie's fear turned to fury. This was her apartment, her sanctuary. She would not allow anyone to invade it like this.

Mattie snatched up the heavy black vase by her bed and hurled it over the edge of the railing, straight at the intruder's bare head.

There was a horrendous crash. The man with the gun crumpled to the floor, his gun skittering across the wooden surface. The intruder groaned and tried to rise. Mattie grabbed the phone and yanked the plug out of the wall. She raced down the spiral staircase with some vague notion of using the phone as a club.

But she needn't have worried.

Evangeline screamed as she woke up and took in the situation at a glance. Obviously accustomed to emergencies such as this, she leaped up off the couch and began bashing the fallen man over the head with the nearest available object. It was Shock Value Frederickson's brilliantly executed metal sculpture. *On the Brink.*

The man groaned once more and fell back onto the floor.

CHAPTER

Seventeen

"Good grief, Evangeline, be careful with that sculpture. It's going to be worth a fortune in another five years." Mattie had just rounded the last turn in the staircase and leaped off the last step, phone raised on high. The hem of her flannel nightgown trailed behind her as she flew across the room. "Are you all right?"

"Yeah, thanks to you, honey. You're a great one for coming to the rescue, aren't you?" Evangeline, dressed in a skimpy black lace nightie decorated with not-so-discreetly placed black lace roses, lowered *On the Brink* and surveyed the man on the floor. "Anyone you know?"

"Why on earth would I know him? Must be a burglar or rapist or something." Mattie flipped on the nearest light switch and took a closer look at the young, dark-haired man on the floor. He was dressed in black jeans, black boots, and a black pullover sweater. He looked like a movie version of a cat burglar. Or an assassin. "Oh, my God."

"You do know him?"

"It's the man who was following me home in the rain the other night."

Evangeline looked up. "Who is he?"

"I don't know his name. I just saw him behind me the other evening. He was wearing a trenchcoat then, and I had a weird feeling he was watching me." Mattie put down the phone she had unplugged in the loft and reached for the downstairs extension. "I'll call nine-one-one."

She had gotten as far as punching out the number nine when the man on the floor stirred. She hesitated, glancing in his direction. "Do you think we should hit him again, Evangeline?"

Evangeline hovered over the sprawled figure with *On the Brink* held at the ready. "I'll handle it."

The man's lashes fluttered, and he looked first at Mattie and then at Evangeline with dazed eyes. "Bitches."

Be ready to cream him if he so much as moves an inch, Evangeline."

"Too late," the man muttered. "Trap's already closing on Abbott and Taggert. Too late to save them."

Mattie froze. "Trap? What sort of trap? What are you talking about?"

The man's lips thinned in a vicious parody of a death's head grin. "Nothing you can do, bitch."

"What is this trap for Silk and Hugh?" Mattie snapped, her fingers trembling on the phone.

"Like lambs to the slaughter." The man's lashes fluttered weakly and he groaned. "Never know what hit 'em."

"When the police find out what you were up to, they'll take care of everything," Mattie said defiantly.

The man showed his teeth in another deadly grin. "Get real, bitch. As far as the cops are concerned, I followed a whore back to her apartment, and we had a little falling out, that's all. Happens all the time."

"Not in my apartment," Mattie said.

The intruder slid back into unconsciousness.

Evangeline and Mattie traded glances, and then Mattie went ahead and punched out the number of the emergency code.

Silence fell on the room while they waited for the police.

"I guess we should get ready for the cops," Mattie said after a minute.

"Yeah. Look, Mattie, you want me to disappear or something?"

"Of course not. You're staying right here. This is my apartment and you're a friend of mine," Mattie reminded her. "I assure you my reputation can withstand an investigation by the Forces of Moral Righteousness and the FBI combined. That's the beauty of having led a very dull life." She eyed Evangeline's black lace nightie. "Still, it might not hurt if we both put on a robe or something."

Evangeline grinned. "Yeah, wouldn't want 'em

to get any ideas. I'll keep an eye on this turkey while you go find one. I've got something in the suitcase I can use."

Mattie went back up to the loft to pull on her brown chenille bath robe and a pair of fluffy bedroom slippers. She surveyed herself in the mirror and decided it would have been impossible to look any more dowdy if she had deliberately tried.

When she got back downstairs she saw that Evangeline had found a see-through black negligee in her suitcase and was shrugging into it.

Mattie cleared her throat delicately as she surveyed the negligee. "I'm sure the Seattle police have seen just about everything, but there's no sense showing them more than necessary. After all, we do want them to keep their mind on business. Do you want to borrow a robe? I have a spare."

Evangeline looked skeptically at what Mattie had on. "Does it look anything like that one?"

"I'm afraid so." Mattie went to the closet and found the old faded bathrobe. "But we can replace both the one I'm wearing and this one when you take me shopping."

"Well, all right," Evangeline tugged on the old robe with a grimace of distaste. "Speaking of cops, just exactly what do you plan to tell them?"

"I don't know," Mattie sat down on the couch. "We could tell them everything, I suppose, but who's going to believe it? We can't prove a thing about Rainbird or the rest of it. Also, I'm not quite sure how much of his past Hugh wants dredged up. I think we need diplomatic advice."

"Who from?"

"From someone who knows about handling delicate situations like this. My aunt Charlotte." Mattie was already punching in Charlotte Vailcourt's private number, the one that reached her anywhere, day or night.

When Charlotte came on the line, Mattie explained the situation as rapidly as possible. Charlotte's response was immediate.

"Say nothing about the Rainbird connection for now," Charlotte advised. "You're right, we don't know how awkward any of this could be for Hugh or his friend. It's not up to us to start raking up their past, not after all the work they've done to conceal it. Also he wouldn't want us calling attention to whatever he's planning to do on Purgatory."

"I agree. He said it was personal business. What about this creep on the floor? Just another ordinary, run-of-the-mill rapist-murderer foiled by two savvy young businesswomen?"

"Exactly. As far as you know, you are two innocent women who were followed home by a homicidal pervert. These days no one, especially a cop, will even blink at that explanation. Happens all the time. And he probably won't say much of anything at all to the police without a lawyer. It's in his own best interests to keep his mouth shut."

Mattie shuddered. Then she heard the sirens out in the street. "They're here, Aunt Charlotte. I'll call you later."

It all happened just as Charlotte Vailcourt had predicted. The gun was a particularly damaging piece of evidence against the intruder, and

Mattie's pristine background as a law-abiding, taxpaying member of the business community was unassailable.

When the furor had died down and the police had taken their leave, Mattie and Evangeline made tea. Evangeline toasted slices of whole-wheat sourdough bread while Mattie tried to call Hugh.

"No answer." Mattie said, replacing the receiver reluctantly. "I'll try Abbott Charters."

The phone in the office of Abbott Charters was answered on the third ring.

"Yeah?"

Mattie frowned at the chewing noises on the other end of the line. She was surprised how clearly she could hear them overseas. "Is this Derek?"

"Yeah," said Derek. "Who's this?"

"Mattie Sharpe. I'm calling for Hugh."

"I thought he was in Seattle."

"You haven't seen him?"

"Not since he left for his vacation."

Mattie decided not to mention the fact that Hugh's trip to Seattle was not supposed to have been a mere vacation. "What about Silk?"

"Didn't see Silk last night in the Hellfire, come to think of it. Hang on a second." Derek yelled across the room. "Ray, you seen Silk lately?"

"Not for a couple of days at least."

Mattie felt herself getting increasingly tense. "Derek, listen, this is important. If you see Silk or Hugh, please ask them to call me or Charlotte Vailcourt immediately."

"Right. I'll leave a message on Abbott's desk,

and I'll take a note down to Silk's boat. I'll also let Bernard at the Hellfire know. That do?"

"Yes. Thank you." Mattie hung up the phone and looked at Evangeline. "That man who broke in here said Hugh and Silk were headed for a trap."

"Uh-huh." Evangeline spread marmalade on a slice of toast. "Sure did, honey. What are you going to do?"

"I don't know. I can't reach Hugh. No one's seen him, but he should have gotten to St. Gabriel yesterday."

"Could have had trouble with connections."

"Not this much trouble."

"No, guess not."

"I'm worried. Evangeline."

"Don't blame you. But I don't see what you can do except try to get word to Abbott that he might be walking into a setup of some kind."

Mattie jumped to her feet. "I'm going out there."

"St. Gabe?" Evangeline stared at her in amazement. "I don't know if that's such a good idea, honey."

But Mattie was already heading for the closet where she kept her suitcase. "Something's wrong. I can feel it. I told Hugh he should have taken me with him. Damn it. I *told* him. He never listens to me."

"So what else is new? Men never listen to women."

"I've got to go out there and find him. There's a flight at six. If I hurry. I can just make it." Mattie hauled the suitcase out and opened it on

344

the floor. She went into the bathroom and started collecting her toiletries. "As it stands now, I know more than anyone else does about this whole mess, and I can't get the information to anyone who can help. So I'm going to go look for Hugh myself."

"You think he'll appreciate that?"

"Probably not, knowing him. But he isn't here, is he? So there's nothing he can say about it."

"You got a point." Evangeline looked around. "I'll check into a motel or something."

"You're more than welcome to stay here." Mattie looked up suddenly. "Unless, uh, you're planning to go back to work?"

Evangeline grinned. "Don't worry, honey. I never work when I'm in the States. Too risky what with the cops and diseases and pimps with guns and everything else you folks have back here. Relax. When you return, your snow-white reputation will still be intact."

Mattie grinned. "Pity."

It started to rain just as Mattie's jet touched down on the St. Gabriel runway. She made the mad dash across the tarmac to the small terminal along with the rest of the handful of passengers who had been on board.

Inside the terminal building she paused briefly to try another phone call to Hugh's house and the office of Abbott Charters, but there was no answer at either place. Hoisting her suitcase, she went over to see about renting a car.

"You're Abbott's lady, ain't ya?" the man behind the counter asked, peering at her intently.

345

"What are you doin' back here without Abbott? He still in the States?"

Mattie frowned as she picked up a pen to sign the brief contract. "You haven't seen him? He was supposed to be back here ahead of me."

"Nope. Ain't seen hide nor hair of him. Course, he could've come through on the evening flight. I don't work evenings."

"Yes. Maybe that was it." She quickly signed her name and collected the keys.

It took her a few minutes to get the hang of the stick shift in the battered green Jeep, but Mattie eventually pulled out of the small parking lot and onto the main road into town.

In spite of her deep fears, she was amazed at how comfortingly familiar everything seemed. *It was like coming home*, she found herself thinking. But that made absolutely no sense. No sense at all.

She stopped briefly near the harbor to check Silk's boat for signs of occupancy. But there was no one on board the *Griffin*. Mattie hesitated and then stepped into the stern to check the paints and brushes that were sitting near the easel.

The brushes were not even damp. Silk had not been at work here recently.

On a hunch she went across the street to the Hellfire.

"Well, hello, Mattie," Bernard said in obvious surprise from behind the bar. "What are you doing here? Where's Abbott?"

"You haven't seen him?"

Bernard shook his head. "Sorry. Derek said I was to have him call you if I saw him, but he hasn't been here. I thought he was in the States with you. Supposed to be on a short vacation or something."

"He left three days ago. He should have been back here by now."

"Unless he stopped off in Hawaii or one of the other islands to pick up some supplies or see some business contacts. He does that, you know. He has a lot of clients scattered all around out here."

"I hadn't thought of that" Mattie admitted. "But what about Silk?"

"Like I told Derek, Silk hasn't been keeping to his usual routine for the past few days. But I sort of figured that's 'cause Abbott left him in charge of his business, and Silk knows there'll be hell to pay if he tries to run Abbott Charters and drink at the same time."

"Thanks, Bernard. If you see either of them, tell them I'm on the island. I'll be at Hugh's house."

"Sure. You're finally ready to move out here, huh? Abbott said it wouldn't take long."

Mattie wrinkled her nose but declined to respond. She got back into the Jeep. She fumbled with the gears again and headed along the island road toward Hugh's small beach cottage. She was not certain what to do next, but she told herself she felt a little better knowing she was on the scene and not sitting thousands of miles away in Seattle. For all the good it did.

She was beginning to suspect that Hugh and Silk had already left for Purgatory. Perhaps they had rendezvoused in Hades. A cold chill deep in the pit of her stomach made her insides clench.

She had to face the fact that Rainbird's trap might already have closed.

The small driveway in front of the beach cottage was empty. There was no sign of life or recent habitation. Mattie switched off the Jeep's engine and sat for a moment behind the wheel. Her sense of uneasiness was very strong right now. Memories of the horror that had awaited her when she had walked into Paul Cormier's white mansion were vivid in her mind.

No, she told herself, it would be all right. She was not about to walk into another death scene.

But the gnawing anxiety was getting stronger. For a second she considered turning the key in the ignition and driving back into town. But she knew she had to look inside the cottage to reassure herself that Hugh or Silk was not lying dead on the floor within. *She had to know.*

Mattie forced herself to get out of the Jeep and walk to the front door. She had the spare key Hugh had given her in her hand, but the instant she slid it into the lock, she knew she didn't need it. The door was open.

Literally sick with anticipation, Mattie pushed open the door and stared into the empty front room.

She exhaled slowly when she realized there were no dead bodies on the floor. Of course, that still left the bedroom.

Mattie walked slowly through the eerily empty cottage. There was no evidence that Hugh had been here recently—no coffee cup in the sink, nothing in the refrigerator.

She was beginning to think that Hugh had never

come back to St. Gabriel at all. That meant he had probably gone to Hades or even directly into Purgatory. And apparently Silk had joined him.

She was too late. Rainbird's trap had closed.

Mattie opened the bedroom door and found herself looking straight into the barrel of a gun.

"About time you got here, lady."

For an instant she could not breathe. She had been so grateful the house didn't contain any dead bodies that she had not even stopped to think it might contain a few live ones.

She went very still and looked up into the face of the young man holding the weapon. He was not very tall, but he was heavily built and had a cruel mouth and eyes that had probably never been innocent. He was dressed in military boots and khakis, and he held the gun as if he was very accustomed to it. As she stared at him he made a show of flicking the briefest of glances at his stainless-steel wristwatch.

"Who are you?" Mattie managed in a tight voice.

"You can call me Goody. I work for someone who wants to meet you, Miss Sharpe. That's all you need to know."

"What have you done with Hugh and Silk?"

"Me?" The thin brows rose. "Why, nothing. Yet. But they'll be taken care of soon enough. Let's go." He used the gun to motion her back down the hall. "Move it, lady. We've got a plane to catch."

"I'm not going anywhere with you."

The man grinned. "That's what you think. You got two choices, lady. Either you walk outside to the Jeep, or I knock you unconscious and carry you out. Take your pick."

"What if I don't like the options?"

"They're the only ones you've got."

Mattie looked at him and believed every word he was saying. She turned and walked slowly down the hall and outside to the Jeep. Goody stayed three steps behind her all the way.

"You drive," Goody said, glancing once more at his watch.

"How did you know I was coming here to the cottage?" Mattie asked as she struggled once more with the gears.

"We knew several hours ago that Mortinson had bungled the operation in Seattle. He didn't report in on time, so he's out of the picture. Christ, the man must have been a complete idiot not to be able to take out one whore and pick you up."

"That's what Mortinson was supposed to do? Kill my friend and kidnap me?"

The man scowled, looking as if he was afraid he'd said too much. "Forget it. Doesn't matter now. You're here, just like we figured you'd be when we found out you'd left Seattle. We knew we couldn't grab you in the St. Gabe airport terminal or near it. Abbott's got too many friends on the island, and they all know you belong to him. Someone would have noticed."

"Yes." Mattie's mouth was dry.

"I figured you'd check his house sooner or later, so that's where I waited for you. Now, let's move this bucket a little faster. I'm in kind of a hurry."

"Don't you think someone at the airport might

notice the gun?" Mattie struggled with the gears and backed slowly out of the drive.

"No one will be close enough to see us. When you get to the airport, drive straight out onto the service road that parallels the runway. The plane will be waiting."

It was.

Everything went just as Goody had told her it would. The Cessna was at the end of the runway. No one appeared to notice the two people who parked the Jeep on the service road and walked out to board the plane.

That was one of the problems with the casual way things were run out here in the islands, Mattie thought bitterly. This sort of thing would never have happened back home in Seattle. Unauthorized vehicles were simply not allowed out on airport runways back in the States.

The young pilot glanced only briefly at his unwilling passenger. He nodded once at Goody as the gunman latched the door.

"What took you so long?"

"She took her own sweet time, Christ, let's just get this thing off the ground. The Colonel will be getting impatient."

Mattie fastened her seat belt, closed her eyes, and wondered where Hugh was.

They reached Purgatory an hour later. Mattie was once again marched across an active runway and thrust into a waiting vehicle. No one said a word. She was surrounded by three armed men now, Goody, the pilot, and the driver of the car. All wore military-style clothing and all were surprisingly young. Mattie estimated their ages at between nineteen and twenty-three or twenty-four at the most.

Her stress level, already sky high, went up another couple of notches when she recognized their destination. Paul Cormier's white island mansion looked as beautiful this time as it had when she had first seen it.

Mattie got out of the car at the point of a gun and walked up the steps to the wide veranda. The door was opened by a young man who looked as if he ordered his clothes from *Soldier of Fortune* magazine. He had a gun strapped to his thigh.

"This way, Miss Sharpe."

The first thing she noticed was that someone had cleaned Paul Cormier's blood off the white marble. For some reason that made her angry. It was as though some part of her felt the evidence of murder should not be erased until justice was done.

The anger gave her strength. She walked swiftly down the white marble hall to the wide white room that fronted the house. The view of the sapphire-blue ocean through the bank of open French windows was dazzling. She concentrated on it rather than on the man who was rising from a white leather couch to greet her.

"Miss Sharpe. Allow me to introduce myself. I am known now as Colonel McCormick, but I believe you are no doubt aware by now of my previous name, Jack Rainbird."

Mattie turned slowly to look at him, as if she found him a nuisance when all she really wanted to do was admire the view. She let her glance slide critically over him from head to foot.

Jack Rainbird was an astonishingly handsome man by any standards. He appeared to be in his early forties, as Hugh had said, but he had the strong, bird-of-prey features that would not even begin to soften for many years. His eyes were a clear, light, honest blue. His blond hair, graying at the temples, had been precision cut with a razor to lie close to his head. His body was trim and there was a crisp military set to his head and shoulders. He was wearing perfectly pressed khakis. His belt buckle shone and his boots had been polished to a high gloss.

All in all, Mattie thought, Rainbird had the classic heroic look historically associated with a leader of men. That was, of course, undoubtedly one of the many things that made him so dangerous. The other thing was his undeniable sexual charm. Hugh had been right. The man had it in spades. He exuded it like an aura.

Mattie felt the first uneasy twinge of a throat-closing claustrophobia.

"This is Paul Cormier's house," she said boldly, more to counteract her own tension than anything else. "You have no business here."

A smile flickered briefly around Rainbird's finely crafted mouth. "What can I say? Best accommodations on the island, and I like having the best. Besides, our friend Mr. Cormier no longer has any need of his lovely island home."

"You killed him."

"Do you always jump to conclusions, Miss

Sharpe? That is generally considered a dangerous thing to do."

"You killed him. Or had him killed."

"Obviously your mind is already made up. I imagine I owe that to Abbott. He, naturally, would have a somewhat biased view of events."

"Why?"

Rainbird gave her a look that was half amused, half surprised. "Why, because he hates my guts, of course." He walked across the beautiful room to a white liquor cabinet. "May I offer you a drink, Miss Sharpe?"

"No, thank you."

"I was afraid you might be difficult about all this." Rainbird splashed whiskey into a crystal glass. "You've been hanging around with Abbott for too long. The man has poisoned your mind against me."

Mattie took a deep breath and asked aloud the question that was screaming in her mind. "Just where is Hugh and his friend Silk?"

Rainbird smiled at her over the rim of his glass. "Now, that, Miss Sharpe, is what I am hoping you will tell me."

She stared at him, open-mouthed. "You mean you don't know, either?"

"I'm afraid not. And the whole thing is getting to be something of a problem. I never did like having Abbott running around loose. The man's too damn unpredictable. Always does things his way instead of the military way. That was one of the reasons I had to . . ." Rainbird smiled again. "Never mind. That's ancient history."

"Well, you've gone to a lot of trouble for

nothing, Colonel Rainbird. Because I have no idea where Hugh is. And I wouldn't tell you if I did."

"Then we shall just have to put out the word that you are here with me and wait for him to come and collect you, won't we?" Rainbird's blue eyes glinted. "Howard will show you to your room now. You may change for dinner."

Mattie's chin lifted. "I should warn you I don't eat meat."

"Excellent," Rainbird said with a smile. "Neither do I. Gave it up some time ago along with cigarettes. Do you know, I believe we are going to discover a great many things in common, Miss Sharpe. It has been a long while since I have had the pleasure of entertaining an intelligent, attractive woman. And knowing you are Hugh Abbott's will make it all the more interesting."

CHAPTER

Eighteen

It was too much to hope that she would be shown to the master bedroom suite. Mattie thought of the secret panel behind the elegant bathtub and sighed. Hugh had said there was more than one emergency exit in this house. She surveyed the room that had been assigned to her.

It was as lovely as every other room in the gracious white mansion. The windows all opened onto the veranda and a view of the ocean. The walls were strips of white marble interspersed with sparkling mirrors. Mattie tentatively pressed on a few of them to see if by chance Cormier had built one of his escape routes in this room. She had no luck, either in the main room or in the adjoining bath.

That meant her only hope for escape was to finagle a way into the master bath. Mattie's heart sank as she realized that was probably going to be a lot easier to do than she might have wished. She had seen the look in Rainbird's eyes and knew what he intended. Before the night was over, he was going to drag her into the bedroom suite, if only for the pleasure of raping Hugh Abbott's woman.

Mattie opened her suitcase slowly and examined the contents. Too bad she had not had a chance to go shopping with Evangeline before leaving Seattle. It looked like the blue and white striped silk camp shirt and prim little navy-blue skirt were going to have to serve as her seduction outfit.

She stood in front of the mirror for a minute before leaving the room and unbuttoned the silk shirt a little lower than she normally would have. Then she took her hair down and brushed it out so that it danced around her shoulders. It made a lot of difference, she realized. She reached for her makeup kit, wishing Evangeline were there to give advice.

Dinner was served by Howard, who looked exactly the same as he had when he'd greeted Mattie at the door, except that he'd draped a white linen napkin over his arm. It didn't quite go with the gun on his hip. Mattie thought.

She was seated at the end of a long, thick glass

table supported on four legs fashioned of carved white stone. Rainbird was seated at the opposite end. He was wearing a white dinner jacket and a black bow tie. Paul Cormier's beautiful crystal, silver, and china glittered on the table, reflecting the candlelight.

"No need to look uneasy, Miss Sharpe." Rainbird sounded amused. "I assure you, I am not planning to poison you. Enjoy your meal. Howard is an excellent chef. Cooking is one of his many areas of expertise. He is a very versatile young man."

Howard glowed under the praise and watched anxiously as Mattie sampled her rice pilaf. She looked up and saw him watching her.

"It's wonderful." she said honestly.

"Thank you, ma'am." Howard inclined his head.

Rainbird's mouth lifted slightly at the corner. "I'm sure you've made his day, Miss Sharpe. You may leave us now, Howard. I'll call you if we need anything."

"Yes, sir." Howard vanished into the kitchen.

Mattie looked down the table at Rainbird. His elegantly carved cheekbones were highlighted by the soft glow of candlelight, and he looked even more handsome than he had in daylight. "Are all your men as young as Howard and the others?"

"Now, yes. I learned the hard way some years ago that young males work out better in this sort of service. Not only are young men more attracted to the life of adventure I offer, they are more amenable to taking orders. The older we get, the more cynical we become, and the less inclined we are to put our trust in others."

"I see."

Rainbird chuckled indulgently. "Don't look at me like that. Young men are much easier to train and mold. It's a fact of life, Miss Sharpe. Why do you think that the draft age is always set as low as possible? The military has always preferred eighteen-and nineteen-year-olds."

"Because they're more impressionable."

"Exactly."

"Are you always so calculating, Colonel Rainbird?"

"Always." He forked up a bite of vegetable curry and chewed meditatively. "It is the primary reason I've lived this long."

"Is there a secondary reason?"

His charming grin came and went. "I have been blessed with excellent reflexes. They have come in handy on occasion. And not just when I'm fighting with someone."

Mattie blushed and quickly changed the subject. "Do you mind if I ask why you are here on Purgatory?"

He smiled, pouring more wine. "Purgatory, my dear Miss Sharpe, is the perfect home for one such as myself. The government, what there is of it, is most accommodating."

"Because it takes orders from you?"

"Let's just say we all get along very well together here. A live-and-let-live philosophy."

"That didn't apply to Paul Cormier, did it?" Mattie asked softly.

"You may not believe this, but I am truly sorry about Paul."

Mattie held his clear blue gaze. "Did you kill him, Colonel Rainbird?"

A trace of sorrow flickered in the depths of the beautiful sky-blue eyes. "No. I give you my word of honor as an officer and a gentleman, Miss Sharpe. I did not kill Paul. He and I had gone our separate ways over the years, but we were former comrades in arms and I had nothing but the utmost respect for him. I still considered him a friend. I intended for us to be neighbors here on Purgatory."

"Then who killed him?" Mattie blurted out, confused and frustrated by Rainbird's obvious sincerity and undeniable charm.

"I assure you. I made it my immediate business to find out. The culprit was a house servant who decided to kill and rob his employer under cover of the military activity that was taking place on the island. He is presently in the village jail awaiting trial. Justice will be done, Miss Sharpe. Have no fear. I am a man who believes in justice."

She looked straight into his eyes and knew with terrifying clarity that he was lying. "Is that right? Then why did you lead a coup on a perfectly peaceful island?"

"All was not as it seemed on the surface here on Purgatory, Miss Sharpe. May I call you Mattie?" Rainbird did not pause for a response. "The small local government had no military arm, and it found itself threatened by a group of local rene-gades—hoodlums, really—who had obtained a cache of automatic weapons. I came ashore with my men at the request of the president. It is not an uncommon sort of action, Mattie. Small, ineffectual governments such as Purgatory's frequently need the assistance of men such as myself."

"And now you've decided to stay?"

Rainbird nodded. "I see in Purgatory exactly what my friend Paul saw. A lovely, relatively peaceful place where a man who has grown weary of battle may live out his life on his own terms."

Mattie narrowed her eyes consideringly. "What about that man you had following me in Seattle?"

"That man was your bodyguard, Mattie. I assigned him to keep an eye on you while you were involved with Hugh Abbott. Abbott has killed innocent bystanders before and will probably kill again. I didn't want you to be one of the victims. I realize you are not yet prepared to believe me when I tell you Abbott is dangerous, but sooner or later you will see the truth."

It was then Mattie realized for certain what she had suspected earlier, Rainbird did not know she had seen the man break into her apartment and attempt to kill Evangeline. Apparently the Colonel had not yet communicated with his assassin. He would know there had been a failure in his plans, but he did not yet know at what point things had gone wrong.

Perhaps the intruder had not regained consciousness, or maybe he had awakened with convenient short-term amnesia. Mattie had heard that was common in cases of blows to the head, and the man who had invaded her apartment had certainly endured a number of those.

"Forgive me, Mattie," Rainbird was saying, "but may I ask you how you came to be involved with Paul Cormier?"

Mattie considered her words carefully. "He was selling an item from his collection of ancient armor to someone I know. As I was going on vacation in the Pacific at the time, I was asked to pick up the item and take it back to Seattle."

"Ah, yes, now it makes some sense. Perhaps you would like to see the collection? I removed it temporarily while the house was being cleaned, but it is now back in place, and it is very impressive. Do you know anything about antique armory?"

"No." Mattie decided not to mention her aunt's collection. The less Rainbird knew, the better.

"Paul acquired some remarkable pieces. I shall be delighted to show them to you."

Mattie's nerves were live wires of tension and fear by the time the meal drew to a close. Rainbird's charm was like a foul cloud reaching out to envelop her. *Vampire*, she thought nervously as she took a tiny sip of wine.

When the Colonel poured her a glass of brandy and led her down a wide hall to the library, she realized her fingers were trembling. Rainbird did not appear to notice.

"Impressive, isn't it?" Rainbird said as he led Mattie into a lovely room filled with books and glass cases of various sizes and shapes. "The cases are all individually sealed and climate-controlled, of course. Salt air is not good for old metal."

"No, I imagine it isn't." Mattie wandered from case to case, her brandy glass in hand, and tried to look interested in the daggers, swords, helmets, shields, and mail inside. She focused on her breathing, trying to calm herself. When the time came to act she simply could not afford to collapse from stress. She stopped in front of a case that held a single weapon, a sword.

"That is a particularly interesting specimen, isn't it?" Rainbird observed, moving softly to stand directly behind her.

"Yes. I think that may have been the sword I was sent to collect." Mattie felt the old, familiar sensation of walls closing in around her. It was, she realized vaguely, the first time she'd ever had another human being trigger her claustrophobia. Elevators, caves, stress, yes. But not another person.

"Fourteenth century, according to Paul's records," Rainbird mused. He was very close to her now. His knuckles gently brushed the line of Mattie's neck. "Finest Spanish steel." His breath was warm on the bare skin of her neck as he lifted her hair in his hand. "It has a name, you know. *Valor*. A good weapon deserves a name of its own."

"I've heard there's also a legend attached to it." Mattie could hardly breathe. She felt as if she were being suffocated by Rainbird's closeness.

"Ah, yes." Rainbird's fingertips touched her neck with infinite gentleness. "Something about the blade being dangerous for anyone to claim unless they're an avenger after a betrayer, no? Charming curse, isn't it? But the betrayer, whoever he was, has been dead for several hundred years. And so has the avenger who was meant to take up the blade."

"Do you think so?" A shiver of dread went straight down Mattie's spine as Rainbird's fingers trailed across her shoulder.

"Yes. The avenger and the betrayer are long gone. But the blade survives." Rainbird stroked her arm. "It is a beautiful sword, isn't it? A blade made for killing, not for ceremony. Note the clean lines of the pommel and hilt." His hand slid along the curve of her arm. "No useless ornamentation or expensive gemstones. The blade reminds me of you, Mattie. Clean and elegant. Cool on the outside. But forged in fire. Beautiful."

Mattie sucked in her breath in a startled gasp as Rainbird eased closer. His fingers were gliding just inside the collar of her shirt now. She felt his lips move softly, lightly on her nape. The claustrophobia was so strong she was almost sick with it.

"Mattie? You are really very lovely, you know. I have never met anyone quite like you."

She looked up at him, half-hypnotized and fully terrified by the utter clarity of Rainbird's gaze. Mattie realized then why he could look at her with such complete sincerity. It was because he had no concept of conscience or remorse. There was nothing there under the surface, just as she had tried to explain to Hugh. *Nothing there at all.*

This was a man who could commit any crime and feel nothing for the victim. He could look his next victim straight in the eye and smile.

Not like Hugh, she thought. She understood then that Hugh had never lied to her. Not once, not even a year ago.

With Hugh, a woman would always know where she stood—if she was paying attention and not letting the past get in the way.

When Hugh made love, there was no doubting the genuineness of his passion. When he chewed you out, you knew he was mad. When he laughed, you knew he was happy. When he made a commitment, you knew he would keep it.

And if he were about to kill you, Mattie realized, you would know it. He would not smile at you with seductive eyes when he pulled the trigger. All the hellish cold of impending death would be there in his wolf's gaze.

"I find you as fascinating in your own way as I do the sword in that case," Rainbird murmured. "But I suppose that is not so very strange. You are a creature fashioned for passion, and the blade is an object designed for clean, cold violence. Sex and violence are forever linked. Two sides of the same coin. Have you learned that yet, Mattie?"

"No," she said, her throat tight as the walls closed in. "No, and I don't believe you. They are not linked. One is life and one is death."

"Such an innocent." His mouth brushed across hers again. The blue eyes were smiling and intent. "I am willing to bet you have never been made love to properly, Mattie Sharpe. I can see the lack of knowledge in your eyes. You're nervous, aren't you?"

"Yes." That was putting it mildly, Mattie thought.

"I told you that good sex and good violence are linked, but that doesn't mean I like my sex to be violent. Quite the contrary, Mattie. I am a man who likes subtlety and nuance. I appreciate delicate things, and a woman such as yourself is a very delicate creature, indeed. You would find me a very gentle, very considerate, very careful lover. I would take my time with you. All the time in the world."

"Please . . . I . . ."

He silenced her with another feather-light kiss. Then, with a small, endearing smile flickering again around the corners of his mouth, he took her hand and led her out of the library and along the veranda to the master bedroom suite. He did not turn on the lights as he urged her through the French doors. A sliver of silver from the moon angled across the room.

Mattie struggled for composure. The massive white bed in the center of the room loomed in the shadows. "What about Howard?"

"Howard will not bother us." Rainbird smiled his beautiful smile. "Don't be afraid, Mattie. I'm not going to rape you. I don't do things that way. There is a place for violence, but it is not in the bedroom."

"You prefer to exercise the power of seduction?" She tried a small, tentative smile of her own.

"As I said, I prefer subtlety." Rainbird's finger drifted along the vee of her shirt collar. "And I imagine any woman who has spent more than ten minutes with Hugh Abbott would hunger for a little civilized behavior. Especially someone as sensitive and lovely as you, Mattie."

She closed her eyes and took one step backward. She was feeling so nauseated now she was beginning to be afraid she would ruin everything by throwing up in the middle of Rainbird's big seduction scene. "Would you mind very much if I used the bathroom?"

"Not at all." He waved her gallantly toward the adjoining room.

He continued to watch her with an intent, vaguely amused expression as she edged toward the bath. His fingers went to the black tie around his throat.

Suddenly Mattie wondered if Rainbird already knew about the secret panel and had walled it up. Perhaps he was playing some horrible game with her. But she had no choice. She had to try it. It was her only hope of escape. The thought of going back out into that bedroom was enough to make her feel faint.

She closed the door of the beautiful bath, turned on the light, and took a quick glance around. Rainbird's personal items were there now, neatly placed along the white marble countertop: silverbacked combs, expensive after-shave and cologne, a single fresh hibiscus in a crystal vase.

Mattie's eyes glided over the mirror, and she almost failed to recognize the white-faced woman with the huge, frightened eyes who stared back at her.

A soft sound in the bedroom made her flinch. She had to make her move now. Mattie walked over to the sink and turned one of the handles of the silver faucet so that the water splashed merrily into the basin.

She started opening drawers quietly, remembering what Hugh had said about Cormier keeping a flashlight in every room of the house because of frequent power outages. Surely he would have kept one in this bathroom, since it had been planned as an escape room. Cormier was a strategist, Hugh had said. Rainbird would have had no reason to remove something like a flashlight.

She found what she was looking for in the bottom right drawer near the sink.

Picking up the flashlight, she stepped out of her shoes and went across the room to flush the toilet.

Water churned loudly in the fixtures.

It was all the cover she would get. Carrying her shoes, Mattie hurried to the marble bath, stepped into it and pushed on the wall panel as Hugh had before.

For a second nothing happened. Mattie thought the stress would overwhelm her. She simply could not go back out into that bedroom. She would become a screaming zombie here in the elegant bath if she did not escape *right now*.

The panel slid silently open. Mattie breathed a silent prayer of gratitude, hitched up her skirt, and stepped into the darkness. The sense of relief was enough to push aside the mounting sense of claustrophobia for a short time. She found the button on the other side of the panel and pushed it. The panel slid soundlessly back into place.

At that same instant there was a soft knock on the bathroom door.

"Mattie? Are you all right in there?"

Mattie switched on the flashlight, stepped into her shoes, and fled down the hidden hallway. She reached the door that opened onto the jungle and held her breath as she turned the handle.

Half expecting to meet up with one of the armed guards, she switched off the flashlight and stepped out into the night. She stood very still for a minute, waiting for her eyes to adjust. Then she darted into the jungle.

She had only the moon and the lights of the house to guide her. The soft, moist earth muffled her footsteps, but she knew she was making far too much noise in the undergrowth. At any moment one of the guards would surely hear her. She could only hope the crashing surf would give her some protection.

She went straight into the jungle, keeping the house lights at her back. They quickly began to fade, however, as the thick vegetation closed in around her. She had to concentrate on the sound of the ocean and the vague light of the moon to guide her. She did not dare turn on the flashlight.

Ocean on the left. House to the rear. Straight on until you cross the stream.

Rainbird's voice, sounding as if it were magnified through some sort of megaphone, blared out in the darkness.

"Mattie, come back. Don't run away. You won't come to any harm. You can't survive in that jungle, Mattie. There are too many things out there that can kill you. Especially at night. Things like snakes, Mattie. Do you want to find yourself in the coils of a giant snake?"

Hugh had said not to worry, Mattie recalled. There were no snakes in the jungles of Purgatory. Hugh had never lied to her. Rainbird could tell you he loved you while he slit your throat.

She plunged on. When the lights of the house

368

disappeared entirely, she risked the flashlight in brief doses. At one point she scrambled over a fallen log and realized it was the one on which she had torn her silk blouse the first time she had come this way.

She was on the right track.

"Mattie, you're safe with me. You will die a horrible death out in that jungle. Trust me, Mattie. I mean you no harm." Rainbird's magnified voice was fading into the distance.

Hugh had said it would be virtually impossible to miss the stream. *Ocean on the left.*

Were those distant crashing sounds the footsteps of her pursuers?

She batted at the leaves, crawled over vines, pushed rare orchids out of the way as if they were so much noxious garbage in her path.

Mattie stumbled over a vine and went down on one knee. She put out her hand to steady herself and her fingers went straight into running water.

The stream.

Blindly she turned left. Now all she had to do was follow the rivulet of water to the waterfalls.

By now Rainbird would have sent his men out into the jungle on the theory that she would not go far. Perhaps he had assumed she would head for the sea in some primitive instinct to avoid the jungle.

She risked the flashlight again in short bursts of light. She quickly learned it was easier not to subject her eyes to the changes in shadows. Mattie continued her journey with the aid of the moon and wet feet. As long as her shoes stayed wet, she knew she was on the right path.

A familiar roaring sound told her she was approaching the waterfalls. Mattie picked up her pace, hoping she would not fall and twist her ankle. She still had all those caves to get through.

God, the caves.

And then what? she wondered bleakly. Assuming she survived the caves, she could not stay in Cormier's sanctuary forever. She would die of thirst and starvation. But she would worry about escape later. Right now the important thing was to get away from the blue-eyed vampire in the beautiful white mansion.

She would rather die of thirst and starvation in the cavern than lure Hugh to his death, and she knew that was what Rainbird intended.

Mattie burst through the last green barrier and came to an abrupt halt at the sight of the magnificent twin waterfalls bathed in silver moonlight. It was an eerie sight that touched some deep cord within her. There were things on this earth that were more powerful and would last eons longer than Jack Rainbird. And they could protect her from him now.

Mattie went forward and stepped up on the first of the wet, slippery rocks that outlined the foaming pool. She dared not fall tonight. Hugh was not here to catch her.

But this time she was not trying to juggle her purse and a French string bag full of paté and bottles of sparkling water. This time it was a little easier. This time she was a little more determined.

Mattie did not slip. She leaped off the last rock, straight through a shower of water, and found herself in the black mouth of the cave. She flicked on the flashlight and scanned the walls for the marks Cormier had left behind.

Now came the hard part, she told herself ruefully. Now she had to walk through these twisting, turning tunnels of darkness all by herself.

It was worse than any crowded elevator but not quite as bad as having Jack Rainbird try to seduce her in a white and silver room. All things were relative, it seemed.

Twice she found herself turning down wrong corridors, but both times she was able to retrace her steps and find the small white marks on the walls. At several points along the way she wanted to close her eyes, but she did not dare. She might miss one of the white marks.

Her stomach was in knots. Her heart was pounding, and the flashlight threatened to fall from her damp palms. But she could not go back. The only direction was forward. Walking through the corridors was a lot like going through life without an obvious talent. Mattie told herself. You just kept moving forward until you found the right path.

She was getting close to the point of screaming, convinced she had made a wrong turn and was heading toward oblivion, when she caught a whiff of fresh sea air.

"Oh, my God." Mattie broke into a stumbling run.

The air became fresher and laden with the tang of salt. It was going to be all right, at least for a while. Rainbird and his men would never find her here.

Of course, neither would anyone else, she reminded herself grimly.

Obviously she would have to risk a trip back out sooner or later. But perhaps after a day or so Rainbird would not be looking so hard for her. Perhaps he would assume she had either escaped or drowned in the sea or died somewhere in the jungles.

She would worry about getting off Purgatory when she had recovered from this first, mad dash to freedom.

She was running full tilt when she reached the entrance to the massive cavern where she and Hugh had hoped to find Cormier's boat. The flashlight pierced the gloom in front of her, revealing the natural boat basin.

The first thing Mattie noticed was that this time there was a boat tied up at the dock. A swift, sleek, very powerful-looking cruiser.

Before she could comprehend the meaning of the boat in the cavern, a man's arm came out of the darkness and tightened like a steel noose about her throat.

Mattie tried to scream, but the sound was promptly choked off. She dropped the flashlight to struggle futilely with her assailant and felt the point of a knife graze her skin in warning.

"Well, shit," said Hugh, lowering the knife. "It's Mattie."

CHAPTER

Nineteen

Mattie sat on a duffel bag next to Silk Taggert, who was calmly checking over a handgun, and watched Hugh pace the cavern with a restless wolfish tread. The forbidding expression on his hard face reminded her of the one he'd had the night she had called him to rescue her from the bar in Seattle. But this was a thousand times worse, Mattie decided. Hugh was a grenade waiting to be detonated, a sword waiting to be unsheathed.

"Are you sure he didn't hurt you?" Hugh demanded for the fifth or sixth time.

"He didn't hurt me. I told you, he admitted he was looking for you, then he fed me a lovely dinner. He told me he was a vegetarian, but I didn't believe him. Not for one minute."

Hugh gave her a strange glance. "Then what?"

"Then he took me to see Cormier's collection of old weapons." Mattie had already been through this recitation several times.

"And then he took you to the bedroom, Goddamn his soul."

"He didn't exactly drag me, Hugh," Mattie said patiently. "He assumed he was charming me. I let him think he was succeeding. The truth was I went with him because I remembered the panel in the bathroom. It was easy enough to duck in there for a minute or two. Having to use the bathroom

373

is the greatest excuse in the world. And as far as Rainbird was concerned, it was safe to let me go in there. After all, there weren't any obvious exits except through the bedroom."

"Good thinking, Mattie," Silk said. He flicked a glance at Hugh. "Lighten up, boss. She did great and she's here, safe and sound. That's all that counts. Hell of a woman, if I may say so." He shoved a clip into the automatic. "Now you and I got work to do."

"I'll kill him."

"Yeah, I know. But first we got to get to him." Silk slanted a smile at Mattie. "Way I see it, we now got us some terrific inside information. A lot more than we had an hour ago."

"Oh, God," said Mattie, feeling drained. "I don't want you two involved in any more violence."

"A little late to worry about that," Silk said gently. "Don't you worry yourself into an ulcer over this, now. It'll be over before you know it. And then we can all get off this damn island. But it would sure speed things up if you could give us some details."

Mattie looked at him and then at Hugh and knew there was nothing she could do to stop either of them. The next best option was to try to help. "I'm afraid I wasn't paying a lot of attention to that sort of thing."

"Just think back and count all the faces you remember seeing and where they were."

"Well, I do remember thinking a couple of times that there weren't as many thugs around as I would have expected. Maybe half a dozen in all.

I kept wondering where the army of occupation was."

Hugh stood at the edge of the basin of black water and stared down into it. "I told you. There is no army of occupation on Purgatory. No need for one. Rainbird is on the government's side, remember?"

"What there is of it," Silk added. "Never was much of a government here. That's one of the reasons Cormier liked it."

Hugh nodded. "What Rainbird did was classic. He made a brief show of force, handed out a few guns, and created a lot of confusion with a small group of trained men. There was no organized resistance on Purgatory. By the time the initial uproar was over, he had cut himself a deal with the folks who are officially in charge around here. Probably guaranteed to triple or quadruple the island's annual tax base with a corresponding increase in salary for the honchos and everyone else who cooperated. Money always speaks louder than guns in the long run."

"Yeah," Silk said. "You can get someone's attention with a gun, but you keep him on your side with money."

"But what does Rainbird get out of it?" Mattie asked.

"A safe harbor. He probably needs it in order to expand his business interests. God knows what he's into by now. Purgatory is perfect. A tiny, politically independent island of absolutely no strategic importance to anyone where he can relax, kick back, and run his empire."

"Probably had his eye on Purgatory for years

after he realized Paul had moved here," Silk said. He turned to Mattie. "Anyhow, that's one of the reasons why you didn't see an entire army hanging around the place. But there's another reason for keeping the house guard down to half a dozen or less."

Mattie nodded. "Hugh explained Rainbird doesn't trust anyone and doesn't want too many people around him at any one time."

Hugh glanced back over his shoulder. "It's damn tough to find even five or six men you can trust with your life. Rainbird is pushing it by having that many around him, and he knows it. Probably intends to cut back as soon as he feels secure."

Mattie shivered and clasped her hands. "All right, give me a minute to think. There was Howard inside. He was the only one other than Rainbird who was actually in the house. He wears a gun strapped to his hip like some old western gunslinger. And then there was Goody, who was waiting for me at the beach cottage on St. Gabe."

"Shit," said Hugh. "I'll kill him, too."

Silk shot him a disgusted glance. "Shut up, boss. You ain't thinking straight yet. Let me and Mattie talk while you cool down. Go ahead, Mattie."

"Well, then there was the pilot . . ."

Mattie began to talk more quickly as she started to concentrate. It proved easier to recall details than she would have thought. All those years of art lessons and her work as a gallery owner were paying off. She really had developed an observant eye, she thought proudly as she concluded her report. She looked at Hugh expectantly, waiting for praise. She got a glare that under other circumstances would have frozen her socks off.

Silk tried to compensate. "Great job, Mattie." He gave her a slap on the back that nearly unseated her. "One of the best recon reports I've ever heard. This is going to make things a lot easier, ain't it, Hugh."

"Shit," Hugh said again.

"Sometimes his vocabulary is what you might call limited," Silk confided to Mattie.

"I've noticed," Mattie said "He told me once it was a sign of stress."

"Silk grinned. "Is that right? Stress, huh? And here I thought all along it was just on account of he never learned his manners."

Hugh whipped around to face both of them and resumed his pacing across the cavern floor. "We can't move on Rainbird until we get Mattie out of here."

"It'll take two or three hours to get her to Hades. Another two or three to get back here. If we wait that long we'll lose a lot of the advantage we've got right now," Silk pointed out reasonably. "You know it, boss. Rainbird obviously doesn't realize we're on the island yet. He's got his men scattered from here to breakfast looking for Mattie. That means he's as isolated as he's ever going to be."

"I know, I know," Hugh growled, shoving his hands into the rear pockets of his jeans. "But I don't like it. If something happens to us, Mattie is trapped here."

"She can take the boat."

"And do what with it?" Hugh stormed. "She's a city girl. What does she know about boats or navigation? How's she going to start the engine, let alone find her way back to Hades?"

"Excuse me," Mattie murmured, clearing her throat. "I would just like to point out that I may be a city girl, but the city I grew up in was Seattle. My father owned a boat all the years I was growing up. Ariel and I can both handle one. And I can read a chart. I wouldn't get lost between here and Hades if I had to find my own way."

"Well, I'll be damned," Silk said in deeply admiring tones.

Hugh gave Mattie a hooded glance. "Is that right?"

She nodded. "It's true. But I don't want to even think about leaving the two of you behind. Hugh, there's got to be a better way of dealing with Rainbird. I don't like the idea of the two of you going in alone against Rainbird and those half dozen overgrown boy scouts he's got around him. Those are not good odds."

"But we don't care about the boy scouts," Hugh explained quietly. His initial outrage was fading now, and a chilling, emotionless quality was entering his voice. "The only one we have to take out is Rainbird. When he's gone, the boy scouts will scatter fast enough. They're nothing without a leader."

"How will you get into the house?" Mattie asked, wishing she could find a way to talk them out of the whole project and knowing it was impossible.

"I told you Cormier built a lot of emergency

378

exits from his house. They work just as well as secret entrances." Hugh ran a hand through his hair, frowning in thought. "We'll use the one in the kitchen this time."

"Sounds good to me," Silk said. "Get in, get out, and we're off the island before anyone even knows what happened. We'll be eating dinner on Hades."

"Wait," said Mattie, feeling desperate. "Are you sure there isn't some other way to do this? Couldn't you get more help?"

Silk grinned. "Hey, we've got you, Mattie Sharpe. So far you've been more use than a whole company of Marines."

Mattie groaned.

"Okay," Hugh said finally, his tone utterly cold now. "You're right, Silk. This is the best chance we're going to get. Let's go do it."

Mattie stood up. "Hugh?"

"Yeah, babe?" Hugh was crouched beside a pile of equipment, his back to her.

"Promise me you won't take any . . . any unnecessary chances." That sounded stupid. Of course he was going to take chances.

"Sure, babe. No unnecessary chances." He shoved a knife into his boot and checked his revolver.

"I love you," Mattie whispered.

Hugh thrust the revolver into his belt and stood up. "I love you, too, babe," he said absently. His attention was clearly on his preparations, not on the words he had so casually just spoken.

Mattie smiled mistily. He did not even realize that this was the first time he had actually said it aloud. The man could be so dense at times. "I know," she said softly. "I wasn't sure until recently. But now I know."

He glanced at her, briefly surprised. And then he scowled. "About time."

"Yes. Things have been a little confused lately," she murmured apologetically.

"Only because you were confused," he said bluntly.

"You may be right. Just be careful. You, too, Silk. You hear me? I don't want you to do anything that could cut short the brilliant artistic career you've got ahead of you."

He grinned and ruffled her hair with his huge paw as she walked over and hugged him tightly. "Hey, don't worry about me, Mattie Sharpe. You and I are going to get rich together. That's a promise."

"You two can talk about what you're going to do with all your ill-gotten gains some other time," Hugh said, heading for the tunnel that led to the waterfalls. "Let's get this business over with first."

"Right, boss."

Mattie watched as the two men vanished, silent as ghosts, in the caves of Purgatory.

And then she sat down to wait.

Hugh heard the voices in the cavern behind the twin waterfalls and knew that two of Rainbird's six-man bodyguard would have to be taken care of before he and Silk went on to the house. Mattie wasn't going to approve. Probably best not to mention the matter to her later.

He switched off the flashlight and waited for Silk to move up alongside.

"Two?" Silk asked.

"Yeah, I think so."

"Sounds like they're going to try to search these caves."

"Fools." Hugh thought a minute. "Might be easiest to just let them get lost."

"They're probably not that dumb. They'll use a rope or something."

"Rope, huh? Then let's hope they've got enough to hang themselves."

Hugh stepped into a side tunnel that branched off the main one, and Silk moved in beside him. Anyone who came this way would have to walk right past them.

A flashlight flickered in the main corridor. The first man in military fatigues moved past, a rope trailing out behind him.

"You see anything, Mark?" called a voice from the main cavern.

"Nothing. I can't tell if she came this way or not."

"She's probably got herself good and lost already. Rainbird's going to be pissed."

Mark halted and shouted down the corridor. "Miss Sharpe, call out if you can hear me. No need to be afraid. We'll get you out of here." His voice ricocheted off the cavern walls.

Hugh studied his quarry. Mattie was right. The kid was too damn young to be playing mercenary. But, then, Rainbird had always attracted bright-eyed young men who had dreams of being heroes.

Hugh remembered a few of his own youthful

dreams as he stepped out into the corridor and brought the butt of his gun down on the hapless mercenary's head. Mark went down without a sound. Hugh dragged him into the side corridor.

"Mark?" The voice at the other end of the rope was not anxious yet. Just curious.

Silk reached past Hugh and tugged gently on the rope, as if Mark were still moving.

"See anything, Mark?" Another flashlight beam cut through the darkness of the main corridor. "Come on, Mark. What's going on? Where are you? You okay?"

Silk tugged on the rope again, drawing it farther into the main tunnel. The second young man followed it slowly, like a wary fish after a lure. When he went past the side tunnel. Hugh stepped out and used the butt of the revolver a second time.

"Got him." Hugh bent down and dragged the second man into the side tunnel.

Silk moved in and quickly used the rope to secure both unconscious men.

"Well, that cases the odds a bit," Silk observed as they made their way out past the waterfalls. "With any luck the rest of 'em will keep floundering around out here in the jungle for a while, and we won't have to cross their paths at all."

"There's always good old Howard the vegetarian gourmet chef."

The moon was almost gone by the time Hugh and Silk made their way over the waterfall pool rocks and found the stream. There was a familiar oppressive weight to the warm air. Hugh sensed the rain that was on its way.

They followed the stream until the sound of the ocean was clear, and then Hugh angled to the right. He and Silk pushed more or less blindly through the jungle, using what was left of the moon as a guide until the lights of the house came into view.

"No problem," Silk observed. "Plenty of cover right up to the house, itself."

"Let's go."

Hugh fumbled a bit trying to find the hidden entrance that opened inside the pantry. It had been a couple of years since Cormier had taken him on the grand tour of the white mansion. But he eventually found the panel in the side of the wall. It was shrouded in pale white lilies.

Inside the entrance a short flight of steps led up to the darkened pantry. Hugh risked the flashlight long enough to get a feel for the arrangement of canned goods, liquor bottles, and supplies that were stacked on the floor. Silk trailed silently behind him.

Hugh turned the flashlight onto the wall and found the circuit-breaker panel. He hit the switches, shutting off everything. Then he opened the pantry door onto darkness. He and Silk crawled out into the kitchen and waited.

"What the hell?" Rainbird's voice came from out on the veranda, sounding annoyed but not alarmed.

"The electricity has gone off, Colonel. I'll check the panel. Probably blown a fuse."

"Contact the men and tell them to get back to the house immediately," Rainbird snapped.

"But I'm sure it's just a problem with the fuses

or maybe down at the generator. I'm pretty good with that kind of thing, Colonel . . ."

"I said call in the others. Do it now, Howard. And find some flashlights."

"Yes, sir. I think there's one in the kitchen."

Crouched in shadows behind a counter, Hugh listened to boot heels ring on marble. The redoubtable Howard was hastening to obey orders.

"Mine," said Silk in an almost soundless whisper.

Hugh nodded and Silk moved across the short distance to step back into the pantry.

Howard came around the edge of the counter, yanking open drawers and groping inside. Then his gaze fell on Hugh.

"Hi," Hugh said pleasantly

Howard's mouth fell open, and he groped for his gun. Silk stepped out of the closet and coshed him. Howard slumped to the floor.

"You keep an eye on the main entrance," Hugh muttered. "If the rest of them come back, they'll probably come that way."

"Right. Give my regards to Rainbird. Tell him I'm sure sorry he didn't die six years ago."

"I'll do that."

Hugh moved quickly through the gloom of the living room and on down the hall. All of the main rooms opened onto the veranda, where Rainbird was standing. Hugh wanted the shortest approach to his quarry. From the sound of Rainbird's voice when he had given orders to Howard, the library would probably provide the ideal point from which to step out onto the veranda.

As soon as Hugh moved silently into the library, he saw he had calculated correctly. Through the open French windows he saw Rainbird standing with both hands planted on the veranda railing. He was peering into the darkness below him, obviously searching for the men who should have been returning on the double from the hunt for Mattie.

"Howard? Have you recalled them yet? Damn it, I said move, boy. I don't like this setup. Something's wrong. I want every available man back here right now." Rainbird paused when there was no immediate response. "Howard?"

"Howard's busy, Colonel. You know how it is. Always a lot to do in the kitchen." Hugh stepped out onto the veranda, his revolver in his hand.

"Abbott." Rainbird swung around, clawing for a pistol that was stuck in his belt.

Hugh kicked out suddenly, aiming for the pistol. He caught it with the toe of his boot just as Rainbird started to aim. The weapon went flying over the railing.

"Still as fast as ever, aren't you?" Rainbird smiled thinly as he slowly lowered his hand.

"Not quite," Hugh said. "But fast enough to do this job."

"Do you think so? You were good, Abbott, but I was always a little quicker than you, remember? And unlike you. I've stayed in training for the past six years. Besides," Rainbird taunted softly, "we both know you aren't hard enough to pull that trigger on an unarmed man. That was always your biggest weakness, Abbott. That and the fact that you didn't take orders very well."

"You mean not well enough to walk into that

trap you set in Los Rios? Why did you do it, Rainbird? That's the one thing we could never figure out. What was in it for you that made it worth trying to get the rest of us killed?"

"Money, of course. A great deal of money. And the timing couldn't have been better. You, Cormier, and Silk and the others were getting too difficult to control. You were asking too many questions about the jobs. Men who question their orders are useless to a good commander."

"So you decided to get rid of us. I guess that makes sense from your point of view." Hugh smiled bleakly "You were smart to fake your own death when you realized that some of us hadn't died in that ambush. You knew we'd come looking if we thought you were still alive."

"Cormier thought he'd seen a ghost when I came through the door," Rainbird said with satisfaction. "You know, the old man was still surprisingly fast, too. He actually had his hands on that old Beretta of his when I shot him."

"I know."

Rainbird nodded. "So it was you who found him right afterward. I came back to clean up the place later after I'd secured the island. I realized someone else had been here. Footprints in the blood. Two rented vehicles parked nearby and no sign of anyone. And then I got word that you were looking for whoever had killed Cormier. Once you start something, you don't give up until you've finished, I'll say that much for you, Abbott. I knew I had to take you out along with Silk and the woman."

"And a poor jerk named Rosey."

Rainbird shrugged negligently. "He knew too much, and he was going to sell the info."

"You were right about one thing. I wouldn't have stopped looking until I figured out who killed Paul."

Rainbird smiled a gentle, vaguely regretful smile "Yes. I understood that from the beginning."

"It was a mistake to kill Cormier. But it was an even bigger mistake to involve Mattie in this."

"Ah, yes. The very interesting Miss Sharpe. I congratulate you on her, Abbott. She is a woman after my own heart. She has spirit and intelligence. And a certain style. I like that. You'll forgive me if I say I'm rather surprised you had the brains to appreciate her. You were never the sort to understand or admire subtlety in a woman."

"I might be a slow learner Rainbird, but I do, eventually, catch on."

"And have you learned to kill a man in cold blood?"

"I think that in your case I'll be able to handle it."

Rainbird grinned, looking genuinely amused. "No, Abbott, I don't think so. You'll lose your nerve at the last minute. We both know it."

In that instant a shot roared out through the jungle night, shattering the glass in the French window behind Hugh. Hugh fired over the edge of the railing and leaped for the cover of the darkened library.

Rainbird acted instantly, grabbing the knife out of his boot and launching himself after Hugh.

Hugh spun around and raised the revolver. But he wasn't fast enough.

As always. Rainbird's incredible reflexes stood him in good stead. His weight crashed into Hugh, and both men went sprawling on the library floor.

Something sharp slashed at Hugh's arm. He felt the revolver fall from his hand, and then he was rolling swiftly away from Rainbird's knife.

Rainbird came after him, kicking out savagely. His boot caught Hugh on the arm. The pain was not the worst of it. The temporary loss of muscle control in his right arm was another problem altogether. It could get him killed.

Shots crackled from the far end of the house. Silk was returning fire to whoever was shooting from the jungle. Another shot into the library sent a shower of sharp glass hail down on Hugh and Rainbird.

Hugh saw the knife in Rainbird's hand glint briefly in the shadows. He jerked away again, groping frantically for his own boot knife.

But there was not time to grasp it. Rainbird was coming at him again, his killer's smile gleaming in the darkness.

Rainbird had always been faster. Faster and infinitely more ruthless because he took a strange delight in the act of bringing death to others.

Hugh scrambled backward, aware of sensation returning to his right arm. He barely dodged another swinging thrust of the knife as he got to his feet. He found himself up against a display case. Without looking at what was in the case, he smashed the glass lid with his bare hand and reached inside. The jagged edges of glass bit deep. Blood streamed down his arm.

His fingers closed around the hilt of a sword just as Rainbird leaped in for the kill.

Hugh yanked the sword out of the case. It was surprisingly heavy. But the weight and balance felt strangely comfortable, even familiar in his hand.

He brought the weapon around in front of himself and thrust the blade out and up just as Rainbird came hurtling through the air.

The sword sank into Rainbird's chest with sickening ease. A shattering scream rent the darkness and then there was an unholy silence.

For a few seconds Hugh just stood staring down at Rainbird's body. He looked up as Silk came pounding down the hall and into the library.

"He dead?" Silk asked, coming to a halt.

"Yeah. This time he's dead."

"About time." Silk squinted in the shadows. "You okay?"

Hugh nodded.

"Always knew you were faster than him. You just needed the right motivation is all. Come on, boss. We got to get out of here before the rest of those boy scouts get back. Mattie'll have our heads if we let anything delay us."

"I didn't plan to hang around." Hugh realized he was still grasping the sword. He looked down. It was the one he had arranged for Cormier to sell to Charlotte Vailcourt, the one called *Valor*.

Death to all who dare claim this blade until it shall be taken up by the avenger and cleansed in the blood of the betrayer.

"You going to take that sword with you?" Silk asked, already moving toward the door.

"Might as well. Charlotte will like having it in her collection. And I think Paul would have wanted her to have it."

There was no sense trying to explain to Silk that *Valor* felt clean now, Hugh decided as he followed his friend out into the hall. He could not even explain the feeling to himself.

Hugh paused briefly in the doorway and glanced back at the body of the betrayer. Rainbird lay in a widening pool of blood. Hugh suddenly remembered another ancient prophecy. *All they that take the sword shall perish with the sword.*

"You know, Silk. I'm sure glad you and me wised up a few years back and decided to get ourselves a couple of new professions," Hugh said. "Nobody stays fast enough forever."

CHAPTER

Twenty

Mattie stood on the beach in the moonlight and watched the glistening breakers as they rose and fell on the night-darkened water. The lights of Hugh's cottage gleamed in the shadows behind her, but she did not turn around. Hugh was busy on the phone inside the cottage, talking to Charlotte Vailcourt. Mattie had walked down to the beach to think.

Not that she had not already had ample opportunity to be alone with her own thoughts during the excruciating wait in the cavern on Purgatory. The short time that Hugh and Silk had been gone had seemed an eternity. When they had finally shown up with the blood-stained sword called *Valor*, she had known what had happened. She had not asked for explanations.

Without a word she had bandaged Hugh's bleeding arm while Silk readied the cruiser. They had been on their way within ten minutes. Nobody had said much on the long ride to Hades, where they spent what was left of the night with the local doctor, who treated Hugh's arm. All three of them had fallen asleep from sheer exhaustion, risen early, and been on their way back to St. Gabriel by dawn. And through it all Mattie had said nothing of her plans. She had been waiting for the right opening.

"Mattie?" Hugh's voice was soft in the shadows.

She turned and smiled at him. "Finally finish satisfying Aunt Charlotte's curiosity?"

"Yeah, Man, that woman can sure ask questions. But I think everything's under control at both ends now. The guy who broke into your place finally woke up. He's keeping his mouth shut, but the cops have him cold on three or four solid charges, including breaking and entering and assault with a deadly weapon. You and Evangeline sure did a number on him."

"Independent businesswomen have to be able to look after themselves."

His mouth crooked. "You're not exactly a soft little city girl, are you?"

"Tough as nails," she assured him.

Hugh grinned briefly. "Well, I wouldn't go that far. Parts of you are very, very soft. Come here, soft little city girl."

She walked into his arms, and they closed around her. "I'm so glad it's over, Hugh. The time I spent waiting for you in that cavern were the worst hours of my life."

"It's over, babe. It's finally over." His hold tightened. He turned her face up to his and kissed her with the old, familiar white-hot passion.

Mattie gloried in the sheer, overwhelming honesty of the embrace. Hugh loved her. She was certain of that now. All the tension that had set her nerves on edge for the past few weeks was finally gone, leaving behind a wondrous sureness and a sense of rightness that would last for the rest of her life.

Mattie's fingers went to the buttons of his shirt. She undid them slowly, letting her hands slip inside to feel the warmth and hardness of his chest.

"Babe," he whispered in an aching tone as her fingertips found the fastening of his jeans. "Babe, you don't know what you do to me."

"Tell me again that you love me, Hugh."

"Damn, but I love you. More than anything else on the planet." He was unbuttoning her shirt now. "Believe me?"

"I believe you. I should have understood months ago when you first started concocting schemes to see me."

"You can say that again. Wasted a lot of time, babe. But I'll let you make it up to me." He grinned, the wicked smile full of sensuality and loving promise.

"Wait, Hugh." Mattie trembled with desire as she felt his hand glide over her breast and down to her waist. "There's something I have to tell you."

"You're pregnant?" he asked eagerly.

Startled, she looked up at him. "Well, no. Not that I know of."

"Too bad. Maybe tonight, huh?" He pulled her down onto the sand and rolled over on top of her. He unzipped his jeans.

"Hugh, I am trying to talk to you about a serious matter."

He kissed her throat. "If it doesn't have anything to do with something really important like you getting pregnant, it can wait until later." His hand moved down to her hips and he tugged at her slacks.

Mattie abandoned the effort to talk to him. When Hugh Abbott made love, he gave it his full attention. She found herself crushed into the soft, warm sand, her clothes stripped from her in a few swift movements.

And then there was nothing of importance in the whole world except the weight and feel of the big man looming over her, blocking out the moonlight, covering her, sheathing himself in her, filling her completely.

"Mattie"

She clung to him as he carried her away on the wild, passionate ride into ecstasy. It would always be like this, Mattie thought fleetingly, a whirlwind of shattering excitement, a flashing, thundering, crashing, elemental explosion. A wild, free run with a wolf in the silver moonlight.

393

And she would never, ever tire of it.

A long time later Mattie felt water on her toes. She stirred beneath Hugh's heavy weight. "Hugh?"

"What's the matter, babe?" he asked in that tone of lazy satisfaction he always had after he'd made love to her.

"I think the tide's coming in."

"It's okay. I can swim."

She gave him a clout on his arm. "Smart ass."

"Ouch."

"Oh, my God, was that your wounded arm?"

"No, but it could have been."

She relaxed as she heard the laughter in his voice. "Hugh, I really do have to talk to you."

He groaned into her shoulder. "This is about Seattle, isn't it?"

"Well, yes, as a matter of fact. In a way it is."

"Babe, I really don't want to talk about it just now."

"We have to discuss this, Hugh. This is our future we're dealing with here."

"Our future is with each other. Everything else will work out. Eventually."

"You keep saying that."

He raised his head reluctantly and looked down into her eyes. His own gaze was shadowed and intense. "I mean it. I've been thinking about it, babe, and I realize there's only one way to handle the problem we've got."

"There is?"

He nodded. "I'm selling Abbott Charters to Silk. I'm moving to Seattle. For real. I just

394

finished talking to Charlotte, and she says the job is full time if I want it. I told her I did."

Mattie looked up at him and knew he was telling her the truth. "Oh, Hugh." She framed his hard face with both hands and smiled gently. "That's very sweet of you, and I will never forget this as long as I live, but it's not the right answer."

He went very still. "You got a better one?" he demanded fiercely. "Because I'm not letting you go, Mattie. And that's a fact."

"Aunt Charlotte and everyone else is right when they say you belong out here, Hugh. This is the home you've made for yourself. You overcame enormous odds to build a new life out here, and I want to be part of that new life."

"Here?" He stared at her. "You're saying you want to move to St. Gabe?"

"I want to live in that beautiful house you're going to build, and I want to have your baby, and I want to start my own business here. And I want to do it all right now. So I am going to go back to Seattle on the first available plane and sell Sharpe Reaction. And then I will pack up all my belongings and move out here to St. Gabriel."

Hugh looked dazed. "But what kind of business are you going to build here?"

"I'm not precisely sure yet, but I think there's going to be plenty of opportunity for an ex-gallery owner with ties to the West Coast artistic community. I've got a few dreams I'd like to try. I'm going to look into the possibility of starting an artists' colony. A place where people like Shock Value Frederickson can come and get refreshed, maybe. For a price, of course."

"You're going to invite all your artsy-craftsy friends to come out here?" Hugh was clearly appalled.

"They'll spend money, Hugh. Lots of it. They'll love St. Gabriel. And they'll love the idea of a Pacific island art colony. And on the side I think I'll open a tourist-oriented boutique. I'll feature Silk's paintings for starters. And I think I can persuade Evangeline Dangerfield to move out here and set up a clothing design business. I can sell her creations alongside Silk's."

"The mind boggles."

"You've said yourself St. Gabriel is on the verge of getting discovered. I'll make a fortune selling stuff to the tourists while you clean up with Abbott Charters. Silk will made a bundle on his paintings, and Evangeline will be able to go into a whole new line of work. We'll all get rich, fat, and happy."

Hugh laughed softly, turned onto his back and pulled her down on top of him. "Life is never going to be dull with you, babe. I'll say that much."

"Hugh, the tide . . ."

"Like I said, I can swim and I'll take care of you. Trust me, babe."

She smiled and bent down to kiss him full on his beautiful, sexy mouth. "I do."

"About time."

Charlotte Vailcourt closed the folder on her desk, leaned back in her executive chair, and looked at Hugh, who was standing at the window watching the people on the street below. "An excellent proposal, Hugh. You have a talent for organization and planning. I imagine it will stand you in good stead as you build Abbott Charters."

"I learned a lot from you, Charlotte. I appreciate it."

"You have more than repaid me." She paused. "I would like to be able to call on you from time to time as we implement this security proposal. Are you going to be available for the occasional consultation?"

"As long as it's occasional, I think I can manage to fit you into my schedule."

"Thank you," Charlotte murmured with a smile. She glanced across the room to where *Valor* lay on black velvet in the display case. "And thank you for bringing back the sword. It is a fine blade, isn't it?"

"If you like that kind of thing."

Charlotte smiled in genuine amusement. "Well, I don't suppose I need to worry about the legend attached to it any longer, do I? One way or another it seems to have been fulfilled." She gave Hugh an odd, speculative glance.

Hugh shrugged. He was no longer interested in *Valor*. It was a good fighting tool that had been available when he needed it. That was all that mattered.

"What's Mattie doing? Still packing?" Charlotte asked.

"Today she went shopping for her trousseau with Evangeline."

"This should be interesting. I can't wait to see what she's bought under Evangeline's guidance. Imagine going shopping with a professional call girl."

"Ex-professional. Evangeline is a real business-woman now. Mattie says she's bought an industrial-grade sewing machine and about half a million spools of thread to take out to St. Gabe with her. She's planning to ask Silk to design some fabric for her. You know, I think Silk's going to go crazy when he meets Evangeline."

"You're going to have an interesting little group out there on St. Gabriel."

Hugh turned away from the window with a smile. "You'll have to come out and pay us a visit."

"I'll do that. You'll take good care of our Mattie, won't you?"

"Mattie is my life," Hugh said simply.

"All she's ever really wanted is you. Since the day she met you."

"All I ever wanted was her. It just took me a little time to realize it, that's all." An image of Rainbird dying on the point of a sword flickered in Hugh's mind. "You know, Charlotte, unlike some people I could name, I'm getting smarter as I get older."

"That's what makes you a survivor. You've got good genes, Hugh. So does Mattie. When are the two of you going to have a baby?"

"As soon as I can talk her into it."

"Think that will take long?"

Hugh laughed. "No, ma'am. Not long at all. She thinks I'll make a terrific father. Told me so herself," he added proudly. *A real home. The way it was supposed to be.*

"I think you will, too. The world needs more

good men like you. Mattie saw your true potential the day she met you."

Hugh hid what he feared might be a telltale red in his cheeks by glancing at his watch. "I'd better get downstairs to my office. Time for another batch of bug juice. You know, I'm actually starting to like the stuff."

"You like it because you know Mattie spends an inordinate amount of time and energy concocting it just for you."

"That's how I knew for certain that she still loved me," Hugh admitted. "I figured she wouldn't go to all that trouble to feed me right if she didn't care about me. You'll be at the wedding?"

"Wouldn't miss it for the world. Evangeline is designing the bridal gown, I hear. Should be a sight to behold. I wonder if it will be in red."

Hugh was still laughing when he got off the elevator and walked into his office to pour himself a glass of bug juice.

Mattie paid for her cup of herbal tea and carried it over to the table where two extraordinarily good-looking men in their early thirties were waiting for her. Both men were wearing expensive Italian-cut linen jackets over their equally expensive designer shirts and trousers. Both had an air of casual, urbane elegance. Both also had physiques to die for. Mattie smiled to herself. It wasn't every day a woman got to sit down with a couple of hunks like this.

"Gentlemen," she announced as she put her tea

down on the table and seated herself on a delicate wire-frame chair, "do I have a deal for you."

"We're listening," one of them said equably.

"You've got our full attention," the other murmured, sipping cappuccino with languid grace.

Mattie proceeded to lay out her plans in precise detail. She ran through the bulk of her proposal and then added a rider. "There's just one other thing."

"Anything for you, Mattie, you know that."

"I'd like a guarantee that for the next two years you will agree to show the works of Flynn Grafton."

"Don't be ridiculous," the first man drawled. "You don't have to ask us for a written guarantee. We would kill for Grafton's work. Saw it at the opening the other night. Fabulous, Absolutely fabulous."

Mattie nodded. "Good. I thought you'd agree. Then you like the overall arrangement?"

"You've got a deal, Mattie," the second man announced. He glanced at his friend. "Right?"

"A deal," the first man agreed, putting down his cup.

Mattie started to say something else but paused when the hair on the nape of her neck stirred. Instinctively she turned her head to see Hugh striding through the small espresso shop. His gray eyes simmered with a vaguely annoyed expression.

"Suzanne told me you were down the street having coffee with a couple of collectors," Hugh said, surveying the two exquisite young gods sitting on the other side of the table. "Just what do you two collect?"

"Anything Mattie says we should." The first man returned Hugh's gaze with interest. His eyes started low and traveled slowly upward to Hugh's broad shoulders. "She has absolutely fabulous taste, you know. We've never gone wrong when we've been guided by Mattie. Do feel free to join us."

"Thanks. I was going to do that," Hugh declared, sounding thoroughly disgruntled now. He dropped onto the seat beside Mattie and glowered at everyone.

Mattie grinned. "Hugh, I'd like you to meet Ryan Turner and Travis Preston. These two gentlemen are currently making a killing as stockbrokers. They have wisely decided to get out of the market while they're ahead and go into something with a little more class."

"Is that right?" Hugh cocked a brow. "Just what are they going to do now to keep themselves in those spiffy duds?"

"They're going to take over my gallery. Meet the new owners of Sharpe Reaction."

"A pleasure, I'm sure," said Travis, his gaze lingering on Hugh's shoulders again.

"Yes, indeed." Ryan murmured. "A great pleasure. Mattie, dear, you do have such wonderful taste."

"Well," Hugh said philosophically, "that's one less thing for me to worry about."

"What's that?" Mattie asked.

"When Suzanne told me I'd find you sitting here with a couple of real hunks, I'll admit I had a few brief qualms. It occurred to me I might find myself having to defend your virtue."

"Oh, God," Ryan said, "I really do love the machismo, don't you, Travis? So utterly primitive."

"Didn't you know?" Travis said to his friend in feigned surprise. "This is the one from Ariel Sharpe's Elemental period."

"That explains it, of course," Ryan said with a sigh.

Hugh looked at Mattie. "You know something? I think I've finally had enough of the wonders of life here in the sophisticated fast lane of the big city. It's time to go home."

"Yes," said Mattie. "I think it is."

Mattie woke before dawn on the morning she and Hugh were scheduled to leave for St. Gabriel. She stretched and slowly opened her eyes, aware of Hugh's heavy, masculine warmth beside her. She glanced at the clock and reached out to touch her husband's shoulder.

"Hugh?"

"I'm awake, babe." He curved his arm around her, drawing her down onto his bare chest. His gaze was sleepy and sexy and full of a very male contentment. "What time is it?"

"Four-thirty."

"Time to get up. We've got a plane to catch."

Mattie smiled and the fateful words she had spoken nearly a year ago came back to her. She said them again. "Take me with you, Hugh. I love you so much. Please take me with you."

His hands caught in her hair, and he dragged

her mouth down to his. "Don't you know I couldn't leave without you, babe? You're my whole world."

This time they both caught the six o'clock flight to St. Gabriel and the future they would share together.

IF YOU HAVE ENJOYED READING THIS
LARGE PRINT BOOK AND YOU WOULD
LIKE MORE INFORMATION ON HOW TO
ORDER A WHEELER LARGE PRINT
BOOK, PLEASE WRITE TO:

WHEELER PUBLISHING, INC.
P.O. BOX 531-ACCORD STATION
HINGHAM, MA 02018-0531